LOOKING DOWN AT his own body, as if from outside it, he became aware of something in the dark water below him. A pale shape, coming closer. A face. At first – such was his disorientation – he had the strange idea that it might be his own. But as it loomed nearer, its features resolved into those of a corpse, its skin and eyes as pallid as a cave fish, its flesh drawn and bloodless, lips and gums shrunk back from its jagged, broken teeth, its long, tangled hair, flecked with the whorled shells of sea snails and silver with their slime, fanned out like lank, oily weed. All over its grotesquely bloated belly and sunken chest, strange eel-like creatures clung and writhed, while pale, lifeless fish-eaten organs lolled from a ragged black cavity in its side. Out of the black water – impossibly – its dead, skeletal arm, almost stripped of tattered flesh, reached towards him, the fingers of its ghastly hand – thin and sharp as bleached fishbones – clawing convulsively at his leg.

ABADDONBOOKS.COM

An Abaddon Books™ Publication
www.abaddonbooks.com
abaddon@rebellion.co.uk

First published in 2011 by Abaddon Books™, Rebellion Intellectual
Property Limited, Riverside House, Osney Mead, Oxford, OX2 0ES, UK.

10 9 8 7 6 5 4 3 2 1

Editor-in-Chief: Jonathan Oliver
Desk Editor: David Moore
Junior Editor: Jenni Hill
Cover: Gerard Miley
Design: Simon Parr & Luke Preece
Marketing and PR: Keith Richardson
Creative Director and CEO: Jason Kingsley
Chief Technical Officer: Chris Kingsley

US ISBN: 978-1-907519-69-7
UK ISBN: 978-1-907519-68-0

Printed in the US

# TOMES OF THE DEAD

# VIKING DEAD

## TOBY VENABLES

**ABADDON
BOOKS**

# PROLOGUE

Skalla sat, his hand resting on the pommel of his sword, his chin resting on his hands, staring at the pile of bodies.

The still-warm corpses steamed in the cool air of the clearing. Behind him, his black-clad men, done cleaning their weapons, stood in silence, waiting – for what, they knew not. Some, perhaps, suspected. But only Skalla knew for certain.

To his right, he heard feet shifting nervously among the damp leaves. That would be Gamli. Like the others, he was impatient to get out of this place. But there was more to his restlessness than that. Skalla had had his eye on Gamli for some time, aware that he had started to lose faith in their masters. More than once he had questioned their orders. It took a brave man to do that, or a stupid one. Skalla knew Gamli was no fool – but he also knew the man's boldness hid deeper fears. Fears that could spread, infecting the others, contaminating them with doubt. That, he could not allow. It threatened everything they had built here.

He ran his fingers through the black bristles on his chin, then up to the scar that passed through his left eye. It ran from his forehead down across his cheek, and had left the eye sightless – milk-white and dead. He pushed at the edge of his helm, relieving the pressure on his forehead for a moment. The scar tissue itched badly today. It always did after combat – the result of the heat and sweat. Not that what had just passed could truthfully be termed 'combat.'

There had been six in all. Perhaps seven. He couldn't remember. They were the ones who had been locked up the longest, those meant to be forgotten. The ones who ran, who broke down, who refused to work, who fought back. The biggest heroes and and the biggest cowards. All the same, now. They had also been kept separate all this time – well away from the various wonders and horrors that had been unfolding. That, Skalla suspected, was one of the real reasons for this little outing to the woods. True, his masters had no desire to waste further food on these lost causes. But they were also wise enough not to waste an opportunity. They would make some use of them, even in death.

And so, they had marched them to this lonely spot, shackled and at spear point, and forced them to cut logs for firewood. They had performed the tasks well, considering their chequered histories – some, almost with gratitude. Perhaps, thought Skalla, it simply felt good to have a purpose again. He had not told them they were gathering wood for their own funeral pyre.

The killing had been quick. Regrettably, the kills were not as clean as he'd hoped. There were struggles, cries, prolonged agonies, repeated blows. From the start, it had not been the most straightforward task. His men had been reluctant to venture into these woods, even during daylight. Then there had been the orders themselves. No damage to the head or neck – that's what their masters had specified. The order had bemused Skalla's men, and in the heat of the slaughter – one could hardly dignify the killing of these unarmed, underfed wretches with the term 'battle' – he could not be sure how closely they had adhered to it. At least one had taken a glancing sword blow across the top of the head – protruding from the heap, Skalla could see his hairy, blood-matted scalp, flapped open like the lid of a chest, the yellow-white bone of the skull grinning through the gore. But it didn't matter now. It was done. They would see soon.

"We're done here," said a voice behind Skalla. It was Gamli. He had stepped closer to where Skalla was sitting. Clearly, he was itching to leave. Perhaps he understood more than Skalla had realised.

"We wait," said Skalla.

"For what?"

"Until we are sure."

"Sure?" Gamli's voice was edgy. As always, he tried to cover it with a kind of swagger. "What is there to be sure of?"

"That they're dead."

Gamli laughed emptily, his throat tight. "Then why not burn them now and have done with it?"

"Are you questioning me, Gamli?" Skalla's eyes remained fixed on the corpses.

A kind of panic entered Gamli's eyes. "Not you. I would never... but the masters. There are doubts about them." He looked around as he said this, as if expecting support from his fellows. None came.

Skalla did not move. "I pledged my sword to them," he said, "and you swore an oath of allegiance to me. You do not question one without also questioning the other."

Gamli stood motionless, robbed of speech.

"Step back into line," said Skalla.

Before he could do so, a sound came from the heap, and an arm flopped out of the tangle. The men's hands jumped to their weapons. The arm hung there, motionless – quite dead. Olvir – one of the three crossbowmen – broke the silence with a nervous laugh. "For a moment, I thought..." He was interrupted by a low groan from the centre of the heap. Skalla stood slowly, hand still upon his sword, and, stretching to his full height, slowly flexed his shoulders. It was part of his ritual before combat.

"Gas. From the bodies," said another of the men, nervously. "They can do that." Olvir began to cock and load his crossbow. The others followed suit.

From deep within the pile came a weird, semi-human grunt, and the whole tangle suddenly shifted. As one, the men drew swords and raised crossbows. The uppermost body – a skinny man, whose abdomen was split open, and whose right arm had been all but severed – slithered from the top of the heap. The hand that had loosed itself from the pile twitched, its fingers inexplicably starting to straighten.

"It's beginning..." said Skalla. The hollow moan repeated itself, and was joined by two more in a kind of desolate, mindless chorus. As they watched in horror, dead limbs moved, arms flailed and grasped, lifeless eyes flicked open.

"This can't be happening," said Gamli. "Not to *them*..." From the heap, one of the men – a solid, muscular fellow who had taken two crossbow bolts through the chest, one of which had pinned his right hand to his sternum – staggered unsteadily to his feet. For a moment, he seemed to sniff the air, then turned and lurched towards them.

Skalla spat on his palms and raised his sword. "Aim for the heads," he said, and swung the blade with all his strength at the dead man's neck. Such was the force of the cut that it sliced clean through, knocking the attacker off his feet and sending his head bowling into the bushes. Already two more were on their feet – the skinny man, his right arm hanging by a sinew, his glistening guts dangling between his legs, and the scalped man, his cap of hair flapping absurdly to one side like piece of bearskin, who Skalla could now see had been killed by a heavy sword blow to the left side of his chest, the upper and lower parts sliding against each other gruesomely with each lurching step. A crossbow bolt hit the skinny man in the shoulder, spinning him round. "In the head!" barked Skalla. As the skinny man resumed his steady progress a second bolt thudded into his eye, knocking him flat. A third flew uselessly past the scalped man's ear. His arms reached out, grasping at Skalla, as another three grotesque figures rose stiffly behind him.

The rest of Skalla's men, momentarily mesmerised by the scene unfolding before them, now threw themselves into the fight. Gamli stepped forward first, grasping the scalped man's outstretched arm and hurling him to the floor. Drawing a long cavalry axe from a strap at his back, he flipped it around and with one blow drove its long, steel spike through the exposed skull. As his other men hacked mercilessly at two of the remaining ghouls, Skalla advanced to finish off the third – a once-fat man with folds of saggy skin beneath his ragged, filthy tunic. Skalla recognised the stab wounds in his chest – wounds that he himself had delivered with his knife. The fat man's left arm – bloody and slashed where he had attempted to defend himself from Skalla's blade – waved before him, his right – bloodier still – hanging crippled and useless by his side. Skalla raised his sword steadily, waiting for the right moment. The man's hand, formed into a claw, swayed and snatched at Skalla, his jaws opening and closing like those of an idiot child, dribbling bloody drool down his chest. Skalla began to swing – but something caught his foot, pulling him off balance. He stumbled and fell heavily onto the damp earth.

Looking at his feet, he saw that the seventh prisoner – his spinal cord severed, his legs useless – had dragged himself along the forest floor, and now, teeth bared, Skalla's ankle gripped in both hands, was gnawing at his leather boot, his blue-tinged jaws opening and closing mechanically like a landed fish gasping for air. Skalla recoiled in disgust, kicking at the ghoul's slavering, gap-toothed mouth – but the tenacious grip held, and over him now loomed the fat man, moaning and clawing at his face. Too close for an effective blow, Skalla abandoned his sword and scrabbled for his knife – but, before he had time to draw it, another sword blade was driven hard into the fat man's mouth, sending him choking and tottering backwards, his teeth grinding horribly against its metal edge. Skalla recognised the hilt: Gamli's sword. Skalla swiftly regained his feet, took up his own weapon once more and brought it down with a crashing blow, cleaving the skull of the crawling man in two. He gave a nod of acknowledgement to Gamli, and scraped the man's brains off his black boot with the point of his blade.

It was over. And his men, thankfully, had escaped unscathed.

"So it's finally happened," said Gamli, surveying the carnage that surrounded them – the men they had hacked down for the second time that day. "Our worst fear has come to life." The others exchanged anxious glances.

Skalla ignored him, wiping clean and sheathing his sword as he hunted around for the head of the first corpse-walker. He would take that back to his masters.

"I'm sorry," said Gamli, bowing his head. Skalla turned to face him. "I will not question you again."

"No," said Skalla. "You will not." And without blinking he stabbed Gamli in the side of the throat with his knife, severing both carotid arteries, then pulled the blade forward through his windpipe. Gamli collapsed in an eruption of blood, his last cry turned to a choked gurgle of air bubbling and frothing from his neck.

As he pumped crimson onto the forest floor, a contorted expression of disbelief frozen upon his face, Skalla looked upon him for the last time. "I did not kill you before only because I needed your sword," he said matter-of-factly, and stepped over the body. The other men drew back as he approached. He scanned their faces one at a time, then sheathed his knife.

"Burn them," said Skalla, the still-living Gamli convulsing behind him. "All of them."

# PART ONE

VIKINGR

# CHAPTER ONE

## FOG

ATLI SHOULD HAVE been home hours ago. Clutching the bundle of gnarled sticks tight to his chest as he emerged from the trees onto the broad curve of the riverbank, he looked south towards the distant, looming shadow of the Middagsberg. His heart sank. It was even later than he'd thought. The low sun, a watery smudge of light in the late summer mist, had long since passed the cleft in its summit, and was already half-way to the mid-afternoon daymark – the ragged edge of tall pines puncturing the horizon on the mountain's shallow western slope. For a moment he imagined his father looking up at the same line of trees, his face livid with anger, cursing his son's name.

He would get a beating again. It was part of the routine.

He shivered, turned his eyes resignedly to the ground, and kicked idly at the wet, grey stones that littered the bank, the smell of the damp wood in his nostrils. The threat of his father's stick across his back should, he knew, be sufficient incentive for him to head back home in good time. That was certainly the intention. But it just made him all the more determined to stay away. And the longer he put off his return, the more severe became the inevitable punishment – and the more gloomily reluctant he became. A vicious circle. "Like a dog chasing its tail," his mother used to say. It had been eight winters since she'd passed, when Atli was barely five years old, but he still recalled her words from time to time, although her face was now lost to him.

It had been this way almost as long as he could remember. He often wandered by the water now, dreaming of change, escape – something, *anything* – but where that change might come from, even he could not imagine. And as he dreamed, and his father fumed – increasingly at odds with the world, as well as his own son – each grew more distant from the other, more stubborn, more deeply entrenched, until Atli had begun to fear where it might ultimately lead.

He flicked a loose stone with his foot so it tumbled and splashed, coming to rest in the shallows at the water's edge – the edge of his world. These waters were their protection. That's what his father always told him. To Atli, however, they seemed more like a prison. To the north, through the woods and beyond the village, was the river Svanær. South of the village – and on whose banks Atli now stood – the wider, meandering Ottar. Each provided them with plentiful fish and formed a barrier against overland raiders and outlaws. To the west, on the spur of land that dwindled to a point where the two rivers met, was thick forest with good hunting – accessible only from their village. To the east, the fertile land and rich pasture upon which they'd built their farms rose to distant, rocky fells – a natural discouragement to any who did not already know the paths, and which had long proved its worth. As his father had said so often, it was the land that supported them, and the land that kept them from harm. Atli thought of all the times he had sought solace down by the water's edge, and wondered how often, had the river not been here to protect them, he would have kept on walking until that familiar landscape were left far behind.

There was one threat the land did not keep them safe from, however; a danger that tormented his father's mind and had become the subject of repeated, dire warnings. River raiders. Pirates. *Vikingr*. "If you see *vikingr*," his father said, "you must *run*. Run as fast as you can. They are bad men. Desperate men. They will cut a man's throat for the fun of it – and much worse. They steal everything that isn't nailed down. Even the animals. They dishonour and kill women. They eat children. I have heard it! Remember, you must *run* – and warn the village. But make no sound!"

"How will I know them?" Atli had asked.

"You will know them." His father had nodded with a kind of portentous unease. "They will come from the river. And you will know them…"

There hadn't ever been a raid in these parts. Not even further downriver was such a thing heard of these days – at least, not as far as Atli knew. And anyway, if he did encounter *vikingr*, the one thing he wouldn't do was run. He would beg to be taken with them.

He sighed and gazed longingly across the still water – or, at least, as far as it would let him. In the last few hours a thick shroud of fog had rolled in from the estuary. Following the course of the river upstream with eerie precision, it hovered silently over the river's surface now, mocking its shape, obscuring the tall trees of the opposite bank as it thickened the air. Dead. Impenetrable. Ungraspable. *Like a ghost,* thought Atli. *Like the creeping ghost of the river.* Images crowded his head from old stories his father had told – of whispy spirits escaping from the bodies of the dead, of glowing smokes and fogs seeping out of mounds and barrows and taking terrible, half-recognised shapes that sucked the life out of the living. Another chill ran through him. He kicked at the stones with a sudden anger, as if to banish thought with physical action – any kind of action – to kick his childish night-terrors away. He refused to succumb to the anxieties and superstitions that had taken over his father's life. He refused to live in fear. Every day now he saw it in his father's eyes, and it made him ashamed.

Superstition had been the other half of Atli's upbringing. When he was young, the stories had seemed magical – dwarves and elves that lived in the earth and forged great gifts of gold, spirits and serpents that lived in the woods and the water, gods who turned men's fortunes, playing cruel tricks on the proud and bestowing blessings upon the brave. Although, in his heart, he had never quite believed in their literal truth, as others seemed to, they nonetheless had their own reality – one that he loved. They existed in another world. And they were an escape from his own.

Then, after his mother died, the tone of the stories changed. Each one became a warning. Another stick to beat him with.

All manner of irrational fears seemed to take over his life. His father became obsessed with death. At wakes – where most were content to drink and share good memories – he cut a gloomy, troubled figure, repeatedly warning those present to take precautions against the corpse's potential return. He would insist upon an open pair of iron scissors being placed on the chest of the deceased, and always afterwards could be seen sprinkling salt along the threshold. It was protection, he said, against the *draugr* – the undead – who returned to inflict untold horrors upon the living. In regions to the south, there was talk they were on the rise. He'd heard it from a merchant who refused to go near the place.

Privately, many scoffed at him for wasting such precious commodities. Others simply laughed at his ways. Once, when he was too young to know better, Atli had asked his father if it wouldn't be a *good* thing for his mother to come back. Wasn't that what they all wanted? A weird terror burned in his father's eyes. "Try to understand," he said, his voice trembling. "It is not *they* who come back, but something else. Something terrible." His eyes widened. He spoke in a hoarse whisper, as if afraid of being overheard. "You would wish to see her again. You would welcome her in when she came knocking at night.

But it would not be the mother you knew. Imagine a lumbering, soulless mockery – heavy with the stench of decay, her body bloated, distorted, monstrous in proportion, her heart empty of feeling, her head a foetid shell, her eyes dead as a fish's, her only emotion a blind envy for the living whose flesh she is driven to devour, crunching the bones, drinking the blood in great gobbets..."

The image haunted Atli's nightmares for years.

Then, in his eleventh year, he had come to his current realisation. It was fear, not anger, that drove his father. And that, ultimately, was why he hated him. It was not because he was a bully, (not only was he bigger than Atli was, but bigger than most of the men in the village), nor because he thrashed him on a regular basis. He hated him because he was a coward. Atli knew that he bore the brunt of the man's frustrations only because he could not offer any resistance. His father beat him not just because of what he did or didn't do, but because of all the other people and things in life that he was too afraid to confront – chief among them, Atli had begun to suspect, himself. His own weakness. The weakness to which the father knew his son's eyes were no longer oblivious. The weakness which Atli doggedly refused to inherit.

He trudged to the edge of the river and stared momentarily at his own indistinct reflection in the water, then kicked another pebble and watched the ripples break it apart.

Vaguely he wondered what was going on back at the village. Not long ago there had been a distant clamour of shouting from that way – some sort of argument that was best avoided, probably. Recently, a fight had broken out over a pig which had wandered into a neighbour's house and eaten a cabbage that had been cut for dinner. Bera, the woman of the house, had demanded compensation for her loss. Yngvar, the pig-owner, had countered by accusing Bera of trying to steal his pig. After a lot of shouting, during which Bera had cracked Yngvar across the temple with a wooden ladle, it ended with a rather fearful Yngvar conceding that his pig had probably wandered of its own accord and Bera accepting a quantity of pig dung – some of which had already been deposited in her house – in payment for the cabbage. Such were the heady thrills of farm life.

Now, Atli could see there was also a thick column of dark smoke coming from that direction. Perhaps they weren't so desperate for his kindling after all. Gripping his bundle under one arm he crouched down to pick up a smooth, wet pebble, and hurled it at the water. It was swallowed instantly with a loud plop. He screwed up his face in frustration, grabbed another, flatter stone and, crouching lower this time, aimed it at a shallow angle. It skipped once, twice, three times.

Good. But he knew he could do better. Seven was his record. It needed a certain kind of stone, though. His eyes darted about the shore by his feet, among the wet pebbles and grit and occasional patches of green weed that waved in the lapping water. A perfect stone caught his eye – nicely smooth and flat, with a notch in its edge for his forefinger. He snatched it up, aimed, and let his arm sway back and forth for a moment, rehearsing the arc of the throw. Then... Snap! Cracking his whole body like a whip, he let the stone fly. He knew from the moment it left him that it was a perfect throw. The shimmering stone skipped across the smooth water, dipping like a dragonfly, weightless – three, four, five – until finally enveloped by the fog. In the stillness of the afternoon he could still hear its sound: six, seven, eight, nine... ten?

That couldn't be right. Yet still it kept going. He'd lost count, but stood, holding his breath, ears on stalks. He could still hear the surface of the water being broken. A fish? No. A steady rhythm. He'd swear to it. But different now. Surely the fog must be playing tricks? No, there was definitely something. Another sound, that had at some point merged with the first. Slow and steady. And not receding, but coming closer.

Atli fought against the images of wraiths and phantoms that suddenly flooded his mind. His father had warned him the fog brought terrible things. It was the cold breath of Niflheim – of Hel itself. Who knew what horrors travelled within it? Atli got a grip of himself. Such things were not real – or, if they were, they were not part of his world.

But the sound kept coming all the same.

A sequence, continually repeating, echoing weirdly in the dull air. A splash of water. A hollow clunk, like wood against wood – but somehow multiplied. A creak. Then again. Splash. Clunk. Creak. Over and over. He bit his lip, frowning hard, straining to penetrate the grey murk. He knew this sound – but couldn't place it. It grew closer. His mind raced. The hairs on his neck prickled in slow recognition. Involuntarily, he began to take slow steps back from the water.

Then a great shape loomed out of the fog.

The head and neck of a dragon.

Gliding straight at him in a moment of surreal silence, the dragon's huge bulk bit into the grit and pebbles of the shore and drove part way up the bank with a crunching of wood, stone and water before coming to rest just yards from Atli's astonished face. He was dimly aware of the loose bundle of twigs falling one by one from his enfeebled hands. High up and to the left, a figure emerged from nowhere and landed heavily on the rocks and shingle. A tall man, broad-shouldered, beardless, but spiked with blond stubble, ice-blue eyes glinting behind the eye-guards of a steel helm.

*Run,* said a voice in Atli's head. *Run as fast as you can.* But he could not move.

The man took three steps towards him – mail-coated, rings shimmering in the feeble light, circular shield strapped to his back, gold-hilted sword drawn and ready – so close that Atli could make out the pattern-welding on the gleaming blade. A hint of a smile flickered across the man's face, his sword point hovering barely an arm's length from Atli's chest.

Another figure – a giant of a man – heaved itself over the right side of the ship, making the ground shudder as his feet sunk into shore. This one was equipped much like the first, but for his simpler helm whose rim rested on his heavy brow, and the dew-damp fur of some grey creature wrapped across his shoulders and tucked into a wide leather belt. Dark, deep-set eyes peered from amongst unruly black hair and beard, fixed intently on the boy. He spat in his palms, and, holding Atli's gaze, reached over his left shoulder and drew forth a broad-bladed axe.

Behind him, another man landed on the shore. And another...

One by one they spilled over the sides and crunched and splashed down onto the riverbank – twenty, thirty, more – until the grey stone beach and misty shallows around the dragon's oaken hull were filled with men, some trudging shoreward from the deeper water, emerging from the fog like ghosts – grim-faced, steel-helmed, girt with hide and mail, until, finally, it seemed the whole river's edge shimmered with the glint of weapons.

Though he had never seen such a thing in his whole life, Atli recognised them instantly.

Not ghosts.

Worse.

*Vikingr.*

# CHAPTER TWO

## THE CREW OF THE *HRAFN*

BJÓLF ERLINGSSON TOOK another step towards the boy, eyes fixed on him, sword steady. He gave a nod towards the ground. "You dropped your sticks, little man."

A rumbling laugh ran through the assembled men as the lad crouched and began to gather up the scattered firewood. Bjólf watched the farm boy with amusement as he tied up his bundle – stick-thin legs and crude, ill-fitting clothes, no doubt cut from the roughest, itchiest, shittiest blanket in the place; the blanket even the dogs rejected. The look of it, the smell of it... It all seemed so familiar. It was at times like this he was reminded exactly why he'd left that life behind all those years ago. True, the plundered cottons and silks to which he had since become accustomed may have meant him facing danger and death on a daily basis, but it seemed a fair trade. Hel, how those bloody blankets had itched!

"Are you from the village?" he demanded. The boy nodded hastily, jumping at the sound of the man's voice. Bjólf rested his sword casually over his shoulder – looking momentarily like a wayfarer with his bundle of belongings – and scanned the treeline ahead, taking note of the path that disappeared into the wood. He nodded towards it. "How far?"

"Six hundred paces..." In spite of his obvious efforts, his voice sounded thin and reedy.

Gunnar Black-Beard shifted his axe from one hand to the other. "Hm. The boy can count."

*Fisherman*, thought Bjólf. *Counts the fish for his father.* He knew all about that. Most of his men knew it, in one way or another. And those who denied it most perhaps knew it keenest of all. Bjólf turned back to the lad. "You have animals there? Food? Valuables?"

"Animals... and food. Not the other."

"We'll have to make do with that," sighed Gunnar.

Godwin snorted dismissively, resting his hands and chin on his massive axe. "Everywhere the same. You'd think there was no decent treasure left. How's a man to make a living?" A few of the men muttered at his words.

"Have I ever let you down, Godwin?" Bjólf shot back. He didn't give him a chance to answer, but turned to the boy again.

"Any weapons there?"

He shook his head.

"Then we go," said Bjólf. And with that he made a sudden move towards the boy, his sword raised threateningly over his shoulder.


I'M DEAD, THOUGHT Atli. *I've told him what he needs, and now he's going to kill me.*

In the moment that followed, he involuntarily pictured the heavy blade slashing downward and across in one movement, the catastrophic moment of contact stretched out into a slow, dream-like sequence – the sword's edge striking his left shoulder, parting the flesh, shattering the bone and not stopping until

22

it had come clean through to the opposite side of his chest, severing his head, shoulder and right arm in one continuous action.

Curiously, it was not fear that took hold of him in that weirdly suspended moment, but a kind of anger. With tears suddenly stinging his eyes, he inwardly cursed his own inability to act – cursed this last, lost opportunity – and wondered abstractly whether he would remain conscious long enough to gaze up at his own lopsided, headless corpse, its insides still pumping, and see it sway and fall.

Without warning, the beardless warrior thrust out his left hand, ruffled his hair with a gruffly dismissive laugh, and gave a nod to the giant alongside him. Then, to Atli's great surprise, the entire party of men began to move rapidly up the shore, the ring of metal against metal filling the damp air. Slowly, the realisation dawned that the man had no intention of spilling Atli's blood on the dull, grey stones of that lonely beach. There was, as far as Atli was concerned, a far more terrible fate in store.

He was going to ignore him.

Atli couldn't stand it. With a mixture of anger and desperation, he whirled around to the rapidly receding throng and called out: "I could lead you!"

As one, the group stopped. The captain turned and stared at him. There was a chuckle and a murmur among the men. "And why would you do that?"

Atli felt his face flush red. He strove to find an answer, but under the hard stares, no words came. Then one among them spoke up – his voice little more than a hoarse whisper, his words clipped and strange. The men fell silent at the sound of it.

"My people tell a story of a boy who offered to lead raiders to his village..." The owner of the voice stepped forward, drawing a long, curved knife from a fringed leather sheath on his belt. His general shape was unremarkable – a little shorter in stature than the majority of the men, perhaps – yet his appearance was unlike anything Atli had encountered; his clothes and cap made of skins from no animal Atli had ever seen, and his dark body-armour – like the segmented carapace of a cockroach –

formed from toughened strips of hide sewn together in wide bands. The man's hair was dark, his nose upturned, his hairless face broad and flat with skin the colour of beeswax. The wide eyes that now bored into him seemed permanently narrowed, as if in the glare of the sun, and, as the figure loomed closer, the complexion that had appeared smooth from a distance revealed itself to be so covered with spidery creases that Atli could not honestly tell if the man was twenty summers old or a hundred. Something in his otherworldly aspect caused Atli to shudder. As the thin blade swayed near the boy's pale, exposed neck, the man bore his teeth in a strange smile. "He led them to their deaths..." The breath stopped in Atli's throat as if it were held in the man's fist.

"Enough!" called the captain, giving an abrupt flick of his head. Wide-Face acknowledged it with a sly grin and turned slowly away, silently sheathing his blade. Atli, suddenly able to breathe again, gasped, his head swimming.

The beardless warrior stared at the boy for a moment, his eyes seeming to narrow behind his eye-guards, then turned back to his companion. He didn't need to speak. They'd known each other too long for that.

"Personally, I'd sooner have him where I can see him," said the giant, shrugging.

The captain nodded slowly, then made a sudden, exaggerated half bow, and extended his arm dramatically towards the woods as he did so. An invitation. Atli stared at him for a moment, incredulously. "Lead on, little man."

At their captain's gesture, the men parted. It was true. He really meant for him to lead them. Atli stumbled nervously past the silent ranks, his bundle of sticks still tucked under his arm – all eyes again upon him. As he advanced, he was now able to take in the grim array of figures for the first time; no longer the shadowy, grey shapes that had emerged from the fog, but distinct, real. Faces that were scarred and weatherbeaten and spoke not only of years lived, but of miles travelled, of things seen, of battles fought. All men who worked the earth and the sea were hardened to life, with muscles like twisted rope and faces carved from aged applewood – but these had something else, something that Atli had not seen.

They had no fear.

Those closest now stood out to him, startling in their detail. There was, of course, Long-Axe – the one they called Godwin – bare-chinned and impressively moustached, his blackened helm with long bronzed nasal and cheek-guards, and his mail coat almost to his knees; and the unnerving Wide-Face, the ageless one, dressed head to foot in animal hides, still fingering his knife, his eyes glinting darkly. There was Curved-Sword – a slender, fine-featured man in long robes and armoured hauberk like the scales of a fish, his helm pointed, his short hair black, his skin dark, his sword long and thin and curved like a scythe, and near him – in utter contrast – One-Ear, wearing quilted body armour reinforced with leather and no helm at all, his face and head shaved to stubble, his lips scarred, his shield rim battered, his spear notched, and his left ear missing its top third, looking for all the world as if someone had taken a bite out of him. Opposite them, Red-Hair, his rust-red mane and beard standing out sharply against his thick cape of green wool, clasped with an ornate bronze brooch, his helm and breastplate of dark, hardened leather, a spiked mace slung over his shoulder, and near him, Two-Axe, barely taller than Atli, but at least three times as wide and built like an ox, his face entirely obscured by a masked *grimmhelm*, his armour of tarnished metal plates joined with leather thongs, and, unlike all the others, no shield – just a heavy axe hanging from each large, calloused hand. And, perhaps weirdest of all, there was Grey-Beard, a gaunt figure of a man in heavy, brown, hooded robes, simple conical helm on his head, from his belt hanging not only his sword but such a variety of knives as Atli had never seen in one place, in his hands a long ash spear, in his face a dark, puckered hole where one of his eyes should be – a vision, it seemed to Atli, of Odin made flesh.

They formed a terrifying company. Yet, as Atli walked, a confidence grew in him – increasing with each step. *They trust me*, he thought. *I have their respect...* It was the first time he had inspired such a thing in any man, let alone such men as these. But as he reached the head of the troop, there was a sound of movement immediately behind him. Before he had time to react, he felt something whip around his neck and pull tight. Clawing at it, he turned in shock.

With his free hand, the captain was twisting the decorated scabbard of his sword, from which issued a thin, looped leather strap – the baldric from which both sword and scabbard, until recently, had hung – now taut like a ship's rope.

Atli was tethered like a dog.

"My apologies," the man said with a smile. "But you know these woods, and doubtless can run a good deal faster than us in your attire..." The men laughed once again, and once again Atli felt the blood rush to his face. "Now, lead on. Where you go, we follow."

And with that, he gave the strap a sharp flick. "*Hyah!*"

Atli staggered forward in a daze, his mind only now starting to grasp the grim reality of what was about to happen.

# CHAPTER THREE

## THE VILLAGE AT TWO-RIVERS

As the company moved swiftly up the beach toward the trees, Atli looked back to the river. The swirling mist was creeping onto the shore now. From it, the tall slender prow of the longship stood like a lonely sentinel.

Feeling strangely numb, he pulled at the strap around his neck as a sharp prod from the captain's sword urged him on. He spoke without thinking. "There's no-one guarding your ship."

The big one laughed. "Everyone knows what a dragon-ship means. No one who values their life will go near."

"But what if they have no fear? What if they are stronger?"

"Then we don't want to meet them, and they're welcome to it!"

It seemed these men even approached the prospect of failure with a kind of boundless confidence – certainly far beyond anything the people in his village possessed. Except, possibly, Bera. Now, that was a revelation... Atli had always found her a cantankerous, difficult sort, her stubborn ways typical of the old folk hereabouts. Yet, he began to realise, she was as different from her fellow villagers as a wolf from a goat. She had no fear – of others, of the world, of herself. Yes, that tough old widow was was more like these *vikingr* than most of the surrounding menfolk could ever hope to be.

Whether she or anyone else would live to see tomorrow was the one question Atli was now trying to put out of his mind.

THE MOMENT THE men entered the shade of the trees, they fell silent. Shields were hurriedly hoisted off backs, helmet straps pulled tight and empty hands filled with weapons. All knew this was the most hazardous part of the raid. Forty *vikingr*, armed to the teeth and with the advantage of surprise, were more than a match for any village, no matter how bold its population. But there was always the unknown, the unpredictable. Regardless of careful planning and advance information, none could be completely sure what they would find, nor who or what they would encounter first. By chance they might run into another from the village, as they had the farm boy – but this time, perhaps, the stranger would scream or shout, or run from the attackers and raise the alarm. In this way, even the smallest child could treble their casualties.

The path narrowed as they drove deeper into the forest. No one spoke. Only the scratch of branches and brambles against wood and metal and the rhythmic pounding of their feet – made heavy by arms and armour – accompanied their swift advance. The sharp smell of damp pine and bruised bracken filled the air. All knew that being forced to move in single file by tangled bush and shrub made them vulnerable. From beneath the eye-guards of his helm Bjólf's eyes instinctively scanned every tree and shadow, calculating where he would place archers, a trap, men with spears. Hemmed in and spread thin as they were, they would be easy prey for an enemy who was prepared.

But Bjólf knew they would not be.

There was to be little finesse about this attack. No sophisticated strategy, no circling around to seal off escape routes. Bjólf knew there was nowhere – and no one – for the villagers to run to. Today, it was about speed. They would hit hard and fast, taking what they could while their quarry was still reeling from shock. A single hammerblow. He was proud of the fact that, in the past, they had often achieved this without a single casualty.

Looking ahead, he gave a tug on the lad's lead and spoke in a cautious whisper. "Little man... six hundred of your paces or six-hundred man-paces?"

"M–my paces."

"Then we're close."

Up ahead, the trees were already beginning to thin out and, beyond, Bjólf could see gaps of light where the forest gave way to a clearing. For an instant, a light breeze brought the unmistakable scent of smoke and pigs to his nostrils. He pulled at the strap around the boy's throat, jerking him to a sudden halt, and raised his sword. As one, the rest of the company stopped.

Listening carefully, but hearing nothing, Bjólf gestured them forward slowly. They spread out in the dappled light as the close undergrowth gave way to a more even covering of ferns and wild garlic, its thick aroma filling the air. Here and there, a few plants still in flower dotted the forest floor. They paused again, their target now visible from the cover of the trees.

"Fjölvar!" hissed Bjólf. The lean, thin-faced young man came forward. He was one of the least armoured of all Bjólf's crew, with no more than a hide coat upon his back and a soft leather Phrygian cap upon his head. From his back, he unslung a bow, ready strung and almost as long as its owner. From his belt hung a quiver thick with arrows, some fletched with white goosefeathers and some with the mackerel-striped brown of a pheasant. The man's eyes – close together, and peering from either side of a narrow, beaky nose – remained firmly fixed on the boy.

Bjólf turned to Atli. "We'll take things from here," He removed the strap from around their guide's neck and slung it back over his shoulder. "Don't run." As he said this, Fjölvar placed a white-feathered arrow with a barbed iron tip on his bowstring.

Crouched behind the abundant tangle of grasses that marked the edge of the trees, Bjólf and Gunnar looked out upon the village. Ahead, speckling the gentle hill that rose before them, was a scattered collection of thatched houses and barns, each accompanied by small, crudely constructed, but sturdy animal pens. Beyond, across the undulating landscape, stretched acres of lush pasture and growing land, some patterned by rows of cultivation, age-worn paths and the occasional, winding fence. From each dwelling curled a peaceful whisp of woodsmoke, and, between them wound a muddy, heavily-trodden track which disappeared over a rise, beyond which lay the rest of the settlement, ultimately bounded by the northern river. It was an idyllic scene – but for the thick column of black smoke coming from over the rise, and the complete lack of any signs of life.

"Where is everyone?" said Bjólf.

"And where's their livestock?" replied Gunnar. "I can't even see a chicken."

"Do you smell pigs?"

"I *smell* them. I just don't *see* them."

Over to their left, just beyond the nearest dwelling, a muddy hog pen lay empty, its gate tilted and broken. Up on a distant slope, in a far corner of an enclosure, a single sheep stood, the only fleck of white upon the hillside. A living thing, at least. To its lonely, urgent bleating, nothing responded.

Gunnar grabbed the farm boy by the shoulder and gave him a shake. "What's going on, boy?" The boy looked at the weirdly empty village, then back at Gunnar, bemused and speechless. The baffled, anxious expression on his face did not reassure them. Gunnar narrowed his eyes, surveying the unnervingly still scene.

"I don't like the look of that smoke." A gust brought the smell to their nostrils again – but there was something else detectable in it; something acrid. From somewhere, caught on the same wind, came the sound of a woman wailing. "You sure about this?"

Bjólf wasn't sure. But what was certain was that they needed supplies of meat, drink and grain at the very least if they were to continue on. He pursed his lips. "Go in fast. Get what we need. Get out."

Gunnar nodded. Bjólf hefted his shield – red-painted – off his shoulder and spoke without turning to his men.

"Finn – you take the left." Wide-Face face nodded. "Godwin you take the right. Gunnar, Thorvald, Kjötvi, Magnus and Úlf – you're with me." Two-Axe, One-Ear, Grey-Beard and another huge man with blond plaits and arms like hams strapped into leather arm guards moved in to join Bjólf and Gunnar.

There was a moment of silence, all muscles tensed, then at a signal from Bjólf, they broke from the trees.

# CHAPTER FOUR

## BLACK SMOKE

SWIFTLY, SILENTLY, THEY moved on the village. Finn and Godwin's companies took each flank, and, as they approached the knot of buildings, the two bands began to disperse, pairs of men splitting off and bursting into each dwelling, while Bjólf and the others headed straight for the heart of the village, weapons raised, eyes alert.

The men moved swiftly from house to house, their passing accompanied by the sounds of crashing from within as beds and chests were overturned. "Nothing," called one, emerging back into daylight. They moved on to the next.

"Nor here..." called another.

"Try the barn," called Gunnar.

"Empty."

"The chests have been broken open..." spat Finn, striding out of the nearest house.

"There must be someone here," said Gunnar. "I smell cooking." So did Bjólf. But there was something about it, different from the honest smells of stew and woodsmoke.

"Keep looking!" barked Bjólf. But his sense of unease was growing.

"Blood," said Kjötvi. Bjólf followed his gaze and saw a trail of fresh gore, and signs that something had been dragged. An animal?

"Rich pickings, you said..." hissed Gunnar, as more men emerged empty handed.

"It was a reliable source," Bjólf shot back. "He's never failed us before."

"Bjólf!" came a voice. It was Finn, emerging from one of the farthest dwellings. In his outstretched hand he held his sword. From it, hooked over the blade, hung a small iron scythe. And, still gripping the scythe's crude wooden handle, a severed hand.

Gunnar scanned the empty village and sniffed the air again in agitation. "There's something very wrong here."

Up ahead, Bjólf suddenly became aware of a single figure, right in the middle of the muddy track. A big man, ragged, staggering slightly, eyes and nose streaming, a mixture of blood and soot smeared across his forehead. He stopped dead when he saw them.

Without hesitation, Bjólf marched up to him, sword raised. But before he could do or say anything, the man collapsed to his knees, sobbing.

Bjólf stared at him. "Get up!" he shouted. "Get *up!*" Slinging his shield on his back, he grabbed the man's torn tunic and hauled him to his feet, his sword blade against his throat. "Answer me quickly. Where are your valuables? Your food? Your animals? Don't think you can hide them from us. We know all the tricks – and trust me, you *will* give them up."

Inexplicably, the man began to laugh.

"We have nothing!"

"They all say that," growled Gunnar.

"No, you don't understand..." He choked out the words between bouts of sobbing laughter. "There's nothing left! They took it all!"

Bjólf's blood ran cold.

"'They'?"

The man frowned and looked from one to the other. "Moments ago. *Vikingr* like you." He pointed a shaky hand towards the far end of the village. "You just missed them."

Bjólf and Gunnar stared at each other in disbelief.

"Regroup!" shouted Bjólf, a note of unease in his voice. "And stay close." He grabbed the man roughly by the shoulder, spun him round and shoved him onward.

As the party of men followed the curve of the wide track, adrenaline still pumping, a group of ragged women and children came into view. Several of the women were on their knees. One pulled at her own clothes and wailed hysterically at the sky. Beyond them, a great fire raged. At first, Bjólf could not make out what it was about it that brought back buried memories. Then the wind gusted, carrying a smell of burnt meat and tallow. And he realised. What he had first thought to be thick branches in the huge pile of wood were the twisted limbs of men. Bodies were heaped one upon the other, crackling, spitting, bubbling. Sizzling fat dripped into the earth, bones cracked, body parts popped and spat and sent jets of steam into the smoky air.

"Gods!" breathed Gunnar. "What happened here?" But it was plain to see. Whoever had raided the village had hit them hard and fast. Efficient. Seasoned. Merciless.

On the pyre, something moved – still alive. Bjólf shuddered.

"Is this how you treat your dead here?" said Godwin, barely able to hide the revulsion in his voice. "You should show more respect, give them the proper rites, or they will surely come back to haunt you."

"No! We have to burn them." said the big man. He gesticulated wildly as he spoke and clawed pathetically at Bjólf's sleeve, a hysterical tone to his voice. "We must send them up quickly. To *stop* them coming back. It can happen. I've heard of it! It's the only way to be sure..."

Some of Bjólf's crew – battle-hardened though they were – were visibly unsettled by the man's words and the weird, grisly scene. But Bjólf knew it was not fear of death or physical threat that got to them. It was something much worse. Something harder to fight.

"This is a bad omen," said Finn.

"Ah, he's lost his wits," said Bjólf dismissively, and spat in the mud. "Do you blame him?" He was well aware there were superstitious men among his crew – warriors and sailors were the worst for that. But he needed to keep them focused. He turned to Gunnar, speaking now so the others could not overhear. "Can you believe this? No raids for years – no one even knowing it was here – then two at once! This is not turning out to be a good day."

Gunnar sighed heavily, surveying the chaos. He could tell by the damage to the bodies that those who hit this place knew exactly what they were doing. And that was not all. "Could've been worse," he said wistfully. Then, after a thoughtful pause, added: "We might've run into him ourselves."

Bjólf eyed him for a moment. "Then you're thinking what I'm thinking..."

Gunnar nodded.

"Grimmsson." Even uttering the name made Bjólf's teeth clench.

"Looks like his work."

"It couldn't be anyone else." Bjólf waved his sword in frustration at the bodies heaped on the crude funeral pyre. "Look at this mess! These peasants are not the sort to resist. But killing five or six straight off as an example... That's his way." Gunnar nudged the big man with his axe. "You! How many were there?"

"More than I've ever seen. Seventy or eighty at least."

"And the sail of their ship – what colour?"

"Red!" wailed the big man, a bubble of snot bursting beneath his nose as he whimpered at the memory. He flung a wild arm past the fire and smoke, where the village broadened out and dipped down to the bank of the northern river, whose waters were clearly visible. "That's where they came... Took everything. Then off upriver. Just like that. They've ruined us!"

He fell quivering to his knees.

There was no doubting it, then. For Bjólf, it was yet another reason to detest his rival. Not that he needed one. He hated everything about him. His brutality, his arrogance, his massively inflated ego. And, most of all, that *fucking red sail...* Only Helgi Grimmsson was possessed of the kind of vanity – not to mention bad taste – to have an entire ship's sail dyed red. The man had too much money and no honour. Unfortunately, he seemed to attract an exceptionally large number of men – all of whom were as dishonourable, foolhardy and dangerous as him. And with the opportunities for freelance operations dwindling as more regions came under the sway of kings, it was becoming increasingly likely that they would run into Grimmsson's sadly far larger vessel. And that, Bjólf knew, was a confrontation that he could not win.

"Got the same tip as us, I reckon," muttered Gunnar.

"And got to it first..."

"Payback for Roskilde..."

Bjólf stared dejectedly. But, in spite of everything, he was counting his blessings.


As THE *VIKINGR* launched their attack, Atli had crept cautiously from his hiding place at the edge of the trees and made his way into the village. Everything that had been so familiar for so long – for his whole life – suddenly seemed strange. A kind of panic gripped him. There was no sign of Yngvar's pig, nor of his fowls. Tools lay here and there, as if suddenly abandoned. He had seen the warriors advance ahead of him, and heard their shouts to one another, seen the disarray as he passed dwellings with their doors swinging open. But nothing had prepared him for the sight that finally greeted him: the spitting flames, the acrid smoke, and the stunned looks on the faces of all gathered there. What had happened here? As he approached, a pair of cowed figures appeared on the track. Bera, her face set in a grim expression, and a younger woman who Atli knew as Úlfrún, her features deathly pale and weirdly blank, as if suddenly deprived of the ability to show emotion. They were dragging something between them on a blanket. A body. As they struggled past dejectedly, the head flopped out from its wrappings, its lifeless eyes seeming to gape at Atli. It was a horrific sight: the right cheek purple and swollen almost beyond recognition from some massive blow, and the lower jaw hanging completely off, swinging horribly as they plodded along.

It was Yngvar.

Atli watched as the women shuffled on towards the fire, Bera's gaze catching his. It seemed to cut through him. He felt sick and confused, not understanding what had happened. As he drew closer to the pyre, through the wafting, bitter smoke, he saw, near to the captain and his big companion, a pitiful figure crouched upon the floor. The man had his head in his hands, but Atli recognised him immediately.

BJÓLF WATCHED BERA and Úlfrún heave the limp body onto the fire, sending a shower of sparks into the air, their faces red from its fierce heat. A blackened skull rolled out of the heap, smoke billowing from its eye sockets.

"Old woman," said Bjólf, a note of pleading in his voice, "why are you doing this? It's madness."

Bera stared back at him and shrugged. "What else can we do?"

He regarded his men, then the villagers. "Well, we'll take some firewood at least. It's better keeping the living warm than the dead."

The big man on the ground looked up, a slightly crazed expression upon his face. "Oh yes, why not?" He laughed, and stood up. "Take it all! Take our homes!" And with that he rushed to the nearest house, trying to pull pieces of wood off it in a frenzy. "Take this! We've no need of it now! Yes! Burn it! Burn it all!" Clawing hopelessly at the solid door and frame, sweat flying off his fevered brow, he succeeded only in tearing off a few meagre strips and several of his fingernails before finally collapsing once again in a sobbing heap. Bjólf and Gunnar watched with a mixture of pity and contempt.

"You can have mine."

Bjólf turned to find the farm boy, standing, arms outstretched, holding his bundle of sticks towards him. The big man on the ground gawped up at the boy in shock, struck dumb. He returned his father's gaze in silence. As boy and man faced each other, the resemblance was suddenly clear. Both Gunnar and Bjólf noted the look that passed between them, and understood.

Bjólf nodded slowly, a flicker of a smile creeping across his face. "Take it back to the ship," he said, packing the boy off with a slap on the shoulder. He looked back once, then ran headlong towards the forest, the bundle under his arm. The boy's father raised his head slowly, tears welling up in his reddened eyes, and held Bjólf's gaze. "A curse on you and all your kind," he said in a hoarse whisper. "May all you've killed return to claim you." And with that, his head fell again.

Bjólf watched him in silence for a moment, then turned to his men, determined to make the best of the dismal situation. "Let's see what we can salvage from this mess and get out of here..." Then he muttered to Gunnar, with a nod towards the father: "... before we all end up as crazy as him..."

Gunnar shrugged. "Maybe he's not so crazy."

Bjólf stopped in his tracks. It seemed Gunnar, for all his old-fashioned ways, still had the capacity to surprise him. "He's throwing his neighbours on a bonfire to prevent them rising from the grave. These are hardly the actions of a sane man. Someone of your religious convictions should at least deplore the lack of ceremony."

"Maybe there's something in his stories."

"Or maybe," said Bjólf dismissively, "he's suffered brain sickness as a result of a serious blow to the head." He turned away once more.

"I'm just saying I've heard of such things, that's all. The dead coming back, I mean."

Bjólf stared back at his friend.

"It was from a merchant..." began Gunnar defensively, his face reddening. "Last time in Hedeby." He raised his hands in an apologetic gesture. "I'm only telling you what he said." Bjólf looked from Gunnar's face to those of his men in amazement. One or two gruffly acknowledged Gunnar's words.

"I met a man last month who said he'd seen it with his own eyes," said Godwin. "South of here. Dead men walking. Refused to put ashore, even though his crew was parched. Face was white as a swan's back when he told me."

"Everyone's heard tales of *draugr*," added Úlf. "And more often, of late."

"Tell me you don't believe all this," said Bjólf. "Stories to scare children!"

"The people there told of fire-drakes flying in the air, and the sea boiling – terrible portents." Godwin added.

Magnus stared at the pyre, its flames glinting in his eye. "The gospels tell of such things." A few men murmured in agreement. "They say that when the dead return, it is a sign of the coming Apocalypse. The end of all things."

Gunnar nodded solemnly. "Ragnarók."

Bjólf looked from face to face in silence. "Horseshit! Will you listen to yourselves? The dead coming back! You sound like old women! One bad raid and suddenly you're doubting everything." They stood, heads hanging, like chastised infants. He pointed at them with his sword, sweeping it slowly from one side to the other. "We've seen more death than most. Never yet has someone I've put down with my sword got up again." He fixed his steely eyes on each one of them in turn. "So, tell me, has any one of you, ever, in your whole life, and with your own eyes, seen a dead man walk?"

Magnus shuffled his feet uncomfortably. "I know it's in your bible-book, Brother Magnus..." said Bjólf irritably, not looking at him. "But *actually seen...*"

None spoke, their eyes cast down. Bjólf turned on Gunnar.

"And you, of all people, should know better than to listen to merchants' tales. They spend half their time going to places that are just like everywhere else, and the other half inventing things designed to make them sound more exotic."

"Like 'rich pickings' you mean?" grumbled Gunnar.

Under normal circumstances, Bjólf – rarely at a loss for

words – would have countered Gunnar's comment with an even more withering reply. It was the kind of exchange upon which their relationship was largely based – a relationship only made possible by an underlying, mutual respect. But just now, he seemed not to have registered Gunnar's words. His mind was elsewhere, his expression changed, distant. Beneath his helm, a frown creased his brow. "Coming back..." he muttered to himself. Gunnar looked at him, puzzled.

"You say the raiders who came before us went *upriver*? What is upriver?" Bjólf shook Atli's father roughly by his shoulders. The man just stared at him, vacantly. "They went upriver to see if there was anything more worth having. Is there? *What is upriver?*"

"Nothing." Bera stepped forward, her head raised, her gaze unwavering. "Water. A bend in the river. Then rocks."

"Rocks?"

"A ford. Beyond the fells." She waved her hand vaguely at the eastern horizon.

"Deep enough for a ship?"

"Only if you have a crew happy to drag it."

Bjólf and Gunnar looked at each other.

"It's fully-laden," said Bjólf. "They won't be dragging that ship over any rocks."

Gunnar's expression became one of slow realisation. "They're coming back..."

"We have to get out of here."

In haste, they turned to leave, Bjólf rallying his men to him. As they did so, Gunnar glanced back towards the river. His face fell.

"Too late."

# CHAPTER FIVE

## HELGI GRIMMSSON

No SOONER HAD the distinctive, spiked prow of Grimmson's ship loomed into view between the banks of dark trees than his men were pouring ashore, spilling over the garishly-painted gunwales and swarming up the grey, stony bank. They pointed and shouted, some shaking their weapons with movements that, from a distance, seemed wildly exaggerated – almost absurd. For a split second, Bjólf and his crew stood stunned – then, instinctively, and as one, tensed and tightened, locking shields, shoulders hunched, weapons gripped, muscles set, as their fate flung itself headlong towards them.

"Orders?" barked Gunnar.

Bjólf hesitated.

"It's two to one at least," came Kjötvi's voice.

"If we stand, we die," added Godwin.

"I thought we all returned from the dead nowadays," said Bjólf, tersely. Still he did not move.

Godwin gave a grim smile. "Let's not put that to the test just yet, eh?"

"Nothing focuses the mind like a blade in the belly," said Gunnar, then added – more urgently this time: "Orders?"

Bjólf knew there was only one choice. But the thought of showing his back to Grimmsson – of running... It stuck in his craw. Anger welled up and pride gnawed at him. His teeth clenched until he felt they would crack, the paralysing knot of indecision burning in his chest.

Grimmsson's men – many with their clothes awry and bereft of armour – were now pounding up the track, red-faced, the fire from the previous raid still in their eyes and the new fury on their faces clearly visible, their hurled insults already striking the ears of their quarry, their footfalls shaking the earth.

An arrow glanced off the rim of Úlf's shield and was sent high into the air. It was now or never. Steeling himself for the inevitable humiliation of retreat, Bjólf raised his sword and took the breath to give the command, when... A harsh cry from the depths of the advancing army brought the thundering horde to a shuddering halt. Bjólf froze, holding his breath, sword aloft, every sinew taut. From either end of the rutted village track the two sides eyed each other in a tense, eerie silence. For the first time, Bjólf became aware that the villagers had disappeared – no trace of them remained, except those whose corpses still crackled and spluttered upon the fire. Then the ranks of the opposing army parted, and from them stepped Helgi Grimmson himself.

He stopped a few paces from his men. Built like an ox – and, Bjólf knew, with a personality to match – Grimmsson stood, stripped to the waist, his shirt tied loosely around his middle, looking for all the world like a man called forth in the middle of a wash. He was armed only with a long, grey throwing spear and, like the majority of his men, had neither helm upon his head nor mail upon his body. Clearly, this encounter had caught them by surprise, with their guard down, basking in the glory of a successful raid. Equally clear was the fact that they had not had the time – or the inclination – to equip themselves before confronting Bjólf and his crew.

"He wants to talk..." muttered Bjólf, barely able to conceal his own disbelief.

Gunnar frowned. "But why?"

"I could take him," said Fjölvar, a white-fletched arrow ready on his bow.

"No!" said Bjólf, and, lowering his sword, took two steps forward. "Let's see what he wants."

For a moment the pair stood face-to-face across the yards of hoof-churned mud, behind one a knot of armoured men in tight formation, behind the other a steaming, panting horde. Bjólf debated within himself how best to approach this previously undreamt-of dialogue. Open with a joke? Grimmsson had no sense of humour. An expression of defiance? Unwise, under the circumstances. Keep it simple, perhaps. Firm and direct. Polite.

No sooner had Bjólf settled on a form of words than Grimmsson flung his arms wide and bellowed to the sky at the top of his lungs. "ODIN!" The sound echoed off the distant, mist-wreathed mountains. Rooks croaked in alarm in the far treetops. "To you, I dedicate this... my enemy's DESTRUCTION!" And with a great, bestial grunt he hurled the spear high over the heads of Bjólf and his men.

There was to be no hesitation this time. "Run..." hissed Bjólf – and as they turned, a great roar rose again from the throats of their foe.

What followed was chaotic and confused. With the slope in their favour as they pounded over the rise and back towards the trees, Bjólf's crew made good headway against their pursuers. But as Grimmsson's men charged down the same incline, unencumbered by mail and equipment, the gap began to close. When Bjólf and his men hit the trees, arrows, axes and other projectiles were already thudding around them. There was no time to look back. Bjólf flew along the path, lashed by branches, occasionally catching glimpses of members of his crew ahead of him, and dimly aware of others crashing through undergrowth to his left and right. The forest muffled the savage cries of their enemies. It became impossible to judge distance. Bjólf could no longer guess how close he was to capture or death. He only knew to keep running.

As the path widened and the trees became more scattered, he knew at last that he was nearing the south river – and the safety of their ship. Up ahead and converging on either side of him he could now see dozens of his own men. From the left, Fjölvar flew out from a tangle of brambles and overtook Bjólf with incredible speed, face scratched and bleeding. A long-bladed spear whizzed after him as he hurtled past, missing by an arm's length and sending a chunk of bark flying as it caught the trunk of a beech tree. To the right, Kjötvi – running full tilt – suddenly cried out and fell with a heavy thud, bowling over and over in an eruption of leaves and pine needles. From behind, crunching through the forest like a giant, came the hulking figure of Gunnar who, without stopping, grabbed Kjötvi's padded tunic, hauled him to his feet and set him back on course for the beach before Kjötvi had time to realise what had happened.

Finally, his lungs bursting, Bjólf broke out of the trees. Ahead, a few were already at the ship, their shoulders to the prow. More joined them, heaving at the old, heavy timbers. The final stretch down to the water's edge seemed to expand like a bad dream. Bjólf felt his feet – made clumsy by exertion – stumbling over the uneven stones, then sinking into the rough, grey shingle as he grew closer to the shore. Finally, close to the water, the ground firmed up; he put on a burst of speed and cannoned into the ship with his shoulder. It shifted against the grit. Gunnar slammed into it with a great roar, and the ship slid another five paces. With the cries of their pursuers ringing in their ears, the gathering men heaved at the hull. It began to move easily now, further with each effort. Turning, Bjólf saw that the first of Grimmsson's men would be upon them before they made clear water: at least five – the youngest and fittest – were already half way down the beach. But these few had run so swiftly, with such eagerness, that they were now alone – unsupported by their slower comrades. And they were without shield or armour.

As his men splashed deeper into the river, heaving the ship away from the shore, Bjólf did something his pursuers did not expect. He turned and ran at them. Bjólf barely had time to register the lead attacker's shocked expression before delivering a devastating punch to his face with the iron boss of his shield, knocking him flat and sending his axe flying. Without pausing, Bjólf swung round with the full weight of his sword and caught the second attacker across the face, his blade smashing through his teeth. He felt hot blood splash across his cheek and bits of tooth rattle off his shield. The man's momentum carried him forward, and he careered drunkenly for several more paces, his smashed, almost severed head gurgling and gushing as he finally collapsed face-first onto the rocks. He was dead before he hit the ground.

A third had gathered his wits and was on Bjólf before he had time to prepare himself, aiming a huge swing of his short axe at Bjólf's exposed shoulder. Instinctively, his head turning in anticipation of the impact, Bjólf punched upward with his shield and caught the full force of the blow. The axe blade cut through the wood of the shield, narrowly missing his left forearm, and was firmly wedged, gripped by the grain. Without stopping to think, Bjólf heaved violently with his shield, giving his assailant two choices: keep a grip on his axe and be pulled to the ground, or let go and lose his weapon altogether. The man – a wiry character with a spiky, brown beard and a missing front tooth – surprised Bjólf by immediately letting go. The man was now unarmed, but he had his feet and he was alive.

At once, Bjólf sensed he had a bold and unpredictable opponent. Without hesitation, knowing the urgent need to end this, he aimed a killing blow at the man's exposed head, but as he did so, the man surprised him again, charging at him, grabbing at the embedded axe and almost wrenching both axe and shield from Bjólf's grasp. The sword blow came down wildly but with full force, missing his opponent's head but finding another target. As Bjólf struggled to steady himself, he saw the man stagger back, staring with a strange, blank expression at the cleanly cut stumps where his hands had been, his thumping, battle-charged heart pumping the lifeblood from him, a splash of steaming red upon the dull, grey stones.

Now Grimmsson's men were coming in their droves. Bjólf

turned and, not daring to look back, ran headlong for the ship – now floating free of the beach, hastily deploying oars like the struggling legs of a great insect. As he neared, splashing into the water, his throat and lungs on fire, he saw Fjölvar perched on the dragon prow, bow drawn, and aimed directly, it seemed to Bjólf, at his head. The bowstring sang. The arrow hissed past – so close, Bjólf felt the wind from it brush his right cheek. Behind him was a stifled cry; something heavy fell, catching his heel, and the sword that had meant to cleave his skull clattered past him into the rocky shallows. With moments to spare before Grimmsson's men overran them, Bjólf flung his shield over the bow of the ship and Gunnar' reached down, grabbed his hand, and hauled him aboard.

Panting heavily, his head throbbing, Bjólf lay flat on his back on the deck as the ship headed into the safety of deeper water. Bathed in sweat, his armour weighing upon him, he watched as more men joined Fjölvar at the prow to pick off Grimmsson's men with their bows. Then, as the ship turned slowly downriver, he stood, threw off his helm and surveyed with relief the receding mob left behind on the riverbank. Nodding wordlessly, he slapped Gunnar on the shoulder.

Gunnar nodded back. "I see you had to go back for a souvenir." Bjólf followed his gaze. Upon the deck was his cloven shield, the axe still embedded in it, and, still gripping it, one of the pale, lifeless hands of its owner.

He looked back over the heads of his crew, now settling into an even rhythm as Úlf, who had taken the role of *rávordr* – the watch position by the mast – called the strokes. Bjólf's eyes darted from man to man, only now realising that not all were on board.

"Hallgeir?" he called.

"Spear in the back," panted Finn.

"And Steinarr?"

Magnus Grey-Beard answered him. "I saw him fall on the rocks as the shore was overrun. He was last out of the trees."

Bjólf cursed under his breath. It was not their way to leave others behind. He remembered that, before the raid, Steinarr had been complaining about a loose shoe. Quite likely, it had been the death of him. Bjólf gazed through the mist towards the ugly horde on the stony bank, wondering at Steinarr's fate. Then, another distant cry went up, and before they were finally swallowed up by fog he saw Grimmsson's men turn again and make for the trees.

It wasn't over.

# CHAPTER SIX

## THE WHALE ROAD

GUNNAR IMMEDIATELY SENSED something was wrong. "You hurt?
Apart from your pride, I mean..."

Bjólf, still staring back upriver, ignored his question. "I need
you to take the helm."

"Thorvald has it."

"It's going to need more weight behind it..." Gunnar frowned.
Bjólf spoke without turning. "They were heading back to their
ship. In haste. The north river joins us up ahead – and it flows
faster than this one." Without another word, Gunnar turned
and hurried towards the stern.

Bjólf climbed high in the prow, arm wrapped around the
dragon's neck. "Úlf! Full-stroke on the oars!"

Some of the men – until now laughing and joking with relief,
blood still fizzing in their veins – looked at one another in
concern. A silence fell.

"We're not out of this yet," added Bjólf, a sense of foreboding in his voice.

With a terse nod, Úlf changed to a new chant – a song, this time, slow to begin, but gradually picking up the pace, from short-stroke, through steady-stroke, until the men were rowing at the limit of their abilities. The ship creaked and cracked, lurching forward as each pull on the oars ploughed its timbers on through the water. The song told of sailing north to Tronhjem – a cheerful song of homecoming. It was the one Úlf always used when speed was required. They needed a cheerful song then; rowing at full-stroke meant they were rowing for their lives. At other times, when the rowing was more leisurely, the men would often raise their voices together, but this song was always sung alone.

Leaning hard into the steer-board, praying to Thor that the old leather of the rudder-band would take the exertion, Gunnar steered the straightest possible course through the bends of the river, taking the ship as close to the banks as he dared. Magnus and Godwin, not needed at the oars, positioned themselves amidships to port and starboard, signalling to Gunnar at any sign of rocks or sandbanks, while Thorvald, relieved from his position at the helm, had taken up a section of planking just behind the mast-fish – the huge block of oak that held the mast – and stood waist-deep below the deck, wooden scoop in hand, ready to bail when they hit wilder waters.

None spoke. Only Úlf's voice rang out, strangely muffled by the fog, its beats matched by each dip of the oars.

His eyes straining as they struggled to penetrate the fog, Bjólf could finally make out the swirling waters where the north river joined immediately ahead. They would pick up some speed here, but would also find out if they had escaped the wrath of their pursuers. If they could not see each other in the mist, Bjólf knew they were safe.

As the ship pulled past the dwindling promontory of land separating the two rivers, the current caught the ship and turned its bows away from the mouth of the north river. Looking upstream, struggling to see past the mast and stowed yard and sail, Bjólf could see nothing in the grey gloom. He breathed a sigh of relief. But as Gunnar pulled against the steerboard, straightening the line of the ship, he heard a faint cry in the distance, and – as if from nowhere – the gaunt shadow of Grimmsson's ship hove into view. Up by the stark dragon's head, holding aloft a burning torch, the unmistakeable figure of Grimmsson himself. Before him, just visible on the front edge of the prow, thick iron spikes projected forward like great thorns, a gesture of contempt – and a hint of what was to come – for any vessel that got in their way. Another of Grimmsson's affectations. Another reason to detest the man. Yet Bjólf could not deny the tenacity of his crew. How they had made up the distance so fast, he could not imagine. But there was no time to think about it.

"Row! Everything you've got!" he roared. Similar cries went up from Grimmsson's ship. It would be a race all the way to the estuary and the open sea.

A pair of arrows, their tips aflame and sticky with pitch, flew towards them, falling short and hissing in the water near the rudder. "They mean to make a fire-ship of us." bellowed Gunnar. "We need to stay out of range!"

"I'm not ready for a funeral just yet," roared Bjólf, and leapt down from his position on the prow. He raced the length of the vessel, eyes wide, willing on the straining muscles of his crew as he passed. "Come on!" he cried. "Leave the bastards standing!"

Úlf had abandoned his song and was now shouting the strokes, pushing them faster, faster.

Bjólf stood by Gunnar, looking back from the stern at their dogged pursuers with a deep frown, the defiance from seconds before now turned to consternation. "How did they do that? Fully-laden, with a poor start and a crew that ran over twice the distance, and still they're right on our tail."

"They must really hate us!" cried Gunnar, leaning hard into the rudder.

Bjólf turned an eye to the bronze weather vane on top of the mast. He knew they could easily outrun Grimmsson's ship under sail. But, in such weather, a decent wind was a remote hope. Up above, the bronze vane swung loose, the black ribbons tied to its edge flapping limply.

With thirty-two oars and now only thirty-eight men – including himself – there was no chance of respite for any but a handful of his crew. Each man could normally manage around a thousand strokes before needing rest, but at this pace, their backs would start to break at six hundred. He only hoped it was enough.

As they pulled away from the mouth of the estuary the fog thinned, the jagged coastline curving away into the murk on either side of them. "This is where it begins," said Bjólf, and turned towards the bow again.

"Which way?" called Gunnar.

Bjólf pointed straight ahead. "The open sea." He swung past the mast and headed back to his position at the prow.

Gunnar stared after him in alarm. Ahead, the flat, leaden grey swell of the ocean heaved beneath a shroud of luminous mist.

"In this? It's madness!"

"Let's hope they feel the same," called Bjólf, and gave a disconcertingly wild laugh. Somehow he seemed to thrive in such moments of desperate adversity.

As they left the protection of the estuary, the ship began to rise and fall on the swell, every timber protesting at the conflicting pressures of oar and ocean, salt spray stinging hands and faces. At the crest of the first steep wave, several of the men in the bows failed to connect their oars with the water and missed a stroke, falling into the men behind them. Hastily they regained their positions, slotting back into the rhythm. Bjólf could not hope for a better crew. But it unsettled him to be heading out from shore into such deep, rolling seas – he'd seen a longship break its back on the swell once, out on the merciless waters of the North Sea. Light and flexible as they were – shallow of draught and slim of build – longships were not at their best in the open ocean. He knew that Grimmsson, with his larger ship and heavier cargo, was at far greater risk. Yet Grimmsson also had more fresh men to relieve his rowers. It would be a battle of wills now. A game of bluff. Bjólf had only one chance, but it meant gambling everything they had.

As the ship rode up the swell, Bjólf looked down onto the pursuing vessel as if from the side of a great valley. They were riding the seas more heavily than Bjólf and his crew, it seemed. The distance between them was growing. The hull of the ship creaked and gave an agonised groan as it tipped again over the peak of the swell, making Grimmsson's ship disappear completely before rising once more above them. The spray cascaded over the bows; Thorvald bailed ceaselessly, the seawater slopping past his feet, keeping time with the rowers – and, amazingly, given the circumstances, humming Úlf's tune to himself. Bjólf felt the timbers shift and twist against each other once again and gritted his teeth. He knew this ship better than any man alive – it was the vessel left to him at the age of only twenty, given to his uncle Olaf years before in recognition of his services to Haakon the Good of Norway. Bjólf never knew the full story, nor the nature of the services (it was the one thing of which Olaf never spoke); all that was certain was that they had earned Olaf the undying hatred of no less than Eirik Bloodaxe, doomed king of Jorvik.

This, then, was one of the great old ships – but for the mast, and a few repaired strakes on the starboard bow, built entirely of oak, and shapely as a swan. She had journeyed to the kingdom of the Rus in the east, and south as far as the Arab lands. She had sailed into Constantinople, and made landfall in Ireland, Normandy, England, the Orkneys and the kingdom of the Franks. She had proved her worth in battle against men, wind and sea, and been Bjólf's true home for the past ten winters. But even he could not be certain of her limits. He would only know them when she finally tore herself apart. Gazing up pleadingly at the dragon's head, he slapped the thick timber of the prow. "Keep it together, old girl. Just a little longer..."

His crew were close to the limit of their endurance now – arms and backs straining, veins and muscles standing out like whipcords, teeth clenched, breaths coming hard and fast. Most had not had time to remove their armour before the chase. Sweat poured off their brows. But, by some miracle – a miracle of muscle and grim determination – they were continuing to pull ahead.

"We have them!" hollered Bjólf. "A few more strokes, and they're dead in the water." The words seemed to drive his men to even greater exertion, a last burst of defiance. Yet, no sooner had he uttered them than one of the men – fourth rower from the port bow – collapsed.

Kjötvi.

As he fell forward, limp and strangely pale, he hit the man in front, knocking him off his stroke. His own oar flailed uselessly, clashing with the two behind. Other oars down the line clashed and faltered as the rhythm broke on the port side. The ship heaved and rocked alarmingly as the uneven pressure of the oars began to turn her. Gunnar fought with the tiller. If they hit the swell at a bad angle, they were in trouble.

Bjólf leapt forward and, as Magnus hauled Kjötvi clear, took control of the oar. Around his feet, the deck was dark and sticky, the froth from the sea spray stained red. Kjötvi's blood. "Pull!" he cried, as the men fought to re-establish the rhythm. "*Pull!*"

The ship straightened. Bjólf heaved on the oar until he felt it would crack, driving his men on, spurring them to one last effort. After what seemed a lifetime, the waters broadened and smoothed, and Grimmsson's ship gradually receded into the fog, until, finally, only the distant glimmer of the torch remained as evidence of its existence.

"Rest!" called Bjólf. The men collapsed over their oars, gulping at the air. A few whooped and cheered in triumph. Bjólf hushed them. Moving astern, he squinted at the faint orange glow in the fog. Bjólf spoke to his expectant crew in hushed tones. "Keep it quiet. And nothing over the side – you can bet Týr's right hand they'll be on the lookout for that. If you have to piss, you piss in a pot." There were nods all round. Some were only now able to throw off their armour, groaning at the pain in their exhausted limbs. He broke into a smile, allowing himself to feel a glow of satisfaction for these men who placed such trust in him. "Good job."

With that, he kicked open a long, rather battered sea chest, flipped his own mail shirt over his aching shoulders and bundled it inside. Pulling out a thick blue cape, he fastened it around him with a bronze brooch, and, slamming the chest shut, gazed at the lid for a moment, lost in thought. In the surface of the wood – once the colour of a fresh horse chestnut, now bleached by sun and scoured by salt – were delicate carvings of the hero Sigurd slaying the dragon Fafnir. They were in the old style. The chest had once belonged to his uncle, and – despite his father's efforts to keep his eldest son focused on the farm, and the wayward brother at a safe distance – had always inspired him as a child, whenever his uncle came visiting from his voyages. Bjólf had imagined himself as the dragonslayer, travelling the world and doing great deeds; a proud and noble warrior. While the reality of adult life had proved a little more complicated, there were fleeting moments when that childhood dream seemed once again to flicker into life. Despite the terrible misfortunes of the day, this was one of them.

"Is there a plan?" said Gunnar, breaking the spell.

"We gather our strength. Then we row with a half-crew, taking shifts of five hundred strokes, until we lose that..." He pointed toward the stern, where the flame of Grimmsson's ship was still dimly visible.

"And then?"

Bjólf surveyed the blank, still greyness that surrounded them on every side. "One thing at a time."

# CHAPTER SEVEN

## KJÖTVI THE LUCKY

KJÖTVI LAY ON the raised deck at the prow, deathly pale, his lips tinged with blue, but for the flickering in his eyelids, the very image of a corpse.

"Will he live? asked Bjólf.

"He's lost a lot of blood," said Magnus. "His skin is clammy." That was a bad sign. Magnus had propped Kjötvi's legs up on a chest to slow the flow of blood and, using a small collection of delicate iron tools spread out on their leather wrapping, was now engaged in cutting open the ragged, blood-soaked material to reveal the wound on the lower part of Kjötvi's left leg. As he carefully snipped and peeled away the wet, sticky fabric, a flap of flesh fell open, spilling thick gobbets of half-clotted blood on the deck. It looked for all the world as if someone had tried to carve a neat slice from Kjötvi's calf, mistaking it for a roasting joint. "A blade caught him from above," said

Magnus, indicating the line of entry with the flat of his hand. "Very sharp. Very deep. But the battle-fire was in him. Probably didn't even feel it."

"In the woods...." said Gunnar, nodding. "A throwing axe flew past my ear and bounced off his leg. I helped him up."

Magnus examined the angle. "Stopped against the bone. He's fortunate to have kept his foot."

"Kjötvi the Lucky," muttered Gunnar. He did not appear so lucky just now, lying there, half dead. But then, mused Gunnar, half dead was better than all dead.

With delicate movements, compensating for the slow rise and fall of the ship, Magnus peered into the depths of the wound, tentatively opening up the sliced muscle tissue. He squinted hard with his one good eye, a pair of iron tweezers between his steady fingers. "There's something I need to..." Before he could finish his sentence, blood suddenly began to flow again, dripping through the fingers of Magnus's supporting hand. "Ach! We could do with more light here."

"We could risk it, for Kjötvi's sake," said Bjólf.

"Wait..." said Magnus. He knew time was not on their side. Holding his breath, he reached deep into the wound with the tweezers, then emerged with a short, yellow-white sliver of bone between its tiny jaws. "That's where the axe stopped," he said, exhaling heavily. "At least that won't stay rattling around inside him." Without further delay, he pressed the sticky halves of the wound together and, gesturing for Gunnar to place pressure upon it, began to bind up the leg with strips of linen.

Gunnar looked thoughtful. "That could have been my head."

"His bad luck was your good luck," said Bjólf.

Magnus sighed. "Were we ashore, I'd seek herbs to aid the healing. As it is... It's in God's hands now." He silently blessed his patient, kissed a small wooden cross hanging from a thong of leather around his neck and tucked it back into his brown robe.

Stooping, Gunnar picked up the small shard of bone, chipped off Kjötvi's leg like a piece of whittled wood. Studying it between his great thumb and forefinger, he shuddered inwardly, wiped it clean on his sleeve, then tucked it in the small leather bag hanging from his belt. He looked up to the featureless dark sky and muttered to himself. "Gentle Eir – listen to the pleading of this faithful old fool and care for our battle-weary friend." Drawing his knife, he pricked his thumb and let a drop of blood fall onto the deck.

Bjólf placed a hand on Magnus's shoulder. "Do what you can," he said, straightening up. "And do not trust too much to gods, or miraculous resurrections."

He walked with Gunnar, picking his way past the men, huddled between their sea-chests, wrapped in thick woollen capes and furs. After their momentary victory, the fall of Kjötvi had put them in a melancholy mood. The fog clung to them, making everything damp with beads of moisture. At the small steering deck, Bjólf relieved Finn at aft watch and stared with Gunnar out across the darkening sea. For a long time they stood and watched in silence, the only sounds the lap of the water, the creak of the timbers and the occasional isolated cough from a member of the crew. The swell was longer and more even now, and night was almost upon them. Of Grimmsson there was no sign. Not even a glimmer in the failing light.

"Must've given up," muttered Gunnar.

"Can you blame them?" said Bjólf, blowing through his hands, his breaths turning to fog. "They'll be feasting on roasted pork and lamb tonight. On dry land. And where are *we*?"

"Hey, we're alive, aren't we?"

"No, really..." said Bjólf squinting at the featureless gloom surrounding them. "Where *are* we?"

"No sun. No stars. No moon." Gunnar sniffed the cold air, then licked his finger and held it aloft. "No wind... No land in sight. Not even a horizon. No creatures in the sea, nor birds in the air." He shrugged. "It's anybody's guess."

"And what would your guess be?"

"My guess would be no better than yours," he said, then, after a moment's hesitation, added: "But Kjötvi would know."

Kjötvi the Lucky was *kentmand* – one who had a deep knowledge of the seas. He was also the unluckiest person Bjólf had ever met; one of those for whom fate seemed to deliver ten times the misfortune of ordinary men. It had become a standing joke among the crew. In the past, some had expressed reservations about even having him on board. In the course of their current voyage, he had lost his father's helmet in a well, his mail coat overboard, his sword and half his ear. But the one thing Kjötvi had never lost was himself. He knew the currents of the air and the water – and perhaps others yet more subtle – better than any man. 'Wayfinder,' they called him, and it was this uncanny ability that persuaded even the most superstitious of the men to accept him. If Kjötvi could not find a way, they would say, there was not a way to be found. Others said the gods had played a cruel trick, granting him exceptional powers of foresight and sensitivity to the ebb and flow of the world, but taking half of his luck in payment.

"Kjötvi..." said Bjólf with a sigh. And then there was Hallgeir and Steinarr. "This has not been a good day." He dug absent-mindedly at a large splinter in his left palm – where and when he'd got that, he had no memory – then, with a deep sigh, pulled his cloak tighter and stared out again into the nothingness that surrounded them.

"You know what's hardest to take?" he said dejectedly. "Grimmson's men didn't even bother to put their armour on. Do they really have such a poor opinion of us?"

"I think it's more a measure of their blind hatred."

Bjólf looked sideways at him.

Gunnar shrugged. "Basically, you pissed them off so much, they didn't even stop to think."

"Well, that makes me feel better."

"If you were so worried about feelings, you probably shouldn't have taken their plunder right from under their noses that time at Roskilde."

Bjólf couldn't resist a smile at the thought of it. Now *that* was a good day.

"I don't like to run, Gunnar," he said. "What is it the *Hávamál* says? 'The fool believes he'll live forever by running from battle – but old age gives no peace, even though spears might spare him.'"

"No one likes to run at the time. You'll be glad of it tomorrow." Bjólf looked unconvinced. "And anyway, you did for... what? Two of them?"

"Three."

Gunnar looked at him thoughtfully. "The thing is, I know you're not really angry because you ran. You're angry because you hesitated. But that proves it, you see?"

"Proves what?"

"You didn't run to save yourself. You ran to save your crew. Left to your own devices, I have no doubt you'd be lying hacked to bits back there, your blood feeding their crops – most likely having taken Grimmsson and several others with you."

"That hesitation cost two lives."

"Steinarr most likely lost his shoe. Hallgeir let himself get fat. Their time was up. And they died fighting."

"And Kjötvi?"

Gunnar shrugged again. "The *Hávamál* also says: 'Better blind or crippled than burning on a pyre.'"

"Better still to be in one piece."

"Ah!" Gunnar threw up his hands in disgust. "Your problem is you think you can change everything. Bend it to your will. Me? I know perfectly well I can change nothing. I follow the thread of my fate, knowing it was set down long ago."

"I cannot believe that. A man's life is his own."

"And that, my friend, is why you are our captain." Gunnar laughed and clapped his huge hand on Bjólf's shoulder. "Maybe that's your fate. To give *them* something to think about." He thrust a thumb out towards the surrounding emptiness as he spoke, at some vaguely-situated dwelling place of the gods.

Bjólf allowed himself another wry smile. For some reason – he had no idea why – the mood of one of them was always unfailingly up whenever the other's was down. He was glad there was one thing that could be relied upon. But as he continued to look out into the nothingness, some words drifted back to him. '*May all you've killed return to claim you...*' He wondered at the curse, and the broken man who had uttered it.

"How many do you suppose we have killed over the years?"

"Hmph! A small army."

"It has not always been something to be proud of."

Gunnar sighed deeply. "That, I grant you."

"Ever feel we're getting too old for all this?"

"All the time. For this life you're always too old or too young. Never exactly the right age."

"It was easier in the old days. Now there are too many earls and kings taking over, pushing people around. Hardly any opportunities left for free enterprise."

Gunnar stared into the dark water. "Norway and Denmark under one king. The White Christ replacing the old religion. The world is changing – everything being drawn to one centre. Even Harald the Blue-Toothed gives up on the ways of our ancestors. And Hedeby and the Danevirke overrun with Germans! I can't help but feel that a great age is coming to an end."

"Maybe it's time we got out."

"I must admit, the prospect of a quiet farm somewhere is starting to look increasingly attractive."

"I never thought I'd find myself thinking that. Or agreeing with you. Maybe after this, one more, then we quit. Agreed?"

Gunnar nodded slowly. "Agreed."

Bjólf spat in his palm and slapped it against Gunnar's. "Our fate's our own, old man." He waved vaguely in the direction of the gods, mocking Gunnar's gesture. "Let *them* concern themselves with someone else for a while." Gunnar grinned and shook his friend's hand heartily.

As he spoke, Magnus approached, an urgent look in his eyes. For a moment, Bjólf feared the worst. Magnus waved away Bjólf's concerns.

"He wakes from time to time," he said. "This is good. But he drifts between this world and the next. And he has no warmth in his body, for all the blankets and skins we pile upon him. Hot food or drink is what he needs now."

"We could all use some of that," said Gunnar.

Bjólf looked out again at the blank, grey night. "What we need is land. Gunnar – tell me straight: what are our chances?"

Gunnar shrugged. "If a breeze comes up, it might be enough

to take us southwest. Then we hit the coast of the English and get slaughtered like pigs. Or, perhaps, the current will be stronger and carry us north. Then, potentially, we miss landfall altogether and end up frozen to our oars for all eternity."

"And the bad news?"

"Well, if we row..."

"We're rowing blind..." said Bjólf, nodding.

"... and, at worst, we run straight back into Grimmsson. There's a chance he may yet be out there somewhere."

Bjólf sighed again. "So we have no choice but to sit tight until this fog clears and we can get our bearings." He gave Magnus a grim smile. "Looks like it's going to be a long night, brother."

Gunnar clapped him on the shoulder again, and gave a cheerful smile. "Don't worry! Thor loves the foolhardy!"

"Fjölvar!" called Bjólf. "What's our food situation?"

Fjölvar stirred, heaving himself stiffly to his feet, and, weaving past his hunched shipmates, pulled up the loose planking of the deck before the mast-fish. Immediately below was a small collection of barrels and caulked chests, lashed to the mast-beam below to prevent them shifting on the swell. He dug around, half buried below the deck.

"Some barley meal, a little dried meat, salt fish, two barrels of water, several rotting onions..." He dragged a small sack from a chest, peered in, sniffed tentatively, and recoiled. "And I think these once were mushrooms."

Gunnar sighed. "No fresh meat. No butter. And nothing to drink but water."

"It'll do, for a start," said Bjólf. "Thorvald! Finn! Throw the lines over, see what we can catch. There must be something alive out there." The two men set about the task, while Bjólf, striding past Fjölvar to the prow, dragged a bulky, heavy bundle from beneath the fore-deck and undid its wrappings. It clanked as he did so. Kjötvi stirred, his eyes flickering open for an instant.

"Sorry, my friend," said Bjólf. "But you'll thank me for it later." He unfolded a sturdy, black iron tripod – as tall as a man – pressed its clawed feet until they bit into the deck, and anchored each foot with a sack of sand. Then, drawing out a wide, charred metal dish – almost the size of a small shield – he suspended it by three long chains from the apex of the tripod. Above that, from three similar chains, he hung a large, fire-blackened cauldron.

"Now... Firewood." He scanned the length of the ship, a vague memory stirring as he caught sight of a familiar bundle of sticks tucked into the gap under the steering deck. He frowned. "Firewood..." As he looked, taking in the distribution of his men on the deck, he noted a slight list of the ship – so subtle, that another eye could not have detected it.

"Thorvald, are we taking in water?"

Thorvald looked up from baiting the lines with a frown. "No. She's sound."

Pulling his knife, Bjólf strode toward the stern, looked around for a moment, then hauled up a section of loose decking on the steer-board side, barely a pace from where he and Gunnar had been standing moments before. From the cramped, dark space below the deck, a shivering, white face peered back up at him.

The farm boy.

# CHAPTER EIGHT

## THE THING IN THE WATER

Bjólf REACHED IN with one arm and hauled the skinny wretch to face height, then deposited him roughly on deck, still clutching the front of the boy's scruffy tunic in his fist, his knife at his throat. His eyes burned with anger.

"What do you think this?" He shook the boy violently. "Just hop aboard and it's a-viking we will go? Well?" With that he pushed him away.

The lad looked at him in pale-faced shock for a moment, then vomited violently over the gunwale.

Bjólf raised his hands in despair. "This is all we need." The stowaway, recovering himself – though still slightly green – wiped his mouth, and stood swaying awkwardly on the shifting deck, every eye of the crew upon him.

"I... I thought..."

"You thought!" roared Bjólf, pointing at his face with his

knife. "This is not a child's game!"

Gunnar put a hand on Bjólf's arm. "Go easy. I seem to remember you starting out much the same way."

"That was different," spat Bjólf. But he could not hide the note of defensiveness in his voice. He had been twelve when he stowed away on his uncle Olaf's ship. It was the only time he saw Olaf get really angry with him. The storm blew over quickly – but the voyage that followed was tough on the boy, and Olaf spared him none of its hardships. Upon his return, Bjólf's father met him not with with the expected fury and platitudes, but merely silent disapproval. Secretly, he thought the experience would turn his son against the viking life, and back to more serious application on the land. It did exactly the opposite. He thought now of the wrecked village the boy had left behind – the crazed, snivelling man on his knees in the mud – and his anger began to subside.

"Well, this solves the food problem, at least," said Fjölvar. The farm boy looked at him in alarm. "What do you say? Throw him in the pot?"

Bjólf looked the boy up and down slowly and shook his head. "Too scrawny."

"I'll have a leg!" called a gruff voice from the dark. There was a chuckle beside him.

"Save me the liver," said Finn with a smile, tapping the blade of his knife against his knuckles.

"Nah," said Njáll Red-Hair, matter-of-factly, "if it's a young lad, the buttock's the best part." A few of the men snorted with a mixture of amusement and incredulity. Njáll threw his hands apart in mock innocence. "Don't blame me, lads. I heard that one from a Christian bishop." There was an uproar of laughter among the crew, during which Njáll threw a brotherly arm around Magnus and planted a kiss on the side of his head. "And if a Christian man said it, it must be true!" Magnus responded with a sardonic smile. For many of the men, those Christian jokes just never wore thin. Although Magnus was far from the only member of the crew who claimed to follow the White Christ, he was the only one to worship him exclusively, or with any real dedication. For most, he was simply another god to add to the extended family – an additional insurance policy against the perils of the world, and an uneasy bedfellow of Thor, Týr and Freyja. Even for Odo of Normandy – the only other crew member who could justifiably be termed 'Christian'– the faith had been born more out of the pragmatism of politics than of personal conviction.

Bjólf had by now regained his sense of humour, but when he turned to face the lad again, his face was sombre. He raised a hand, and the crew fell silent.

"I don't like people coming aboard my ship uninvited, large or small," he said, gravely. "But since you're here, little man, you now have a choice to make. On this ship, you're either crew, or you're cargo. If you're crew, you work, you follow my rules, and you live and die for this vessel and the men aboard it. If you're cargo... Well, let's just say that the only cargo we find ourselves interested in at the moment is the edible kind."

The stowaway looked nervously from face to face. From somewhere came the sound of a knife blade scraping slowly on a whetstone.

"C... crew..." he stammered.

"Good choice!" said Bjólf, clapping his hands and breaking into a broad smile. "Now we will throw you overboard." And with that, several of the men hoisted the boy like a sack by the hands and feet, manoeuvred him to the port side, swung him twice over the gunwale, and on the third, hurled him far out into the heaving sea.

THE COLD HIT Atli like a stone. The world turned blue-black, the distant sounds of laughter deadened by the icy water that enveloped him. He thrashed helplessly as if in a dream, ears ringing, silver bubbles bursting from him as the pressure crushed against his aching chest. He felt a sickening panic at his sudden inability to breathe, then deeper, existential dread at futility of his situation, at the terrifying scale of the surroundings, as if momentarily aware of himself as a tiny, insignificant speck in the vast, black, implacable ocean. He tried desperately to swim, to reach air, but could no longer tell which way was up or down. The strength drained from his limbs. He flailed uselessly. Then, as shock and disbelief subsided, it was replaced by a kind of detached numbness. A strange calm descended. He seemed to withdraw from his body; it felt insubstantial – nonexistent. For the first time in his life, he knew, with absolute certainty, that he was going to die.

Then, in those last moments, at the point where life and death met, a weird vision came to him. Looking down at his own body, as if from outside it, he became aware of something in the dark water below him. A pale shape, coming closer. A face. At first – such was his disorientation – he had the strange idea that it might be his own. But as it loomed nearer, its features resolved into those of a corpse, its skin and eyes as pallid as a cave fish, its flesh drawn and bloodless, lips and gums shrunk back from its jagged, broken teeth, its long, tangled hair, flecked with the whorled shells of sea snails and silver with their slime, fanned out like lank, oily weed. All over its grotesquely bloated belly and sunken chest, strange eel-like creatures clung and writhed, while pale, lifeless fish-eaten organs lolled from a ragged black cavity in its side. Out of the black water – impossibly – its dead, skeletal arm, almost stripped of tattered flesh, reached towards him, the fingers of its ghastly hand – thin and sharp as bleached fishbones – clawing convulsively at his leg.

A tug on his wrist brought him back to life. He felt a sudden, rapid motion through the water. A rope burned him. Then the distant sounds of laughter and shouting gurgled back into his head, and, as the weight of the world returned, he was heaved back onto the deck, retching and coughing up salt water, and finally lay quivering and spluttering in a pool of his own making like a helpless newborn. With one swipe of his thin knife, Wide-Face – Finn – cut the line that had been lashed to his wrist as the crew had readied him for the plunge.

Atli looked up to see the beardless captain's hand extended towards him. "Welcome aboard the *Hrafn*."

As the cheers and laughter rang around him, muffled by fog, he stood unsteadily – ears popping, water dripping in a pool at his feet. His toes were so cold now he could no longer feel them. He shivered, shoulders hunched, teeth rattling noisily in his head – a sensation he felt rather than heard – staggering awkwardly with every heaving movement of the ship, movement to which the forbidding, sturdy figures before him seemed utterly oblivious. For a moment, in a kind of abstract trance, his ears ringing from the cold and the water, his head battered by the dull thunder of their disconnected voices, he marveled at it – at the way they moved with the ship, as if part of it. Somehow, in this strange state in which he now found himself, they appeared to inhabit a different universe altogether, one in which the laws he knew – those which weighed him down, chilled him to the bone, hauled him off balance – did not apply.

He struggled to process all that had happened to him, but could hardly summon the strength. Somehow, as they had actually been happening, he had taken the day's extraordinary events in his stride, even with all their horrors and hardships. He had held on, kept going. He'd felt proud of himself over that. Strong. But now, just when it seemed he had achieved his long-held dream, now that he was once again safe – or as safe as he was likely to ever be – they threatened to overwhelm him; images and sensations flooding into his brain as if the dam holding them in check had finally burst. His dream had turned to nightmare. He felt weak and alone. Tears stung his eyes, lost in the rivulets of seawater coursing down his face. All he wanted now was to go home, and to sleep.

Back at the village, his resolve had been clear. Leaving behind its bafflingly surreal confusion – so strange and unfathomable that it had seemed to barely touch him – he had made his way back through the trampled, fragrant forest to the longship. There was nothing left for him there, no reason now to stay. He was a victim in a village of victims. But he would be that no longer. If he was to die, let him go down fighting like these bold warriors.

Splashing into the shallows along the ship's port side, to which the beached vessel now gently listed, he'd hurled his bundle of wood over the battered, grey-brown gunwale, and hauled himself after it. It was the largest ship he had ever seen, yet once aboard he'd found himself marvelling at how so many men could be accommodated in so cramped a space. From the tall mast – a single trunk of pine – a complex system of ropes stretched all around, some, he could see, wound around wooden cleats at key points along the ship's elegantly curving hull. The central portion of the vessel was dominated by the lowered wooden yard and heavy, furled sail, resting the length of the ship on three supports. Almost as tall as Atli himself, the sturdy posts were topped with horizontal crosspieces shaped to carry the yard and sail – like perches for impossibly large hunting birds.

The main part of deck seemed a chaotic mess of obstacles. Scattered at regular intervals, forming two rows along each side of the ship, were at least thirty long, low chests of various designs, interspersed with numerous boxes, coiled rope, tools and weapons. In the very centre, some distance before and behind the mast, were thick bolts of heavy, folded, striped cloth, tied roughly together with carved planks and poles: tents, for the crew's accommodation when ashore. At either end, some brightly painted shields – several battered and badly split – stood stacked together, with space for many more. On top of it all lay the shipped oars, hastily hauled aboard through the oar holes and laid at an angle towards the stern, ready to be rapidly deployed upon the crew's return. At first, it seemed there was hardly any deck visible, let alone available to walk on. But as Atli picked his way through, it became clear that there was order to this chaos; everything had its place, every bit of space used to best advantage, and – although it was not immediately apparent beneath the abandoned oars – every chest carefully positioned to allow access to any part of the ship, leaving clear pathways down the centre of the vessel for any with a keen eye.

As he passed the length of the furled sail – a vast sausage of dirty, pale, heavy material, criss-crossed with strips of leather – he could just make out glimpses of what appeared to be a dark motif painted or dyed in black upon parts of its surface. An unpleasant, acrid smell of damp rose from it, like wet clothes, mingled with the rank odour of old animal fat. They joined the various other smells that seemed to emanate from the timbers as he negotiated his way aft – fish, rotting seaweed, wet animal skins and stale sweat.

He had to think quickly now. His plan, such as it was, had not extended beyond this point. It was clear that if he was to make good his escape, he would have to hide from his unwitting hosts at least until the ship was in open sea. But where? He stood at the stern, near to the steering board, looking back over the deck, mentally probing every nook or cranny he could find. It seemed hopeless. On this crammed deck there was barely space to hide a rat.

Panic was starting to rise in him. What if there was nowhere? What if the returning *vikingr* were to find him there, and, laughing, simply deposit him back on the shore, back in his everyday life, and leave, never to be seen again? He could not bear the thought. Then, as he stepped back, he felt a portion of the deck shift under his weight. Crouching to examine it, he noticed a small hole cut in the planking, just big enough for a forefinger. He poked one in, and pulled.

A section lifted like a hatch, opening into a dark confined space below, among the ship's ribs. It was damp and dark with tar and smelt like urine. But it would do. Partly filling the space was some sort of bulbous cage made from withies, broken and useless – a bird or animal trap of some kind, he supposed. Further over, a tiny carved effigy of a god, wrapped around with twisted straw, had been nailed to the inside of the keel. Atli abandoned his bundle of sticks, climbed in, and, shoving the trap further under the deck with his feet, nestled against the clammy timbers, pulling the hatch back over him.

He couldn't tell how long he had waited in darkness, listening to the lap of the water. He had been aware, at some point, of shouting in the distance, and the pounding of feet on shingle. Then, quite suddenly, the deck above him had burst into life with the hasty, heavy tread of the crew, and the rumble of oars being thrust into position. There had been urgent cries all around – some so close, he could hear them swear under their breath.

The planking creaked and shifted. Further away, the shouting grew to a roar. There was the clash of metal against metal, and the space around him suddenly reverberated with the grinding of wood and gravel. The ship was moving. Then the vessel freed itself and began to heave to and fro, pitched forward with each pull of the oars. There had been laughter. For a time the motion had even seemed leisurely. Then another shout had gone out, and the ship had begun to lurch more violently, the rhythm of the oars building in speed until everything around him creaked and cracked as if the ship was about to break itself apart. Somewhere to the right of him, the heavy wood of the steer-board had clunked and groaned against the outside of the hull. Amongst it all, inexplicably (at first, he thought he had imagined it) a voice had begun to sing. Suddenly, up ahead, he had seen daylight. Someone further down the ship had raised a section of planking. Surely they could not know he was here? He had gripped the ship's ribs tightly, then, holding his breath against imminent discovery.

But no discovery came. And, as the rise and fall had grown greater, a more urgent fear began to grip him. In the darkness, with each inevitable plunge leaving his stomach behind, he had tried to brace himself against the relentless, increasingly violent motion, clinging to the slimy timbers until he felt his knuckles would burst, repeating over and over the prayer for protection that his father had so often used when they were fishing out in the estuary, and which Atli had never before believed.

It had got significantly worse after that.

The torment that followed had seemed endless; the heaving of the ship so extreme – the inexorable climb on the swell, the sudden drop like a stone, the shuddering and cracking and groaning of the timbers, like howls of agony – that he felt sure he could not survive it. He could not understand how men could go to sea in such conditions. Even in his terrified state, it had made him angry to think of it. Surely, he had thought, whatever was going on outside his wooden prison must be the most treacherous, the most violent of storms? It was only the onset of seasickness that had finally taken his mind off the danger. He had spent the rest of the journey not so much fearing for his life, as wishing for death.

Time had blurred, then. He only remembered becoming aware, somehow, that the swell had diminished – and then, without warning, the scowling face of the ship's captain had appeared, framed in the dim rectangle of the open hatch. Then he had been quivering on deck, facing the stares of the crew – and before he knew it, engulfed by the numbing cold of the sea.

And then there was the thing in the water.

The memory came back, chilling him to the core. He could no longer judge whether it had even been real. As he swallowed, his ears popped and crackled again. Water ran from them, and the sounds of the ship, the sea and the men – now busying themselves with the fishing lines – returned with a disconcerting clarity, sharp and bright in his aching head. He felt himself fully back in their world, stunned and helpless, and only dimly aware of a throbbing pain in his calf where four rows of parallel scratches stood out, angry red weals against the white flesh.

# CHAPTER NINE

## THE NAMING OF NAMES

STANDING SILENTLY AT the stern, the captain kicked open a chest and rummaged inside, pulling out a worn leather belt and short blue tunic embroidered in red and white at its edges. He looked at them, thoughtfully, then back at Atli in his soaking, sagging excuse for a garment. "These were Steinarr's. They would pass to his family, but he has none, so they pass to me. And I am lending them to you." He threw them at the boy. They were soon followed by some brown leggings, and finally an old pair of fur-lined boots which Atli, arms now full, fielded clumsily with his feet. Still shivering, too weak and cold to question it, he immediately changed into them, heaving his old, sodden tunic over his head. It slapped in a heavy, soggy pile on the deck. The new clothes were warm against his skin, more comfortable than anything he had ever worn. The boots, incredibly, were a good fit. Steinarr, whoever he was, must have been a small man. Atli felt the life returning to his toes, to his whole being. It wasn't just the warmth, he realised. It was something else. These were the clothes of a warrior. It was as if they were giving him new strength, new purpose. He felt like a king. For the first time in his life, he was somewhere he belonged.

Bjólf looked him up and down, critically. "A little long, and a bit baggy here and there, but more fitting for a member of this crew." Atli pulled at the belt, fastened as tight as it would go, but still falling about his waist. Steinarr clearly had been a rather slender fellow, but nowhere near slender enough.

"Do you have a knife?" Atli said.

The captain stared back at him in amusement. "Slow down, little man. You're not quite ready for battle just yet."

Atli felt himself blush. "It's for the belt. To make holes."

The warrior laughed and rummaged in the chest again, unearthing a small, sheathed eating knife, which he tossed to Atli. "Don't lose it. It's valuable." Atli gazed in wonder at the ornate handle. He had never seen such a common implement made with such care and skill. It was carved with an intricate, interweaving knotwork pattern in what he assumed – never having encountered walrus ivory before – was some kind of bone. He drew the knife slowly from its simple, brown leather sheath and marvelled at the blade; thin and slightly curved, with a very fine point. It had, at some point in its life, acquired a notch in its edge, close to the handle (what story lay behind that, he wondered?) but otherwise, the smooth metal had all the appearance of having been lovingly cared for, polished, sharpened and re-sharpened over many years. He immediately set about his belt, twisting its sharp point into the tough, brown leather.

"Ah, give the boy a proper weapon," called the giant with a laugh. "He's one of us now!" The words gave Atli an instant glow of pride – so much so that in his distraction he almost drove the knife into his palm. He hoped no one noticed.

"The captain considered his words, then slammed the chest shut and rose to face Atli once more. "First things first. Swords must be earned. For a sword to be given, an oath must be made, and for an oath to be made, one must first have a name."

Atli stopped fiddling with his belt and stared nervously at his new captain.

"Bjólf, son of Erling." He pressed his palm to his chest as he spoke. "And this" – he slapped his hand against Gunnar's shoulder – "this is Gunnar, son of Gunnar. Imagination was not his father's strong point."

Gunnar snorted in gruff acknowledgement. A few of the men nearest them chuckled.

"He is *skipari*," continued Bjólf, "first mate of this ship. Make sure you stay on the right side of him, and do whatever he tells you."

Atli had no idea what to do when meeting a fellow warrior – should he make some kind of greeting? Grasp the man's hand? – and instead just stood uselessly, tongue tied, shifting from foot to foot.

"I'm guessing you've not strayed far from home before, little man," said Bjólf. "Am I right?"

Atli nodded, while trying to exude an air of confidence. He did not wish to admit that he had barely been out of sight of his village.

"Well, your travels begin today." He turned and began to pick his way between the men, several of whom were now occupied with catching whatever vaguely edible creatures the ocean was willing to give up. Atli hurried after him, staggering awkwardly with each movement of the ship and trying not to trip over men, ropes, and the vast array of strewn objects upon which he constantly threatened to bark his shin or impale himself. All around, the crew – each seeming to know their purpose on the vessel without the need for communication – busied themselves with all manner of tasks, most of which Atli could only guess at.

"Half the world is right here on this vessel," continued Bjólf. He gestured to a tall, clean shaven man with black hair and olive skin, the one Atli had called Curved Sword. "Filippus, from Byzantium. You know of it?" Atli, not wanting to admit he had not, made a non-committal kind of sound. "A great city. Many *sjømil* from here. Perhaps you'll see it one day." Filippus gave an elegant nod of his head. Bjólf raised his eyebrows and puffed out his cheeks. "He has a father, so we're told, who has a name, but none of us can pronounce it." There was a hearty laugh from a thick-set man with short-cropped hair nearby.

"Odo, son of Theobald," said Bjólf, clapping the laughing man on the back. "From the land of the Normans. Good fighters. Bad haircuts." Odo half smiled, half scowled back at him, his fellows – Filippus among them – now laughing at his expense.

Bjólf continued to call out names left and right – Thorvald, Úlf, Njáll, Egil, Kylfing – more than Atli could hope to remember. Bjólf gave a friendly kick, in passing, to a lean figure of a man who was crouched at the foot of the mast, seemingly trying to untangle a fish line with his teeth. "Skjöld, son of Jarl. He's an Icelander." Skjöld made to grab Bjólf's foot, but the other was too fast for him. "He'll tell you all about that forsaken place. Just don't ask him to recite any poetry unless you've a couple of days to spare."

At that, a smelly, wet rag flew past Atli and slapped Skjöld full in the face, raising a cry of disgust from the victim. Bjólf rounded on the culprit. Atli recognised the grinning, thin-faced man as the bowman from the forest. "That's Fjölvar, son of Mundi. Don't upset him. He's the cook."

Bjólf moved swiftly onwards, a further cascade of names flowing from him as he picked his way past men of every size, shape and demeanour – Lokki, Odvar, Salomon, Gøtar, Farbjörn, Hrafning, Arnulf, Halfdan, Ingólf, Áki, Eyvind – all with father's names and, more often than not, a less than complimentary nickname too – Ham-Fist, Flat-Nose, Hairy-Breeches, Crow-Foot – the list went on until Atli felt his head start to spin.

Bjólf then came to one Atli remembered. Long-Axe was sat on his sea-chest, running a whetstone along the blade of his axe. Passing behind him, Bjólf placed his hands on the man's shoulders. "And this is Godwin, son of Godred. From England, no less. Nice place. Good growing land – though I don't think he'll be returning there any time soon." Godwin gazed back at Atli, implacable as ever. "He had a slight misunderstanding with some of his kinsmen..."

"They are no kinsmen of mine," said Godwin flatly. Atli felt the man's hard eyes bore into him.

"A good man to have at your side in a tight spot," said Bjólf, back on the move. Before Atli turned away, one of Godwin's eyes winked, and he even fancied he saw a smile flicker beneath the great, sandy moustache.

"And this is Finn," said Bjólf, pulling the man's fur hat roughly over his eyes. Wide-Face said some words of protest that Atli did not understand and pushed it back where it belonged, then returned to baiting his line with what looked to be thin strips of dried fish skin. "He's from Finnmark, in the far north, and his real name is more of a mouthful than raw reindeer balls."

"Lávrrahaš Hætta!" protested Finn. "Even our littlest children can say it!"

Bjólf shrugged. "'Finn.' But of course – you've met already..."

Finn eyed the boy with a smile, skewering the dried fish on a hook. Atli edged around him cautiously, bumping into a great iron dish hanging from a tripod of metal, which rocked and clanged as it swayed on its chains.

They were almost at the bow now. As at the stern, the long, slow pitching of the ship was more extreme here, so much so that Atli struggled to keep his feet, even though Bjólf seemed immune to its influence. Ahead, crouched over a pale, lifeless figure, squeezing a dribble of water onto the blue-white lips, his head partly hidden by a cowl and his thick brown robes draped in folds around him, was Grey-Beard.

"This wise man is Magnus, son of Ingjald. Doesn't fight much. Good healer, though. A Christian man, but we don't hold that against him." Magnus looked up with a half-amused grunt. Atli stared back, his eyes drawn inexorably to the dark, empty socket where the man's left eye had once resided.

"If you are injured, Magnus will put you back together. He was once to be found rotting in a monastery in the middle of nowhere, but he grew tired of the reclusive life. And I know what you're thinking." He whirled his index finger in front of Magnus's face and mouthed a word: "Odin..."

"Ah! Not that again!" Magnus waved his hand dismissively and turned back to his patient.

It was, indeed, exactly what Atli was thinking.

"It's a curious irony, to be sure," said Bjólf. "The Christian man who is the very image of the All-Father."

Magnus turned to look at Atli, and a smile creased his brown, whiskered face. "Well, you look a little more presentable than you did."

Atli had thought Magnus a startling presence back on the riverbank, in the shadow of battle, but now he saw him like this, smiling warmly, it seemed hard to believe he could inspire anything approaching fear. Atli cursed his own stupidity. What use would he be to the crew if he let such childish superstitions get hold of him?

"And this," said Bjólf, crouching, his knees cracking, "is Kjötvi, son of Björn. A finder of ways. We call him 'The Lucky.' Not so lucky today." His face became suddenly grave. He looked up, staring distractedly at Atli's new clothes for a moment, lost in thought. "But luckier than some."

The approach of Gunnar broke the spell. "The fog is thickening. Maybe rain later. Could make for better light tomorrow."

Bjólf nodded, and gazed at the flat featureless sky. He stood suddenly, addressing Atli. "Now you have our names, we should have yours."

"Atli."

"Son of...?"

"Just Atli."

From where he stood, Gunnar saw again the tightening of the boy's jaw at the mere memory of the parent he had left behind, the anger contained within his refusal even to name him. His mind went back to his own childhood – to the harsh words and harsher blows he had suffered from his own father. One day, when he was big enough, he had turned on the old man, wrestled him to the floor and held a knife at his throat. To his great surprise, the old man had broken into an uproar of laughter, and insisted on them both breaking open the mead he'd been saving for Yule. Things were much better between them after that.

"Well, Atli Just-Atli," said Bjólf. "I have a job for you."

# CHAPTER TEN

## NIGHT, WOOD AND FIRE

ATLI PULLED THE stick against his bent knee and felt the satisfying snap as it yielded to the pressure. Placing both halves on the deck, he rested the end of one on the middle of the other, then gave the raised half a sharp whack in the middle with the hand-axe he had acquired earlier that evening. It immediately cracked in two. He fed the two smallest parts into the fire that was now crackling away in the broad, blackened metal dish and watched them catch and spit in the glow, relishing the warmth. The cauldron of water swaying on its chains above was at last starting to steam.

All along the ship, the men were hauling up lines to examine their catch. Now and then one wrestled with small fish – haddock, Atli thought – some of which flipped and slapped on the deck. High on the prow, a man with no front teeth whose name Atli could not remember stood looking out to sea. *Sundvordr*, had

Bjólf called it – bow watch. Below him, on the forecastle, Kjötvi lay, tended now and then by Magnus, while closest to Atli, now wrapped in a smooth skin coat lined with thick fur, Finn scanned the dark water silently, the finger of his right hand tucked under the taut fishing line that disappeared over the side and into the inky black swell, sensitive to the slightest movement. Atli found his own gaze continually returning to this strange figure. He was Sami – so Gunnar had told him; a reindeer herder from the far north, where there were year-round snows. This one had been a shaman of his tribe before the lot of them had been killed by raiders. Somehow, he alone had survived. Powerful with magic, Gunnar said. Atli had already noticed that the attitude of the other men was different towards this one. Though jovial and direct, as they all were with each other, they kept more of a distance from him. There seemed an unusual kind of respect, or perhaps fear. Despite his continuing efforts to fight the superstitious dread that had made his family life so miserable – efforts bolstered by the welcome pragmatism of his new captain – something about this man made Atli edgy. Something unnerving, dangerous – like a feeling half remembered from a dream. Or perhaps it was just Gunnar's story that had disturbed him. He poked the fire, and set about the wood again with his axe. Never mind. At least there should be some proper food soon.

Not long before, Atli had watched as Bjólf had set the fire. It was a familiar ritual – one he had seen perhaps a hundred times before as part of his father's regular routine – yet here performed with such elegance and efficiency that it was somehow rendered fascinating again, as if seen entirely anew.

First, Bjólf had snapped one of the thinnest of the dry sticks into short lengths, then, smashing one of its ends to splinters with the flat back of an axe, placed it in the charred middle of the great metal dish, on top of a handful of straw Fjölvar had brought from a box beneath deck. On top of that, he had piled more small, kindling-sized pieces of wood, then, from the bag on his belt, he had drawn a small pouch, from which he had pulled a tuft of what looked like wool – flax, Atli thought it was – and tucked it into the straw. Rummaging further in the pouch, he had then produced a lump of flint and an elegantly shaped metal tool whose purpose Atli did not recognise – smaller than a palm and something like half a belt buckle, it was completely flat along one edge, the other delicately fashioned with intertwined dragons, the long, snaking necks curving outward and back towards the centre so their heads met in the middle. Its purpose was soon to become clear. From the pouch, Bjólf had taken a small piece of what looked like black felt – Atli recognised it as *hnjóskr*, or 'touchwood,' something his grandfather had once been renowned for making – and, gripping the flint in the upturned palm of his left hand with the touchwood held between his fingers, began to strike the exposed surface of the stone with the flat edge of the tool. Sparks flew. A firelighting steel. Bjólf repeated the blow over and over, moving the touchwood around in relation to the flint, altering the angle of striking to direct the now steady flow of sparks towards it. Wisps of smoke and the sharp tang of flint filled the air. Within a few moments, Bjólf had cupped his hand around the strip of touchwood, and Atli could see that its rough edge was glowing. Transferring it swiftly to the flax tuft, he blew gently until the glow caught the flax fibres and, with the nurturing of another few breaths, made a tiny flame. The flax flame caught the straw, the straw the wood splinters, the splinters the kindling, and, before long, a respectable fire was flickering and swaying before Atli's eyes. Bjólf had stood then, saying: "Keep this fire going, no matter what." Then, as he had turned to go, added: "And don't set fire to the ship."

As he was leaving, Fjölvar had returned with the big cauldron, now full of water, and hooked it back onto its chains above the fire. For a moment it had rocked and swayed dangerously, its contents slopping about above the still-meagre flame. Fjölvar tapped the cauldron with his knuckle. "Every man aboard is depending on you," he said, encouragingly, then, with a single slap on Atli's shoulder, had made off, back to a small area near the mast that he was now using for food preparation.

The first thing Atli had realised, once things had settled down, was that he was faint with hunger. Somehow, the events of the day had managed to keep his mind off his stomach, but suddenly, he felt his head swimming. His hands shook as he fed wood into the fire, his stomach tightening as if it were about to cave in. The mere mention of food had brought him crashing back to the reality that not a morsel had passed his lips since early morning. It had been a rough meal porridge with some dried fish in it. The fish had had a particularly rank taste today – it could get like that when the weather wasn't good for drying – but right now Atli would have given anything for a bowl.

"Here." Atli had jumped at the voice beside him. It was Gunnar. He set down a bowl of drinking water, and then, reaching into a black leather bag – of a type that all the men seemed to wear at their belts – he drew out his huge fist and held it towards the boy. Atli offered his cupped hands, and into it was deposited a huge handful of hazelnuts, shrivelled berries and small pieces of what looked to be dried meat. "Keep your strength up," said Gunnar with a curt nod. He stood awkwardly for a moment, scratching at his black beard, then, with a grunt, turned and went.

At first, Atli had simply stared at the small feast, almost too exhausted to eat. Then a wave of hunger overwhelmed him again. Having no hands free, he simply shoved his face into the mix and chomped on it like a hog. The sweet bitterness of the hazelnuts and sharpness of the berries made his saliva run like a dog – his cheeks ached with it. Then came the pungent, deep flavour of the meat. It was the most delicious thing he had ever eaten. Its effect was like magic. Within moments, he felt his strength and his resolve returning – enough to realise that here, now, food was a commodity too valuable to squander. Half the mixture remained in his cupped hands; it would be wise to pace himself. But, as he looked up, he realised the fire was already dying. Scooping the remaining half of the mixture into his left hand, he shoved a stick into the dwindling blaze then looked around for somewhere to put his precious food. He eventually drank the bowl of water, put the dried mix into it, then turned his full attention back to the fire, piling up the embers with another stick and coaxing it back to life with his breath.

Bjólf, who had been watching from a distance, smiled at the

boy's ingenuity. He'd be alright. They could adapt to anything at that age – it was the best time to go to sea. Or maybe he was just getting sentimental in his old age.

A thought struck him. Returning to Steinarr's chest, he pulled something from it and made his way back to the prow.

The sudden slap of leather on the deck had given Atli another start. At his feet lay a bag that had been repaired in one corner, with a bronze clasp and two straps that had been designed to fit neatly over the belt now at his waist, and of the same brown leather. "You'll be needing that," Bjólf had said, towering over the crouching boy. "Unless you want to keep all your possessions in a bowl."

Atli had wasted no time in putting the bag where it belonged – on his belt, next to his shiny new knife. And it had not been the last gift of the evening. Later, when he had been struggling to break some of the thicker pieces of wood, another of the crew – the one called Thorvald; a short, stocky fellow – had taken pity and given him the axe. Its owner, he said with a laugh, had no further use for it; a trophy of their battle on the beach. But before Atli could ask him further about that, he had gone. It had made his task easier, that much was certain, but, more importantly, it had made him feel trusted, one of them. A warrior. When not in use, he tucked the axe proudly, if a little awkwardly, into his belt, and became all the more determined to make this the best cooking fire the crew had ever seen.

Atli's great worry now was his supply of wood. He had tried to make it last, while getting the best blaze he could to heat the water as quickly as possible – for his hunger, and, he supposed, that of the others, demanded more than dried fruit and nuts – but already, half of it was gone. How long did they want him to keep this going? Until the cooking was done, certainly. But how long would that take? And how much longer after that? An hour? Two? All night?

Emboldened now– and realising he must act before the need made itself too keenly felt – he built up the fire as much as he dared and set off on a foraging mission about the ship. As the men worked around him, sometimes ruffling his hair or making a quip about his size, his eyes darted about in the darkness, searching for anything – anything at all – that might keep the fire going. He found the shattered remains of a shield – Godwin indicated with a stern nod that he could take the boards from it – and then, remembering the broken trap below the boards, in his old hiding place, sought permission to drag it up and put it to better use. As word spread about his quest among the crew, more offerings came – an old broken chest, a pail that had rotted through, a couple of warped spear shafts, an oar that had split its blade and been sitting below deck ever since. Up in the bow, Atli had seen a choice piece – a big, roughly conical chunk of oak, about the length of his forearm, tucked into a gap at the edge of the planking, beneath the prow. He had pulled it out and was about to add it to his hoard when he saw Magnus shaking his head discreetly.

"That's part of the ship," the old man whispered.

Atli returned it without a word.

# CHAPTER ELEVEN

## A GRIM CATCH

BY THE TIME he was done ferrying his spoils to the fireside, Atli had fuel enough to last a night and a day at least, and plenty of work for his axe. Breaking up the wood proved an arduous task, but it was one that his mind and body welcomed; his limbs ached with it, but it was a good ache. He felt somehow connected. Focused. Useful. Before he realised where it had come from, a saying of his father's drifted into his head: "Good firewood heats you up twice – once when you chop it and again when you burn it!" Atli attacked the wood harder and tried to shake the memory from his head.

He had saved until last what he knew would be the most difficult – the tough, thick wood of the broken oar – and had only just begun the painstaking task of chopping it into usable lengths when a sudden movement nearby caught his eye. For nearly the whole time he had been working, Finn had been sitting practically motionless astride his sea-chest, chewing silently on a strip of dark, unidentifiable dried meat, the taut fishing line that stretched over the gunwale tied to the nearest of the three upright bird-perch-posts behind him. Some time ago, he had removed his right boot, and for the past hour had sat with his bare right foot propped up on the long chest, and the line between his toes, waiting, Atli supposed, for the twitch of a fish. Now, something had Finn's full attention. He was sitting bolt upright, his mouth stopped mid-chew. For a moment he remained utterly frozen, his gaze focused somewhere out there, where the line met the sea. Then, never once taking his eyes off the line, he eased his foot off the chest, stood up and carefully replaced his boot. Atli saw the line slacken for a moment, then suddenly tighten again. Finn gave it a gentle pull. It responded, pulling so tight, so fast, it reverberated like a bow-string.

"Something here..." he called, still chewing. Close by, two other men – Thorvald, and the one called Njáll Red-Hair – stood; a third – Eyvind – abandoned the tub of water in which he was meticulously washing his neck and shoulders and moved to join him.

"It's big," said Finn.

Eyvind tested the tension of the line. "Cod, maybe. Good eating. I've seen them as big as deer."

"Bigger," said Finn.

Eyvind laughed. "It's not a fishing contest, north-man!"

Finn's eyes remained fixed on the point where the line disappeared below the surface of the water, a frown creasing his heavy brow. Reaching down, he flipped open his sea-chest, dug out a pair of tough, reindeer skin gloves and pulled them on. "Not fish," he said.

Eyvind chuckled again. Thorvald and Njáll looked at each other in bemusement.

"Well, what else is it going to be out here?" asked Eyvind, spreading his arms wide and surveying the blank desolation that surrounded them. "Sea serpent?"

Finn said nothing.

"Whale?" muttered Thorvald, squinting at the slowly heaving sea, trying to penetrate the thick fog.

"Seal maybe?" ventured Njáll.

"Not seal. Or whale," said Finn. Then, after a pause, added: "Nothing I know."

Thorvald and Njáll exchanged anxious looks. "But there's nothing in the sea you don't know," said Thorvald.

"Something different here."

By now, the small knot of men had attracted Bjólf's attention. "If it takes four of you to haul it in," he said, approaching them, "I'd be more worried about it eating us." But the looks on the faces of Thorvald, Njáll and Finn immediately killed the humour in his voice. "What is it?"

"Something out there," said Finn, nodding towards the black waves.

Bjólf frowned deeply.

"Before you ask," said Njáll, "he doesn't know what." Bjólf looked uneasy at his words.

"Well, let's just wind it in and have a look," said Eyvind matter-of-factly. He picked up the winding frame, and, leaning forward, went to hook it into the line, but, at that moment, as if responding to his words, it fell slack at his feet. Eyvind tugged on it gingerly, and met no resistance. He pulled harder. It kept coming.

"So much for your prize cod!" said Eyvind. "That'll be more hooks lost." And, taking up the limp line he started swiftly reeling it in by hand, letting it fall in a wet heap at his feet. "Just got caught on something, that's all. Some old bit of flotsam or..."

Before he could finish the sentence, the line whipped through his hands with such speed it sent a mist of salt spray into the air. Eyvind howled in agony as the line sliced through the flesh of his palms. As it snapped taut, his body jerked violently forward and he collapsed to his knees, blood coursing from his right hand, the trembling arm stretched out awkwardly before him in a curious, twisted gesture. For a moment, the stunned onlookers struggled to make sense of what had just happened. Then it became clear. Without thinking, Eyvind had wound part of the line around his right hand; now, pulled tight, hauled seaward by whatever lay below the surface, it had him caught like a rabbit in a wire trap, suspended between post and gunwale, cutting him to the bone. If the line were to break now on the seaward side, he would be saved, but if it snapped behind him, he would either he dragged into the sea or have the flesh stripped from his hand. Finn was the first to act, flying past Eyvind, grabbing the line with his gloved hands and pulling with all his strength, his feet braced against the gunwale. The line slackened. Eyvind fell back. Thorvald and Njáll leapt forward in an effort to free him, desperately trying to untangle the line from the afflicted hand.

"Cut the line!" called Bjólf. Thorvald pulled his knife, but before he could act the line whipped through Finn's gloved grasp, sending the smell of salt and burning hide into the air as it snapped taut again and sent Thorvald's blade flying. Eyvind fell forward once more, screaming with the pain like a trapped animal, desperately trying to pull with his free hand as Finn fought to get a grip and, baring his white teeth like an animal, tried to bite through the line.

"Cut it!" bellowed Bjólf, searching urgently for a blade, any blade. The commotion had caught the attention of the entire crew now.

Atli, stunned and horrified by what had occurred in the past few seconds, stood helpless. Only when Bjólf called out for the second time did he realise that he alone, of all those within reach, had within his grasp the means of Eyvind's salvation. The axe hung idly in his hand. With everything seeming to slow as if in a dream, he stepped forward, and raised his axe.

Without warning, as if a spell were suddenly broken, Eyvind and Finn fell back with a crash onto the blood-soaked deck. The loosed line whipped backwards over the gunwale, and something – still attached to its end – flew from the water, arced high in the air with a trail of salt spray, and landed with a wet thud on the deck next to them.

Atli glanced at the axe – still in his raised right hand – then, in the moment of stunned silence that followed, at the dumfounded faces of the crew. Bjólf stared at the thing on the deck, a look of disbelief on his face. Behind him, Gunnar looked on, his characteristically stern features now fixed in an expression of horror. Njáll took a step back. On the deck, Eyvind, nursing his hand, shuddered, and scrabbled to get away from it.

Atli looked. At first, he struggled to make sense of the weird, white shape in the gloom. It was like no fish he had ever seen, and certainly did not seem large enough to have put up such a struggle. Then his reeling brain saw it for what it was. The hand and forearm of a man – or what had once been a man – its grey flesh bloodless and nibbled by fish, its skin bleached by the sea and barely covering the extent of bone and wasted muscle beneath, its elbow ragged with gristle and tendon as if freshly wrenched from its joint. Wrapped around its length was the remainder of the tangled, hooked fishing line.

The first wave of recognition was followed by another, but of a worse kind. With all that had happened, Atli had had little trouble consigning the ghoulish apparition in the water to a place somewhere in his imagination, a place of safety. But now, he knew for certain it was real. It was out in the world – here, on the ship, amongst them.

Bjólf pushed past Thorvald and Njáll and knelt over it. "Give me the axe, boy."

Atli passed the weapon haft-first over their grisly catch, never once taking his eyes off it, then hopped back again, putting as much distance between him and it as honour would allow. Bjólf prodded the skeletal limb, turning it over slowly. A length of limp, green weed entwined its white, bony fingers, now curled skyward like the legs of an upturned crab. A putrid smell rose from it. Around its wrist, Bjólf now noticed, was a twisted bracelet, tarnished green at the ends, its plaited strands coloured black and red.

"Gunnar?" called Bjólf. The big man stepped forward. Bjólf looked at the axe for a moment, turning it around in his hand. "The former owner of this... he left something else behind. What did you do with it?"

"Over the side. Back in the estuary."

"Could this be it?" Bjólf prodded the forearm again.

Gunnar shook his head. "It is... different. This one, there's more of it. And anyway, this has been in the water longer."

Bjólf nodded. "A drowned sailor then? The rest of him down there somewhere?"

"Must be."

"A drowned sailor who pulls," growled a voice. It was Finn. "I felt that line. The dead do not fight back." A few of the men muttered, unsettled at his words.

"This is bad," said Úlf, shaking his head. "The raid. That madman at the village. Steinarr. Hallgeir. Kjötvi... And now this."

"Enough!" Snapped Bjólf, rising to his feet. "We've all seen dead flesh before. Enough to know we should thank our lucky stars we're better off than this wretch." He gave the limb a kick. "He's half eaten by fish. That's what pulled at your line."

Several among the crew nodded or exclaimed in agreement as he spoke, some nudging the more superstitious among them. But, in the very next moment, a gasp came from all their throats. Expressions fell in horror.

Bjólf followed their gaze, and recoiled. The thing on the deck was moving.

Its fingers twitched, writhed, then slowly curled into the palm, its forefinger last to join its fellows, as if beckoning to all those who beheld it. Atli backed away involuntarily, suddenly aware, once again, of the angry scratches upon his calf.

Bjólf raised the axe and brought it down hard, cutting the line. Without a word, he picked up the limb and hurled it out to sea.

"Haul in all the lines," he said, his face and voice grim. "Let's eat."

# CHAPTER TWELVE

## THE CORPSE-PICKER

IT WAS NOT long before Fjölvar was serving up steaming portions of fish stew from the cauldron over Atli's fire. The catch had been fair. The fish was sweet and tender, some barley meal and dried cod had gone into the pot to add substance, and Fjölvar had even managed to rescue enough of the onions to give flavour to the broth. And, most of all, it was hot. Atli had lapped it up hungrily, burning his mouth in the process, but unable, for the moment, to think of anything else. Magnus, meanwhile, had succeeded in spooning some of the hot liquid between Kjötvi's lips, and the stricken man was soon eating as hungrily as his fellows, miraculously returned to life by the brew. Eyvind's wound had been bound, and by great good fortune he had escaped permanent damage. He would be left-handed for a while, but it would heal, and he would still have the use of his fingers. Only Gunnar had had the nerve to grumble.

"Needs salt," he'd said.

Thorvald laughed and gestured to the surrounding sea. "Help yourself!"

Gunnar gazed out at the dark water that hid the rotting, drifting remains of their mysterious visitor, then back at his fish. He said nothing. Despite the welcome luxury of a hot meal, there were few among them who, while swallowing the white flesh, had not thought of the pallid corpse that, until recently, had shared the same domain as their dinner.

After that, the atmosphere remained subdued. The fog hung about them still, like a thick, blank shroud; a physical manifestation of the depressed mood. The ship heaved slowly on the swell as if rocked by an invisible hand. A fine rain fell for a while, and there was not a single one among them who did not yearn for dry land beneath his feet. Men exchanged short words now and then as necessity required, but otherwise kept their thoughts to themselves. No one spoke further of the thing in the sea.

Atli ran his fingers gently over the weals on his leg and thought over and over of the ghoulish nightmare that he now knew lay somewhere beneath them. Not far away, Bjólf sat hunched against the gunwale, a thick sheepskin around his shoulders, his head bowed in dark meditation. Atli wanted to go to his captain and tell him that he had seen it, that it had been real. But he did not have the nerve to penetrate the heavy silence that had descended. Instead, he concentrated on keeping his wood store dry, and feeding up the cheering, crackling flames.

His mind began to drift. Already drowsy from the meal and the glow of the fire, wrapped in a damp but warm woollen cape – another posthumous donation from Steinarr – he allowed his lids to droop and close. The minute he did so, exhaustion washed over him. He tried to fight it, forcing his eyes open, telling himself of his responsibility to ship and fire. But again his lids became heavy, sinking once, twice… The third time, he gave in to it. *Just for a moment,* he told himself. *Just a few more seconds…*

Immediately, fevered images began to swim through his tired brain – images of the thing in the water – lifeless but moving, suspended in icy darkness beneath the hull, grasping at him. In a world somewhere between nightmare and daydream, he imagined it clawing its way up the side of the ship, its sodden, ragged, wrecked form slithering and rattling over the gunwale and onto the deck, squirming in the wet like some ghastly newborn, then tottering unsteadily to its feet, staggering towards him while the crew slept on, oblivious.

Sounds came to him too. Somewhere between asleep and awake, beyond the lapping water and the creaking of the timbers, he thought he detected another sound. Like something scratching slowly, repeatedly against the hull. Like nails dragged against wood.

A sudden movement nearby shocked him awake. He looked around, dazed, unsure how long he had slept. The fog had thinned considerably. The fire was low, its light barely penetrating the gloom. He tucked some kindling into the embers and, as it began to catch, threw on a few more chunks of wood. As he did so, he heard a movement behind him. A strange kind of movement – the same, he now understood, as the one that had jolted him awake. It was a sort of shuffling, flapping sound, something at once utterly alien, and yet uncannily familiar. It sent chills through him. For a moment, he did not dare move. Then came a horrible exclamation, something between terror and disgust. He whirled around. A pale face hovered in the dark extremity of the prow. Near it, an unidentifiable black shape flopped and scratched. For a moment, Atli's eyes – fresh from the fire – struggled to adjust to the shadows.

Then he saw it.

Kjötvi, his face as white as a ghost, his eyes wide as shield-bosses, was staring in horror at a big, black shape that was pulling at his leg. His bandages lay unravelled and strewn about the deck, and a great bird – black as soot and big as a cat – was holding a red, wet length of... something... in its beak, something that was still attached to Kjötvi's calf. It was the flap of flesh that the axe had failed to remove, far too great a prize for a meat-hungry raven to leave behind. It yanked at it repeatedly, each time eliciting a stronger cry of pain and revulsion from its victim, while Kjötvi swiped at the creature weakly, as if trying to swat a gigantic fly.

By now, Bjólf and several of the crew were on their feet, the growing flames of the fire illuminating the bizarre scene, shadows flickering and dancing like ghosts against the timbers of the bow. Fjölvar had strung his bow and already had an arrow upon it, the bird in his sights.

"No!" said Bjólf, shoving Fjölvar's arm roughly aside. The arrow loosed, hissing over Atli's head and disappearing far out into the foggy ocean. Fjölvar glared at Bjólf with a mixture of anger and shock – then suddenly understood. No one moved.

The raven hopped and loped and flapped about, clinging doggedly to the precious bit of meat, the blue-black sheen of its feathers reflecting the flickering light of the fire. Kjötvi, wide awake now, kicked at it desperately with his good leg, looking to his shipmates for aid, not understanding why it would not come.

"To oars!" whispered Bjólf, not once taking his eyes off the black, ravenous creature. "Quickly."

The bird momentarily lost its hold, then flapped and jumped as Kjötvi's foot tried to connect with it again, its hunched form croaking angrily at him. He flailed again and missed – then, seeing another opportunity, it darted back in. It snapped and pulled. Kjötvi cried out. Then again. The creature suddenly tottered backwards and flapped off, up onto the figurehead where it perched victoriously, teetering against the swell, a glistening red strip of Kjötvi's leg in its bloody beak.

The crew, meanwhile, had snapped into action, swiftly deploying the stacked oars. The tips of the port set, Atli now saw, were painted red, the starboard oars tipped with yellow, and each one – slightly different in length from its neighbour to compensate for the curve of the ship – carved with one of sixteen runes to indicate its position. Within seconds, the oars were out over the water, the crew ready.

Bjólf, surveying the scene with growing satisfaction, and turning back to the prow, ran suddenly at it, clapping his hands noisily. "*Hyah! Hyah! Hyah!*" The raven took off and swooped ahead and to port, while Bjólf leapt past Kjötvi, up into the ship's prow and pointed triumphantly after the flapping black shape. "Follow *him!*"

The ship lurched forward as Gunnar called the strokes, Thorvald at the helm guiding the ship along the raven's path. Bjólf noted with satisfaction the faint glow of dawn on the horizon, off the starboard bow.

"I didn't feel it,"gibbered Kjötvi, looking up at Bjólf. "I didn't feel it. I just woke up and it was there..."

"We're just glad to see you alive again," laughed Bjólf.

Kjötvi shuddered as Magnus set about binding his wound again. "It's not right, to still be alive and to have part of you pass through a raven!" He looked at his leg. "I'll never get that back!"

"Your sacrifice was not in vain, my friend," said Magnus.

"You saved us," said Bjólf, beaming. "Trust Kjötvi to find the way!"

The raven, much faster than its sea-going namesake, soon disappeared from sight. But such birds would not stray far from land, and now they had a bearing from the distant glimmer of the sun too. Nevertheless, a tense silence fell as Bjólf stared intently into the eerily glowing fog, trying to read shapes within it. For the space of about sixty strokes, nothing appeared. Then, quite suddenly, a half imagined band of dark, ragged forms emerged dead ahead. Rocks. Grey cliffs. A coastline.

The cliffs were precipitous and inaccessible, but, to port, were broken by a wide, sheer-sided inlet.

"There!" called Bjólf. The oars pulled in steady rhythm. Thorvald heaved on the creaking rudder.

Leaping down from his vantage point, Bjólf bounded past Atli, then snatched up a pail and hurled its contents over the fire, extinguishing it immediately. A hiss of steam shot up as the water hit hot metal. Atli stared at the sodden ruins in utter disbelief, the wreck of the fire that he had nursed through the night.

"Wh-why did you...?" he stammered, wide-eyed.

"We don't want to announce ourselves until we're ready," said Bjólf, weaving his way back towards the stern. "Don't look so downcast, little man," he called as he went. "The long night is over. And tonight we eat and sleep on land!"

As one, the men cheered, relieved that the worst of this ill-fated raiding trip – and the dark matter of the previous night – was at last safely behind them.

# PART TWO

*DRAUGR*

# INTERLUDE

THE RELENTLESS SUN beat upon Bjólf's back, making his tunic sticky with sweat. It was low in the evening sky now, but still ferocious. In the three weeks that had passed since embarking on their southward journey the heat had been steadily increasing, and the past few days had been the hottest he had ever known in his short life. Like standing over a forge night and day, his uncle Olaf said. Bjarki, Olaf's trusted *skipari*, claimed that further south the sun was fiercer still. He had seen lands where everywhere the soil had turned to dust, where there was no rain and not a single leaf of green. How people lived in such conditions, Bjólf could not imagine.

The voyage had been hard. By the end of the previous week the sun had burned Bjólf's skin raw, and the wind had rubbed the salt spray into the worst afflicted parts of his face, leaving his lips cracked and blistered. He was healing now – his skin unevenly brown and peeling – but for a while had been delirious with it, feeling as if his skin were on fire. One night, just as Bjólf's fever was hitting its peak, they had put ashore at a small, dusty port where the houses appeared to have grown out of the dry earth like anthills and the bustling throngs of merchants seemed to be perpetually shouting; words that were harsh and alien to his ears. He remembered the sights, sounds and smells like disconnected images from a dream: dark faces lit by the flicker of firelight; cries in a dozen unknown tongues; the smell of hot coals, raw fish, stale sweat, fresh garlic, spices and vinegar; drums and wailing pipes and voices raised in song. He remembered strange loping creatures that snorted and stamped and dropped their dung, or capered and flapped at the end of a chain: a dwarf-like creature covered in hair with arms and hands and a face like a shrivelled man; a squawking bird that spoke whole words, all colours of the rainbow; a black bat hanging from a perch, as big as a seagull. His uncle bought him wine, some skewered, charcoal-grilled meat, and black berries that looked to Bjólf like the small plums his mother used to gather, but which were hard and oily and bitter-tasting. The wine – his first taste of this great, southern luxury – was good, and he wolfed the food down, ravenously hungry, but nonetheless also strangely disconnected, and no longer entirely able to tell what was real, and what the creation of his fevered imagination. He had lain awake all night, sweating and shivering and drifting in and out of maddening, repetitive dreams, desperate for the clear, cool air of the open sea.

Now that the fever was past, the burning flesh calmed, he stood at the prow of the ship under full sail, feeling the cooling air and the fine salt spray on his skin, able at last to appreciate the beauty of this ocean that held such a fascination for his otherwise unsentimental uncle. In these waters, it seemed, one barely had to lower a net into the waves for it to be blessed with creatures that made good eating, and never had the sea and sky seemed so blue, nor the shore glowed with such colours as they did in these long, late evenings. At moments like this, even the crushing heat did not seem so bad.

But there was another, deeper kind of contentment. Although his frame had yet to fill out with muscle, Bjólf was tall and broad for his thirteen winters, at least on a par with the shorter members of the *Hrafn*'s seasoned crew – none of that stopped jibes about his size, of course. But, as he stood shoulder to shoulder with Svein, on watch at the bow, he felt that he had grown in other, more important ways upon this journey. Ways that could not be mapped or measured.

Yet, despite everything that had happened to him, there was one more experience, one more milestone that this trip had to offer. It was something that he had long known would come, but he anticipated it with increasing dread.

"Sail!" called Svein, snapping Bjólf out of his reverie. Olaf stepped up to the prow and curled a hand around his right eye.

Bjólf looked. At first, he could not be sure what he was looking at – just a flash of brilliant white in the far distance off the port bow – but as his eyes found their range, the dark smudge beneath resolved into a distinct shape. As they cut through the waves in their steady advance he could make out a vessel; compact, with one – no, two – square, white sails. It bobbed in the water, apparently without direction, both sails flying in the wind.

He saw his uncle's face crease into a frown as he squinted at the horizon.

"What're they playing at?" muttered Bjarki behind his shoulder.

Even with his limited experience, Bjólf could tell something was wrong. He could see now that one of the sails was only partially secured, flapping limply at one of its corners in the steady breeze; the other had seemingly come completely adrift of its sheets and billowed uselessly from the yard, occasionally catching the sun as it did so.

"Who are they?" asked Bjólf.

"Arab traders," said Bjarki. "From the East." He nodded directly ahead.

Bjólf could now just make out figures on the deck – dark-skinned faces and arms, heads and bodies garbed in white – waving in their direction.

"Arab traders in trouble," snorted Svein, dismissively. "Either their fathers never taught them how to sail, or they have worse problems on board."

Distant raised voices now carried across the water as the westerly wind ebbed. Although Bjólf could make out none of the words, there was no doubting the tone. They were cries for help.

"What do you think?" said Svein.

"Attacked, maybe," ventured Bjarki.

Olaf narrowed his eyes, rubbed his thick beard and gave a grunt. "That's what they want us to believe."

Bjólf frowned at his uncle. Olaf seemed to sense his question without once taking his eyes off the horizon.

"They're no merchants," he muttered.

"Who then?"

"Pirates."

Svein nodded. "A trap." Without a word, he reached down beside his sea-chest and began to strap on his sword. Olaf gave a curt nod to Bjarki, who turned and gave a shrill whistle towards the helm. The tanned and weather-beaten faces of the crew looked up to see him make a concise gesture – a single slap of his clenched fist against a flattened palm. It was a signal Bjólf had seen only twice before, when arming for a raid. There was a creak deep in the timbers of the ship as it changed course directly for the Arab vessel. Olaf made a sudden turn and headed back along the length of the ship.

"But, how can you be sure?" said Bjólf, hurrying after.

"If they'd been attacked, they'd be dead. But since they have a good many able-bodied men on board, alive and well, one has to ask how they got this far if they can't even secure a line."

Bjólf, alarmed, gawped at his uncle and then towards the nearing vessel. "They intend to trap... *us?*"

Olaf gave a deep, rumbling laugh. "No! They don't intend that." He stopped and stared back at the other ship for a moment. "They don't yet realise what we are."

His uncle gave another hoarse grunt, then resumed his purposeful march.

"The sun is behind us," he continued, stopping at the place where his sea-chest stood. "They see only a silhouette of a square sail. They assume we are a trading ship returning to the East – exactly what they are pretending to be." He hauled out his coat of mail "Fully laden. Easy prey, especially when coming to the aid of another we believe to be in distress."

"So, what do we do?"

Olaf shrugged matter-of-factly. "We go to their aid." He flipped the mail coat over his head, shook it down over his huge body and began strapping his wide belt around it. "No reason to disappoint them." In a few swift moves he had slung his sword over his shoulder and tucked his axe into his belt. All around, without a word, men were doing the same, checking blades, passing out shields and tightening helmet straps. "Better arm yourself, little man," said Olaf. And with that, he took up his battered helm and headed back towards the prow.

Bjólf hastily grabbed his weapons and scurried after, struggling with belts and straps as he went. He recalled the words of his uncle a few days before, when they had first entered these calm, blue waters: "Take care," he had said. "Our people inflicted great damage upon these regions in past years, and some hereabouts have long memories."

"But... What happens when they realise who we are?" Bjólf called nervously. Olaf stopped next to Svein at the prow.

"They just have..." said Svein.

Bjólf looked again towards the Arab ship. The urgent babble of voices was clear now, but the pattern of movement on board had entirely changed. Instead of waving in distress, their attention had now turned inward. One of the sails had already been secured, and the rest dashed about in a bustle of frantic activity, some shouting impatiently at each other. Just one man – their lookout – was completely motionless; a strange, still point amidst the mayhem, staring silently back at them. Bjólf could just begin to make out his features. It seemed to him the man wore an expression of barely concealed horror.

"Hoy!" called Olaf, standing high on the prow. Despite the Arabs' haste in securing the other sail, it was clear the longship would be upon them before they could get underway. Some turned and began more wild gesticulations. Voices called out urgently. Olaf's booming voice answered in what, to Bjólf, seemed disconcertingly friendly tones.

"What's going on?" he asked. He thought he had caught odd words – it was not the Latin his uncle was teaching him, but the Byzantine Greek that was spoken so widely in this region.

"They are saying there is plague of some sort on board, that we should stay away," said Svein.

"Then, should we not just go around?" said Bjólf. Svein said nothing.

There was barely any distance between the two vessels now. Olaf called out again, even more cheerily this time. Svein chuckled at his words. "Now he's saying we have many healers on board, who can release a man from his sickness."

"Do we?" said Bjólf, bemused.

"Oh, yes," said Svein. "Though it may not be quite the release they are after."

Bjólf frowned. But before he had a chance to even ask the inevitable question, Svein had drawn his sword.

"Better get ready," he said, bracing himself against the gunwale.

With that, the helmsman leaned hard on the rudder, bringing her right alongside the Arab ship. The crewmen on the halyards dropped the yard, several more on the deck reefed the sail in one rapid, fluid motion, and the hull of the dragon ship butted violently against the Arab's bow. As it did so, to Bjólf's utter amazement, Olaf launched himself from the gunwale and landed heavily with both feet upon the enemy deck. A space instantly cleared around him, like a stone dropped among swarming ants. For a moment the man stood, regarding them in silence on the swaying deck, towering over all around by at least a forearm's length. Bjólf could make out their faces now – gnarled and seasoned, much like Olaf's crew, but with skin of every hue from the palest brown to the darkest black – what some of the older Norse crewmen referred to as 'blue men.' Among them were expressions ranging from nervous dread to simmering defiance. One stepped forward, speaking rapidly, and, Bjólf thought, with barely contained agitation, despite a fixed smile, gesturing repeatedly at something on deck, something Bjólf could not see.

"They are telling him to return to his ship, that it is too late for healing," said Svein. Then, craning his neck, added: "It appears the Nubian fellow at their feet is already dead."

Bjólf raised himself as far as he dared, high enough to glimpse a long body in robes of white and tan, stretched out and motionless on the Arab's deck, the dark skin of his face tinged with a deathly, ashen pallor. But already hooks had been thrown over the side of the Arab ship, pulling it tight alongside, and other members of Olaf's crew were now clambering over, while Olaf himself continued to smile at the increasingly nervous Arab sailors.

"Stay close, young cub," said Svein. "I promised your uncle I would keep you alive." And with that, he too slipped over the side. Bjólf followed, his hand on the old sword his uncle had given him and which, as yet, had not shed blood, his eyes nervously scanning the rows of faces that greeted them. Their fingers twitched towards weapons, their tense bodies edging back and forth, keeping their distance from the silently invading Northmen.

Bjólf felt his knees shake. Cold beads of sweat trickled down his sides. Now, with his ship behind him and his feet on this unknown vessel, he had never felt so exposed. He wished to turn – to check his ship was still there, at least – but did not dare.

Looking around slowly, still smiling, Olaf picked up a pail from the deck, and took two steps toward the dead Nubian, ignoring the shouts of the Arabs' leader. Others inched away at his approach. Then, as he looked back at the dead man, Bjólf happened to notice that the deathly pallor of his face was entirely absent from his hands. Finally, he understood, and knew for certain what was to come.

"Time for the cure," muttered Svein. Olaf hurled the contents of the bucket over the Nubian's face. The man roared and leapt to his feet in a fury, easily matching Olaf for height, shaking his head violently, white powder running off his face, his gold-ringed hand grasping a huge curved sword that had been concealed beneath his body. Eyes blazing, he lunged forward, and as one the Arab crew flew at the invaders.

Several fell in that first moment. Less armoured than their Norse opponents, with no helms upon their heads, a few among the Arab pirates succumbed immediately to well-aimed blows. A single strike of a sword or axe to the head was usually enough to settle the matter, but many of the viking's body blows were turned by concealed armour. The fighting that followed was intense and bitter. For Bjólf, it lived as a confused memory, the details of which were fractured and blurred. He remembered men wrestling for their lives all around him, falling in spilt blood, the white robes stained red. He saw Olaf dispatch one with a swing of his axe, catching the small wiry man with the flat of the blade against the side of his head with a sickening crunch and propelling him clean overboard. Near Olaf's feet was the big Nubian, motionless, blood on his head. Then Bjólf was buffeted by something – other men, struggling in each other's grips – throwing him off his feet and knocking the wind out of him. Someone stepped on his left hand with all his weight. He felt a bone crack. Through the pain, he recovered his senses and looked up to see the Nubian, somehow up again and almost upon him, staggering, his blade raised. As it swung wildly at him, Bjólf scrabbled desperately backwards. Something caught his forehead a glancing blow. He crumpled, his head swimming. Afterwards, he remembered being suddenly on his feet again – how, he had no idea. There was a ringing in his head, and he was blinded in his left eye, but he was up, alive and alert, his sword still in his hand. The chaos continued all around, and the Nubian swung at him again. Having no shield, Bjólf parried with his sword. The two blades met with a jarring crash, sending both singing out of the their owners' hands to clatter on the wooden deck. Bjólf staggered back as the Nubian went at him again, hands reaching out towards him, grabbing his throat. He could smell the man's sweat. To his left, he was dimly aware of Svein, sword drawn, trying to fight his way towards them, but suddenly blocked by a small man with a halberd, screaming at the top of his lungs. No help was coming. Without thinking, Bjólf unsheathed his knife and lashed out blindly. The Nubian's eyes suddenly widened, his grip on the boy's windpipe loosened, and with a horrible, rattling groan he slid to the floor, taking Bjólf's knife with him, stuck fast between his ribs. Bjólf stared into the man's face as he gasped his last breath, the life leaving his eyes.

In minutes it was over. Every Arab pirate was dead. The deck swam with blood. In a daze, Bjólf watched it wash back and forth with the roll of the ship. He felt the gash on his left brow from the tip of the Nubian's sword, realising now that it was only the blood in his eye blinding him. A lucky escape. Olaf's men relieved the hold of its plunder, which was considerable. His own crew had got away with only minor injuries. Tonight, they would celebrate. Bjólf would be singled out for special treatment; he had made his first kill. And he was alive. They would drink mead, and sing songs, and make oaths. Olaf would honour him with a new sword – the sword once meant for the son he never had.

The memory faded, but some things remained. Through the middle of Bjólf's left brow there would now always be an angled scar where no hair grew. His right hand would ache in cold weather. And for years he would dream of the face of that Nubian, rising from the dead to kill him.

# CHAPTER THIRTEEN

## THE GREY LAND

As the sun rose, the *Hrafn* made its slow, steady progress inland, a half-crew keeping a slow stroke on the oars. The grey walls of the deep fjord towered above them on either side, shrouding them in shadow, and, despite what the raven had promised, offering no place to make a landing, and precious few signs of life. Save for some smears of slimy green algae close to the water's edge, no growing thing seemed to have gained a foothold on the steep, forbidding crags. Occasionally, a large bird flapped and cried out at the brow of the cliff, and the eyes of the men flicked nervously upward, scanning its broken edge. Weapons were kept ready for fear of other eyes watching, but mostly it was the unnerving, dead stillness of this place that made them tense, and kept them keen. Even Kjötvi, though still weak, was awake and alert. Then, after a while, just when it seemed the sun might break into the depths of this lifeless chasm, another thick fog rolled in. Different, this time, seeming to come not from the sea, but to creep out from the landward side, to seep out of the rock itself, heavy and tinged with sickly yellow. It clung to their clothes and made all aboard shiver.

For a long time, no one spoke. Only the sound of the oars accompanied their progress. They hugged the shore on the port side, close enough to keep it safely in sight, but just far enough to keep their oar-tips clear of the rocks. The surroundings were beginning to have a strange effect on all aboard, making them sullen and listless. The lack of any other sound save those of the ship itself had a curiously disorientating effect. Bjólf could not even judge the passage of time with any certainty, and found himself counting oar-strokes in an effort to combat the sense of disconnection from the world.

Gradually, the terrain began to change. The cliff wall became less sheer, more broken. Here and there, in the few, tiny bays where life had at some time taken hold, twisted roots wound their way through fissures in the rock. Occasionally, there were spiked, leafless limbs of trees – grey as the stone to which they clung – that reached out and trailed the tips of their warped, gaunt branches in the water, some choked with the sinewy remains of old, colourless ivy. At the port bow, Bjólf scanned the forbidding land for even the slightest offer of a place to make landfall. But everywhere the cliff was too sheer, the rocks too treacherous. He heard a grunt at his shoulder.

"This is bad," said Gunnar, speaking in a whisper.

"We'll find a place," said Bjólf. "It's just a matter of time."

Gunnar shuddered. "You follow a raven, you should not be surprised that he leads you to a land of the dead."

"That bird saved our skins, Gunnar." He turned to his old friend, frowning. "What's wrong with you?"

Gunnar could not place the feeling. He shrugged. "Maybe it was a bad omen. Coming from nowhere, out of that fog."

Bjólf sighed. "Gunnar, this ship is called 'Raven.' We have a raven on our sail. The weather vane atop our mast is shaped like a raven's wing. If you're really so superstitious about that particular bird, you joined the wrong ship."

"They're different! We all know what the raven is. A Corpse-Picker. A Death-Follower. And he doesn't just follow death; he casts death's shadow. It's no coincidence the All-Father has them in his service." Gunnar pointed discretely towards the heavens once more as he spoke, as if afraid someone out there might notice."

Bjólf laughed. "Gunnar, I can't believe the Old One sends his personal ravens to earth just so they can have a peck at Kjötvi's leg."

"Ah, you're mocking me!" barked Gunnar. "You don't know what schemes are being played out, what fates we may have spun for us." He shook his head in dismay. "You never did have respect for the old religion."

"What faith I have is in these two hands," said Bjólf irritably, raising them before Gunnar's glowering brow. "And I have no time for omens." He turned them, then, in a conciliatory gesture. "I've no greater respect for any man, Gunnar. You know that. But... It's just a bird."

"It's not *just* –" began Gunnar, but thought better of it. He had never won this argument, and never would. "I'm just saying. One should not tempt fate."

"Fate will come whether I tempt it or not," said Bjólf, his voice as hard as steel. Gunnar kept silent. Upon this one point, at least, both could agree. Bjólf thought for a moment, then added: "Anyway, it was a crow."

Gunnar growled, doggedly refusing to crack his face at the joke.

"Hoy!" hissed a voice.

In his position high on the prow, Fjölvar was pointing up ahead. As Bjólf peered into the murk, he could just make out the beginning of a long bend in the waterway off to the starboard side, and with it another change in the landscape. The sheer cliffs – whose dominance had evidently been diminishing for some time behind the fog – were finally giving way to a gentler shore, the dead rock to ever more thickly tangled forest, whose boughs and thickets overflowed and tumbled into the water. Up ahead, the overhanging foliage – as dense as Bjólf had ever seen – still presented an impenetrable barrier to their landing.

Yet here and there, where the knots of vegetation occasionally thinned, there were glimpses of a swampy land beyond, bringing the hope that landfall could not be far away.

"There!" said Fjölvar. His eyes were sharper than most, but finally Bjólf saw it: a tiny sheltered bay, little more than the length of their ship, where the small closely-knit trees stood back a little from the water's edge and presented a thumbnail of solid ground – albeit covered in thick tangles of bramble, hawthorn and mossy roots. At the nearest end, half in the water, was a huge boulder that seemed to bear no relation to its surroundings, as if dropped there by a passing giant. Bjólf gave the signal to Úlf, at the helm, to take them in.

"This forest is old as the hills," he said to Gunnar. "Must be teeming with game."

"I'd feel better if I could hear it," said Gunnar, still evidently unnerved. He turned and hauled up a length of rope from the deck, at the end of which was a large iron hook, and slung it over his shoulder. "Nevertheless, I volunteer to go ashore, if only for the forgotten pleasure of relieving myself on dry land."

Úlf steered the ship into the tiny, still cove as Bjólf's crew shipped their oars. Gunnar made ready at the gunwale, and as the hull rasped and crunched against submerged stones and roots, he made a jump for the strip of shore. It was not the most elegant of landings. He came down short, his feet splashing in the filthy, green water hidden beneath the mesh of roots and creepers, then, in trying to step forward to steady himself, snarled his toe in the tangle and pitched forward, landing heavily on his front and barking his shin on a tree root. The crew guffawed.

"Dry land, Gunnar!" called Bjólf.

Gunnar struggled to his feet, hauling the ship's line back over his shoulder and muttering to himself as he fought through the knee-high web of foliage to firmer ground. Finally, he rose up onto what was evidently a solid bank, veined with thick, tuberous roots, made a great show of stamping his feet upon it, then turned and raised his arms in triumph. All aboard the ship gave a cheer.

Suddenly aware of the uncertainty of their surroundings, Bjólf turned and gestured for quiet. The laughter died down, the occasional lingering chuckle echoing away to nothing in the still air. "Now, just get on with it!" he called.

"First things first..." replied Gunnar, throwing the grappling-hook and line on the ground and hitching up his tunic. The foliage steamed as he emptied his aching bladder. "Ah, that's better. You can't beat a good piss in the open air with the earth beneath your feet!" He shuddered as he finished, the muffled sniggers of the men behind him and the splash of his own water before, and another sound caught his attention.

It came from within the trees.

At first, he thought it must be the groan of the ship's timbers, somehow cast ahead of them by the strange nature of this rocky fjord. Then, he heard a distinct movement directly ahead. He stared hard into the dark shadows of the forest, trying to penetrate them, but could see nothing. Fastening his clothes, he stepped forward gingerly, pushing apart the thorny outer branches at the forest's edge.

"Gunnar?" The voice was Bjólf's.

Without looking back, Gunnar raised his hand in acknowledgement, but it was a gesture that also called for silence. If there was game here, he didn't want to scare it off. What he wanted most was to sink his teeth into it. His mouth watered involuntarily at the thought of its succulent flesh. As he took a step forward into the woods themselves, he frowned deeply, his eyes becoming slowly accustomed to the gloom. There was a dead, still atmosphere amongst these trees – like none he had ever encountered – the boughs of the trees, where they were visible at all, covered in clumps of ancient moss, dusty, crumbling layers of lichen and the choking, skeletal remains of old ivy. A sudden, sickening stench of organic decay wafted over him. Some stinking bog in the forest's interior, he supposed. He shuddered again. A twig snapped to his right. Whatever it was, it was near, but the vegetation was so close, so dense and dark, he was barely able to glimpse anything beyond a couple of paces. *Stupid*, he thought. *What can I do about it now, anyway, with no spear and no bow?* He was about to turn back when something big crashed unsteadily through the thicket with a great, unearthly groan, its face suddenly emerging from the mass of thorny suckers and grey leaves, barely an arm's length from his own. Gunnar, who had seen every terrible thing that deprivation and savagery could deliver, reeled in sickened horror at the sight of it, staggering backwards through the bushes and clear out of the woods to the thin, tangled strip of shore.

He had only a fleeting moment to take in what he had seen.

It was the face of a man – or what had once been a man – its skin quite gone, like something flayed alive. But he could hardly believe that what lurched towards him in those woods was actually alive. The veins, sinews and musculature were not only uncovered, but bloodless, misshapen and eaten away like rotten, wasp-gnawed fruit. It was – he could not doubt it, for he had seen enough of them in his life – the face of a long-dead corpse. Beneath it, hung in limp, wet rags, was a body so ravaged that the impression was of a skeleton barely held together by its liquifying gobbets of grey, slimy flesh, its extended right forearm so stripped of meat that he could clearly see between the exposed bones. Yet its hand grasped, its yellowed eyes without lids twitched in their sockets, staring madly at him, and its lipless mouth snapped, the blackened, loose teeth clattering horribly against one another. Gunnar had hesitated just long enough to see it take two quivering steps towards him.

GREETED BY THE comical sight of the big man tottering wildly backwards out of the undergrowth, Bjólf broke into a laugh. "Gunnar?" His old friend stopped dead. Bjólf's smile faded. "Gunnar...?"

"We have to get out of here," said Gunnar in a monotone, then resumed backing away, his eyes fixed on the trees.

"What is it?"

"Something bad here." He was ankle deep in the water now, stumbling against roots.

Bjólf scanned the treeline, but could see nothing.

Gunnar splashed towards the ship and heaved himself up and over the gunwale, his face pale. He spoke in short, urgent bursts. "Some... pestilence... a man. Half dead. More than half..." He fixed Bjólf's eyes with his own. "We have to get out of here."

Bjólf had never seen Gunnar like this. He turned back to the tangled wood, thinking of his crew's desperate need for fresh food and water. "Are you certain?"

"I saw it, this close" said Gunnar, grasping Bjólf's arm. "It was a man. Eaten away. Dead. But alive... I saw it, up close."

Bjólf stared at his friend, then back at the trees.

"I saw it too." The voice came from behind him. It was Atli. So quiet had he been these past few hours that Bjólf had almost forgotten he existed. Now, the eyes of the entire crew were upon the boy. He spoke confidently this time, as if relieved to unburden himself of the matter. "Not here. Back there. In the water. A man. Dead... and alive." Several among the tense crew shifted nervously, recalling the thing pulled up on Finn's line.

Bjólf eyed the lad with a mix of concern and anger. When it came to their survival, he trusted Gunnar beyond all men. But he had no patience for superstitious talk. He gestured towards the blank wall of foliage. "But there's nothing..."

His voice trailed away as a weird, strangled cry – neither human nor animal – rose from the depths of the forest. Then another, off to their left, like the wheezing of broken bellows. The whole crew tensed, hands on their weapons, eyes scanning the trees. A third, baleful groan came – close by, this time. Then the sound of movement in the undergrowth; something moving clumsily, not caring whether it was heard. Not the way any animal moved.

And another, deeper in the trees.

And more, to the other side.

"Get us out of here," said Bjólf.

The men snapped into action, extending the oars and

pushing the ship away from the bank – slowly, slowly – all eyes on the dark trees, no sound but the creak of the ship and the unidentified groans echoing in the dead air.

"D'you see them?" Gunnar asked Fjölvar, his eyes frantically searching for signs.

"I see nothing," said Fjölvar. At that, the leaves shook, and something crashed in the thicket. Bjólf's men heaved on the oars to pull them into clear water.

"Let's hope they can't swim, whatever they are," muttered Fjölvar. But there was hardly a man aboard now who was not thinking of that thing in the water.

"The line!" called Thorvald. Bjólf looked. He could just make out the rope Gunnar had abandoned on the shore, its outline snaking through the water from the ship to the forest's edge. It was drawing tighter as they moved. Thorvald, at the port bow, tugged hard upon it, sending a line of spray into the air. "Hook's caught fast on the roots."

Without a word, Gunnar took the coil of rope from him and threw the whole lot overboard. "Go!" he said. A few of the men looked questioningly from Gunnar to Bjólf.

"Do as he says!" barked Bjólf. He gave Atli a hard look as the oarsmen settled into their rhythm, then stalked off towards the stern.

Atli was glad to have said what he did. He felt a closer bond with Gunnar. But he had not liked the look Bjólf had given him. Turning away from the ill-fated shore as Úlf took the ship out at a sharp angle, he looked across the starboard gunwale, into the yellow fog, one arm wrapped around the thick mast.

Then, for the second time in as many days, he saw the towering head of a dragon charging out of the fog towards them, the iron teeth on its prow just moments from biting into their hull.

# CHAPTER FOURTEEN

## THE DRAGON'S TEETH

WITH A DEAFENING crunch the bows of the oncoming craft hammered into the *Hrafn*, striking at an oblique angle just ahead of the steer-board. The battered vessel tipped violently, her starboard side lifting crazily, her port side almost driven below the waterline, the mast whipping through the air as every timber and rivet cracked and groaned in protest. It was only Atli's grip on the mast that saved him from being hurled against the port strakes. The shuddering impact had thrown three of the crew clean off their feet, and as she righted herself, Grimmsson's ship – fully laden, and far heavier than Bjólf's even when empty – ploughed on inexorably, its ironclad, brightly-painted prow raking along the *Hrafn's* side, shearing two oars outright, the splintered shafts flying from the hands of their owners and smashing into the backs of the oarsmen before them, crushing one – Gøtar the Swede – hard against the gunwale. He gave a short, stifled cry as the air was squeezed out of him.

What happened in the next few minutes was to shatter any remaining illusions Atli may have had about the realities of life among the *vikingr*. Men on both sides scrambled for any weapons that came to hand, while Grimmson's crew – looking every bit as confused by the collision as Bjólf's – reached out to the rival ship, grasping over the gunwale. It was clear to Atli that they intended to board. Then he heard Bjólf, who had been standing at the stern and was one of the closest when the two ships clashed, suddenly roar with terrifying ferocity, flying at the invaders with a huge axe, which he swung in great arcs around his head. The battle-cry set a fighting spirit spreading like fire through the men, and they surged forward to meet their foe. This time, they would not shrink from battle.

It had taken some moments for Bjólf to recover his senses after the shock of the impact. But the instant he understood what had happened, he had thrown himself into the attack. The thoughtful, circumspect man who Atli knew was quite gone. Bjólf launched himself at the first of the invaders – a huge fellow with food in his beard, who was fearlessly straddling the gap between the vessels and already had one foot on the *Hrafn*'s deck. It was a gesture for which the man would pay dearly. Bellowing like thunder, driven by a burning anger, Bjólf swung the axe high above his head and brought it down with every ounce of strength, severing the man's leg above the knee and embedding the blade in the boards. Without hesitation, he heaved it free, hefting its bloodstained blade in great wheeling curves, as the man – pale as a ghost – tottered backwards aboard his ship, leaving his leg behind, his face contorted in utter disbelief. Flying so fast at the end of its shaft that the air hummed around him, Bjólf's blade caught another square under the chin, then cut straight through and around to take the head of a third, each exploding in a spray of gore. The head bounced and rolled on the deck, leaving a crimson trail in its wake.

The rest of Bjólf's crew, meanwhile, had not stood idle. They knew well that once aboard, the invaders would have the upper hand, and had grasped anything they could to fend off

Grimmsson's men. Led by Gunnar, who had driven his spear into two men before Atli had time blink, and spurred on by the shouts of Godwin the Axeless, a solid row of defenders had formed rapidly along the gunwale where the two ships touched, each one wielding a weapon to keep the attackers at bay: spears, boat-hooks and oars – even an iron anchor, swung wildly by a Norwegian called Háki the Toothless, who struck one man a terrible, crunching blow across the jaw. All these weapons were thrust mercilessly at the enemy crew, inflicting horrible injuries on the invaders. This was no time for chivalry. Behind them a second rank of men had formed; led by the short but formidable figure of Thorvald Two-Axe, who cast colourful insults above the clamour. They armed themselves heavily with helm, shield and blade. Magnus Grey-Beard, meanwhile, scurried the length of the ship, tending wounds as best he could, while Finn and Fjölvar, perched on the prow, picked off the loftier among their opponents with their bows. As the battle raged around him – so close that flecks of the blood of their foes splashed upon his face – Atli stood sweating, rooted to the spot, still hugging the mast and gripping his hand-axe in terror, the shouts of pain and fury ringing in his ears.

In the fight that followed, it was the aggressors' own impatience that proved their greatest downfall. In their hunger to engage the enemy, and with an arrogance known only too well to Bjólf and his men, they had armed themselves for attack, taking up swords and axes: weapons suited to close combat – close combat that they were now denied. They struggled to raise spears, shouting bitter obscenities at their foes. In frustration, some threw axes and clubs, one of which sent Kylfing sprawling on the deck. But the place where the prow of their ship overlapped the *Hrafn* was small, and in their eagerness they had become crammed against their own gunwale, with those behind unable to wield their weapons to any effect, and those in front trapped between their fellows and the vicious, thrusting points of Bjólf's men.

\* \* \*

AT THE STERN, finding his opponents' resolve had mysteriously melted away, Bjólf took up the huge, sweaty, severed leg of his first victim by its blood-soaked bindings and heaved it back at his attackers in contempt. It crashed into the chest of a broken-nosed man with a braided beard and then fell at his feet; he staggered unsteadily and promptly vomited over it. Among the attackers, Bjólf realised, a space had cleared where he stood. None now dared to face him, filled with fear at the mere sight of this man, his body bathed in their blood. Up at the prow of the enemy ship, in the midst of the melee, he finally caught sight of Grimmsson. Spying his rival, his sword held aloft, Grimmsson turned and fought to make his way towards him, keen to settle the score, but his own men hemmed him in, he shoved and struck at them in exasperaton.

Bjólf saw his opportunity. Grimmsson's men had not been given the chance to get their hooks into Bjólf's ship, and already the gap near the *Hrafn*'s stern was widening as the two vessels drifted in the current. Grabbing an oar he shoved hard at the hull of Grimsson's ship. "Come on!" he cried. Several in the second rank of defenders – including Thorvald and Finn – immediately lowered their weapons and took up oars to push.

UNDER THE SUDDEN exertion the ship slid away from the attackers, and as the gap widened, Gunnar and his men joined the effort, planting their oars and spear-shafts against the side of Grimmsson's ship and heaving with everything they had. Grimmsson's crew, furious that their quarry were breaking free, hacked and hammered at them, trying to dislodge the forest of poles that were pushing them apart. But already, in the fore section of the *Hrafn* where there was clear water on both sides, Úlf had hastily mustered the men, and under the power of almost half their oars, they were now pulling steadily away.

At the enraged bellowing of Grimmsson – red-faced and streaked with sweat – part of Grimmsson's crew scrambled to their own oars, while the remainder, fuming and outraged, sent all manner of axes, arrows and other missiles raining down upon the deck – even a boot bounced off the yard. On this occasion, however, his crew – less disciplined than Bjólf's men – were far slower off the mark.

"Give it everything you've got," called Bjólf as they began to pull away from their pursuers. Gunnar heard him muttering under his breath, then he seemed to spy something in the water, and in the next moment was kicking off his shoes and throwing off his bloodstained tunic.

"What is it?" said Gunnar. He scanned the water where Bjólf had been looking, but could see nothing. "This is a Hel of a time to change your clothes..."

Bjólf simply smiled and threw off his shirt.

Gunnar gawped at him. "What in Frigg's name are you doing?"

"Going for a swim," said Bjólf, then added: "Don't wait for me."

Without another word he slid over the port side, hidden from Grimmsson's ship, and disappeared under the water. Dodging down as a fresh volley of arrows hissed past, Gunnar stared after the dwindling trail of bubbles in astonishment.

Grimmsson's crew were getting into their own rhythm now, but already there was a full length of clear water between the vessels, and the *Hrafn* was gathering speed. For what seemed an impossibly long time, an increasingly anxious Gunnar saw no sign of Bjólf. He had no idea what his captain could have in mind. He only hoped it wasn't some stupid, final act of defiance. A hero's death and an eternity in Valhalla were all very well, but on the whole he'd rather that his old friend lived, to drink and laugh and fight another day right here on Earth.

Then he saw him. In a dangerous and unexpected move – to which their pursuers were entirely oblivious – he had emerged right in front of the toothed prow of Grimmsson's ship, and, as it advanced toward him, flung his right arm up and caught hold of the lowest of its iron spikes. For a second he clung there, just above the waterline, a rope held fast between his teeth. Hurriedly, he wrapped the rope around the spike and knotted it tight. And finally Gunnar understood. His eyes at last picked out the slowly tightening line, stretching from the prow of Grimmsson's ship back to the root-snarled shore from which he had only recently fled.

Bjólf waited for the next thrust of the oars and flung himself forward, his powerful arms plunging into the water, legs kicking for all they were worth. Gunnar knew Bjólf was a strong swimmer, and with his first great spurt was even pulling away from their pursuer, but it couldn't last; within a half-dozen strokes they would be upon him.

Bjólf was caught between the two vessels now, his enemy starting its creeping advance toward him with each pull on the oars, his salvation drawing further from reach. A shout went up from Grimmsson's ship. Several arrows zipped through the water, narrowly missing their new target. On the prow Grimmsson himself appeared, and grabbed the bow from the archer there. He wanted this pleasure to himself.

"A line!" called Gunnar. "Get me a line here!"

Eyvind hurried to him, a wet length of rope coiled around his shoulder, which Gunnar grabbed and hurled out into the water as far as it would go, wrapping the rest around his arm and waist. Bjólf spied it as it snaked out from the stern. But, fast as he was, Gunnar could see it would be two or three strokes at least before he would make the rope. And that would be too late. They were picking up rhythm and speed now, bearing down on Bjólf, and by some great effort even gaining on the *Hrafn*. Another arrow flew from Grimmsson's bow and shot into the water a hand-width from Bjólf's head – so close that Gunnar caught his breath.

Then, just moments before the barnacle-crusted keel would have driven over him, the vessel made an inexplicable turn to port. Grimmsson looked around in confusion and alarm as the helmsman fought with the tiller. The line was now pulled tight, the ship's momentum pulling it round in an arc towards the shore. "Hold fast..." muttered Gunnar through clenched teeth, a prayer for the resilience of the rope going out to Thor. "Hold fast..."

It was all Bjólf needed. In the next moment, he grasped the line, wrapping it around his wrist, and Gunnar hauled upon it, and he and Eyvind heaved him up out of the water. "What kept you?" said Gunnar.

Bjólf looked back, just in time to see Grimmsson's ship – nearly broadside-on now – crash into a knot of overhanging branches, both Grimmsson and its prow disappearing into the jumbled, prickly mass as it finally struck the shore and shuddered to a halt.

There was a roar of fury and a final hail of arrows and other missiles, most of which now fell far short. But just when it seemed they were out of range, Oddvarr, who had taken up his oar near the stern and was in the process of cracking a joke at Grimmsson's expense, caught a spear clean through the shoulder. Hurled with what must have been exceptional force, it passed out the other side and stuck in the deck, pinning him in place at his rowing station until Magnus and Eyvind were able to break the shaft and free him.

In response, his eyes blazing with anger, Bjólf picked up by the hair the head of the man he had felled and hurled it with all his strength at the receding vessel. Atli heard it thud sickeningly upon Grimmsson's deck – a grim reminder to all who would seek to take this ship from its captain.

He stood in silence for a moment, dripping on the deck, his lungs aching with the effort. Once again, they had prevailed. But as he and Gunnar watched the other ship melt into the fog, a curious change came over its crew. New cries went up. A kind of panic seemed to take them. And, just before it finally disappeared from view, it appeared to both men that the crew had turned savagely upon each other, as if gripped by a kind of madness.

# CHAPTER FIFTEEN

## WAR TOKENS AND WOLF'S FOOD

"A FAIR FEW rivets rattled loose along the steer-board side," said Úlf, half hidden below the planking. "Caulking's gone in places. We'll need to get some tar on that."

Crouched at the edge of the raised planking, Bjólf looked on anxiously as the big, heavily muscled man – the ship's *filungar*, learned in the ways of ship-building – continued his examination of the hull, ankle-deep in water. Behind him, Grimm the Stout, who fully lived up to his name, and Áki Crow-Foot, a lanky Dane from south of Ribe, bailed water steadily, while all around a three-quarter crew kept up a brisk pace at the rowing benches. Having no replacements for the two lost oars had meant moving one from port to starboard. They would be fine rowing that way for the time being, fifteen oars a side, although Bjólf knew there was not a man aboard who was not praying for a breath of wind.

"The timbers?" he enquired.

Úlf frowned and ran a huge hand along the point of impact. "Ribs and thwarts are sound..." He grunted and nodded to himself. "Top two strakes are cracked, but they will hold."

Bjólf sighed with relief. He was still master of his own vessel, they were not sinking, and compared to the terrible damage inflicted upon their impetuous attackers, their casualties had been light. Bjólf had often had occasion to curse his acute sense of caution – a trait reflected in his crew. But not today.

Úlf stood and slapped the gunwale where Grimmsson's ship had struck. "We picked up a souvenir, though..." Above the water line, projecting through one of the oak strakes and held so tightly by the wood it had completely plugged the hole it made, was the sharp tip of a rough iron spike, snapped off Grimmsson's prow. "He bit off more than he could chew this time!" chuckled Úlf.

"Well, I hope the raven left a bitter taste in his ugly mouth," quipped Grimm, and patted the deck affectionately.

"Was it his intention to ram us, do you suppose?" said Gunnar from the helm.

Bjólf straightened and shook his head, moving to join him. He stared back out into the fog. "If it had been, we would not have got off so lightly. I think they were as lost as we were." He shrugged. "Pure chance."

"Some chance!" scoffed Gunnar. "I don't believe in chances. Not like that, anyway. Across that expanse of ocean, in all that fog..."

"Please, Gunnar," Bjólf raised a hand in protest, "don't give me the 'destiny' speech."

Gunnar merely shrugged and raised his palms and gave a familiar smirk that said: *As if I would...*

Magnus approached then, his face strained and tired. He spoke in low tones.

"Mostly small wounds. Gashes and broken ribs. Two were struck by arrows, but the damage was small. And Kjötvi lost a finger in the fight." Bjólf and Gunnar exchanged looks of disbelief at the man's singular misfortune. "He is well – he rallies," said Magnus. "But three others will not see home..."

Kylfing had taken a club full in the face, and though he had at first had fought back despite his entire visage having swollen up like an inflated pig's bladder, he soon after became suddenly dizzy and slurred of speech, and fell into a sleep from which he would not awaken. Then there was Oddvarr, who had taken the spear, and his fellow Swede, the big Gøtar, who had been crushed behind one of the oars as the other ship struck. For one, the fight was already over. The other's breathing was laboured, and periodically he coughed up blood – each bout worse than the one before, and causing such pain that the colour drained from his hands and face when the fit was upon him. A broken rib had pierced his lung. Magnus hung his head as he described what each sensed was inevitable.

"There is no remedy within man's power," he said. "But, I can give dwaleberry to ease his passing."

Bjólf nodded. There was nothing to be said.

Magnus shrugged. "They are beyond my help now." Then he nodded in the direction of the mast. "It's him I'm worried about..."

Bjólf followed his gesture and saw young Atli: pale, trembling, his white knuckles still gripping the shaft of his axe, his other arm still clamped around the mast. He gave the briefest of laughs at the sight of it. "We'll sort him out. Just see that Oddvarr, Gøtar and Kylfing have what little comfort we can give."

Magnus nodded and left Bjólf and Gunnar to their thoughts.

"We must do right by them," said Gunnar. "Give them a proper burial."

"And we shall," said Bjólf. "But we must put more distance between us and Grimmsson first. Just to be certain. Although..." He looked back into the fog.

"You're thinking about what happened on that ship after it hit the shore," muttered Gunnar. "Do you think they turned on each other, or...?"

"Or?" Bjólf looked at Gunnar. Gunnar said nothing. But each knew what the other had in mind. "I need to hear from you exactly what you saw in this forest," said Bjólf. "And to talk to the boy, too. Away from other ears – for the moment, at least."

Gunnar nodded in silent acknowledgement.

"First," said Bjólf with a sigh, "let me see if I can prise our young recruit from the mast."

# CHAPTER SIXTEEN

## *STEINARRSNAUTR*

"Little man?"

The words caused Atli to start violently, snapping him back to the present. For some time – he did not know how long – he had been unable to tear his gaze from the places along the gunwale where the battle had raged, marked by the dark stain of blood. Now he stood, hunched, feeling small, and stared at Bjólf, his eyes filled with confusion and fear.

"Are you hurt?" asked Bjólf.

Atli shook his head.

"Do you wish to leave us? You're free to go your own way."

Atli, not needing to look at the uninviting shore to arrive at an answer, shook his head again, though less vigorously this time.

"I have never seen a battle..." he said.

"As you see, it is not all adventure and glory. Not even in victory."

Atli frowned, felt sick. "Is it always... like this?"

"You do what you need to."

An sob suddenly escaped Atli's lips. This was not the life he had imagined. He tried to contain himself, embarrassed before the other men, tightening his grip on the axe in an attempt to stop his hand shaking.

Bjólf nodded. "You think this might have been avoided. The bloodshed..." His voice suddenly changed, becoming stern, charged with the same steely defiance Atli had seen during the fight. "Understand, boy, they meant to kill us, and to take this ship. They had no mercy in mind, and expected none in return."

Atli knew he spoke the truth. Yet, as he spoke, each blow of Bjólf's axe blade replayed itself in Atli's mind – a parade of faces at one moment filled with passion and vigour, and the next... His face drained of blood, and for a moment he felt he would vomit.

Bjólf slapped his hand suddenly against the mast, making Atli start once again. "This ugly pile of wood... It is no mere chattel. This ship is my livelihood, my home, my family. And these men are my kin, for I have no other I value as much. I am bound to them, as they are to me. Who threatens them, threatens me. And who does so incurs my wrath."

Atli nodded, saying nothing. Tears stung his eyes; tears of anger, now, at his own feebleness.

Bjólf took a deep breath then, and, leaning in, spoke in softer tones: "You may not believe it, but I know what it is you are feeling. I have felt that fear in my own stomach, and on this very ship. There is no man here who has not, and none will think the less of you for it."

"I will do better. I will learn."

"Yes. You will." Bjólf slapped the boy on the shoulder. "And I have just the thing to help you in your quest." With that he made towards the stern, stopped after a few paces, turned and looked back at Atli. "Well? Are you coming or not?"

Atli slipped his aching arm from around the mast and followed.

At the stern, just below the steering deck where Gunnar still stood at the helm, Bjólf had several long chests, at the centre of which was his own; the fine, carved box adorned with dragons that he had inherited from his uncle. To the left was Steinarr's, from which Atli had already gained much, and to the right another of exceptionally dark wood, polished and left plain, but with ornate, green-tinged bronze hinges. All stood open.

Bjólf reached into the black box. "First," he said, rummaging noisily inside, "something to keep you alive." And as he straightened up, Atli saw his hands were filled with bunched swathes of linked mail. "This was Hallgeirr's. He would not mind me lending it out."

"He never liked that shirt anyway," grunted Gunnar.

Ignoring him, Bjólf held it aloft. "Belt," he said to Atli, nodding in the direction of his waist. Atli took a moment to realise what Bjólf meant. "As soon as you are ready, little man, this stuff is heavy..." Hurriedly, Atli undid the buckle and let it fall to the floor. "Arms," said Bjólf. Atli raised them. Bjólf heaved the mail over the boy's hands and let the gathered folds of linked metal fall down over his body to just above his knees.

Atli felt his legs bow at the weight hanging on his shoulders. He had never imagined a garment could be so heavy. But then, had he never seen mail so close up, let alone dreamt he would one day be wearing it himself. Where he came from, you only had such stuff if you were wealthy, and nobody was.

"It was always short, but Hallgeirr was taller..." Bjólf looked him up and down. "I think we have a fair compromise. Good?"

Atli nodded, and even managed a smile. "Why did Hallgeirr not like it?"

"Cheap stuff," said Gunnar dismissively, his arm wrapped around the tiller. "Always complained the links were too large. Said it was too noisy."

"Noisy?"

"Bad for sneaking up," explained Bjólf.

"But what if I need to sneak up?"

"One step at a time, little man," frowned Bjólf. "A moment ago you had no mail at all. Now you're getting picky."

Gunnar chuckled.

Atli looked thoughtful for a moment. "Does mail make you..." – he struggled to find the word – "invincible?"

Gunnar laughed. "No, nothing can do that. Everybody dies."

"And, in case you didn't know, Gunnar is the man responsible for morale aboard this ship – if you can believe that," sighed Bjólf. "But there is one more thing." He looked down into Steinarr's sea-chest. "The other half of the story. Something to make you a true warrior." From the chest, he lifted a long, fine-hilted seax, sheathed in red-stained leather. Drawing it for Atli to see, he held it across his outstretched palms. It was sharp on one side only, like a knife; a narrow, straight, fullered blade, but thick and strong at the back and angled at the end to a sharp point. The grip was girt with black leather, the bronze hilt plain, the matching pommel lobed in three. Along the blade, before the fuller, a repeating diamond pattern had been etched, and close to the hilt the bright blade was marked with runes. Though the whole thing was barely the length of just the blade of Bjólf's sword, it was a handsome weapon. Atli's eyes glittered at the sight of it, all thought of the bleakness of battle, for the moment, quite gone.

"One does not lend swords," said Bjólf. "One can only give them. I therefore give this sword to you, but in doing so, call upon you to make an oath, if you are ready to do so."

Atli nodded.

"Kneel and place your right hand upon the blade," said Bjólf solemnly. Atli did so. "Do you swear on this blade the unbreakable oath of kinship and loyalty to this ship, its crew and its captain, Bjólf, son of Erling, to use this sword in its service and for its protection, and never to spill the blood of your kin?"

Behind Bjólf, Atli saw Gunnar mouth the words: "'I, Atli, do swear it...'"

"I, Atli..." he began. He hesitated, a dim thought coalescing in his mind. Then he raised his voice again, stronger this time. "I Atli... Son of Ivarr... do swear it..."

Gunnar smiled at the words.

"I call this blade *Steinarrsnautr* – Steinarr's gift," said Bjólf, passing him the sword. "Remember the name, and never put yourself more than two paces from it."

"Something we could all do to remember," muttered Gunnar, recalling Bjólf's use of Godwin's axe.

"Now," said Bjólf in hushed tones. "We must talk, you and I, about this thing you saw in the water."

# CHAPTER SEVENTEEN

## THE ROAD TAKEN

IT WAS ONLY gradually that Atli realised what his new treasures meant. As they talked, the weight of his situation began to bear down upon him as palpably as his new mail-shirt. But now, like the mail itself, there was something oddly comforting in the burden, and while he felt a rush of sheer terror each time he even thought of putting his sword to use, its presence also reassured him. In this company, dressed as he was, he felt himself speak a little more assuredly, move a little more naturally with the ship and stand a little taller.

"Then we are agreed. There is some pestilence in this land," said Bjólf.

"I have no need to agree anything," said Gunnar, his patience wearing thin. "I saw it with my own eyes."

"But some *pestilence*. That was what you said. A plague of some kind?"

"I suppose," shrugged Gunnar. "But unlike any I've seen. And we've seen many, you and I."

Bjólf nodded gloomily. "And you are certain of what you saw?"

"Odin's beard! For the last time... It was like something yanked out of a grave; a puppet of rotten flesh and bones! Just as the boy describes. And don't forget those moans, you yourself heard those."

"Could they have been something else? An animal of some sort?"

Gunnar threw up his hands. "If that was an animal then you can drop me in a cauldron and call me a Celt."

"Well, this makes sense of the merchant's' tall tales."

"And perhaps, too, of our old friend back in the village." Gunnar gave Atli a swift sideways glance as he spoke, then added: "Of Ivarr..." Atli felt mixed feelings at the vindication of his father's actions. He chose to remain silent. But he was glad, at least, that Gunnar had chosen to honour his father with a name.

"There's one good thing to come of it," sighed Bjólf. "If the poor wretches you saw did stray onto Grimmsson's ship, then that crew will have more pressing things to worry about than us."

"It seems the bad luck was in our favour."

At that moment, the voice of Finn called out from his position at the prow. "Hoy! Up ahead – a fork in the channel."

Bjólf hurried to the bow, with Atli close behind, as the steady rhythm of the oars drew them through the fog, closer to the place where the waterway branched off, off to port. Splitting off at an angle and heading back in the opposite direction from that in which they were now travelling, it was far narrower than the fjord in which they now found themselves – but still a good size for their ship. It was also considerably more inviting. The banks were greener, it even seemed the sky beyond was lighter, and they could see slight eddies around the confluence – signs of the gentle current against which, thus far, they had been rowing.

"So," he said. "It seems we have a choice. Keep on inland within this fjord, or turn back down this tributary, and perhaps on to the sea. What say you, little man?"

Atli looked ahead at the forbidding, indistinct gloom of the fjord, then back at the leafy, gently sloping banks that lined the waterway to port. "This is like the rivers of my home. Its forest has a kindlier look than hereabouts. More the kind of place I would wish to be if I wanted fresh meat and game."

Bjólf nodded. "More hopeful of a landing place, too. And everyone has had a bellyful of rowing, and it's easier to roll a stone downhill than up. Bring her about!"

Slowly the *Hrafn* was turned into the gentle current, and the men, every one of them glad at the boy's decision, were finally able to ease up on the oars. "Don't let her drift!" called Gunnar. "I can't steer her if you drift!" All jeered at his protest, but Úlf, relieving half the rowing crew, made sure the remaining men kept up a gentle pressure on the oars.

It was not long before all spirits were lifted. The surrounding banks, though swampy, were green and verdant, the fog was clearing with every stroke of the oars, and soon the haze was pierced by glimmers of sunlight and the sounds of birdsong. Finally, there began to appear subtle signs of human habitation: a thick wooden post among the branches at the water's edge, once a mooring for a boat; a long wicker basket, abandoned now by the side of the river, but meant for trapping eels; in a stark, half-dead ash tree, old sacrificial offerings to the gods – skeletal remains of pigs, sheep and birds nailed to its mossy boughs.

Bjólf stepped up to the prow then, and, taking up the thick, conical wedge of wood that Atli had once thought to put on his fire, climbed up past Finn to the dragon's head and knocked out two pegs from the point where the neck joined the prow. For the first time, Atli realised that the head – intricately carved, and once painted in bright colours, though now faded and chipped almost down to the dark, bare wood – was an entirely separate piece.

To Atli's great surprise, Bjólf then tilted the dragon's head backwards until it came away completely in his hands. He paused for a moment, patted the dragon's forehead affectionately and muttered "Sorry about the 'ugly pile of wood,' old girl..." Then he kissed his fingers, pressed them on the dragon's head, wrapped it carefully in sacking and laid it gently in the crook of the prow. "We are not on a raid today," Bjólf explained, seeing the questions creeping across Atli's face. "So, we take her down to show we have no warlike intent. No point making enemies until we know what we're dealing with."

As he was speaking, Finn, looking ahead, had spied something. He nudged him, and gestured downriver. Just visible in the distance, on the river's left bank, was a clearing around a muddy bay, and beached in the mud several small boats.

"However," Bjólf continued, "there is no advantage in appearing weak."

He turned and gave a shrill whistle to the crew. All looked to him. And without another word he raised his arms to head height and struck a clenched fist against the flattened palm of his left hand.

As Bjólf strode astern to arm himself, all around threw open chests and set about the same task. The air was filled with the chink of mail and the glint of helms and blades as hauberks were thrown over heads, straps tightened and quivers filled. Shields and spears were passed out from their places on the deck, while amidst the clamour came the sound of whetstones honing sword and axe.

Among the men, Gunnar spied Kjötvi, up and about and making his own preparations, despite a near total lack of armour with which to prepare. His leg was bound, his left hand wrapped in a bloody bandage so he struggled to buckle his belt, yet it seemed to Gunnar that, aside from the obvious injuries and the near permanent look of consternation upon his face, that he was the very picture of rude health. That was just the way of things, he supposed. Some men could trip on a bucket and that was the end of them. Others could be trampled by a dozen horses and get up afterwards. Kjötvi, uniquely among men, seemed to combine the worst of one and the best of the other. It was certainly a strange kind of half-luck that he had.

Gunnar approached him. "Sorry about the, er..." He nodded in the vague direction of the place where Kjötvi's left index finger had once been.

Kjötvi shook his head in disbelief. "I put my hand on the gunwale for one moment. The two ships' hulls clashed, and..." he shuddered at the memory.

Gunnar reached into the bag on his belt and pulled out a small, yellow-white sliver. "I have something. Something to return." He handed it to a bemused Kjötvi. "The shard of bone that Magnus removed from your leg," explained Gunnar. "I kept it safe. It's not much, but it seemed to me you'd already lost enough for one trip."

Kjötvi took the bone fragment, and, closing his fist around it, gave a smile of deep gratitude.

Atli – already kitted out with mail and sword – had meanwhile hurried back to his small heap of belongings at Bjólf's command. As he fastened his belt, from which hung his leather pouch, eating knife and axe, Magnus approached, in his hands a simple steel helm with a straight nose-guard. He held it out to Atli.

"Gøtar asked me to give you this," he said. Atli took it from him, momentarily lost for words. Like the mail, it was far heavier than he had imagined. Responding to Magnus' encouraging nod, he lifted it and placed it carefully over his head, uncertain how he was supposed to tell whether it was a good fit or not. His head rattled around inside the metal casing like a clapper in a bell. Magnus raised a finger, then reached inside his tunic and pulled out what looked like a woollen cap. "Here," he said, "you need one of these." And with that he took off the helm, then, having pulled the tight-fitting cap onto Atli's head, put it back over the top. Atli shook his head from side to side again. It was a snug fit now. Magnus smiled and rapped a knuckle on the front. "Better!"

Atli beamed. "I should thank him..."

Magnus shook his head solemnly. "He has passed. But this was his last wish."

Atli's face fell at the words.

"He knew the life was leaving him," said Magnus. "The helm was no protection when his time came. But he hoped it might help you live out longer days."

And without another word, he turned and left Atli standing in silence. The boy could not put a name to the feelings he felt at that moment. Never had he experienced such a mix of pride and sorrow. That a man who he barely knew – a warrior – had spent his last breath upon him... As he thought of the lives these many forge-fashioned works of metal had known – these things, everything he owned, that now were part of him – his feelings resolved into a steadfast determination, a decision about how his own life should be. Whatever he did, wherever he went, he would strive to honour them all – Steinarr, Hallgeirr, Gøtar and the rest.

# CHAPTER EIGHTEEN

## LANDFALL

"Make ready!" called Bjólf. He, too, was fully fitted out with war-gear now, more than Atli had ever seen: fine mail-coat gleaming, gold-hilted sword at his side, short seax hanging cross-wise beneath his belt, a bright blue cape over his shoulders and clasped by a gleaming gold brooch, and over that, at his back, a red-painted shield with bronze decorations on its face, and a bearded fighting axe. In his right hand he held an ash spear, its long, leaf-shaped point glinting in the sunlight. Only his helm hung from his belt, to show his intentions were not hostile.

Every one of the other men was similarly attired, each in their own fashion, but all contrived to invoke awe in those who confronted them. In the short time this had taken, the ship had closed upon the boggy harbour, and half the crew kept up the pressure at the oars as Thorvald, who had taken the helm, guided her in. Gunnar now stood alongside his captain at the prow, his great, grey wolfskin across his shoulders.

"Ymir's breath..." he muttered, looking out at what greeted them. "What is this?"

Atli moved forward to get a better view. In many ways, what he saw still greatly resembled the river approach to his own village: there was the natural harbour, the gently sloping shore leading up from the water, providing a good landing place for boats, the protective banks of trees and foliage on either side. But where his home was all pebbles and shingle, here the bay was lined with dark estuary mud giving way to thick grass that, but for a worn yet oddly neglected path, swathed the long, gentle slope far inland to the boundaries of the forest, only occasionally punctuated by an outcrop of jagged, grey, moss-covered rock. And, where the woodland around his village was, he now thought, welcoming in character and pleasing in scale, the forest here was massive, thick and brooding, its gigantic forms seeming to pile up and press in on either side, ancient boughs that hung so far out over the edges of the water that one could hide a whole army beneath them. Dotting the muddy shore were five small boats – one filled with greenish water, and one so old and uncared for it had rotted through to its ribs and sat, half sunk, like a forgotten carcass. And there, way ahead up the slope, at the far end of the untended path, the first sign of human settlement; a towering rampart of whole pine trunks, higher than a house, curving away on either side until it disappeared behind the screen of trees, at its centre a crudely constructed but formidable pair of gates hanging between rough wooden watchtowers, the whole length of its top edge lined with thick, sharpened stakes.

The men shipped the oars and, in silence, the ship slowed and came to a gentle stop as its keel eased into the mud, its prow sliding part-way up the marshy bank. Four men hauled up a long section of the deck that served as a gangplank and rapidly extended it from the port bow to more solid ground.

"Úlf," called Bjólf. "Take Eyvind, Guthmund and Ingólf and form a watch. We do not leave anything unguarded here."

"And keep vigil over our fallen brothers," added Gunnar gruffly, his eyes scanning the sky. "We've fed enough ravens today."

"Amen," muttered Magnus under his breath.

With their captain at their head, the party tramped down the gangplank and gathered on the shore, Atli making sure he was close behind Bjólf and Gunnar. It had only been a day and a night since he had first trod the deck of the dragon ship, yet now it was the solid ground that felt unfamiliar beneath his feet. He staggered unsteadily, unconsciously anticipating its rise to meet him. Even in this sodden state, it seemed strangely unmoving and implacable – a memory from an age ago that already his body had forgotten. As he moved across the muddy ground with the other men, he felt the full weight of arms and armour pull down upon him – the warrior's burden.

THE ASSEMBLED MEN made an imposing sight – something no foe, no matter how fearsome, would wish to tackle lightly. Yet Gunnar surveyed the scene with trepidation. There was a strange air of abandonment about the place. In the mud, near the waterlogged rowboat, a familiar, grisly shape caught his eye. A human skull, bulging out of the dank-smelling mire. Nearby, the same colour as the mud in which it lay, the stark, curled claw of a ribcage. Gunnar nudged Bjólf, but Bjólf had already seen them for himself.

"What in Thor's name is this place?" whispered Gunnar. "Is it deserted, do you think?" Thoughts of plague and pestilence still played on his mind.

Bjólf said nothing, but simply pointed to a patch of sky immediately above the stronghold's wall. A thin column of grey smoke curled upward from its interior. Gunnar hardly knew whether to be glad or sorry.

"We go!" Bjólf called, and they began the march to the gates, mail and war-gear clashing as they went.

"So," said Gunnar, close to Bjólf's ear. "How do you want to handle this?"

"Carefully. Does that meet with your approval?"

"Does Idun have apples?"

"Remember the old saying: where we can't raid, we trade."

"Trade? With what?"

"Our hands. Our wits. Our swords." Gunnar looked skeptical. Bjólf merely picked up the pace. "We have few choices, big man. Let's see what we can make of it."

"What we can make of it..." he grumbled, then nodded towards the stockade. "What do you suppose inspired someone to make *that*?"

"Perhaps a need for men just like us."

Great, grey clouds had begun to move rapidly across the sky, casting huge, solid shadows that rolled across the landscape like striding giants. Gunnar felt the wind on the side of his face. "Hmm! *Now* we get a breeze!"

Picking their way up the path, making no effort to conceal their approach, they saw no signs of life besides the trail of smoke. The path itself had been used over years, that much was clear – and here and there it seemed the damp, overgrown grass may have been trodden or parted by something – but whether any man had come this way in recent days was impossible to tell. They pressed onward without a word, crushing the covering underfoot, the grass giving up its sweet, moist scent.

Finally, the great stronghold, an endless row of stout pine trunks, loomed above them. Still nothing stirred. Bjólf halted before the bulwark.

"What now?" said Gunnar.

"We do what any well-mannered man would do," said Bjólf. "We knock."

And with that, he strode straight up to the gate and, raising the blunt end of his spear, hammered hard upon it five times.

He stepped back. Then, at the lookout point atop the left of the two watchtowers, a face appeared.

"Who are you?" snapped a voice.

"Well, at least he speaks our language," muttered Gunnar.

He was an old man, bearded and grey, his rheumy eyes squinting and blinking ceaselessly behind his quivering bowstring. Not the most obvious choice of lookout, thought Bjólf. Little wonder their approach had not been spied earlier.

"I am Bjólf, son of Erling, captain of these men."

"State your purpose!" Even from here, Bjólf could hear the old man's wheezing.

"Please, friend, lower your bow. Only I'm afraid you might let go and accidentally kill one of us."

The man's bow dipped and trembled, his grip on the arrow faltering. Several men in the front rank of Bjólf's company winced as it wavered in their direction. "We require provisions," continued Bjólf. "Grain, meat and ale..."

The bow drooped immediately. A look of terror had passed over the man's face. "You are Skalla's men?"

"No." Bjólf noted the look of relief that transformed the watchman's features. "But perhaps there is something with which we could help. A trade..."

The old man frowned. Other voices could be heard behind the stockade: one harsh, one less so, both female. The old man responded to them, then disappeared from view. The tone of the discussion turned to one of bickering, in which the watchman seemed to be coming off distinctly the worst.

"They must not get many visitors," said Gunnar.

In another moment, the face of an old woman, well-dressed, her hair in a fine linen hood but her expression sour, bobbed up and glared at them, then after another bout of babbling, another female figure appeared, and stood for a moment studying them, silent and unmoved, framed by the timbers of the watchtower.

The second woman had quite different qualities – qualities which Bjólf and his men were quite happy to regard at greater length. Her neck was pale and slender, her features fine and well-proportioned, her dark chestnut hair drawn back in two elegant plaits which were wound at the back, a slim band of green and gold brocade across her forehead. From a belt about her slim waist hung a bunch of iron keys. No peasant, this one, thought Bjólf. Though little more than twenty summers, he would guess, she held her head like a queen, and looked down upon this daunting band of men with no hint of fear, a hard frown upon her face.

"What do you want?"

"We have travelled a great distance, my men and I. We wish to speak with the lord of this noble place."

"There is no lord," she said. "I am mistress of its hall."

A few of the men murmured in amazement. Bjólf tried not to show his surprise.

"Then... we throw ourselves upon your hospitality," he said, pressing his hand to his breast, "and hope that we may offer something in return."

"Don't offer too much..." hissed Gunnar.

A frown crossed her face. Urgent, whispered words were uttered somewhere behind the stockade. "What is it you bring?"

Bjólf spread his arms and gestured either side at the fearsome company that surrounded him. "As you see... No more. No less." Then, acting on a gut instinct – the instinct of an opportunist pirate – added, "This 'Skalla' you speak of..."

The woman's expression turned to one of sudden realisation. "Then at last you have come," she gasped, and disappeared from view.

Bjólf stared up at the empty space and, leaning towards Gunnar, allowed a puzzled frown to cross his face. "What did she mean, 'at last you have come'?"

Before Gunnar had the chance to respond, there was a sudden uproar behind the gates, followed swiftly by a great grinding of wood against wood, a chorus of voices joined in effort, and a heavy thud that shook the earth beneath the warriors' feet. And with a deep, sonorous creak, as of something unused to movement, the gigantic gates swung inward. From its opening crept a slender figure robed in green – a two-part dress of exquisite handiwork with fine clasps of gold above and below the breast. She flew forward suddenly, and flung her arms around Bjólf's neck, grasping him tightly to her. In her wake came the old woman, arms aloft, exclaiming tearfully as she threw her own arms about an astonished Gunnar, then, upon her toes, planted kisses on each black-bearded cheek.

Both men stood, disarmed and dumfounded, as behind them the whole company of men struggled to contain their mirth. With the fine scent of the woman's hair filling his nostrils, the soft green fabric of her dress pressed against the unyielding grey metal of his mail shirt, Bjólf turned his head and beamed at his comrade. Gunnar, the old woman's face buried in his chest, glowered back, daring him to speak.

# CHAPTER NINETEEN

## HALLBJÖRN'S HALL

THOUGH HE HAD never encountered her like before, Atli knew at once she was of noble blood. It was not just the fine weave of her clothes, the softness of her skin and the glittering adornments of gold. It was her whole being – the way she spoke, the way she moved. She was also one of the most beautiful women Atli had ever seen, though perhaps, he thought, that was not saying much. There was, above all, a kind of dignity contained within her young frame by which one could hardly fail to be impressed. All the more odd, then, that she should fling herself at Bjólf with such abandon. Had she thought he was someone else? Some long-lost friend? Atli could not fathom it.

As soon became clear, it was not only he who regarded the scene with puzzlement. Looking around at the faces of the others, he read in them all varying degrees of amazement. And so, bemused or not, he found himself able to chuckle along contentedly with his new-found fellows.

"Please, forgive me," she said, releasing her grip on Bjólf, her face flushed, her head bowed, as if with sudden embarrassment. "We had given up hope..." She smiled and wiped away a tear.

As she withdrew her hand, something caught Bjólf's eye. He caught her hand in his. Around her pale, slender wrist was a thing he had seen only hours before, in the grim, fog-bound delirium of that long night on the heaving ocean. It was the simple, solid band of a bracelet, formed of two interwoven strands plaited carefully together – each no thicker than a barley stalk – one blood-red, the other crow-black. For the space of two breaths he stood with her small, delicate hand held between his rough fingers, scrutinizing it intently, a frown spreading across his forehead. "Where did you get this?" he said.

The woman's face reddened. "It was a gift," she said, seeming suddenly downcast.

"It is very distinctive," said Bjólf. "Are there... many like it?"

"One other. But it is lost. As is its owner..." – she struggled to recover her composure, her voice wavering – "my husband."

The old woman, who had now released Gunnar from her clutches, clasped her hands together and gazed tearfully at her mistress. Turning the band around her wrist, momentarily lost in thought, the young woman looked up at Bjólf, cocking her head quizzically. "Why do you ask?" she said. A look of vague hope then lit her features. "You have seen its like before?"

Bjólf slowly shook his head. "No. Never."

Her eyes lingered on him for an instant, then she gathered herself, standing straight and smoothing her hands down her dress. "I welcome you to Björnheim. I am Halldís, daughter of Hallbjörn, jarl of this land."

"Bjólf, son of Erling," responded Bjólf with a bow of his head, then gestured towards Gunnar. "And this..."

She held up a hand, silencing him. Atli was impressed.

"You and your men are surely tired and in need of refreshment after your long journey. And we should not linger longer than necessary outside."

Indicating for them to follow, she turned and moved swiftly towards the narrow opening from which she had come, the old woman scuttling behind. Bjólf and Gunnar registered her nervous glances towards the dark edges of the forest that surrounded them. They exchanged a silent, questioning look – then led the band of warriors between the great, rough-hewn wooden gates to the interior.

What met their eyes as they entered was a bizarre mixture of sights. Within the colossal stockade lay a wide, open space of grass and beaten earth in which were arrayed a great variety of sturdy, wooden buildings, of considerably greater age and quality than that surrounding wall. Up ahead, at its centre, past houses, barns and a forge and dominating the view, stood a huge hall, its great roof curved along its length like an upturned boat. The thick timbers that supported it were sturdy and of exceptionally fine craftsmanship, the gable ends delicately carved with intertwining patterns of branches and vines, all filled with stylised representations of birds and beasts, the richly decorated boards crossing at the peaked roof and finished with the elegantly sculpted, curving heads of horned stags. Rarely had Bjólf seen a hall of such scale and grandeur.

Yet all about, the haunted, hollow-cheeked faces of the rag-tag band of villagers that silently greeted them seemed to tell a quite different story. For the size of this settlement, they were pathetically few in number and curiously devoid of vitality. Ragged, thin and baffled of expression, they were composed of the leavings of society: the old, the crippled, the infirm, the weak of body and mind. Among them, Bjólf counted less than half as many men as women, and of those, barely a single one between the ages of twelve and forty. Halldís' limited retinue – the nobility among the population – were also few in number, and, despite the few trappings of wealth and the healthier disposition that came with it, seemed ill-equipped to protect even this sorry crew. Of them, only Halldís and her companion – the old woman, Ragnhild – seemed to stand out as still stout of heart, undefeated and indefatigable.

Gunnar had been wrong – the place was not deserted. But the

dead, stultifying air of emptiness and desolation hung about its neglected beams and rafters as surely as if it had been left in the keeping of ghosts. A deep, portentous thud sounded behind their backs as the gates were pushed shut, and a huge bar of wood was heaved into place by its weary-looking custodians. For good or ill, Bjólf, Gunnar and the rest were now captive within this strange, necrotic netherworld.

Yet, as they ran the gauntlet of these blankly staring spectres, both sides stunned into an eerie silence by the sight of the other, a change seemed to come over them. Slowly, as if waking from sleep after taking a draught of bitter wormwood, some of the spectators seemed to come to their senses, a light returning to their eyes. They began to murmur to one another as they watched the men march past. Their limbs, too, seemed to stir into life, and some hurried alongside as the party advanced, expressions of excitement creeping across their tired faces as, bit by bit, they realised what this awesome band of fighting men might mean to them.

At the near end of the hall, as they approached, stood a lone, hunched figure, whose gloomy presence, in the space of a moment, seemed to suck the life back out of the party.

Dressed in clothes of once fine quality, topped with a cape of charcoal grey, the man nonetheless seemed an ill fit for his clothes, as if he had somehow shrunk inside them, like a piece of air-dried meat. Yet his skin was so pale that it hardly resembled anything that had ever been alive, and his tiny eyes seemed themselves so devoid of colour that they hardly seemed composed of a distinct kind of matter from his face. This was long and lean with high cheekbones. His thin nose projecting from his pallid, bony face like a blunted axe blade. On either side of it hung curtains of long, lank hair – strikingly blond. His thin beard seemed to sprout only from the end of his chin, and hung beneath in straggly tendrils like the roots of an onion.

The only man in this place who appeared of useful age – around thirty summers, Bjólf would guess – he and he alone appeared unimpressed and unmoved by the sight of the warrior band. In fact, it seemed to Bjólf there was brazen hostility in that peevish scowl. He glared dismissively at Bjólf's crew, looking them up and down with as cold and unsympathetic an eye as a slave trader judging a potential purchase, then cast Halldís a similarly hard and sneering stare. Then, without a word, he turned with a brusque and petulant flourish of his cape and stalked off into the shadows.

Halldís turned to face Bjólf and his men apologetically, her confidence somehow shaken, as if mere sight of the pale man had brought doubts to mind. "I am sorry. What am I thinking? The hall is not prepared. There is no fire in the hearth. It has been closed up for some time and is disarrayed – more a meeting hall for mice and spiders than a fitting place to welcome men." She laughed awkwardly, then looked downcast. "It would shame me to show you into my father's hall in such a condition."

"The sky is hall enough," said Bjólf, with a shrug. He looked about him, at the great open space that extended north of the great hall – evidently a gathering place – in its centre a stone well, richly bedecked with all manner of wild blooms. He gazed up at the sun, a hand shading his eyes, fleetingly catching the scent of the flowers on the breeze. A sense of wellbeing washed over him for the first time in many days. "We're men of the outdoors. The air is fresh and the weather is fine. Better to enjoy it than lurk in the dark." He cast a fleeting glance after their skulking friend, now lost in the shade cast by the hall.

Her face beamed with a smile. "Ragnhild, have benches brought out. And prepare the hall." She turned back to Bjólf. "This evening we honour you with a feast!"

A great murmur of approval rose from the men. Ragnhild clapped her hands with glee before hurrying to her task, and a rush of excitement spread through all about as if the villagers were finally awoken from their torpor. "Food..." muttered Gunnar in grateful anticipation, then rolled his eyes skyward. "Thank you, old Troll-Beater, for looking after our needs." And he raised his Mjollnir hammer pendant briefly to his lips.

# CHAPTER TWENTY

## BREAD AND BEER

FOR SOME TIME they sat as the great clouds hurtled overhead, eating the bread and beer that was brought by willing hands. The bread was gritty and tough – poor flour, thought Bjólf, adulterated with acorns or who-knows-what to make it go further – but the butter was sweet, and the beer, though thin, was welcome relief for their parched throats. Ragnhild and Halldís passed amongst them with great flagons of the stuff, raising spirits wherever they went, broad smiles upon their faces.

"So, have you found out what all this is about yet?" said Gunnar.

"Enjoy the moment, old man," said Bjólf dismissively. But Gunnar knew only too well when his friend was avoiding the issue.

"It's plain they think we have come to fight for them," he

said. "It seems we may have survived a battle only to get involved in a war."

"Let's see how this unfolds," said Bjólf. "Perhaps it's in our favour. And if not, well, we restock, make our excuses and get on our way." Despite his cheerful tone, he did not look entirely convinced by his own words.

"At the very least, she should know that we're not the army she thinks we are."

Bjólf looked him straight in the eye. "So, do you want to tell her before the feast, or after?"

Gunnar looked into his beer, then back up at Bjólf, and grunted in assent. He took a great swig, then passed his hand across his wet mouth. "There is something strange here. No young men. The remainder looking like the walking dead, in spite of rich land all about. A wall penning them in like frightened cattle. And a woman lord of a hall!"

"It's not natural!" laughed Bjólf.

"Well, it isn't!" protested Gunnar. He looked about him at the inhabitants of this stronghold, at the haunted expressions behind their smiles. "Are they under siege from the pestilence we witnessed, do you suppose?"

"Maybe. But that doesn't quite follow. You don't fight plague with an army."

"Unless it gets up and walks," said Gunnar.

Bjólf said nothing in return, but simply sat, chewing on his bread, frowning at his own thoughts, and watching Halldís weave to and fro between the benches. He found himself captivated by her. Not that she was the most beautiful woman he had ever seen, but there was... something. A curious mixture of strength and vulnerability that he had not encountered before. As she laughed with the men – at the unashamed joy they took in her company, at their gentle flirting – he nonetheless saw a kind of fragility, even sadness, behind the confident persona she presented. And yet, when she drew apart from them to the heavy wooden table upon which the ale had been set, standing lost in her own thoughts and for the moment distant and melancholy, it seemed that it was quite the other way around – that somewhere beyond that sad demeanour lay a core of defiance and courage. She caught him watching and looked away hastily, busying herself refilling the flagon with ale. He stood and moved to join her.

"We're grateful for your hospitality," he said.

"It is an honour," she replied.

Bjólf smiled, sipping from his horn-cup. "Perhaps you have slightly too high an opinion of us."

"It is not matter of opinion," she said, not meeting his eye. "It is my duty. High-born or low, you are our guests, and deserving of every courtesy. That's what my father raised me to believe."

"A man of ideals. That's a rare thing these days."

"He was a good man," said Halldís, hanging her head, "until this loathsome conflict destroyed him."

"The feud with Skalla?" probed Bjólf.

His words seemed to sting her. She dragged the heavy flagon to her hastily, causing some of the ale to slop out on the tabletop as she did so. Frowning, she mopped at it in irritation. "I do not wish to speak of it." Her voice was hard, angry. "Nor will I have his name mentioned here. It is an obscenity among the people of Björnheim." Then, after a moment, she seemed to relent, and for the first time a look of gloomy resignation came over her. A deep sigh escaped her lips, and she began to speak in slow, measured tones. "They came in black ships from a dark fortress in the fjord, and have grown in strength as we weakened." She looked at Bjólf almost apologetically. "We are far from kings and their laws." She looked away again, troubled by memories. "Unimaginable horrors came in their wake. For five years they have taken our crops and livestock. They have enslaved our men and dishonoured our women. It is more than a feud. It is a curse they have brought down upon us."

"But you sent for help..."

"More often than I can remember. None of our emissaries escaped this valley. Each time the bodies of our people – or parts of them – were sent back to us. They were the lucky ones." She shook her head, as if trying to rid it of the dark thoughts that rattled inside. "Those men... they are few in number, but their masters command a dark magic. And so, as you see, we cower in this prison of our own making."

Bit by bit, Bjólf was beginning to build a picture of this place – of this woman – and their desperate history: the oppressed community, the fallen jarl, the lost spouse. Yet each new piece of information he gleaned, illuminating as it was, seemed only to lead back to the same inevitable question. He thought of the bracelet upon her wrist, and of its twin upon the ravaged body in the sea. The body of the husband that he alone knew was dead. The body that was dead and yet still moved. "I had wondered," he began, "if these walls were measures against the plague we had seen hereabouts."

Halldís stared at him, wide-eyed. "I should not have brought you here," she whispered, and hurried away.

Bjólf gazed after her, more bemused and troubled than ever.

# CHAPTER TWENTY-ONE

## A BOAT

Time passed swiftly for the rest of the crew. Halldís buried herself in her duties as hostess, the beer flowed freely, and all had begun to be lulled by the general good cheer of the occasion when a shrill shout brought them suddenly to their senses.

"Boat! Boat!" It was the reedy voice of a boy waving frantically from the watchtower. Bjólf and his crew were immediately on their feet, heading to the gate, weapons ready. The local people's reaction to the cry was equally swift, but their sense of urgency took them in quite the opposite direction. As Bjólf's crew raced past, mail and weapons ringing, they retreated rapidly, melting away into their homes, terrified.

"Look at them!" said Godwin in disgust. "Like frightened sheep!"

Arriving at the gates, Bjólf hurled himself up the uneven ladder to the covered platform of the watchtower where the young, skinny lad still stood, spotty beneath his straggly blond hair and red-faced, pointing down towards the water's edge.

Before he had even made the top of the tower, Bjólf had heard Úlf's distinctive whistle fade in and out on the stiff breeze that now blew at his back. It was the signal indicating another vessel, yet Úlf had not raised an alarm. Bjólf narrowed his eyes, looking down towards the harbour where his ship sat – at an angle now on the mud, where the tide had left it stranded. At first he did not see it. There was no sign of his men on the ship – they would have concealed their numbers, he knew – but beyond that, there seemed to be nothing unusual about the scene, just his ship, and a few small boats... Then he realised. Out in the water, almost obscured by his own craft, a small boat, sitting low in the water, drifted gently past, apparently brought by the current, its upper strakes and curving bows gaudily painted in a familiar style. He could see no sign of life, but within it was a curious shape, partially covered by a large swathe of dark red cloth. Another whistle went up – the sign that all was clear – and Bjólf saw the characteristic shape of Úlf Ham-Fist stir in the stern, his big forearms reaching out to the water with a boat hook to catch the passing craft.

"Open the gate!" called Bjólf as he threw himself back down the ladder. The gatekeepers hesitated, looking timidly from him to Halldís, who had herself just arrived at the rampart.

"Do it!" she cried.

They set about the task, hastened by several of Bjólf's men who lifted the weighty oak beam clean out of their hosts' hands and tossed it aside. Atli jumped back as it crashed at his feet, then joined them as they heaved on the creaking gates.

Within moments, Bjólf and his band were striding into the harbour mud, where Úlf had hauled the small boat up onto solid ground. The decoration upon it was unmistakable now. It was the row-boat from Grimmsson's ship. As he approached, he saw the big man – who was afraid of nothing on earth that Bjólf knew of – staring down into it, quite motionless.

"What is it?" said Bjólf as he came up alongside, breathing heavily. But he could see for himself now. Inside Grimmsson's boat was a single oar, a large wooden chest girt with black bands of iron, wrapped around with a heavy chain, half-draped with a cape of fine manufacture, and an expertly-wrought Frankish sword, its blade slicked with something black and sticky. Nothing else. It was immediately clear, however, what had caught Úlf's attention. On the top of the chest was a single, clear handprint of blood, still glistening in the early afternoon light.

The other men crowded around the boat, each staring at the strange sight.

"Things did not go so well for Grimmsson, then," said Gunnar. He prodded the abandoned sword-blade tentatively with the tip of his spear. "What is that? Is that blood?"

"If it is," said Godwin, "it's like none I've seen."

"Not from a living man, anyway," said Njáll.

Atli, catching only the occasional sight of the boat between shifting bodies of the other men, shuddered.

"Open it," said Bjólf.

Úlf stepped forward, his mace raised, and gave the iron lock a crashing blow. Bits of metal were sent flying. Bjólf threw off the chain and heaved the heavy lid open. The men murmured in awe at its contents.

Atli at first struggled to get a glimpse of what so impressed them. Then, as they moved, he caught sight of it, glittering in the sunlight. A precious hoard such as he could not have imagined.

Njáll whistled. "Arab dirhems, English silver pennies, Byzantine gold... this is the cream of their booty."

"Such valuables would only be in this boat if someone had been trying to make off with them," said Thorvald.

"Or more likely if the ship was lost, and they were trying to make an escape," added Godwin.

"So, what became of those who loaded it into the boat?" asked Njáll.

"The greater question must surely be what happened to the rest of the crew," said Godwin.

"Dead," said Bjólf.

Thorvald frowned at him. "All of them? The whole crew?"

"Or they fled for their lives. From a threat greater than the lure of this booty."

"Grimmsson's crew doesn't run," said Gunnar.

"And no one lets go a sword like that while they have breath in them," added Njáll.

"Then that leaves only one possible fate," said Bjólf.

"But what could wipe out an entire crew like that?" said Atli.

Gunnar looked about at the dark, blank walls of forest that surrounded them. "There's something out there. Worse than plague."

For a moment all the men looked around them, shifting in anxious silence. The thickening, mountainous clouds finally succeeded in obliterating the sun, casting a chilling pall over the company.

"Looking on the bright side," announced Fjölvar, attempting to dispel the gloom, "in the space of a day we have gone from being poverty-stricken victims of that dishonourable bunch of inbreds to having the greater part of their plunder."

"Perhaps we should quit while we're ahead," mused Thorvald.

"I vote we take what food we can and get out," said Godwin. Several nodded and muttered their agreement.

"We cannot leave," said Bjólf. The men fell silent.

Gunnar frowned at him. "One more successful raid, we said, remember? We have that now. Grimmsson finally destroyed and enough plunder to set us all up for life."

"I am sick to my stomach of running," said Bjólf. "We chose this life to be free from tyranny. Now here we are retreating from it."

"This is not our fight, my friend." Gunnar said. "And it is not tyranny we have to worry about. There is something different here. Something deadly... That wiped out eighty warriors like *that*." He snapped his fingers.

"The people here expect it of us," said Bjólf. Then, after a moment's hesitation, added: "She expects it."

Gunnar's voice hardened. "We made no deal. There would be no shame."

"There would," said Bjólf, tapping the side of his head, "In here." For a moment the two regarded each other, deadlocked. Finally, Bjólf pulled himself away and raised his voice to the rest of his men. "It is your decision. Stay or go?"

For a moment there was silence. Few could honestly say they were for staying, but none wished to speak out openly against their captain.

"Stay," said Atli. The men parted, turning to him.

Gunnar stared in surprise. "*Now* I feel shame. You have an uncanny knack of complicating matters, boy!"

Godwin gave a heavy sigh, nodding in reluctant agreement. "This little man is making us look bad."

"While you ladies are deliberating," interrupted Úlf, giving the hull of the *Hrafn* a slap with his huge hand, "allow me to point out that there's no way we're shifting this out of the mud without nature's help."

Bjólf looked at his beloved ship, held fast.

"How long until next high tide?" he asked, squinting at the edges of the mudflats.

All then looked at Kjötvi. He leaned heavily on his spear, looking back at them awkwardly. Gunnar noticed that he had bored a hole in the sliver of leg-bone and now wore it on a thong about his neck like a talisman. Kjötvi shrugged. "Tide's at its lowest. It'll be another quarter day until it's at its peak again. Around nightfall. Then again in the morning, when it will be high enough to get us off the mud for nearly half the day. But if we are still here at midday tomorrow, we'll likely be stuck again."

Bjólf nodded. "Then the decision is made. For now, at least. We stay put and take stock in the morning. See what another night brings. Which means, gentlemen," his voice rose with enthusiasm and not a little relief, "that tonight we feast!"

There was a mutter of assent from the men, mingled with muted approval. If they were forced to stick around to partake of a feast, well, maybe that wasn't so bad. Catching Atli's eye for a moment, Bjólf gave the boy a smile. He had earned the respect of many of the men today, men not easy to win round.

"We must prepare," Bjólf said. "Bring all weapons from the ship. Everyone is to stay armed." He pointed at Grimmsson's chest of silver and gold. "Stow that aboard, out of our hosts' way. Thorvald – take Einarr, Grimm and Eldi and relieve Úlf's watch here." The men snapped into action, heaving the chest from the boat and clambering aboard the ship. "Godwin?" The Englishman stood at his captain's shoulder. "I want a man up on the ramparts. Keep the ship in clear sight at all times. And have four more men on hand below. I want to be able to open those gates at a moment's notice if need arises, whether we have our host's permission or not."

"One more night, Gunnar," he said, slapping his friend on the back. "Then we see."

Gunnar looked up from beneath creased black brows, his eyes scanning the slowly darkening sky. "A storm is coming," he said.

# CHAPTER TWENTY-TWO

## A FEAST

THUNDER RUMBLED AROUND them as they sat in Halldís's hall, arrayed along the mead benches with as many as would fit in the place. It had turned to a dreary night, with rain rattling on the great curved roof all around them. But the heat from the flames of the great log fire that crackled and popped in the central hearth set all their faces a-glow, swiftly driving out the damp and musty smells of neglect, restoring to life some of the grand and noble feelings of the past – feelings all too many had forgotten.

Their nostrils now were filled with the welcome, warming smells of bubbling stews and roasting meats, Sweet, heady mead had been brought forth, too, served first to Bjólf by Halldís herself. The doughty captain had drained the long, curved drinking horn in one, as tradition demanded, to the enthusiastic claps and cheers of his men. Even Halldís – presiding over the rest of the feast from the high seat at the centre of the hall, her cheeks flushed in the heat – had regained her former poise, and seemed, at last, to appear as one who sat at the heart of a proud community, the worries of the outside world, for the moment, completely banished.

The road to the evening's celebration had not, however, been without its obstacles. There had been a tense moment at the very start, when Frodi – the reeve of the village since the time of HallBjörn, and one of Halldís's most dependable supporters – had thrust himself in front of Bjólf's men just as they were about to troop in and reminded them, politely but firmly, that no weapons were to be carried into the hall. "We feast in friendship and trust," he said, "or not at all." All were perfectly well aware of the rules of hospitality, and the banishment of blades from the feast, but few gave them up willingly. Njáll, the Irishman, who claimed to have seen this very rule exploited to treacherous ends, even squared up to the old man, who nonetheless refused to budge. It fell to Bjólf to resolve the matter to the satisfaction of both sides. All weapons were left outside, but within easy reach, and under guard by one of his own men. Frodi eyed Njáll with some suspicion after that.

When the food was brought, that, too, fell a little short of expectation; a single roast pig, a few scrawny fowls, a leg of ham and – much to Gunnar's displeasure – a fish stew with mussels that was uncomfortably similar to their makeshift meal the night before.

"Mmm. Seafood," said Gunnar, sniffing the stew. Bjólf glared at him. The fare was certainly meagre, even by the standards of the average farmstead, but he had no wish to embarrass their hosts. Although one or two among the crew seemed to take the poor quality of the food as a slight, he understood that this, in all likelihood, represented the very best they had to offer.

"The mussels were gathered today," said Halldís, adopting a cheerful air. "They are at their sweetest now." But Bjólf could see that she, too, was aware that their offerings fell far short of what they would have wished.

"We rarely hunt game in the forest," added Ragnhild. "Not unless forced to do so." Halldís silenced her with a look.

Bjólf stood, then, and raised his mead-cup. "To the mistress of this hall, who honours us with this feast, and to new friendships..." All raised their voices together in the toast. He thought he detected a flicker of a smile upon Halldís' face.

"Thor!" added Gunnar, tipping a drop of drink upon the beaten earth floor before taking it himself – a small offering to the gods. Many about him did the same.

Soon, as bellies were filled, faces warmed and the mead hit its mark, the conversation blossomed, and the laughter grew. A harper struck up and sang a song of the adventures of Sigurd, and then Skjöld the Icelander, very drunk but all the better for it. Before long, crew and hosts were laughing uproariously together like the oldest of friends: Njáll was slapping a smiling Frodi on the back, forcing more drink into his already overflowing cup, Ragnhild was hooting and flapping her apron whilst eyeing up Gunnar with ever-decreasing subtlety, and Fjölvar was engaging the old man from the watchtower in some kind of drinking game at which he himself was very obviously cheating, much to the amusement of his neighbours. Finally, Halldís too, who at first had tried to keep a sense of decorum by pretending not to understand the jokes at Skjöld's expense, gave in to fits of laughter, wiping tears from her eyes. Bjólf was gladdened by the sight of her, feeling, at last, that there was something here worth fighting for.

Among them all just one sat apart, disdainful and humourless. In a far corner, the pale man sipped sparingly at his drink, watching Bjólf intently.

"Who *is* that sour-faced fellow?" asked Gunnar, slamming down his cup in irritation.

"Ah, now," said Fjölvar, perched on the edge of their table. "I have the story on that one, from Klaufi, our short-sighted friend at the gate. Remember?"

"You trust that old fool?" asked Bjólf.

"His wits are still sharp, even if his aim is not."

"It's not his wits I question," said Gunnar. "It's his eyesight. He called Filippus 'Miss'."

"I always said he should grow a beard," quipped Bjólf.

"Fortunately, what he lacks in one faculty, he gains in another.

He may have all the visual acuity of Odin's missing eye, but he is blessed with Heimdall's hearing." Fjölvar bent forward, adopting a confidential tone. "It seems those ears of his take in far more than any around him would imagine, and fortunately it only requires a few ales to get it out of him again."

Bjólf and Gunnar both leaned in closer to hear Fjölvar's findings.

"The lonely man is Óflár, son of Hallthor. He is cousin to Halldís, but while he is very much the son of her uncle, he was not born of Halldís's aunt..."

"Ah, the old story," sighed Gunnar. "One foot in the family, one foot out."

"Well, that matter has long since been forgotten. But it seems that, being the acknowledged son of Hallbjörn's brother, he believes he has been cheated of his birthright by the fair Halldís."

Bjólf nodded. "In other words, he thinks it should be his scrawny arse upon the high seat of this hall."

"I think Halldís graces it rather more agreeably," mused Gunnar.

"No wonder he looks so bloody miserable," said Bjólf.

"He failed to act when the time was ripe, and Halldís, knowing that the hall should not fall empty and feeling her father's loss keenly, stepped forward to assert herself. A popular move, by all accounts. Now he fears that popularity."

Gunnar frowned in exasperation at this pathetic tale. "So what is he doing now? Waiting for her to give up the ghost?"

"He could be in for a long wait," said Bjólf. "The girl is slight, but what she lacks in brawn she makes up for in spirit."

"She had more supporters back then," continued Fjölvar, "men who would fight for her cause, if need be – including Hunding, the one became her husband. But Hunding is lost, and they have since dwindled. And so Óflár bides his time."

Bjólf snorted. "If he intends to wait until all opposition fades away, then all he stands to inherit is a ghost town."

"It is nearly that already," grumbled Gunnar.

"This husband of hers, Hunding," Bjólf said, "what is his story?"

Fjölvar shrugged. "He took a ship to seek aid from the king. Its charred bones were found washed up two weeks later. Of the crew there was no sign."

Bjólf nodded solemnly.

"Soon after," added Fjölvar. "Óflár made a generous offer of marriage to Halldís."

"Clearly a man of tact." Gunnar said.

"She roundly, and rather publicly, rejected him," said Fjölvar, spinning a knife idly upon the table. "He has not forgotten it."

As Godwin approached to join them, Bjólf looked up and, glancing beyond him, caught Óflár's eye with his own. He held his gaze until the other weakened and broke away. "You notice he is almost the only man here isn't either too old or too young to take a wife. Why is that?

Fjölvar looked across at him, too and frowned. "Why, indeed."

"Watch him," said Bjólf.

"Who is this 'Skalla' anyway?" asked Godwin, throwing his leg over the bench and slumping astride it heavily. "Has anyone found that out yet?"

Gunnar grunted as he lowered his mug, dripping beery froth from his moustache. "Hmm! Sounds like a girl's name."

"An *ugly* girl's name," added Godwin.

"None will talk of him," said Fjölvar. "Not even Klaufi." He threw up his hands. "I tried everything."

"I found the same," nodded Godwin. "As soon as the name is mentioned, the gates are shut and bolted."

"All I know is he is the captain of the clan with whom they have their feud," said Bjólf. "A river-raider. But he must hold some terrible power over these people that they will not even talk of him."

"I assume he is the reason for these fortifications," ventured Godwin.

"Perhaps," said Bjólf, staring into the flames that leapt in the hearth. "But if the threat comes only from the river, why does this stockade surround them on every side?"

All four men looked at each other in silence.

"I trust Halldís," said Bjólf. "But there is something they're not telling us. Stay on your guard."

With that he stood and crossed the earthen floor to where Halldís sat. She saw his approach and smiled.

"With your permission, I wish to send some food out to my men on watch," he said.

"Upon the rampart?"

"Aboard my ship. It has been a long, cold night for them, and..."

"You left men aboard your ship?" interrupted Halldís. Her voice and her expression were suddenly changed, her face registering shock at his words.

"Of course."

"It is not safe."

He frowned. "That is precisely why we guard it."

"Your ship is not in danger so long as your men are not on it."

He puzzled over the words. "It is not only our ship that needs guarding. They keep watch over our dead."

Halldís stood in alarm, the colour drained from her face. "You have dead aboard your ship?" Several about her, Frodi included, fell silent, turning to face Bjólf, their expressions grave.

"Three of us fell in conflict with some common sea-pirates."

"Why did you not tell us of this?"

Bjólf stared at her, utterly bemused. "What need was there? They lie, wrapped in linen, bothering no one. And then we will bury them."

"How long has it been?"

"What?"

"How long have they lain dead?"

"Half a day. Three-quarters at most." Bjólf was losing patience now. "But what concern is that of yours?"

"They must be removed and burned," said Halldís. She turned away. "Ragnhild – fetch men and see to it immediately."

Ragnhild made to stand, but before she could move Bjólf stepped forward, grabbed Halldís by her shoulder and spun her back round to face him. "No! You will not touch them."

Halldís glared at him, outraged. Frodi stood, his cool, grey eyes blazing. Godwin and Njáll were instantly on their feet, followed slowly by Gunnar, who towered over them all.

"Three days we let them lie," rumbled Gunnar in the tense silence. "To show respect. That is *our* way, whether it be yours or not."

"Believe me, it is not from lack of respect that I say these things," replied Halldís.

"We have seen how you show respect to your dead," said Bjólf, "from the bones left rotting in the estuary mud."

"You do not understand," she protested, tears welling in her eyes.

"No, I do not! And you have done little to remedy that lack of understanding. We ask about Skalla and your lips snap shut like an oyster. I make mention of the pestilence that we know afflicts this land and you run from an explanation. If I am ignorant, if I am ill-informed, it is only through want of answers – answers that only you in this hall can give, but will not."

For a moment they stared at each other, the great, shadowy spaces of the hall filled only with the hiss and crackle of the fire, and the thrash of rain.

Halldís let her head fall, then began to speak in a quiet monotone.

"When they first came in their black ships, their cruelty knew no bounds. But they were just men, and were as strong or as weak as men ever are. At first, we resisted. They were few in number, and though unused to war, we were a proud people. We forced them to an uneasy truce."

"Then... *Skalla*..." she forced herself to utter the name, "unleashed a new abomination. One day, after many weeks respite, the black ships appeared again. Our men rode to face them. Skalla's crew dragged seven great, long boxes from their ships, and upon prising off the lids, revealed inside bodies of men – or what once were men; huge, bear-like warriors, their flesh grey, the stench of decay about them. Some had once been our own warriors. What this meant, our warband could not guess. Skalla threw a liquid in their faces and his men hastily retreated to their ships. The bodies stirred, staggered to their feet – moving, but the light in their eyes quite gone out. They were *aptrgangr* – death walkers; like the *draugr* in stories of old. But no story could have prepared us. Like ravening beasts they attacked – tore with hands, with blades, with blood-drenched jaws. Our weapons would not touch them. A terrible havoc was wrought that day. Then, when their masters were at last satisfied with the quantity of corpses their hideous progeny had heaped up – the limbs wrenched from sockets, the bones bitten, the flesh devoured in great gobbets, the mud made red with gore – they once more crept forth from their ships. Skalla threw a powder in their faces. Lifeless, they fell to earth. Nailing them back into boxes, they dragged those monstrous berserkers back aboard their ships. Thirty men lay slain. One survived the butchery, his arm left somewhere in that charnel heap. From that day, we did not resist.

"One might think this suffering enough. But the gods, in their wisdom, did not deem it so. We have since become a cursed people, whose dead the earth will no longer hold. Our own land rejects us, as a dog vomits up bad meat. First, the curse was merely passed from one to the other. That, we could control, though the methods were harsh. We were forced to retreat within the walls of this stockade, to abandon the outlying villages and farmsteads to their fate, even the burial grounds of our ancestors. They walk the forests now. But then it began to afflict all who died here. We have returned to the old ways, burning our dead, but in unseemly haste, else they are spat from their graves to wander as restless, mindless monsters, no longer knowing loved ones, driven only by the need to feast on the flesh of the living. This fate awaits us all. And so all of Björnheim cowers in its shadow – doomed, defeated, already dead in life."

Bjólf's men could only stare at her, incredulous. Yet not one could shake the creeping sense of inevitability that hung about her words, the way they seemed to give horrid meaning to the grim details of past days. Even Bjólf himself, still searching for earthly explanations, could see in her eyes that she spoke the truth, or, at least, what she believed to be the truth.

Halldís relieved the silence. "Tell, me, if you had known this, would you have come, or simply thought us mad?"

Bjólf, briefly wondering whether it could indeed be a kind of madness that afflicted this place – and perhaps infected him and his own men too – resolved there and then to reveal his own secret; that they had not come in response to a call for aid – that, in all likelihood, no message had got through, and no aid would ever come. And that her husband Hunding – for whom she still held some hope – had succumbed to some ghastly fate, his body tossed and battered by the eternal churning ocean out beyond the fjord. But, as he drew breath to start his speech, a great crash turned every face to the door. It had been flung back on its hinges; leaves and rain now swirled on the wind, and in the doorway, soaked to the skin, his sword drawn, stood Atli, eyes wide, his face pale as a ghost.

# CHAPTER TWENTY-THREE

## DEATH WALKERS

IT WAS A flash of lightning that had first revealed it, standing stark and pallid against the endless black of the forest's edge. For an instant, the white, forked shape had burned and flickered – and then was gone. At first, Atli had simply blinked back at the featureless night into which he was immediately plunged, uncertain of what he had glimpsed, the intense but indistinct image still seared into his brain, blinding him not only to what he could now see, but also to what he had seen. Then, just as the deep, rolling rumble of thunder had followed the lightning, so the realisation of what he had witnessed gradually grew clear in his mind.

A figure, deathly pale, its ragged clothes offering scant protection against this cold, rainy night – or any night – standing, motionless, half way between the stockade wall and the brooding immensity of the trees. Atli's eyes now strained to see anything in the pale moonlight, which came and went through the heaving cracks in the violently rent sky. But in his mind, the fleeting image slowly asserted itself in all its details, like the blood that comes gradually to a fresh wound. Chief among them was a face. Or that was the best word Atli had for it, at least. For while it had the familiar arrangement of physical features, it was yet lacking something in every one of those details. Its eyes were dark pits, its nose withered and collapsed, its mouth lolling open, devoid of expression. Like a blind, idiot child it stood, its limbs like a doll's, its grey, lifeless visage now seeming to him a kind of horrible mask, behind which was nothing.

It was only then he had realised that the beacon on the *Hrafn*, his only link with the handful of men still aboard the ship, had disappeared.

Moments later he had been stumbling headlong through the wild, rain-lashed night towards the great hall, his mail and weapons weighing heavily upon him, his limbs seeming to move with the agonising inertia of a tormented dream.

As the invaded hall now emptied into the hectic night, Bjólf's men, still dazed with drink, grasped weapons and torches in a chaos of urgent movement, and for the second time that day found themselves hastening towards the gates and the harbour beyond – to face what, none yet knew. Even Atli himself could not be certain. His breathless, fractured exclamations at the door of the hall had been sufficient to raise the alarm and get every man on his feet. Now, as he struggled to keep pace with Bjólf, still gasping from his run and having to shout above the wind and clamour, Atli fought to give an account of the sequence of events that had led to his dramatic intrusion.

While Bjólf and the guests at the feast had been carousing in the mead-glow of the fire's flames, Atli had been stationed upon that lonely rampart, huddled in the icy downpour, helm rattling in the rain, his woollen cape pulled tight against the wind.

The task with which he had been charged was simple – to keep in sight at all times the beacon that had been lit upon the ship. At regular intervals, this torch – mounted upon the prow

– was raised and waved from side to side six times by a member of the first night watch. Should it disappear, or fail to move at the appointed time, Atli was to alert those of Bjólf's crew who who manned the gate below. Of these there were four.

On occasion, one or other of the crew would call up to the watchtower, or come to see how Atli fared. Later in the evening, Salómon had even brought up some mead that had been smuggled out of the hall. Atli supped the sweet liquor, and felt its satisfying warmth seep into his bones. Supposedly these things were done out of simple fellowship, to ease a long and lonely watch. But they were also, he suspected, to ensure he was awake. Either way, he was grateful.

Atli spent long periods leaning on the log parapet, at first gazing toward the ship, where a second, dimmer fire could sometimes be seen – a sign of Thorvald's work, applying pitch to the ship's damaged hull – and then staring out towards the dark trees. Something about them pierced him through with a kind of primeval dread. Though he could barely make out their shapes – or perhaps because of it – his mind swam with restless thoughts of the unnameable horrors that lurked within those deep, ages-old shadows. And yet he kept his eyes resolutely, defiantly upon them. It became a challenge, a test of his mettle, to look upon them unflinchingly, to conquer them and the demons they loosed in his imagination.

It was then that the ghastly apparition had appeared.

For a moment, he had been paralysed with shock. But, slowly, his mind began to rationalise what he had seen. Perhaps the weather had put out the torch, and perhaps the figure he had seen was one of the crew, come to fetch fresh fire from the stockade. Then something happened that he could not explain. He saw a glimmer of orange light dart about near the ship, then suddenly erupt into a great column of flame. And, blinking away the drops of rain that coursed from his helm down onto his face, he began to realise that it had not only the leaping, shifting patterns characteristic of a fire, but a distinct shape. The shape of a man.

As he watched the form with growing horror, he saw that

it was moving. It advanced slowly, steadily, with a kind of staggering gait, its arms reaching out before it. Then, flame leapt up again just within their reach, as if a second creature of fire had been spawned by the first, its shape more wild and disordered this time, and a horrible, agonised shriek tore through the night.

Atli flew to the top of the ladder. Below, his fellows had already registered the scream, and he met a cluster of pale, upturned faces. "Fire!" he shouted, his voice coming feebly and getting lost on the wind. Then again, with more urgency as he pointed over the rampart, "*Fire!*"

Lokki, frozen in the middle of a trick involving three walnut shells, dropped everything and leapt at the bar upon the gate. The others, slower off the mark, were soon upon it, hurling the beam away into the mud and squeezing out through the gate the second it was wide enough for them to pass, torches in their hands.

"Get the others!" called Halfdan. They pounded off into the night as Atli scrambled and slipped down the rain-soaked

rungs of the ladder.

WHEN THE PARTY of men from the feast finally reached the gate they found its keepers, leaning against the gates in desperation, like children pressed against a door, as if such efforts were capable of preventing anything but the most feeble intruder. Godwin and Gunnar thrust the men aside and hauled the gates open. Beyond, no light could now be seen. The fact alarmed Atli. For a moment, he feared he had been somehow mistaken, that he had thrown his new shipmates into confusion for nothing. But at least the ship was not ablaze. Then, with an icy chill, he remembered Lokki, Halfdan and the others. Where were the lights of their torches?

"Farbjörn, Arnulf, Hrafning," barked Bjólf. "Stay and guard the gate." He glanced back towards the hall, where, in the semi-darkness, a lone figure was hobbling, resolutely. "And when Kjötvi gets here, tell him to join you."

With that, weapons drawn, they advanced into the raven-black, cloaks flying, their own torch flames roaring as the wind whipped and pulled at them. Atli could not suppress a shudder at the sound of the gates thudding closed behind them.

The band moved swiftly down the path, long wet grass soaking their legs as they went. They were lighter on their feet without their armour, and emboldened by drink, but each of the two dozen men also had Halldís's words echoing in their ears. Torches aloft, they wheeled around at the slightest sound or movement on either side.

"You say they all followed, boy? All four?" demanded Bjólf. Atli reluctantly affirmed it.

"There should be eight men out here," called Gunnar over the sounds of the storm. "They cannot simply have disappeared."

"Spread out," ordered Bjólf. "And stay sharp."

As grass gave way to mud, another silent, searing flash cracked open the night sky, illuminating the harbour for an instant and throwing out stark shadows: the eerie, slender prow of the ship standing like a lone sentinel, its shape reflected in the shallow water.

"There!" shouted Finn, and surged ahead as they were again plunged into darkness.

They followed Finn's flame as the thunder boomed and wrenched the air. Near the edge of the water, half-lit by Finn's torch, was an irregular shape from which a choking smoke was rising. Finn crouched over it, then recoiled. As the others approached, their light showed it to resemble a body, lying on its back, its arms held before it in twisted, horribly contorted gestures. Every part was burned down almost to the bone, blackened and crusted with what now passed for flesh, smoke still billowing from its cavities.

"Is that a man?" muttered a horrified Gunnar.

"Another here!" called Njáll, splashing into the water, close to the ship. Bjólf, Atli and several others followed. As with the first, whisps of smoke were tugged and whipped from it by the wind, the hiss of heat that issued from it audible even above the storm. Yet this one was far less destroyed – presumably because the water into which it had collapsed had quenched the flames. The lower legs were virtually untouched by fire, the upper body still partly protected by the blackened metal of its hauberk. The helmed head, however, had borne the brunt of the burning. Crouching, Njáll turned it over in the water, cursing as he scalded himself on the still-hot metal of its mail. Magnus knelt by him. The face was blistered and blackened to a crust, the hair quite gone, a steady smoke coming from the helm like steam from a hot cauldron. But there was no doubting its identity now. With sinking heart, Atli recognised one of the crew. "Eldi," confirmed Magnus.

"Hoy!" All turned in alarm at the voice. There, aboard the ship, dimly visible in the feeble light, a figure was clambering over the gunwale. Advancing to meet him, they could see now it was Einarr, one of the ship's watchmen, his eyes wide, his face white and stained with blood. He had lost his helm, and his dark hair – normally in thick plaits – had come loose, its wet strands flying about in the wild air. In his right hand, his sword – gripped as though his life still depended on it – was blackened along the blade by some oily ichor. He staggered. Godwin ran to support him.

"The others?" demanded Bjólf.

Einarr shook his head. "I am alone," he panted, his voice strained. "I stayed with the ship... they went after them. Those things... We threw them off... they could not climb back aboard. But more came... I was the lucky one."

"They?" said Bjólf. "Who? You were attacked?"

At that, Einarr, to the bemusement of his fellows, began to laugh. It grew in volume and intensity, strange and hollow, until finally the moment of hysteria passed and he seemed to gain some measure of control. "By our own men..." he chuckled drily. "The fallen..."

Fjölvar and Finn had meanwhile climbed aboard the ship, looking it up and down.

"You won't find them!" called Einarr. "They've fled the nest!"

Finding little sense in his words, Bjólf looked to Fjölvar and Finn. "Anything?"

But where the bodies of their three dead comrades had been, there now was nothing but a single length of ragged linen, someone's funeral shroud. Fjölvar held it up for Bjólf to see, and simply shrugged, his expression baffled.

Bjólf turned back to Einarr, a deep dread now gripping him. "Where are they? The fallen men? Someone took them?"

"No! *They* attacked us. Our dead." Einarr's eye suddenly caught sight of the blackened, smoking skeleton that lay in the mud, and he fell silent. Staring, wide-eyed, yet half averting his gaze as if not wishing to acknowledge it, he extended his arm slowly and pointed at the thing. "Kylfing."

Bjólf glared at him. "But Kylfing was a corpse," he said. "His flesh grey. The flies on him... we all witnessed it."

"I saw him. And the others too. As clear as I see you now." He turned and looked around as if reliving the nightmarish events. "Oddvarr rose first. We did not see him. He got Grimm from behind, sank his teeth into his neck. Grimm struggled, took both of them over the starboard side, and the beacon too. We heard shouts, running, splashing of water. Thorvald... he went after them, into the darkness towards the trees. Told us to stay with the ship. Then Gøtar came... his eyes were empty, his teeth..." Einarr shuddered at the memory. "Eldi and I fought him – gave blows that should have felled a mortal man. With a spear I thrust at his neck, pushed him over the side. Still he was not dead. We heard him moving in the darkness. Thorvald called to us in the distance then, and it seemed the movements we heard went off towards the sound. Then it was Kylfing's turn, his face swollen, grotesque..."

He moved toward the ship, making wild gestures as he continued his description. "Eldi had a plan. I fought with Kylfing, could not stop him, but forced him over the port side. Eldi was waiting there. He had the pail of pitch that Thorvald had been using, and a brand from the fire beneath. He lured Kylfing a safe distance from the ship, then hurled the pitch over him and set the body afire. But he must also have spilled pitch upon himself. Kylfing did not stop – came at him even as the flames consumed his flesh. The fire caught. Eldi burned as I watched.

"Then there was fighting in the darkness. Out there, the others from the stockade. More of the creatures had come. They showed no interest in the ship. But I could hear them moving. I stayed quiet."

A sound made them all turn, weapons drawn, limbs tense. A splashing of water followed by a kind of grunt. Somewhere, off to the left of the ship, close to the trees, something was approaching. Bjólf strained to see past the torchlight. As the moon broke briefly through the clouds, a pale shape loomed dimly, staggering out of the night. It was weird – unrecognisable. Then a familiar voice called out. Halfdan. As they watched, he came splashing heavily along the edge of the water, sword in one hand, the other struggling to support the stocky, flagging figure of Thorvald. Halfdan raised his sword hand in greeting. "Don't kill us," he called, somehow managing to cling to a grim kind of humour. "We're friendly." Others rushed to their aid. Thorvald was shivering and bloody, but both seemed to have escaped serious harm.

Sheathing his sword, Bjólf placed his hands on Thorvald's shoulders, looking hard into the scratched and bloodstained face he knew so well. He knew if anyone could give a rational account that would dispel Einarr's mad ramblings, it was Thorvald. "Salómon?" Bjólf demanded. "Lokki? The other men..?"

Thorvald, breathing heavily, looked across at Einarr. Something seemed to pass between them then. Thorvald simply shook his head. Halfdan, too, cast his eyes down into the black muddy water, his humour quite gone. "We found Salómon back there, near the trees." Magnus grabbed a torch from Finn and made to move in that direction, but Halfdan stopped him with the flat of a hand upon his chest. He shook his head solemnly. "What is left is beyond help."

"Burned?" asked Gunnar.

"Eaten."

The men stared at each other. Thorvald looked about for a moment, frowning at the silent, sickened faces, as if unable to believe his own words. "I would blame it on wolves or some other beast if I could. But it is not so."

Bjólf scanned the dark edge of the forest, squinting through the rain, trying to make sense of this nightmare. "What of the rest?" he insisted. "Grimm? Hrolf?"

"I searched as best I could..." Thorvald could only shake his head again, then let it fall.

"I saw a body taken off by the river, too far out to reach," said Einarr. He shrugged. "It could have been Grimm."

"Two dead. Three missing," said Bjólf. "And for what?" He glared into the surrounding faces of his fellows. "Whoever this enemy may be, they will pay for the outrage they have visited upon us this night."

There was a grunt of steely defiance among the men. Thorvald looked at him pleadingly. "Swords do not stop them. We have not seen a foe like this before." He placed a hand on Bjólf's shoulder. Bjólf shook it off irritably.

Einarr spoke then, his voice now clear and grave. "You have fire in your blood – the fire of revenge. But know this: death stalks around us. And it will take us all unless we leave this cursed place."

Suddenly the sky was rent by a lightning flash – so close that it set the air crackling, the roar of thunder rolling immediately behind.

"We have company," said Godwin, swinging his axe over his shoulder. Following his line of sight, Bjólf could just make out a random scattering of shadows between them and the torch flames upon the distant rampart – a dozen or so slowly moving forms. He scowled at them, unblinking in the flickering, wind-lashed torchlight, the rain coursing down his face.

Without breaking his gaze he addressed this crew, his voice stern – measured but simmering with fury. "We did not seek to fight these men, but they have chosen to make a fight of it nonetheless. So be it. I know nothing of ghosts and trolls, but whoever, or whatever, these men are, they look to be locked in flesh and bone, just like the rest of us." He drew his sword. "And bone is not as hard as steel."

All around, men readied themselves.

"Forget the ship," said Bjólf. "Let's see what these death-walkers are really made of." And with that, his wind-blown hair whipping in his face, he moved swiftly toward the lurching shadows.

# CHAPTER TWENTY-FOUR

## STEEL AND BONE

As Bjólf ADVANCED, the men following in his wake, his speed quickened. The stride became a jog, and the jog a run, until Atli found that he was struggling to keep pace. The *vikingr* captain flew forward, eyes fixed, head low, sword held wide and ready. It was with sudden alarm that the boy realised he was now hurling himself headlong towards his first battle, unprepared, in rain and darkness, and against a foe who, without the benefit of weapons – for he could see none among their silhouettes – had utterly destroyed several of the hardest men he had ever encountered, and left the survivors with their nerves, and perhaps their sanity, shaken to their roots. He could not yet understand how Bjólf – careful, thoughtful Bjólf – could so hurl himself towards potential destruction. And yet he ran, caught up in the impetuosity of the moment, forcing the fear that gripped him into the straining tendons of his fingers, tightening them around his shield grip and seax, and thanking fate for having this happen while he was on that rampart, in full armour.

FOR GUNNAR, SQUELCHING heavily behind, sword in one hand and axe in the other, Bjólf's behaviour was no longer cause for surprise. He had often joked, over the years, that there were two Bjólfs. There was Bjólf the Careful, the cautious sea captain, the thinker and planner – even, he sometimes thought, the politician. And then there was Bjólf the Reckless. The fighter. The killer. Most of the time, the former held sway. But then, every once in a while, he was pushed by circumstances beyond some invisible limit. That was when the other burst forth. There was no gradual transition. The change was sudden, absolute, devastating. The man became a whirlwind of violence: merciless, unstoppable, and knowing no fear. Gunnar felt a pang of pity for any whose fate placed them in Bjólf's way when the battle-fire was in him. Whether even this would be enough against this new, weird enemy, however, he could not begin to know.

AS THE SWAYING figures loomed out of the darkness, the flickering, uneven light from the crew's torches finally struck the faces of the first few. Several of Bjólf's men faltered, shocked at what they saw – pallid, lifeless flesh, dead, dry pits for eyes, cavernous, hollow cheeks, gaping, shapeless mouths – some with the meat rotted to black, oily pulp, others little more than dry skin stretched over bone. But they had only moments to process the information before the inevitable, bloody clash.

The nearest, directly in Bjólf's path, appeared in most respects surprisingly presentable; his clothes, although bloodstained and muddy, were unworn and of fine quality; his hair and beard neatly braided into plaits in fashionable style, fastened at their ends with short, neat lengths of coloured material. For an instant Atli convinced himself this must be someone come down from the village, that this whole attack was perhaps a mistake. The belief was short-lived. As the flames burned closer, his gaze fell upon the man's half-illuminated face.

One whole side of it was missing – torn away, as if savaged by a wild animal. His left eye hung out, the flesh from forehead to chin scraped off, as if by a great claw. The hair was matted with blood, forming a stark contrast to the still neat coiffure on its opposite side. Below, the left arm was half missing, wrenched away at the elbow, from which clot-strewn shreds of flesh hung, trembling as the creature moved.

In a fleeting moment of incongruous recollection, Atli realised had seen something like it before. Once, the people of his village had found a stranger – they never knew who he was, nor from where he had come – who had blundered too close to one of the bears that lived on the mountain. Felled by a single blow which had ripped through his face and shoulder, he was hauled away by hunters who had warned the creature off its meal. But that man had been stone dead. This man, impossibly, stood before them, gesticulating weirdly with his remaining arm like an uncoordinated infant, a strange, hissing grunt escaping his half-mouth.

BJÓLF allowed himself a split second of doubt before striking. Why had this man not drawn his weapon, or made to defend himself? He had never encountered so unflinching a foe. Was it the sickness that so disordered this creature's mind?

Seeing the ghastly half-grin of the face, he did not stop to question his advantage. Using all his momentum, he swung his sword in a steep arc, bringing it down on the base of the neck with such force that its bones snapped and sprang apart either side of its edge, leaving the body sliced across to the edge of the ribcage. He drew his blood-slicked blade from the cleaved flesh without pause, the nauseating sound of metal scraping bone echoing in the chest cavity. The momentum spun the hapless victim around as he did so. The man's head, right arm and shoulder teetered away from the rest of the body for a moment, revealing a sticky mess of black, half congealed gore, then its legs buckled and it collapsed in an ungainly heap with a horrid, sickening crunch.

Bjólf looked back at his men, sword extended, crumpled body at his feet. As if in response to the sound of the impact, a chorus of groans had come from the throats of the other staggering figures, and they had started dragging their half-dead limbs towards him, clawed hands outstretched, as if seeking revenge for their own lost brother. But Bjólf's men, seeing the fall of the first of them and their captain's expression of defiance, were suddenly spurred to greater boldness.

The night-stalkers were real, but they were not immortal. Nor were they immune to the bite of the sword's blade. With a great shout, swords and axes flying, the first rank of warriors hurled themselves at their expressionless opponents.

As his men engaged the enemy with a clash of steel and bone, something cold gripped Bjólf from behind, throwing him off balance. A putrid smell filled his nostrils. Staggering back, reeling at the sickening stench, he grasped at the thing about his throat, the grip of his fingers slipping against its cold and yielding surface. It was an arm, but so rotted as to resemble little more than bone dipped in oily grease. A horrid, hollow moan sounded in his ear like a cold wind blown through an empty skull. He could hear teeth gnashing and rattling together like a bag of shaken runestones. Tearing desperately at the ruined limb – astounded by the strength still in it – he felt the crack of bone and the snap of shrunken sinew as he heaved it away from him, nearly retching at the proximity of it. For an instant, as he struggled to regain his balance, its clawed hand twitched and grasped convulsively before his face. Another horrid groan assailed him. Then, feet planted firmly, he twisted hard and suddenly, flinging the half-dead thing off him. He whipped around, striking instinctively with his sword. The thrusting blade met little resistance, passing right through the ribs and skewering the man like a pig, through the heart.

For a moment, they regarded each other from either end of the weapon.

Man? Bjólf looked on in appalled disbelief. This was no man. Not any more. The bones – completely exposed where the rotted, colourless rags of his clothes no longer clung – were held together by shreds of gristle and sinew, withered like whipcords, the flesh so advanced in putrefaction that it was now no more than a covering of slimy, stinking jelly. The face grinned perpetually like a mask, its jaw clacking up and down. Within the ribs and body cavity, dark, glistening, shifting shapes lurked; in death this creature seemed to have given rise to whole new forms of writhing, wriggling life whose nature Bjólf had no desire to know. Finally he understood Gunnar's words. It was absolutely as he had described; a puppet of rotten flesh and bones.

The figure advanced towards him. It was not falling. Not collapsing. Not even flinching at the wound – a wound that should have been instantly fatal to the healthiest of men, let alone such a wretched, degraded body as this. As it came, it impaled itself further upon the blade, with no more care than a living man might show pushing through a thicket.

The undead thing before him shifted forward another staggering step, and he felt his blade scrape against its backbone. He was now, he realised, faced with an intriguing philosophical problem. How do you separate a soul from its body, when the body has no soul? There was no time for such conundrums. Drawing the sword rapidly, he swung around and aimed low, at the creature's left leg. Bone shattered. The creature fell at his feet. As it continued to grasp and crawl, as if the injury were no more than an irritation, he stood over it, then brought the blade crashing down upon the skull, its black, oily contents splattering the wet grass.

It did not move again.

"Get them in the head!" he called out. "Do not rely on anything else!"

Then he spat, in an attempt to rid his mouth of the all-pervading tang of festering death, and looked back up to the wooden rampart. Emerging from out of the right-hand bank of trees were another two dozen death-walkers, creeping towards them erratically like damaged beetles.

\* \* \*

ELSEWHERE, THE FIGHTING had been no less chaotic. At first, it seemed all too easy. The foe was slow moving, and even the few who had weapons made no move to use them. Flailing both sword and axe before him – making up in sheer brute force what he lacked in style – Gunnar had cut a swathe through the rag-tag group of figures, knocking three of them flat with as many blows. Others around him had similar success. Only Atli was hesitant, stopping where Bjólf had felled the first of them and staring, horror-stricken, at what remained. But it wasn't so much the battle-carnage it had suffered that horrified him. It was the fact that the elegantly coiffured half-face was still swivelling its one good eye and snapping its jaws.

"Hurry up, little man!" called out Gunnar. "There'll be none left!"

Then came the slow realisation. Only gradually did they discover that, of those they had struck down and left for dead, more than half were regaining their feet. For some, that knowledge dawned late. Both Fjölvar and Jarl were attacked from behind by men who should not have survived their assault. One – a stocky peasant of a man, whose grey, shapeless face looked as if it had slid out of connection with his skull, and who Fjölvar had taken down with an arrow to the chest – grappled him to the floor, then fell on top of him, the fletched end of the arrow catching Fjölvar in the throat. Scrabbling for his knife, choking at the wound, Fjölvar stabbed the man in the neck, then hurled him off and fired another arrow point blank into his eye.

Jarl was not so fortunate. A horrid apparition of a woman – once beautiful, perhaps, but now a ragged, bony wraith with milky, staring eyes – grabbed from behind at his head, catching him around the face with the talons of her flesh-stripped fingers and driving her long, bared teeth into his exposed neck. He cried out, temporarily blinded and trailing blood, while another of the ghouls, utterly destroyed from the waist down, reached up and, biting to the bone, chewed noisily upon his hand. Crashing blows from Gunnar's axe saw both of them off before Jarl succumbed.

It was those with stabbing weapons and arrows who came off worst – and of those, many fell victim to their own shock at their fallen enemies' sudden resurrection. But then Bjólf's cry had gone up, and those with axes – and especially Úlf with his mace, which was rarely aimed at anything but a skull – made quick work of those remaining. Atli, who had not struck a single blow, breathed a sigh of relief.

Then, with sinking heart, he saw the second, larger force of ghouls lumbering between them and the gates. The men drew together again, weapons readied.

"Gods! How many of them are there?" exclaimed Gunnar.

"How many have died here?" muttered Godwin.

"It's the noise," came a voice. It was Einarr. "The noise of battle draws them."

"There will be more of that before the night is out," said Bjólf grimly, staring through the rain at the broken line of silhouettes that swayed slowly, relentlessly towards them. He drew a whetstone from the bag on his belt and ran it along his sword blade, drawing sustenance from its sharp, clear sound. "Take down all in your way. Protect your fellows. Ignore the rest. We'll lose no more men tonight. And remember, aim for the head."

What followed was horribly confused and disjointed in Atli's mind – a nightmare of flickering shadows, teeming rain, roaring torch flames, groaning, leering faces and the sickening crack of steel against skull and jaw. And everywhere the stench of the grave.

At first, the men had formed into a tight group, in which Atli was more than happy to hide from harm. But as the mindless creatures clustered around like pigs at the trough, pressing in at them, surrounding them, the need to disperse became clear. The group broke, scattering the disordered ranks of the enemy as they drove forward, taking them down wherever they could. Here and there, torches were swung with a great roar of fire and a cascade of sparks as they struck their targets. Sometimes, the undead burned briefly in the downpour, flailing, blinded by flame. It did not kill them. But it did provide precious time and a clear target for the decisive blow.

Atli, meanwhile, had decided to skirt around the death-walkers where they were thinnest, far out on the right side. One of the few to have a shield as well as a sword, he was at least comforted by the knowledge that there was some solid linden wood between him and the gnashing teeth of these monstrous creatures. What he lacked, as soon became abundantly clear, was any fire to light his way. In the darkness, the uneven ground between the path and the edge of the trees rose up to meet his feet in every kind of unexpected way, jarring his knees and turning his feet as he stumbled across the rough grass. Cursing his lack of light, he clenched his teeth, held his weapon tight, and kept the torches upon the watchtowers fixed firmly in his sights – beacons he knew would see him back to safety.

As he went, he chanced to look to his left, across the ragged line of men, their torches dimly visible in the thrashing rain. Only then did he understand how fortunate he had been.

At first, he thought it an optical illusion – an exaggerated impression caused by the light thrown from the torches, making their surroundings more immediately visible. But no... there was something else. As his eyes adjusted to the gloom, it became clear from this distant perspective that the crew's torches were actually serving as beacons for the corpse-creatures – that they drew the mindless foe to their intended victims as a candle flame draws a moth. He smiled to himself, then, as he pounded closer to his goal, suddenly thrilled with his own shrewd judgement, and thankful for the fortuitous lack of light which, just moments before, he had so ardently wished.

Suddenly, he barrelled straight into something large and solid. Losing his footing, he bowled over heavily, barking his shin on a rock and thudding onto the sodden ground, his front tooth cracking against his shield, his seax flying off into the dark. The fall, made worse by the weight of his mail coat, had knocked the wind clean out of him. For a moment he lay, crippled and wheezing, trying to get his bearings. There were no lights visible now, and only gradually did he realise that the sticky wetness on his face was not just from rain or mud. He put his hand to it. It was slick and viscous. Had he done himself some injury? Apart from his throbbing shin and chipped tooth he felt no pain. Then a foetid smell stang his nostrils. He felt sick, suddenly struck by the horrible feeling that he had fallen headlong into the rotting carcass of an animal, or worse.

Then the dark object let out a low, half-human groan, and took a faltering step towards him.

As Atli scrabbled to his knees the cloud cover began to break, and the watery light of the half-moon illuminated the scene.

To one side of him, and just a body's length away, towered a massive figure. Broad shouldered and thickly muscled, it was dressed in a simple, plain tunic – white in the moonlight – which the downpour had so completely soaked that it was plastered to its body. From its foot, a long length of muddy cloth dragged, while upon its chest was a great patch of congealed, blood – blood which, Atli now realised to his horror, had left the thick, stinking residue upon his face. He retched, frozen to the spot. Then the clouds cleared further to cast a less broken light upon the pale monster's shadowed visage, and a new kind of horror gripped him.

Long hair hung in lank shreds to the shoulders, a horrible vertical wound made the mangled neck gape open like badly butchered meat, the forked beard was stained with blood which had streamed from the mouth, and now hung from it in quivering clots. But it was the face itself that struck him through like a blade. Though handsome and well-proportioned, it had been rendered gaunt and ugly by death, its flesh as grey as ash, its lifeless, unblinking eyes expressing nothing. But Atli recognised it, nonetheless.

It was Gøtar.

Atli was struck by the insane thought that the man had returned to reclaim the helm that now sat upon his head, to mete out a horrible revenge on the foolish, arrogant boy imposter who dared to dress in the garb of a warrior. It was action that pulled him past that paralysing fear. The hulking mockery made a sudden lunge for him with its huge, muscular arms, a ghastly wheezing cry rising from its ruptured throat. With shock and alarm, Atli was awoken from his horrified trance to the reality of his surroundings. He dodged and looked about him, desperately aware that if others heard the sounds, they would be drawn to him too.

And then he realised he had no sword.

He did not even think about drawing his axe. Instead, some other instinct caught hold. As the creature lurched toward him again, he raised his battered shield and charged at it with every ounce of his strength. The iron shield boss crunched into the death walker's chest; with all the weight of body and mail behind him, Atli slammed his shoulder hard against its wooden boards. To his surprise, he did not stop dead against that great column of flesh, but kept on going. Stumbling clumsily as the obstacle gave way before him, he fell, rolled over in the dark, wet grass, righted himself and, unharmed, scrambled to his feet. The great figure crashed backwards onto the ground with all the crushing force of a felled tree, its limbs flailing and twitching like a freshly slaughtered ox. Panting with the effort, his head spinning, he tried to think what his next move should be. Dozens of disordered thoughts – incomplete or too fast to properly grasp – cascaded through his mind. Out of the chaos, one clear, urgent thought came. *Run*, said a voice in his head. *Run, run, run!*

He fought to stir his trembling, leaden limbs, unable to take his eyes off the stirring, groaning thing that he knew would be on its feet in moments, its head wobbling, turning toward him. He finally broke the paralysis, took a step backward, and his heel met something hard and sharp in the grass.

*Steinarrsnautr.*

Once again, something swifter than thought took him over. In the next moment he found himself poised over the great beast, sword raised high above his head, hardly knowing how he got there. He had one final, chilling look into the hollow, empty eyes of the man whose dying thoughts had been of generosity towards him. Then, with a force that left Atli shocked, as if it somehow came from outside of him, the heavy blade crashed down upon the creature's neck, chopped through the throat and jarred against breaking bones. Black blood spilled.

Such was the second passing of Gøtar, son of Svein.

When he thought back on it later, Atli could remember nothing of the journey to the gates of the stockade. His feet simply pounded the earth without thought, as if somehow independent of the fact that his heart was bursting out of his chest, until the nightmare was far behind him and the huge pine logs that represented his salvation towered over him. The mindless rhythm was fuelled by a chant repeated over and over under his struggling breath, the words of which he was barely conscious: *I'm sorry... I'm sorry... I'm sorry...*

AT THE GATES, the men had gathered – breathless, soaked from the storm, their weapons dark with the blood of their enemies. Bjólf beat upon the massive timbers with the pommel of his sword, then stood back and squinted up through the stinging flecks of rain at the watchtower.

"Open up!" he bellowed.

Behind Bjólf and his men, all was now silent. But before them, beyond the rampart, voices could once again be heard raised in argument. Among them, though almost drowned out by the chaotic bickering of numerous unidentifiable men and women, the familiar tones of the crewmen Bjólf had ordered to stay at the gate, now raised in anger.

Gunnar and several other of the men on the outside of the stockade looked anxiously at the dark line of trees, aware that there was fresh movement there. But before Bjólf could raise his voice again, a head appeared at the top of the watchtower. It was the old man, Klaufi.

"Open the gates, old man!" called Bjólf.

"I cannot," said Klaufi. Bjólf stared back up at him in disbelief.

Klaufi merely shrugged. "It is forbidden to open the gates without the express permission of..."

Bjólf's curt reply cut him off. "Whatever gods you follow, you'd better start praying to them, because unless you open these gates right now..."

It was Klaufi who interrupted Bjólf this time, even as the

sounds of the distant death-walkers in the edges of the wood crunched and crackled in their ears. "My hands are tied. I must abide by the laws laid down by the council of the hall of... of..."

His voice trailed away. But it was not words that had stopped him. Down below, Bjólf's eyes blazed with a furious flame, his sword raised at the end of his muscular arm, its point directed at Klaufi's neck as if to take the old man's head, the wrath on his darkened face so palpable, so extreme, that the old man felt it might somehow strike him dead with a mere glance.

"Open these gates, you old fool," rumbled Bjólf, his voice cutting through the dying storm, "or, by the gods, my final act upon this earth will be to hack them to splinters and watch the dead tear the living flesh from your wretched, worthless bones."

At that, Gunnar gave a terrifying roar and charged at the gate, sinking his axe into the timber with a shuddering crash that sent chips of wood and bark flying. Klaufi stepped back in dread as the watchtower swayed. Godwin came forward next, axe held high... then Thorvald... then ten more axes with stout arms and strong backs behind them, ready to batter the gates to oblivion.

Before they could strike, another pale, alarmed face appeared above. Halldís. She was panting, breathless.

"They're our guests!" she cried at Klaufi. "Our allies! For Freyja's sake, open up!"

There was a clatter and a rumble behind the timbers, and the gates swung open. Bjólf's men poured in, casting hateful glances at the mob that had assembled there. A space cleared around the warriors.

Kjötvi stepped forward, his good ear bloodied. "They tried to stop us," he said. Farbjörn, Arnulf and Hrafning were close behind, each of them showing the signs of having been in a struggle. "Things got a little heated," continued Kjötvi. "We stopped short of using weapons. But some were not so considerate." His hand went to his right ear, which, Bjólf could now see, had had its top third sliced off, making it now almost a perfect match for the other. Bjólf looked around at the suddenly quiet crowd, baffled by this turn of events.

Hrafning read the look in his eye. "It was him stirred them up," he said, and nodded towards a pale figure that lurked at the back of the motley throng. Bjólf just had time to catch sight of the sickly, self-satisfied features of Óflár before he melted away into the shadows.

"Would you like me to gut the little weasel?" muttered Gunnar. But Bjólf – cautious Bjólf – raised a hand to stop him.

Others from the hall arrived – at their head, Frodi pushed through to the front of the crowd, looking on mortified and apologetic. Here, at least, a man with some sense of honour, thought Bjólf. The crowd then parted for Halldís, down from the watchtower, who wore a similar expression, though perhaps tempered by other, more complex feelings as she looked at Bjólf. She stepped up to him.

"Do not blame them," she said. "They have lived in fear for too long, for reasons that you now begin to understand."

"Yes, I begin to," said Bjólf, his voice hard and unsympathetic. He turned his back on her and faced his men. "We leave at first light."

Halldís stared at him in disbelief, and, stepping forward, grabbed his arm and spun him around. "You cannot leave." There was urgency – even yearning – in her voice.

"Can I not? I am master of my own destiny."

"But your task here is not done," she pleaded, a note of anger entering her voice. "You came to help us."

He took a step toward her, forcing her to back away from him. "We are not the men you sent for. We never were. Our coming here was pure chance. Our leaving, however, is a matter of choice."

"You accepted our hospitality," muttered Frodi, glowering. "We thought you honourable men."

"Think what you like," replied Bjólf. He would get over Frodi's accusations. But Halldís' despair stung him. He turned again. "We will sleep tonight wherever we are welcome." He gestured to the gate. "Out there, in our ship if we must."

"No!" said Halldís. She checked herself, then let her gaze fall, despondently contemplating the churned mud at their feet.

"You are still our guests. You have my father's hall."

At this, the old woman Ragnhild suddenly lurched forward from the crowd, her arms raised in a weird gesture, her eyes rolling back in her head, a long, loud groan escaping her lips. Bjólf was ready with his sword but, to his surprise, she then pulled a small soft leather bag from inside her gown, tipped the contents upon the ground and fell to her knees. With her face still raised to the heavens, she passed her hand over the small, white tablets of bone that lay scattered in front of her. Runestones.

"Is the old woman a runecaster?" asked Gunnar, frowning at this unexpected outburst.

"Our seer is dead," said Halldís. "But Ragnhild has the gift."

The old woman pulled at her hair until it hung about her wildly, wailed once more, then cast her eyes over the scattered runestones.

"I see it!" she moaned. "The hidden purpose of the women at the well, the immortal *dísir*. It is clear, our salvation comes in the shape of a ship. I see it marked out in flame! Upon it are the great warriors from other lands who will deliver us. The enemy will be destroyed, the curse wiped out, and the victors shall live forever as esteemed heroes to us all!" She looked up at Bjólf, a great smile spreading across her face. "You will not leave us. Your fate is here, Bjólf son of Erling. You and all your men. And it is good!"

Bjólf looked her in the eye for a moment. "Let me show you what I think of fate."

And with that, he turned and walked away.

# CHAPTER TWENTY-FIVE

## THE LEAVE-TAKING

"WHAT DID YOU, as a man of religion, make of that?" said Bjólf to Gunnar as the crew strode off to gather their possessions.

Gunnar thought about his answer for several moments as they ran the gauntlet of bemused villagers. "Frankly?" he said, finally. "Utter bollocks. If that woman has the gift, then the emperor of Byzantium can wear my arse for a hat."

Bjólf smiled. "Don't hold back, Gunnar. Tell me what you really think."

"I think that the sooner we're out of here, the better off we will be."

Bjólf clapped him on the shoulder. "For once, big man, we are in total agreement."

Back at the hall, the men passed out the mail, armour and remaining weapons that had been stowed in the small, dark antechamber at its entrance. All understood that, this night, whatever the etiquette of the hall, they would sleep with their weapons close at hand. No one interfered with their activities. Halldís was nowhere to be seen, and all the others maintained a discreet distance. Atli, still shaking from his ordeal, looked forward to a few hours of warmth and sleep by the hall's great hearth and some of the leftovers from the feast.

Bjólf looked over those who were injured. Thankfully, all were minor wounds. The one significant exception was the horrible wound upon Jarl's neck, where the female death-walker had taken a piece of him. That would require Magnus's expert eye. In many respects, Jarl had been lucky; the bite had stopped just short of the parts that would have threatened his life. But, although Jarl refused to show it, Bjólf knew that the ragged tear had left its victim in excruciating pain. And then there was the question of this strange pestilence. Had it been passed to Jarl? Bjólf did not wish to think about that for the moment. Jarl had maintained a kind of dogged, forced good humour since they had returned to the safety of the stockade, as if he too wished only to put it from his mind.

Bjólf turned from him. "Magnus?" he called. "There's a patient for you here." But the old monk was nowhere nearby. Bjólf sighed impatiently and scanned the low-lit interior of the hall. "Magnus?" he called. But there was no reply. No movement.

Others began to look around. Only gradually did they realise that Magnus was not among them.

"Has anyone seen him?" called Bjólf, his sense of unease growing. "Has anyone seen him since we came back through the gate?"

No one had.

They searched for hours beyond the stockade wall, all the while watching and listening nervously for more of the shuffling, vacant ghouls. Having learned the lesson from their earlier encounters, each man went about his melancholy business in silence, thankful that the rain had abated. But for a distant scuffling or groaning carried on the breeze, there was no more sign of the death-walkers that night. Yet all secretly feared what they might find.

The sky was beginning to lighten when they discovered him. It seemed he had doubled back in an attempt to outflank the lumbering enemy, and while clambering over a large outcropping of rock near the left bank of trees had fallen into a cleft in the grey, moss-covered stone. He lay awkwardly in the narrow, grave-like gap, his temple smashed and bleeding, his eyes rolled back in his head, his breath barely perceptible. He had fallen victim not to the death-walkers, not to his own valour or to some rash, foolhardy act, but to nothing more than a meaningless accident.

They took him to the hearth, tended his wounds and kept him warm. Fjölvar knew a little of the healing arts, and did what he could. Halldís sent her most learned practitioner – a crook-backed woman with a knowledge of herbs – but herself remained distant. The cruellest irony was that the only one who really knew how to deal with such a grievous wound was Magnus himself. Magnus the Healer. Magnus the Gentle. Magnus the Wise. There was knowledge in him that would be forever lost.

Bjólf sat with him for the rest of the night. Atli, though exhausted and craving sleep, sat up too, Magnus's shallow, rasping breaths marking the time until they were to leave.

In his long and colourful career, spanning more voyages than he could recount, Bjólf had experienced all manner of farewells. Some were joyous and celebratory, some marked by tears and anguish. A good number were accompanied by the battle-roar and clatter of weapons, while yet others were silent and stealthy, watched only by the plashing fish and the ravens that croaked among the dawn treetops.

But never had he known a leave-taking so bleak, so dismal.

The villagers, for the most part, remained in their homes. Bjólf and his men – kitted out much as they had been for their dramatic arrival the previous day, but now curiously drained of the pride and bold defiance that had once inspired in them – set out in silence beyond the stockade, largely unregarded. Four men carried the unconscious Magnus between them in a makeshift bier. Though all knew it, none spoke of the fact that he was dying. All loved the old man too much to admit it.

It was not until they were upon the path leading down to the muddy harbour that the full extent of the previous night's carnage became clear. All around them, from one bank of trees to the other, dozens of bodies – or parts of bodies – littered the ground, all hacked and hewn and in various horrid states of mutilation and decay, a ghastly, stomach-turning stench hanging about the place, too heavy for the morning breeze to carry off. Twisted limbs stuck up into the air, some in tortured gestures. Rocks and grass and mud were occasionally stained with the black ichor, the gentle undulations of the landscape jarringly pockmarked here and there by shapeless heaps of gore, or denuded bone from which the flesh had slipped or been slashed. It was as if, in that one night, the dead of ages had been hauled shrieking from their graves, wrenched apart and scattered about to be picked at by birds and beasts. But there were no beasts to pick at this flesh, and not a single bird sang.

The fog had lifted. The sun shone. But all served only to make the horror the more immediate, the more inescapable. The final atrocity was the fact that what little had remained of Salómon and Eldi from the previous night had now completely disappeared – taken by whom, or what, none could tell. Of the others – Grimm, Lokki and Hrolf – nothing more was ever seen again. The night had swallowed them. As they made the final approach to the ship, through bone-strewn mud and water, all tried not to imagine the fates of their fellows, or shuddered visibly at the unwelcome thought.

As the last of the rainwater was bailed, the oars were thrust out and the vessel rowed into the river where it was turned slowly downstream, Grimmsson's rowing boat towed behind. Bjólf stood at the stern, noting with a bitter pang of despair the gaps in the rowing benches, doggedly refusing to turn back towards the stockade. Had he done so, he might just have made out the solitary figure of Halldís upon the rampart, a blue cloak wrapped tightly around her against the cold morning breeze as she gazed at the gradually departing ship, a look of empty desolation upon her face. But it was the certain knowledge that she alone was watching that kept Bjólf's back turned on the village of the daughter of Hallbjörn.

It remained so until long after the place was gone from view.

# CHAPTER TWENTY-SIX

## THE RESURRECTION AND THE LIFE

THEY HAD BARELY departed when Magnus finally gave up the ghost. For hours afterwards they followed the winding course of the river in silence, the wind in their faces. The channel became broader, the turns longer and more meandering, and here and there it began to fork off into other tributaries, some of which were near-choked with overhanging trees and creepers. But, bit by bit, the banks became more favourable to the presence of men; the vegetation thinned, seeming to spring forth with a more youthful vigour. No longer the impenetrable, primordial murk of the cursed land they had left behind, but fresh and inviting, the penetrating sunlight clearing the airy forests of the dank moulds and fungi that had weighed so heavily upon the air of that weird domain. To port, far beyond the trees, the land rose to craggy, mountainous uplands whose jagged tops shimmered in a hazy morning mist. Beyond them, Bjólf surmised, lay the steep-sided fjord which led to the site of their encounter with Grimmsson's ship. Yet nearby, the banks' edges were shallow and inviting, the grass lush, the soil dark, the trees lofty yet not oppressive, their branches filled once more with the songs of birds.

It felt like emerging from a nightmare, and yet, even this began with the end of a life.

Looking down upon the neatly wrapped corpse of Magnus, Bjólf called out to his crew.

"Heave to!"

Thorvald leaned on the tiller. The men shipped the oars, and Finn threw out the anchor. They would land here and rest a while. Perhaps hunt some game. And, most of all, they would give Magnus a decent burial. He, at least, would be properly laid to rest. It would not quite be the funeral he deserved – no array of rich accoutrements to accompany him to the next world (in truth, Bjólf was uncertain what warrior trappings, if any, were appropriate to the Christian heaven). But the spot was tranquil and beautiful, with dappled sunlight and scattered clumps of fragrant herbs here and there – the very ones the old man had once so carefully gathered to ply his craft – and Bjólf knew that, to Magnus, this would be worth more than all the wealth and ceremony of a king.

With the ship safely anchored a short distance from the shore, Bjólf took his place upon the steering deck, the body of Magnus at his feet, and turned to his men.

"I am no religious man, but Magnus followed the White Christ, and while I profess no knowledge of gods or their ways, it is only right that we honour him in his own manner, out of love and respect for the man we knew." A general mutter of approval passed through the assembled company. "But also, I wish to pay him my own tribute, this last time. There are others for whom I would like to have done the same, others we have lost. I cannot stand over their bodies and speak words of praise at their deeds. We have been denied that right. And so, my words over this, our most recently fallen, go out in honour of them all." He paused for a moment, head lowered, thinking carefully about the form of his words.

"Magnus was a great friend. A fearless man and a generous one, whose skills in healing we all have had reason to thank over the years. Some of us live today only because of him." There were nods of assent. "I remember when we first found him, locked in a filthy cell, drunk and baying for the blood of his abbot – branding him a coward and a hypocrite in the foulest possible language..." Another laugh, more raucous this time. "This was not what I had come to expect of a Christian monk. The very next moment, he was telling us where the abbot's silver was hidden and begging to be taken away from that hell-hole. Somehow I sensed we had found – what can I call it? – a kindred spirit. He began as our guest, became our friend. Our teacher. Such were the qualities of the man..." Bjólf cleared his throat, looked suddenly self-conscious and uncertain, then pressed his flattened palms together awkwardly in an unfamiliar gesture. This was to be, he hoped, how Magnus might have wanted it. His eyes sought out Odo amongst the men crowded on the deck. Odo nodded discreetly to confirm that Bjólf was doing it right.

"Man comes from earth, and returns to earth," Bjólf began, hesitantly. He'd heard parts of the sacred book from Magnus many times before, but now he was starting to wish he'd listened more closely. It all seemed to jumble together in his head. "We commend his soul to... to... the hall of Christ..." Was that right? He recalled that Christ and his men were sailors, but what else? He searched his memory, trying to find somewhere in it the sound of Magnus's voice. "Long may he feast there... at the... last supper of his God..." A groan came from somewhere. Was his attempt at this really that bad? He pressed on, regardless. "And revel in that heroic company... until the great day of his... earthly resurrection." Yes, now he remembered. A familiar phrase popped into his head, as if Magnus himself had uttered it in his ear. He spoke it triumphantly: "The Christ told his men, 'I am the resurrection and the life'..."

As he spoke the words, a second, greater groan came from the deck. With it was a sound which seemed utterly incongruous – the slow tearing of fabric. Before Bjólf could grasp what was happening, the front few rows of the crew recoiled suddenly, crashing into those behind, and an ungainly white shape seemed to loom out of nowhere. It staggered drunkenly before him, shreds of stretched and rent linen unravelling and falling away from its face as the thing within emerged like a moth from its silken cocoon.

Magnus. And not Magnus.

Bjólf was momentarily paralysed, not with fear, but with disbelief. Others seemed similarly stricken. In the weird, still silence that followed, the eerily frozen company stood tense and motionless, expressions of horror and incredulity upon their faces, as the ghoulish figure wearing their friend's features swayed uneasily before them, its arms still part-swaddled by the remains of its wrappings. Its head turned stiffly, twitching, taking in its surroundings like a ghastly newborn. Its feet shuffled and it lurched suddenly around to face the body of men. At the sight of them – of this great feast of flesh – the expressionless mouth lolled open, spilling drool upon the gnarled wood of the deck. From it came another horrible, imbecilic wail.

Shrunk against the gunwale, half-slumped in horror, Atli scrabbled backwards at the sound as if to put more distance between him and this new nightmare. Next to him, the old, rusted spare anchor – the very one Háki the Toothless had swung with such crushing effect at the jaws of Grimmsson's men – shifted noisily at his elbow and fell flat against the boards. At the sound, the dead parody of Magnus turned, baring its teeth, and lunged at the boy.

Atli flung himself out of the creature's way as several men – snapped out of their reverie – jumped forward in an attempt to restrain it. As they did so, its arms finally sprang free of its linen bindings and flailed about wildly, catching one or two across the face. They reeled back, but more waded into the fray, grabbing at it in a disordered melée of shouting and thrashing. The thing turned on anyone that came near, fearless, thoughtless, punctuating the uproar with the sharp clatter of its teeth snapping at their flesh.

Many now had weapons drawn; seaxes and knife-blades flashed in the sunlight. Yet many who would not have hesitated under other circumstances – who had survived past battles only because of their lack of hesitation – were suddenly afflicted by a crippling doubt. This was Magnus. Wise Magnus. Gentle Magnus. Was he alive after all? He walked. He moved. Could he not be crazed with fever? Might he not be saved? Even as the ghastly, pallid mockery lurched before them, evoking all the horrors of the previous night, misplaced hope stayed their hands.

Bjólf stepped forward, then, sword drawn. "Get back!" he called as he strode towards the wild brawl, blade raised and ready over his shoulder. The men immediately scattered, knowing their captain would not wait to strike his blow. The creature whirled around, saw his approach, and even as Bjólf swung at it, flew at him with no regard for its own welfare. The sudden move caught Bjólf off guard; he tried to redirect his blade as it sang through the air, and caught the creature across its raised arm with a clumsy strike. The thing staggered and crashed against him. Bjólf fell as its severed arm – still moving – thudded on the deck next to him, splashing thick, foetid fluid across his face.

The thing was still on its feet, looming over him. Some of the men, the spell broken, had snatched up spears and poked at the writhing figure. But its eyes were fixed upon Bjólf. Ignoring the spear-points, it cried out again – a hollow moan of blind, ravenous hunger. Drool dripped upon Bjólf's chest.

Gunnar, meanwhile, had grabbed the nearest thing to hand – the iron chain that had come aboard with Grimmsson's treasure chest. He swung it around his head in a great circle, its heavy length clinking and roaring in the air. The others stepped back at the sound, and he made his move. The iron links caught the thing a heavy blow on the side of the head, wrapping around its neck, and Gunnar hauled the creature towards him with a roar and threw loops of chain about its body, pinning its arm against its chest. He spun the creature around and looped the chain through itself before pulling it tight at its back. "Finish it!" he cried out, gripping the thrashing ghoul from behind in a bear hug. Thorvald broke from the crowd, his heavy axe in his hand.

Then, just when it seemed it was over, the fiend smashed its head back into Gunnar's face. He staggered back, letting go his grip, blood pouring from his nose. The thing teetered sideways, away from Thorvald, its remaining arm wriggling free again, the long chain dragging after it.

CROUCHED BY THE gunwale, Atli looked up once more at the thing that had been Magnus, stumbling above him. This time, his mind was clear. This time, it would be different. Out of the corner of his eye, he had seen Bjólf scramble to his feet. A look passed between them as Bjólf hefted one of the oars. Atli understood. "Hey! Over here!" he cried. The creature whirled around and made for him once more. Atli did not move this time, but pressed himself hard against the gunwale until the very last moment – human bait for the monster. In moments the thing was almost on him. As its hand grasped for his face he dropped, curling himself into a ball. The full weight of the oar, swung with all Bjólf's strength, cracked against the creature's back and sent it flying forward, stumbling over Atli and tipping head-first over the side.

The weight of its iron bonds dragged it swiftly beneath the surface. As the loose chain rattled along the deck, Bjólf caught hold of it and wrapped the end around the brace cleat. The chain pulled tight, and Atli peered tentatively over the side, into the churned, weedy water that had swallowed the creature. But of Magnus there was now no sign.

Bjólf clapped Atli on the shoulder with a grateful nod, even allowing himself a hint of a smile. He did not say anything. But that silent recognition meant the world to the boy.

Gunnar approached, shaking the dizziness from his head. He scooped up some water from the river and splashed it over his face and beard, then spat, and snorted the remaining blood out of his nose noisily.

"You should know better than to put your face in the way of someone's head," said Bjólf.

Gunnar simply made a gruff rumbling sound deep in his throat, one of his more subtle means of expressing annoyance. He wiped his big forearm across his mouth, and then stared at the few tiny bubbles that broke the surface, a dark and brooding look upon his face.

"Kylfing. Gøtar. Oddvarr. Now Magnus," he said. "They were all dead, of that there can be no doubt. And yet..."

Bjólf raised his hand, silencing the big man, and turned and leaned on the gunwale, staring at the place where the still quivering chain disappeared beneath the water.

"We've all seen it now," he muttered, gazing into the impenetrable, green-tinged depths, his expression dark. "The dead return." He sighed deeply. "I needed to see it with my own eyes. That is my own failing." Gunnar shrugged, as if this were not such a bad failing to have. Bjólf spoke slowly, in calm, even tones. "This was how Grimmsson's ship died. The ones you saw in the woods, they not only attacked his crew; they took the pestilence aboard. Passed it on."

He looked along the length of the *Hrafn*, and amongst the men spied a solitary, motionless figure sitting slumped, head hanging, his face pale and with a clammy sheen of sweat.

"Watch Jarl," said Bjólf.

He searched further, found another whose eyes were fixed upon the same subject, as they had been since departing the vale of Halldís and Hallbjörn. "And watch Einarr too. His wits have been shaken since last night. Who knows what master he follows now." Gunnar, his heavily browed eyes scanning the ship, gave a curt grunt of acknowledgement.

"But what of Magnus?" he said after a long pause. "He suffered no bite. No wound at the *draugr*'s hand. And Kylfing and the others, too..."

"It is among us," Bjólf said, nodding slowly, his voice grim, resigned. "As with the dead of Hallbjörn's clan – they leave their graves regardless of the manner of their death. It is in the air. In their blood. In us. Now we carry this curse with us, wherever we go." He turned to Gunnar. "There is no escape, old friend."

Gunnar stood in silent thought, then exclaimed defiantly. "Pah! So what if death stalks us? When did it not? Nothing is changed. We do as we have always done – fight to stay alive!"

But Bjólf was not cheered by the words. He spread his hands out before him, reviewing every mark and scar, as if suddenly baffled by his own flesh. "We're dead already."

# CHAPTER TWENTY-SEVEN

## THE END BEGINS

ATLI CREPT AWAY from Bjólf and Gunnar, simultaneously appalled and numbed by their words. They had not known he was listening, had not even noticed him lingering there. That was the one advantage of being the least among the crew. Yet the knowledge had not helped. Instead, it had crippled him. He wandered the length of the ship not knowing what to think, let alone what to do. Here he was, starting out in life, yet already marked for death, doomed never to rest, never to ascend to the great halls of the warriors.

All about him, men muttered darkly. They had not been party to the same exchange, but they were not fools. Many had already drawn the same conclusions. Here and there, strange stories sprang up. They spoke in hushed tones, huddled in small groups.

"Kylfing used to say that among the Rus they told of a night-time blood-sucker," whispered Farbjörn to those gathered around him. "It was said a cursed man, or one who died in disgrace might become one, and that the affliction was passed on by its bite." At these words, all eyes slid sideways to where Jarl sat. He stared vacantly at the deck, making no movement but the occasional febrile shiver. None sat with him.

Though doing so gave him a sickening feeling of shame, Atli gave the man a wide berth as he passed.

"My cousin has sailed far and wide out in the west," said Skjöld the Icelander to another small knot of men. "He says there is a deadly disease out there in the icy wastes in which the victim comes back to life for a time and can divulge secrets about the future." Several around him nodded as if they knew this to be the truth.

"We should have asked Magnus," said one, shaking his head. "We have squandered a valuable opportunity."

"What's the point?" scoffed Njáll dismissively. "Our future is clear enough." But few shared the Celt's cheery fatalism.

At the far end of the ship, another man sat alone. Einarr stared the length of the vessel, two swords upon his lap – his favoured blade, and an old notched weapon of his grandfather's – both of which he sharpened with a steady, obsessive purpose.

It FELL TO Bjólf to finally break the sombre mood. Stepping up to the steering deck, he addressed the crew, his message straightforward, the words brusque and practical. "We rest now. Go and hunt. Then we'll eat and drink ashore." Pausing for a moment, he cast a cautious eye upon the forest, and added: "Keep your weapons about you. Tonight we sleep aboard ship."

None argued the point.

A rope was swiftly set up between the ship and the shore by which they could ferry themselves back and forth in the boat, and within only a few hours, men were returning from the woods with raised spirits. The hunt had been good: there were game birds of all kinds – pigeons, plover, lapwings and grouse, as well as several duck and a wild goose. Some had trapped hares, and Fjölvar, by a stroke of good fortune, had almost walked straight into a deer. Thanks to his skill with the bow, it was soon destined for the spit. Hazelnuts, berries, wild celery, nettles and a variety of herbs had been gathered, too – but the greatest prize was brought home by Úlf, who emerged red-faced and covered in stings, proudly holding aloft the crushed remains of a bees' nest, dripping with that most luxurious of commodities – honey. His arrival drew a cheer, and as Thorvald set about making the fire, a few men even began to sing as they sat and plucked the feathers from their dinner.

It was then that Finn, seeing Bjólf alone, approached him. "I beg your permission to stay ashore tonight," he said. Finn's mood was sombre and subdued, even by his own cool standards. But Bjólf recognised the look in his eye, a look that had come upon him before at times of trouble or doubt.

"You have it," he said.

"You have not asked me why."

"You have your reasons."

Finn allowed the faintest of smiles to flicker across his thin, straight lips, gave a brief nod, and made for the boat.


BACK ON THE *Hrafn*, Atli was crouched upon the deck. He had been charged with scrubbing the boards clean of the gore that had been spilled upon it. Had, in fact, been abandoned there until the job was done. Exhaustion from lack of sleep had nearly got the better of him. The sound of the rowing boat hitting the side of the ship made him jump out of his reverie. Watching quietly, he saw Finn step aboard and, approaching his sea-chest, draw various strange objects from it. Chief among them was what, at first, appeared to be a large wooden bowl, but proved to be a drum, the skin painted with all manner of strange images and symbols: birds and beasts and stylised figures of men, and a host of bizarre, spindly signs and characters at whose meaning he could only guess. Finn tapped its taut surface with his finger. It rang out a clear, resonant note. Seemingly satisfied with its condition, he rummaged further in his chest and drew out a small bundle of cloth, in which were wrapped a metal ring and a smooth length of animal bone. He wrapped them up again carefully, and placed both bundle and drum in a skin bag which he slung over his shoulder. As he turned to make his way back to the rowing boat, he caught sight of Atli. The boy looked away and scrubbed fiercely. When he looked up again, Finn was towering over him. For a moment, each looked at the other. Then Finn spoke in quiet tones.

"I go to listen to the earth spirits, seek their guidance. For that my feet must be upon the earth. I do not know what they will say, or what they will ask of me. But if I do not come back, tell them this is what I did. That I did not leave willingly, but acted out of love for this ship." Atli nodded, wide-eyed. With that, Finn turned and left.

All ate well that night, but, few slept soundly. From the dark shadows of the shore, the hollow sound of Finn's reindeer-skin drum beat its lonely, melancholy rhythm on through the dark hours. Most aboard understood what that meant, though none would speak of it. And beneath them, somewhere in the weedy waters, another sound – one that Atli recognised – further disturbed their restless slumber. It was the never ceasing *scrape-scrape-scrape* of Magnus's fingernails clawing against the wood of the hull.

THE MORNING – SUNLIT and beautiful as it was – brought a new and unexpected horror. So withdrawn had he become from the rest of the crew that none could remember for certain when Einarr had ceased to be among them. A search of the shore at first yielded nothing – then Finn appeared from the woods, looking haggard and drained, and directed them to the spot.

"I kept the wild beasts from his body," he said.

In a clearing, beneath a tall pine, Einarr's lifeless, bloody corpse lay. Hanging from a branch high above was a length of rope, and at its end a curious contrivance formed of two swords. Each was lashed to the other close to the hilt, their blades uppermost, like a half open pair of scissors. A short way up, another length of rope was twisted around the crossed blades to prevent them parting further, and it was to the middle of this that the line to the branch had been tied. The lower part of it and much of the tree were splashed with blood. Einarr had evidently placed his head between the blades, tightened the rope behind his neck, and jumped from a lower branch. It had decapitated him instantly, like a pair of shears snipping off a flower head. It was, for him, the only certain solution. Finn had heard the sound, and stayed with the body until morning, when the boat would return.

Bjólf surveyed the scene with a mixture of pity and contempt.

"What do you want done with him?" said Gunnar.

"Leave him to the birds," said Bjólf bitterly. "Nothing we can do will bring any honour to this."

Bjólf then went and spoke with Finn for some time, away from the others. Gunnar watched Bjólf's face as he responded to Finn's muttered words, listening intently, and wondered what it was that passed between them.

When they returned to the ship, news came that Jarl, too, had passed. None had checked on him during the night or made efforts to tend his wound. As Bjólf approached the pale body, its expression haunted and tortured even in death, he saw that the crew maintained a wide space around it – and not, he knew, out of respect. Without hesitation he took up Godwin's axe, swung it high in the air and brought it down upon Jarl's neck. His head sprang from his body and rolled towards their feet, spilling fresh gore upon Atli's carefully scrubbed deck.

Bjólf leaned on the axe and looked each one of them in the eye. "I would expect any of you to do the same to me." He handed the axe back to its owner. "Set his body in the boat and let the river take it. He was a man of the sea. Let him return there in peace." And he headed towards the prow.

"What now?" called Thorvald.

"Now we go back."

"Home?" came a hopeful voice.

"To Björnheim and the hall of Halldís."

There was consternation among the men. Even Gunnar looked at him in surprise. Bjólf stood upon the foredeck, facing his crew.

"Finn! Tell them what you told me."

All eyes turned to the Saami shaman. He spoke in a clear voice. "Our future lies with Halldís and the men of the black ships. There can be no doubting it."

The grumbling of the men surged again; some in protest, others suddenly less certain. Many believed implicitly in the power of Finn's magic. Bjólf raised his hands to silence them once more.

"I speak with no spirits. No gods. But for what it's worth, I am of the same opinion." There was further muttering of discontent, but Bjólf raised his voice again. "This tyrant Skalla, and his men, they are the source of this scourge. But they also possess its secret." He paused as the men became suddenly silent. "A secret that we can take from them."

So that's it, thought Gunnar. He has a plan.

"We cannot fight the power of a black wizard!" called one.

"He is no wizard," spat Bjólf, angered at the words. He strode back and forth as he spoke. "The white powder. The clear liquid. Halldís spoke of these things. Skalla controls his death-walkers with them, just as Magnus used herbs to heal. And Magnus was no wizard." There was a murmur of agreement. "Skalla is just a man. And if he can control this pestilence, then why not we?"

Bjólf turned to Finn once more.

"Tell them..."

"The spirits showed me a vision of their island fortress split apart and consumed by fire."

The murmuring grew in volume again.

"Do you still doubt that we can do it?" Bjólf called out, as if daring them to believe it. "Do you?" He drew his sword and ranged its glinting point before them.

"Leave now if you wish. You're all free men. But for good or ill, this ship sails south." He pointed southward with his blade, then swept it over their heads, arm outstretched, his voice rising with vengeful fury as he spoke. "The secret lies within that fortress. Bow to this curse if you like. But that's not my way. I mean to fight it, to fight until my muscles tear and sinews snap, to cut out its stinking black heart and see that stronghold ruined and in flames!" Some of the men roared their approval. "At the very least, I mean to do some good before I die." His voice grew quiet again, his face grave. "If you find that meat too rich for your tastes, go now, and let no more be said of it."

Gunnar drew his sword and raised it silently, slowly into the air. Without hesitation, Atli drew *Steinarrsnautr* and did the same. Njáll and Godwin joined them. Then Fjölvar, Odo, Thorvald, Úlf... One by one each man raised his blade aloft, every one showing his pledge, until the deck was a forest of glinting steel. Bjólf raised his own sword in salute, and as he did so a sudden breeze moved the gilded vane upon the mast, turning it southwards.

"The wind is with us," called Bjólf. "Raise the sail! To the south, and Skalla's ruin!"

A great cheer erupted. Immediately the men dispersed, each to his task. Shouts went up all over the ship, and men hauled on lines, muscles standing out like whipcords. The yard was heaved up the mast, the great sail unfurled, the great black image of a raven filling the sky above them.

As the rush of activity continued Finn approached Bjólf, and spoke to him in quiet tones. "You did not tell them everything, about what the spirits revealed."

"They showed you victory," said Bjólf. "That's all I need to know."

"They also said that none of us would leave fjord of the black fortress for a thousand years."

Bjólf looked Finn in the eye, then without a word turned and strode towards the tiller where Gunnar stood, staring indecisively at the chain that was still wrapped around the brace cleat.

"What about him?" said Gunnar, a note of indignation in his voice. "We cannot just leave him to writhe and flail in the depths for eternity. It is Magnus! Our friend!"

"Magnus is long gone," said Bjólf. And with that, he unfastened the chain and let it slip over the side. He watched it disappear like a snake into the water as the men made ready to turn back to the land of the death-walkers, and their grim appointment with Skalla.

# PART THREE

---

*RAGNARÓK*

# INTERLUDE

SKALLA SAT IN the great hall's late gloom, elbows on his knees, one hand held against his wrecked left eye. He felt strangely detached from all that had happened to him – oddly unmoved by his injury, or the loss of half his sight, even as his good eye watched the blood which soaked his sleeve and oozed through his half-closed fingers, drip into a thick pool upon the beaten earth of the floor. An image of a clawed hand flailing towards his face flashed through his mind. He shuddered at the resurrected memory of its bone scraping against his.

That feeling, too, would fade, in time.

Twelve nights had passed since the first one came. The creature had been drawn by the sounds of their feasting, bitter with envy, perhaps, at the pleasures of honest meat and ale and the promise of lusty embraces that it was now denied; enraged by the voices joined in song, the joy of fellowship, the celebration of life. It was a life-hater from the misty margins of this world, of neither earth nor Hel; a lost traveller between life

215

and death who had no lord and bore no arms and was immune to the bite of human blades. Dead, and not dead. A hate-filled monster. A demon.

Such was the opinion of his master. It was, so Skalla had begun to realise, calculated to cast the conflict in a more heroic light.

To him, the act had no more heroism than the killing of a rat. What was certain was that this guest had come with a wholly different kind of feasting in mind. At least, thought Skalla, it displayed a sense of humour – if sense it had at all. He had reason to doubt that, though. It seemed to him they were driven by only the basest instincts. He had observed their movements the past several nights, as one invader had become two, then five, then seven... He had watched as the first of them to invade the hall had struck the guests through with shock and dread, how its bloody assault upon the nearest of them had happened before any knew how to respond, and how all had made repeated, futile attempts at restraining it, having no weapons to hand, while the woman Arnfrith had screamed over and over in confused horror, begging them not to harm her late husband. That man had been killed by some beast whilst out hunting, they said. Now they knew better.

He had watched each successive night as the clamour of feasting had drawn more of them, the dead of previous nights returning as if in some nightmare, and wondered at the dogged refusal of Hallbjörn to admit weapons or to quit the hall, even when his guests were dwindling in number and those that persisted were getting eaten alive.

And he had watched, especially, during that last desperate fight, when the *draugr* had proved too numerous for the newly-posted hall-guards to repel, seeking confirmation of his conclusions before taking action. And even then, his actions were by way of an experiment – a confirmation, or otherwise, of a theory. The crushing blows to the heads of three of the fiends with the heavy iron poker – the same one with which he had tended the fire for so many years – provided the confirmation he sought. Each of their skulls had been smashed outright with a single impact, felling them immediately – the last achieved in spite of his grievous wound.

The fact that it had also saved his master's life was pure coincidence.

"You have served me well over many years," said Hallbjörn. "And never more loyally than today. You fought when others fled." He turned, walking in a small circle, avoiding a patch that had been churned to red mud in the struggle. "Perhaps it is time to talk about your future."

"Future?" said Skalla.

It was something he had had little reason to think about. He had trained himself to avoid it over the years. What had been the point? How was his wretched future to be any different from his wretched past, consisting as it did of the same tasks, the same hardships, the same endless succession of days?

"About your *freedom...*" added Hallbjörn. He spoke with great gravity, emphasising the final word as if it were a potent charm, and carried in its utterance some magical, transformative power.

"Freedom," repeated Skalla. He rolled it around in his mind, muttered it again, as if considering it from different points of view might somehow endow it with life. It remained as dead as earth. The notion, after all, was meaningless. It seemed as though every free man assumed the idea would mean so much more to a lifelong slave such as him. They were wrong. "Freedom to do what?"

Hallbjörn laughed, a note of irritation in his voice. "Why, to do whatever you wish. To remain here. Or to make your way in the world, if you so choose."

To remain here. To work exactly as he had been working, no doubt. Or to venture out there, to what? With what? What kind of choice was that? It was, thought Skalla, the kind of generosity that only a wealthy man could think worthwhile; a gift that, to one with nothing, meant nothing. An act of benevolence that, in truth, gave more to the giver.

But then, perhaps there was something out there that had caught his interest, after all. Something no one could have expected. And something of which Hallbjörn was unlikely to approve.

"What would you have me do?"

The question clearly pleased Hallbjörn. "We must go to the source of this pestilence and stamp it out," he said, his voice suddenly charged with a stern gravity. The voice of destiny, thought Skalla. The voice of an imagined saga, told in an imagined future around this very fire. "I *ask* that you join me in this quest."

So that was it – the great honour that Hallbjörn was now bestowing upon him. To fight and die for his jailer.

In truth, Skalla had been thinking quite a bit about the source of this pestilence. Since the great firestorm, the night it all began, he had overheard increasingly wild stories about the mysterious island in the fjord and the dark, magical powers that had begun to emanate from it. Skalla did not believe in magic, even as he had watched the dead of the clan of Hallbjörn stagger back into the hall, the marks of their deaths still upon them. In them, he saw no curse. Just another process to be understood. He knew the world for what it was: dead matter, mindlessly shifting in space, grinding the pathetic creatures that scuttled between its cracks with as little thought as a millstone gives a weevil; a relentless chaos of struggle and death, from which only the deluded sought escape through desperate belief in the beyond. Skalla had never had the luxury of such childish notions. Creation was material to be used, held at bay, bent to one's will. Only then could fleeting pleasures, brief moments of satisfaction, be wrung from it.

And what did he care whether dark or light? Two sides of the same coin. Dark, light, day or night – he was equally a slave whichever held sway. The lash raised the same weals, whether brandished by a good man or a bad.

But power – that which dictated whose hand was on the lash... that interested him greatly. It was something he had hardly known. Yet, for that very reason, he felt he knew it more keenly than any of the pampered, overindulged free men who passed him by each day; men who, through years of familiarity, failed to even register his presence. That, too, could prove an advantage.

Yes, there was a power growing upon the island, that was certain. He had seen it challenge Hallbjörn in his own hall, shake his authority to its roots, turn the laws of life and death upon their heads, bringing fear to those who had for so long fancied themselves fearless. It had struck ruthlessly, coldly, without passion or anger and with no regard for etiquette or honour. And for that reason, Skalla knew, it would win. In the past twelve days Skalla had become aware of an entirely different future from the one that, until now, had seemed inevitable. In his mind's eye he now saw something he thought never to see: the fall of the power of Hallbjörn in this land, and the rise of another.

Skalla looked up at Hallbjörn, removing his red, blood-slicked hand from his torn left eye. He saw his master wince at the sight of his injured face, then hastily regain his composure, his kindly, benevolent expression. The reaction gave Skalla a curious glow of satisfaction. He had never before cared how he looked. No woman would look at him, not even the slave girls from whom he had once forced brief, empty pleasures, before such things had ceased to seem worth the effort. But they would all notice him now. Perhaps even fear him. And fear was the greatest power of all.

This would be his way, now. Where others saw a curse, Skalla would find opportunity. And the greater opportunity – the one that had begun to emerge out of the fog over the past few days – finally stood before him, clear and unassailable.

"Odin gave an eye in exchange for wisdom," he said, holding Hallbjörn's gaze. "Perhaps, now, I too see the future more clearly. See what must be done."

"Good." said Hallbjörn, smiling. He turned and went to the high seat, and from behind it drew out a sword in a gilded, richly embossed scabbard. He turned and approached Skalla, carrying the sword before him with great reverence, laid flat across his upturned hands. Its hilt and pommel were of gold, with fine cloisonné inlay of garnets and blue millefiori glass, its grip made of alternating rings of silver and whalebone. This was a great sword from the old times, the only battle-blade permitted in the great hall. But this one ventured into battle no longer. Even in the desperate conflicts of past nights, it had remained sheathed. It was a sword of ancestors, meant for the giving and taking of oaths, upon whose blade – and the blood it had spilled – such oaths were made inviolate.

Hallbjörn, still smiling, drew the great blade and, laying its scabbard gently upon the ground, held the sword before him towards Skalla. Only gradually did Skalla grasp the nature of the honour that was to be bestowed upon him. He was to be given his freedom, and the opportunity to swear his allegiance to Hallbjörn. To be given the status of a warrior.

To Hallbjörn's surprise, Skalla reached forward and took the sword by the grip. Without expression, he swung it from side to side, judging its weight in his hand. Hallbjörn half laughed, frowning at his slave's ignorant action, went to correct him. Before he could do so, Skalla swung the blade with all his strength, severing the old man's head. The expression on its face as it left his body and bounced sizzling into the fire was one of utter disbelief.

Yes, it was a good blade. Sharp enough. It would serve him in his new purpose.

This new power would need men. An army. And an army would need a captain. So why not him? They cared not for status or protocol. But he had to move quickly, before another saw the chance. He would gather others around him – slaves, like himself, who had suffered under the yoke of the old ways. They would accept his authority. He would exploit their bitterness and resentment, fashion a force of men to offer to the new regime that was rising in the fjord, and in doing so turn the tables on their masters.

Skalla glanced down without feeling at the headless body of the man who had once owned him. Taking a step back from the spreading pool of blood, he looked up at great beams of the hall that would one day be his, and, sheathing the great sword in its magnificent golden scabbard, shoved it roughly through the worn, dirty leather belt fastened about his greasy tunic and stalked off into the night.

The first blow of the new order had been struck.

# CHAPTER TWENTY-EIGHT

## THE RETURN OF THE RAVEN

THE SAILING WAS good; their passage swift. Beneath the great raven – bulging before the wind, wings outspread – their expressions were grim. But, as they were carried southwards towards their fate, there was a growing defiance upon the brow of each and every man. They had witnessed much in the past few days – seen a possible future presented to them in the grisly fates of their less fortunate comrades. But, with their quest now set, they were now determined. Swords were sharpened, axes honed. They would not end like Magnus, or Jarl, or Einarr. They would fight until they were victorious, or until death took them. And each man silently pledged that he would not leave another of his fellows to suffer the living death.

When they once again stood before Halldís and her court, with Bjólf at their head, they were very different men. There was no pretence now. They came fully armed and armoured, sweeping aside protests as they entered the hall.

"We come to war," Bjólf had said, "and go nowhere unless equipped for war."

Halldís had allowed it. That tradition, noble as it was, had cost them enough lives.

"We thought you lost to us," said Halldís. Her voice was cold, but Bjólf fancied he detected more than a hint of irony in it. Well, he could hardly blame her for that.

"It seems things once thought lost have a habit of coming back."

"Some more welcome than others." She paused, keeping him guessing another few moments. "We are glad at your return." Her expression warmed, a flicker of a smile crossing it – even, he thought, something mischievous, flirtatious. "Tell us, what was it drew you here again?"

"We have a new purpose," he said. She raised her eyebrows, questioningly. "Before we came merely to trade, knowing nothing of your plight."

"And now?"

"We come to fight. To destroy the black ships and put Skalla in the earth. To fight our fate. The fate that afflicts us all."

She held his gaze for a lingering moment, knowing now that Bjólf's crew laboured under the curse of undeath that, even as his ship had been leaving, she had hoped they'd escaped.

There were murmurs of approval at Bjólf's bold announcement. Ragnhild beamed with joy. At Halldís's shoulder, Frodi held Bjólf's gaze and nodded slowly in satisfaction. At last, it seemed, the two men had come to an understanding. Bjólf was glad to have regained his respect.

Then a pale, joyless figure stepped forward from the rest, regarding Bjólf and his men with a sideways look. Óflár the Watcher. Óflár the Patient.

"You seriously believe you can alter the course of fate?" he said. His voice was thin and reedy, its tone as pinched and mean as his person. He extended his long, skinny hand in the direction of the distant harbour. "Why not try to change the

222

course of this river while you're at it?" Several members of the court sniggered at that.

"I have seen the course of a river changed," responded Bjólf calmly silencing the doubters. "I have also seen blocks of stone piled high as mountains in the deserts of the south. And a great wall, as high as three men and twenty *sjømil* long or more – the whole width of England. Men did these things. Men who did not shrink from challenge. Who did not sit comfortably at home, who did not amount to nothing merely because they refused to question what was thought impossible."

Óflár's milky eyes narrowed to slits. His supporters among the assembled throng shuffled their feet uncertainly as he passed before Bjólf in silence, then circled and stalked slowly back. "You have great confidence in your powers where before you had none," he said, then turned on the rest of the crew as if probing for signs of weakness. "Is this the view of you all?"

Gunnar cleared his throat and shrugged. "My noble captain and I do have rather differing views on the nature of fate," he said.

Óflár allowed himself a thin smile at this. The big man's tone changed as he fixed the pale figure before him with glowering eyes. "But better to fight than to cower."

Óflár's pale fists clenched. Frodi did not attempt to hold back his smile.

"Are you with me?" called Bjólf to his crew.

"Aye!" came the shout – strong and clear, all voices as one, the sound ringing about the rafters of the great hall.

"You have your answer," said Bjólf.

Seething, his mouth downturned like a spoilt child, Óflár slunk back into the shadows.

Halldís stepped forward then. "We cannot avoid what fate places before us," she said. "Yet I believe that an intelligent man may moderate what fate brings, if he is clear in his mind and is prepared to seek the help of friends."

Bjólf nodded in acknowledgment.

"You said that Skalla had power over his death-walkers," he said. "We mean to take that from him. It is the one hope for the salvation of us all – my crew and your people."

Frodi raised his eyebrows, impressed at what he heard. "It will be a hard fight," he said.

"That is the only kind of fight we understand," responded Bjólf with a half-smile. "But we need to learn all we can about our enemy. Numbers, weapons, the kinds of men they are..."

"We can tell you all we know," said Frodi. "But you may be able to see some of that for yourself, and sooner than you think."

Bjólf looked from Frodi to Halldís, a frown upon his face.

"Skalla comes to collect his tribute once a month, after the first day of the full moon," explained Halldís. "And it is full moon tonight."

Bjólf and Gunnar exchanged glances. They would need to plan quickly.

"When does he come?" asked Bjólf.

"Midday. When the shadows of the stags upon the gable point their horns at the well."

"What strength?"

Frodi spoke this time. "Always one ship with at least twenty men. Several armed with crossbows. Fearsome weapons."

"Yet those behind them are poor warriors, for the most part," added Halldís. "No match for your men. But..."

"But" – Frodi took up the point – "they have their *draugr* berserkers..." He hung his head and sighed. "Against them, I am afraid, there is little defence."

"Everything has its weakness," said Bjólf. "Theirs is a white powder that Skalla carries about him." He allowed his eyes to linger upon Halldís for a moment, then turned to his crew. "We shall lie in wait, watch from the forest's edge. See what we can see. Take them if we can." He turned back to the mistress of the hall. "Perhaps we can force this to a swift conclusion."

At this, Frodi stepped forward. "If we are to fight, you can add my sword to those of your men."

More came forward then, each pledging to stand with Bjólf. He nodded and smiled in grateful acknowledgement. True, the men were old, but their will was strong, and they knew their enemy.

Gunnar grunted. "And what if more of those death-walkers come sniffing around while we're crouched among the trees?"

Bjólf looked at him with fire in his eyes. "We point them at Skalla," he said.

# CHAPTER TWENTY-NINE

## SKALLA

ATLI PEERED OUT nervously from the thick tangle of undergrowth, his sword drawn, the smell of sweat, rotting wood and rank estuary mud in his nostrils. At first he had laughed when he saw the men smearing the stinking mud upon their helms; then Gunnar told him it was to prevent their position being given away by the glint of metal, and he had swiftly followed suit. That was his first lesson of the day.

Ahead of them, beyond the trees, the harbour was a picture of peace. It had been that way much of the morning. The grisly remains of the slaughter of the death-walkers had been cleared, and now the sun shone down, the grey-green water sparkled, and the wind sighed in the trees. Only the total absence of birdsong attested to the abnormal nature of the place.

He shifted to relieve the cramp in his foot, and cursed as

he caught his thumb on a bramble thorn. To the left of him, Godwin gave a nudge and raised a single finger to his lips. Atli reddened, and stuck his thumb in his mouth.

The harbour, as yet, was empty of life, devoid of threat. But there was still the forest. What lay in there, and what might emerge, none could say for certain. Had they destroyed all the *draugr* that night? Most of them? Or were they merely the first – the advance guard of a vast, stumbling army of blood-hungry flesh-eaters?

Atli tried to imagine how many had died here since the world began, to picture them all returning – hundreds, thousands of them. How far back could this curse reach, he wondered? Years? Generations? Did it have the power to animate even the dried up bones of ancient ancestors, whose ways in life would now seem strange?

He looked behind him, past the great huddle of crouched and armoured men, into the depths of the forest where no sunlight penetrated. He had lost count of the number of times he had done that today. Gunnar, immediately on his right, caught his eye, and pointed forwards. Atli blushed again, and turned back towards the harbour. Of course, nothing could approach them through that great thicket without announcing itself, and the death-walkers were hardly models of stealth. But Atli's nerves were already getting the better of him. The waiting was becoming unbearable; he wanted to piss, but did not dare, he felt dizzy and sick, his heart pounding in his chest, his stomach clenched into a ball, every muscle in his body as tight as a harp-string and ready to snap. He had come through the long night of the death-walkers. But this was different. This, if it came to it, would be his first real battle.

He tried to banish all such thoughts from his crowded head, and focus solely on the task, on the empty scene before him. Part of him wished for the black prow of Skalla's ship to come soon and end this torment. Another wished it to be put off as long as possible.

\* \* \*

PREPARATIONS HAD BEGUN immediately their meeting in the great hall had concluded. The older volunteers among Halldís's people had exhumed their long-idle weapons, and set about honing them back to life. Some trained and sparred, trying to coax dim memories of battle back into their limbs. At Frodi's suggestion, Bjólf had set Úlf to thickening their shields with a double layer of boards – protection against the crossbows whose power Frodi knew only too well.

The greatest task had been that of concealment of the ship. Some had argued for simply mooring it downriver, away from the fjord, from which all assumed Skalla was to come. But Bjólf was against it. What if this one time, for reasons they could not anticipate, Skalla were to come from the other direction? Some suggested hauling it ashore, into the stockade – but all knew that even over level ground, that was a back-breaking task. Fjölvar and Finn were in favour of hiding it in the thick vegetation of one of the half-choked inlets they had passed. But if they were going to do that, suggested Bjólf, why travel so far? Why not do the same thing right here? He pointed out the huge trees that draped their branches into the water on the north side of the harbour, opposite their proposed vantage point. Might not their ship disappear behind those?

A hasty survey showed it to be possible. Without delay, the men removed tents, sea-chests and weapons from the ship to the stockade. Only the great box of booty remained, stowed below deck. Bjólf did not trust their hosts that much just yet, and it was more than an afterthought that had him set Finn, the stealthiest among them, the task of keeping watch on Óflár. With the inner branches cut away, the mast was lifted from its housing in the mast-fish and lowered, and the ship carefully floated behind the huge, overhanging screen into the great cavern of tree and leaf. After a few hours work – and some judicious dressing of the branches – it was as if the *Hrafn* had never existed.

That night, Bjólf and his men had pitched their wooden-framed tents in the clearing before the hall – a great circle of them around a central fire of spitting pine logs. Haldís had food brought, to which they added some of the spoils from the previous day's hunt. Still, it was a modest feast compared to that night downriver.

"They are keeping it from us," complained Finn as they sat chewing bread around the crackling blaze, the bright painted colours of the tents glowing in the flickering light. "The good food," he explained, seeing the question upon Bjólf's face. "I have seen it, when I followed Óflár. He went to a large store-house, to check something. So I made it my business to check it too." He swallowed a tough gobbet of bread, gesticulating with the remaining piece as he spoke. "Food. Everywhere. Grain. Dried meat. Whole carcasses of mutton and beef hanging. They have deceived us!"

"It's no deception," said Bjólf. Finn frowned.

"Tribute for Skalla," explained Gunnar. He spat a piece of gristle into the fire and dug at his teeth with a finger. "It's what is to be collected tomorrow. Not destined for our table, nor that of Halldís."

Finn bit at his bread again, disconsolately.

"What else did he do?" asked Bjólf.

Finn shrugged. "He is a very boring man. After the store house he went to another hut and fed a bird in a cage. He put it on his arm, then watched it fly about. Then he went home and drank alone."

"Clearly a man whose company is in great demand," quipped Gunnar.

"Keep watching him," said Bjólf. Then they had turned in, to gather strength for the next day's encounter.

It was Fjölvar – far out on the right flank and closest to the point of approach – who heard them first. The whispered message was passed down the line, as very shortly Atli heard them too. It was the same sound he had heard the day the *vikingr* came out of the fog. The steady dip and heave of oars, the clunk and creak of wood against wood. He strained to see past the closely-packed helms ranged to his right, through the foliage to the river. But he could make nothing out. To their left, up at the stockade, a shout went up. Someone in the watchtower had seen them first. Atli had a moment of panic at not being able to see their enemy and leaned forward, and Gunnar hauled him back.

Then the black ship slid into view.

It was long and lean, its timbers so dark they appeared pitched inside and out, the stark figurehead not a thing carved of wood, but the great, horned, empty-eyed skull of an aurochs. And, behind it, standing high upon the prow – there could be no doubting it – Skalla. He was clothed head to toe in black, the tunic of thick leather and covered with blackened, interlocking plates of metal; a foreign, unfamiliar style of armour. Above the angry scar that slashed through his dead left eye, his helm gleamed with the sheen of black flint. But the fine sword at his waist was sheathed in gold.

Up at the stockade, the gates had opened, and from them now issued a rabble of spindly figures: a ragtag band of people from the village, carrying Skalla's spoils, headed by Halldís and two elderly armed guards, whose presence, thought Bjólf, could be little more than symbolic.

"The exchange will be swift," whispered Frodi. "Skalla does not waste time on pleasantries."

As they watched, the oars were shipped, the vessel run up almost to the water's edge and a long gangplank extended to the shore. Skalla strode down it then, followed by four black-clad men. They positioned themselves at the edge of the grass, unnervingly close to where Bjólf and his men lay hidden. Frodi had been right – Skalla's followers were not the most fearsome specimens of manhood. But what they may have lacked in physical presence, they made up for with their formidable weapons. The crossbows that were slung about them were like nothing any of them had ever seen; awesome in appearance and flowing in design, the material black and gleaming like carved obsidian.

Halldís stopped a short distance away, the nervous villagers placing their cargo on the ground before her. She did not bow her head in welcome as was her usual custom. Her expression today was cold as stone. Skalla gave an abrupt signal, and several crewmen scurried down the gangplank and set about loading the goods. No word was spoken.

BJÓLF LEANED IN close to Gunnar's ear. "I count twenty-five men at most. If we hit them fast enough..."

Gunnar gripped his arm. Immediately, Bjólf saw the source of his alarm. A second ship had drifted into view – identical to the second, but for the ram's skull upon its prow. Bjólf read the agitation upon Halldís's face, sent desperate thoughts in her direction, whispering to himself through clenched teeth. *Don't look around... don't look around...*

Halldís stared straight ahead. The second ship sat back in the harbour, its dark crew scrutinizing the transaction upon the shore.

"It's still us against twenty-five if we're fast," whispered Gunnar; trying, for the moment, to put the crossbows out of his mind. "By the time the others got to shore..."

It was Skalla who silenced him this time.

"Your face gives much away," he said, regarding Halldís. His voice was hollow, empty of expression. In the trees, hands tensed around weapons. A passionless smile creased Skalla's face. "You wonder why we come in such numbers."

"You do as you wish," replied Halldís, struggling to sound indifferent.

"Yes," said Skalla. "I do." He removed his gauntlets and turned around slowly as the last of the cargo was loaded, presenting his back to her. "I have heard that a ship came here. A ship with many warriors."

Bjólf cursed under his breath.

"Someone has betrayed us..." hissed Gunnar. He glared at Frodi. Frodi looked back at him in shocked bemusement.

Halldís maintained her composure. She stood in silence for a moment, as if weighing alternatives in her mind. Finally she spoke.

"It's true," she said. Skalla turned to look her in the face, surprised by her words. "We killed them," she continued.

"Poisoned their food, cut their throats as they slept and burned their bodies. Perhaps you saw the smoke?"

Skalla stared at her in amazement, then a hoarse, rasping laugh escaped him. "You really are full of surprises. You certainly have far more about you than your father ever had." Skalla fingered the pommel of the gilded sword as he spoke. Halldís bit her lip, refusing to be drawn. "Since we are forced, in these harsh times, to dispose of our dead before our dead dispose of us, there is no evidence to verify your story." He sighed. "Convenient." His eyes bored into her, searching for weakness, and then he turned away, suddenly. "Well, it seems you missed one..."

He waved his black gauntlets, and two of his men heaved a third, heavily muscled figure from the ship onto the gangplank, dragging him ashore by the ropes that bound his wrists. Every one of Bjólf's men gaped in astonishment at Helgi Grimmsson. They shoved him forward, and he staggered and fell to his knees, a stone's throw from where Bjólf was concealed, his face beaten and bruised.

"This is the only one we have encountered alive," said Skalla. "We found him wandering in the forest. So far he has proved most unco-operative."

He prodded Grimmsson with his boot, and Grimmsson spat upon it, the spittle mingled with blood. Skalla laughed again and turned back to Halldís. As he did so, Grimmsson looked up, and for a moment seemed to catch Bjólf's eye, deep in the undergrowth. Bjólf, staring back in disbelief, felt the hairs on the back of his neck prickle. Yes, it was true. Grimmsson had seen them. He gripped his sword and shield, prepared in the next moment to hear their presence proclaimed, for desperate fighting to erupt, the advantage of surprise utterly lost.

But something quite different happened.

As he held Grimmsson's gaze, he saw the big man, his eyes blazing, give a brief but urgent shake of his head, then tear his attention away. It was distinct, but subtle, such as Skalla and his men would not notice from behind.

"What was that?" whispered an astonished Gunnar.

Bjólf could hardly believe it himself. "He was warning us. Warning us not to attack."

"But why? They know we are here."

"No," said Bjólf. "They're not certain."

As they watched, Grimmsson staggered to his feet, and, turning, lurched towards Halldís. "You killed them, you bitch!" Halldís reeled in shock at the outburst. Skalla hauled on the rope, pulling Grimmsson back from her as one would an unruly dog.

"He seems to know you. I believe this one may be their captain. An unfortunate loss; he could have served my masters well. But I need to make an example."

He signalled once again. Two men hurried ashore and drove a stake deep into the ground near where Halldís stood, securing Grimmsson's rope to it with what seemed excessive care. Others, meanwhile, heaved three great, black oblong boxes down the gangplank, dragging them to within a short distance of where Grimmsson was now bound.

Grimmsson spat again in contempt, taunting them, a crazed look in his eye. "You'd better kill me well, Skalla, or by the gods I'll come back and bite your pox-ridden bollocks off!"

That defiance was soon to be shaken. With nervous hands, the men had prised off the lids – some visibly recoiling from what was revealed inside – and now retreated hastily to the refuge of their ship.

From his vantage point, Bjólf could not see what lay within. But Grimmsson could, and across his face flashed an expression Bjólf never imagined he would see upon his old rival; a look of uncomprehending horror.

Skalla drew a small flask from inside his tunic, and called out to the villagers. "Stand back, or you will all die."

They did not need telling twice. Halldís withdrew hurriedly. Others simply turned and fled towards the stockade. Skalla threw a clear liquid from the flask into the boxes, one after the other, then backed slowly away towards the ship, watching intently.

In each box, something stirred. There were groans. A thud.

A weird, deep growl – half-human, half-beast. The sound of nails clawing against wood. The first of the boxes shuddered violently, then jumped as if from some powerful impact. And from it, bit by bit, moving awkwardly, rose a huge, hulking figure of a man. At least equal to Grimmsson in size, its body was thick and muscular, but as grey and dead as the grimmest of the death-walkers. On its chest it wore a battered leather hauberk, scored and stained by battle, and here and there, the bloodless, green-tinged flesh showed signs of wounds that had been crudely repaired with stitches of rough, yellowed thread. The sutures strained and pulled the flesh as the creature stood and flexed its massive arms, a low rumble in its throat. A close-fitting helm obscured most of its features – but red eyes glowed from within the shadows, and a gaping mouth hung open in the tangled, gore-spattered mat of its beard. It wore no sword, this warrior, and carried no shield. But around its waist was a heavy chain, and from its right hand hung a battle axe of immense proportions, held in place by two iron nails.

So awe-struck was Grimmsson by this ghastly figure, that its two companions were on their feet before he realised – each as big as the first and in the same close-fitting helms; one in a ragged, rusting half-coat of mail, the other hung about with what had once been the whole skin of a wolf. The first had the wooden shaft of a great hammer nailed to its palm. The second had no weapon familiar to a warrior, but to the bones of both hands were bolted vicious iron claws.

The first looked about, sniffed at the air, turned a full circle with an unsteady gait as if not yet awake, and stopped, facing Grimmsson. Bjólf's rival could stand no more. "Come on then!" he bellowed at them, making as if to attack, heaving so hard on his rope that the stake threatened to pull free, his voice charged with renewed contempt.

It was the last coherent sound he ever made.

The first of the berserkers made a loud snort like a bull, and with a sudden burst of ferocious speed, like wild dogs let off the leash, all three flew at Grimmsson.

Flailing fists pummelled and tore, teeth snapped and snarled, and blood and gore was flung about with such savagery that in moments the living man was reduced to splintered bone and shapeless shreds of glistening, pulsing tissue.

Skalla stepped forward, dipping his hand into a small, black lacquered box, which hung on a cord about his shoulder. All three of the ogres turned at the sound of his approach, parts of Grimmsson still hanging from their champing mouths. Showing no emotion, Skalla stood his ground as they turned upon him, and in one swift movement flung a spray of the white powder across their faces. Instantly, as if felled by elf-stroke, the three colossal figures stiffened and crashed to the ground, dead as a ship's carved figurehead.

Bjólf, Gunnar and the rest looked on in shock and awe, the smell of fresh, hot blood and torn flesh carrying on the air. The attack was over so fast, the destruction so complete, that none yet knew how to react. A sword blow, the impact of an axe, the stab of a knife – these things they understood. But for such utter, instantaneous devastation to be wrought upon a living body... It was beyond their comprehension.

Skalla snapped his fingers. His men – no less terrified, with appalled expressions on their faces, one retching – crept back reluctantly and, faces averted, began to load the lifeless, blood-soaked hulks back into their boxes.

Some distance away, Halldís finally dared to put her hand to her face. A spot of Grimmsson's blood came away on her pale finger. She swayed, her face drained of colour.

Skalla looked around, almost as if he had expected some intervention, then faced her again. "Well, perhaps you told the truth after all," he said, nodding slowly, his cold eyes upon her. "I will not underestimate you again." With that he turned, preparing to leave, then again changed direction, as if having one last thing that he wished to say. "Oh, I nearly forgot – if they are all dead, then they won't be needing their ship, will they?" He signalled to the captain of the second vessel, out on the river, and from it a hail of flaming arrows was unleashed upon the great overhang of trees, within which was hidden the *Hrafn*.

Gunnar leapt up in fury, his axe ready to split Skalla's skull, but Bjólf grabbed his belt and hauled him back down before he could give their position away. He shook his head despondently. "Even if we could take them and their berserkers, the other ship would make it away and warn the rest."

Gunnar slumped back, defeated. As they watched, the great trees burst into flame. Beyond their branches, Skalla's arrows had already ignited the sail, and the hungry blaze now leapt and licked along the planking of the deck.

"It's just a ship, Gunnar," whispered Bjólf, still restraining him. But both knew he did not believe it.

Without another word, without looking back, Skalla strode up the gangplank and the black ships departed, leaving undreamt of ruin in their wake.

Bjólf and his men finally crawled from their cramped hiding places, spirits crushed, horrified beyond measure at the sights before them. A few instinctively rushed to the ship, splashing into the water with the thought of effecting some kind of rescue. But it was all too late. All were turned back by the intense heat of the blaze, whose eager shoots now reached to the very tops of the trees. The branches upon which the fiery tendrils climbed crackled and spat and fell burning into the water, a huge column of thick smoke billowing above. Reflected in the steaming water, the blackening shape of the *Hrafn*'s elegant prow stood like a silhouette in the great roaring torrent of flame – its timbers, marked with the deeds of ages, steadily consumed, its memories forever lost.

Bjólf hauled off his helm and let it drop to the ground, barely able to comprehend what had happened. His mind kept spinning back to the tantalising moment when the powder had been there, right before them, almost within their grasp; the moment before everything was suddenly snatched away.

"I should have been on board," he muttered, the flames from the fire reflecting in his eyes. "I always thought it would be my funeral ship."

Lacking the words to ease his friend's torment, Gunnar poked at the edge of the circle of mangled flesh with his axe. "Grimmsson saved us. All those years of sniping and fighting, and he saved us. Why?"

Bjólf shrugged, tearing his eyes from his dying ship. "Honour amongst thieves." He looked back upriver, in the black ships' wake. The wind gusted, changing direction, carrying the smoke across the sun and throwing his face into shadow. "Perhaps because he had encountered something truly evil, such that our similarities suddenly seemed more important than our differences."

Halldís approached, her face drawn. She looked up at Bjólf, her hand upon his arm, mouth open but empty of words, shaking silent tears from her eyes. The sight of this man crushed by defeat was almost more than she could bear. He took her hand, drawing comfort from the contact, and gave a forced smile of gloomy resignation.

"We must leave," she begged. "The noise will have attracted death-walkers."

In silence, the men trooped back to the safety of the stockade. Last of them was Bjólf, who hung back just long enough to see the exposed ribs of the great old ship devoured by the flames.

# CHAPTER THIRTY

## KING ÓFLÁR

As THEY HAD trudged up the hill and on through the village, thoughts of the day's events had begun to consolidate in Bjólf's mind. He had not remained defeated for long. Despair had turned to melancholy, melancholy to bitterness, and, by the time they reached the great hall, to a murderous rage.

"We were betrayed," he snapped as he strode back and forth before the mead benches, his sword still in his hand. Its blade swept through the air as he spoke. Even his friends were keeping a respectful distance from him now.

"But who?" said Halldís, exchanging a look of deep unease with Frodi. He turned and stared into the hearth, his face dark and brooding.

"I know on whom I would place my wager," he muttered.

"But, more to the point, how did they pass the message?" added Gunnar. "No one here would go by land, and we know none went by boat."

"Their information was scant," said Godwin, "or many of us would doubtless be dead by now, torn apart by their berserkers."

"They had the chance," nodded Frodi.

"But they did not take it," frowned Bjólf. "They did not know everything. Grimmsson was able to mislead them. They were warned – about us, about the ship – but did not know what else might have passed." He rubbed his chin, and looked up to the rafters as if somehow seeking inspiration there. *Come on, Thor... Odin... anyone...* he thought. *I've neglected you all these years, I know, but I'll take any help I can get, whether you exist or not.*

A vivid childhood memory came to him, then, quite unbidden: of his uncle's hall – a far more modest affair than this – and of the sparrows that used to nest among the beams. During feasts, they would swoop down and steal scraps from the tables. In time, they became so tame they would even take food from Olaf's huge hand. He smiled at that ridiculous image. The old man loved those birds. Such a thing could not happen here, in this lifeless realm. He had not seen a single bird since they had arrived.

Then he turned, fixing Finn with a look of frightening intensity and pointing at him with the tip of his blade.

"This bird that you saw Óflár feed," he said, his voice like thunder. "He let it fly free?"

"Yes," said Finn, shrugging.

"What kind of bird? A hawk? A hunting bird?" He did not think Óflár the kind to have a pet.

"No... Eating bird. What do you call it?" He flapped his arms and imitated its sound. "Coo-coo-coo!"

"A pigeon!" exclaimed Gunnar. The men looked at each other in sudden comprehension.

Bjólf turned, brow furrowed in fury, fingers clenched so tight around his sword grip his knuckles were white, and stormed out of the hall, leaving the great door swinging behind him. Moments later, he was back again. He strode up to Halldís and grabbed her by the hand. "Show me where Óflár lives!" he demanded, and charged out once again, dragging Halldís behind him.

"This should be interesting..." said Gunnar. All hurried after them.

Óflár took his time answering the irate pounding at his door. When he did so, he opened it the merest crack and peered out, suspiciously. "What is the...?"

That was all he had the opportunity to say before Bjólf kicked the door in, smashing Óflár's face and sending him flying back against a wooden pillar. As the pale man lay whimpering pathetically, snorting like a pig through his crushed, bleeding nose, Bjólf strode into the house, grabbed Óflár by his greasy hair, and dragged him out into the courtyard. He did not stop, but passed by his waiting crew and continued on towards the stockade gate, the snivelling screams of his writhing baggage drawing more and more people from their homes.

"Nothing to worry about," Gunnar reassured them. "Just sorting out a little rat infestation."

Bjólf, his anger growing, tugged harder, causing Óflár – bumping along the ground on his skinny rump, his hair almost wrenched from his head – to shriek all the more.

At the gate, the one-armed blacksmith, who was boiling nettles in a pot over a small fire, saw him coming, Halldís hurrying behind him, and the best part of Bjólf's crew behind her. Bjólf did not look like he was going to stop. Jumping to his feet, uncertain what to do, the blacksmith looked from Bjólf to Halldís and back again.

"Open the gates!" she called. The blacksmith and his fellow gatekeeper – a stout older man with no front teeth – fumbled with the heavy bar. Bjólf dumped Óflár on the ground and strode over to the blacksmith's bubbling pot.

"What is this?" he barked.

"Er... s-stingers," stuttered the blacksmith as they heaved the beam from the gates. "An infusion for my... Wha – ?"

But before he could say any more, Bjólf snatched up the pot, strode back to the wriggling form of Óflár and emptied the boiling contents into his lap. Óflár howled, pungent steam rising from his groin. Bjólf looped his arm through the pot's handle, took hold of Óflár's thin locks once more, and, with an expression of fury and disgust, marched out of the gates, dragging his screaming captive down the path to the harbour, where flames still licked at the jagged, sunken carcass of his ship.

HALLDÍS STOPPED AT the gates. None stepped past where she stood. Gunnar looked at her, questioningly. "Do you want us to..." The sentence ended in a kind of half nod towards the receding figures.

Halldís shook her head. "Let him deal with this in his own way."

"I don't understand," whispered Atli, embarrassed by his own ignorance. "What did Óflár do?"

Gunnar gave a grim laugh. "Pigeons are not only for eating," he said.

Atli, still confused, looked from one face to another.

"Messages, boy," said Godwin. "They also carry messages."

ALMOST AT THE water's edge, Bjólf hauled Óflár into the very centre of the circle of gore and released his grip. Óflár fell face first into human blood and offal, then recoiled and cried out in shock and revulsion, slipping in the slime, covering himself in it.

'This is your anointing," said Bjólf, a manic look in his eye, and strode about him. "Now prepare to ascend your throne!"

Grabbing him by the scruff of the neck, he dragged the wailing, writhing Óflár towards the stake, sat him roughly against it, and trussed him up with the ragged, blood-caked rope that had once bound Grimmsson.

"This is your mantle!" he bawled in Óflár's ear, pulling the bonds tight.

Óflár screamed in torment, his returning senses finally

beginning to grasp the full horror of his situation. He struggled feebly and looked about in panic. At the edge of the forest, upon the northern side, close to the water, could now be seen three death-walkers, their gait jerky and uneven, drawn from the forest by the sounds of death, the smell of blood.

Bjólf held the pot aloft and hammered hard upon it with the hilt of his sword. It rang out loudly like a crude, muffled bell.

"Come one, come all!" he cried. "Attend the court of King Óflár the Great!"

On the south side, now, another death-walker was visible. Bjólf turned and bowed to the whimpering, pleading creature at his feet. "Your majesty," he said, and jammed the nettle-pot roughly upon Óflár's head. A strange, humourless smile crossed his face. "You wished for a kingdom of your own. Well, now you have it. This is your kingdom." He gestured wildly with his sword blade. "And these your subjects!"

Óflár stared wild-eyed at the flames, the blood, the empty-eyed creatures that now stumbled towards him, sobbing and kicking ineffectually, like an infant. Bjólf straightened, staring down at Óflár with contempt. "I leave you to their wise counsel." With that he turned, and walked away, back to the stockade, where the distant screams were finally lost in the wind.

So ended the brief reign of Óflár, son of Hallthor.

# CHAPTER THIRTY-ONE

## OUT OF THE ASHES

FOR HOURS AFTERWARDS, Bjólf sat brooding in the watchtower, staring out towards the vast, blackened hole at the forest's edge, beneath which the embers of the ship still glowed. None dared approach him. Even brave Klaufi, whose watch this should have been, would not go near. An anxious Halldís had asked Gunnar to keep an eye on his friend. He hardly needed telling to do that, but he reassured her he would. Bjólf's men, meanwhile, lurked outside their tents in a state of dejection. Cheated of the opportunity to strike at Skalla, their only other means of attack now taken from them, they sat around the fire, dazed and directionless, and waited – for what, they knew not.

Then, when the smoke had finally ceased to rise, Gunnar looked towards the tower and saw Bjólf gone. Atli was sent clambering up the ladder, and found nothing but a knotted rope secured to the support and lowered to the outside. Off in the distance, he could see Bjólf trudging past Óflár's stripped bones, heading for the vessel's charred remains.

Some time passed before Bjólf was seen again. He called out at the gate, and when admitted marched in without a word, soaked through, a sack over his shoulder. Gunnar could not tell for certain what it contained, but it was something large and rounded in shape.

"We thought you had gone for the treasure," he said, striding alongside his captain and eyeing the sack with a curious frown.

"That can stay at the bottom of the river," said Bjólf. "No good to us here."

"Hmm," Gunnar nodded. "Probably all melted into one great lump, anyhow." Bjólf did not reply. "So, er... what's in the bag?" Gunnar tried his best to sound casual, but acting was not his strong point.

"You'll see."

When they reached their encampment by the great hall, Bjólf dumped the sack on the ground. His men gathered without any word needing to be spoken. Halldís and Frodi, deep in conversation with Godwin and Fjölvar, cut short their discussion and hurried over, Halldís forcing her way to the front.

Bjólf looked around at them all and smiled briefly at the company, then tucked his thumbs into his belt and began.

"We know now what this Skalla is about. He has formidable weapons, that much is clear. But our will is the stronger." There was a mutter of approval. "You are aggrieved at having been robbed of the chance to stand against him. I know that. You want nothing more than to heft your weapons at him and his kind. I know that too. He thinks us destroyed. That is in our favour. Now the time has come to make our attack upon him."

With that, he upended the sack, and a big, heavy lump of wood thudded onto the ground. Charred, sodden with river water, but still sound and clear in shape – the dragon's head from the *Hrafn*. Bjólf picked it up and held it before him. "She has passed through fire. But she will sail again."

A murmur passed through the men. "But how?" exclaimed

Gunnar, wondering, for a moment, whether his old friend had finally gone mad.

"We need more than a figurehead to carry us," said Njáll.

"Our ship is ash and embers," added Godwin. "Our only means of attack gone!"

"No!" said Bjólf, his eyes gleaming. "There is another..."

The men stared at each other in bewilderment, dumbstruck.

"Grimmsson's ship..." said Atli. He had spoken aloud without thinking, without realising he was doing it. The men looked at him in amazement.

"Grimmsson's ship," said Bjólf with a slow nod of his head, grinning broadly at the boy. A buzz of excitement suddenly gripped the crew; they chattered feverishly, some even laughing, enlivened by new possibilities.

"It was tethered," said Fjölvar. "It should still be there..."

Godwin nodded. "The death-walkers have no interest in ships. We know that much."

"But what if Skalla's men have discovered it?" said Kjötvi.

Úlf shook his head. "They knew of only one ship when they came today."

"We must act quickly," added Bjólf, "and get to it before it is found."

"How?" said Odo.

"We walk." Bjólf pointed past them all, towards the far end of the village, and the dark trees that lay beyond the stockade. "It lies southeast of here." He looked at Halldís. "A small bay, marked on one edge by a great boulder, half in the water."

"Ægir's Rock," She nodded. "I know it."

"How far?" asked Gunnar.

She shrugged. "A day. I can direct you. To the island in the fjord, too."

"But... the *forest*?" said Eyvind, a note of doubt in his voice. They had learned to fear the place in the last few days.

"The going would be hard," acknowledged Halldís. "The forest is dense, and the death-walkers wander its shadows."

"But they are lumbering beasts," said Gunnar. He hefted his axe. "We can handle them."

"Those 'lumbering beasts' wiped out Grimmsson's entire crew!" said Kjötvi.

"And Grimmsson's crew, we must assume, have joined their ranks," added Godwin. A few muttered their concern.

"But they were not prepared," said Bjólf. "Nor were we, that first night. But we know our enemy now."

Thorvald, who had survived the long vigil upon the ship when so many had perished, stepped forward, nodding. All fell silent. "We fared badly in our first encounter. But we learned quickly. They are slow, their behaviour simple. They do not hide the sound of their approach. On open ground, they can be easily seen. In the forest, easily heard. We have this one chance. My vote is to go."

Thorvald's words carried the weight to convince the doubters. "So, we have a plan!" announced Gunnar with delight, and gave his captain an almighty slap on the back.

"Gather provisions," called Bjólf. "And sharpen your blades. Tonight we sleep, and dream of wanton women. At first light we march to Skalla's ruin!"

# CHAPTER THIRTY-TWO

## THE STRANGER AT THE GATES

THE NEXT MORNING, the men assembled outside the great hall, fully armoured once more, strenghtened shields and bags of provisions upon their backs, helms hanging from their belts, and every weapon they could carry strapped to them. The preference was for heavy blades and clubs; few trusted to stabbing weapons on this trip. There were thirty of them in all, including the boy Atli, whose burden on this occasion was even greater than the rest. Bjólf trusted any one of them with his life, but it was a sobering thought, too often on his mind, that when they had first come to these shores, they had been forty strong.

A handful of men from Halldís's retinue had volunteered to join the raiding party, as Bjólf had expected they would. He admired the courage and determination of these men, all in the twilight of their years, and, despite being doubtful about their suitability for so arduous a mission, accepted them graciously.

They had suffered under Skalla for years; this, he felt, was their right. Their addition brought their numbers up to thirty five. Frodi was to stay, under strict instructions from Halldís, though it was clear that it rankled with the tough old warrior. A shame, thought Bjólf; he suspected this one would have proved a fearsome addition to the warband.

With a face like thunder, infuriated at having been denied a place – but kitted out for battle to honour those who were going to the fight – Frodi arrived with two stewards to escort Bjólf and his men to the gate on the far, landward side of the stockade. From here, they were to head into the forest along an old herding path, then strike out south-east for the shore of the fjord – and, they hoped, Grimmsson's waiting ship. Bjólf looked around, expecting to see Halldís nearby. He could not imagine that she would not be here to see them off. Yet it became clear that, for reasons known only to her, she had not come. Though he did not show it, his heart sank at the realisation.

Little was said. With curt nods of acnowledgement on either side, they set off, passing through an as yet unfamiliar part of Halldís's domain. Here, the houses and farmsteads were more scattered, the land increasingly dominated by agriculture. Penned animals and enclosed pasture jostled with a patchwork of cultivated fields in which were grown every kind of crop. Not a scrap of land was wasted. Yet, despite the impression of plenitude this gave, the skinny peasants who watched wide-eyed as the glittering band of warriors tramped past showed that this land, reduced as it was by the limits of the stockade and the demands of Skalla, struggled to sustain them.

Before long, they had reached the far boundary of the stockade wall, beyond which the dark edge of the forest loomed once more, appearing now more vast and threatening than ever. The old south gate, though clearly once the twin of the western entrance that opened to the harbour, now presented a very different demeanour. It stood like a monument to their self-imposed imprisonment, every aspect of it speaking not so much of neglect – though neglected it had certainly been – but of fear. It was impossible to tell when anyone had last dared to pass this way – it could not have been longer than the few years that the stockade had been in existence – but already the forest had begun to reclaim the great boles that had been so insolently torn from it. Invading ivy had forced its way between the trunks, its clinging fronds winding their way around the whole length of the wall, and around the gate itself had crept up the outside of the watchtowers, choking the lookout posts and tumbling over the top of the barrier in a great green wave, bringing with it a tangled profusion of briar, holly, elder and hazel. This whole section of the wall was dark with shadow, and it was only gradually, as his eyes adjusted to the gloom of this forgotten corner, that Bjólf became aware of a figure pacing slowly back and forth at the foot of the left tower, arms folded, head bowed and obscured by shadow.

At first, Bjólf assumed him to be a guard. But what was the point of that? No one came this way, and there seemed no possibility of ascending the watchtower. Besides, although his stature was modest, his dress and equipment were far beyond anything Klaufi or the blacksmith had to offer. Over a green tunic and brown leggings was a shimmering coat of mail, at his waist a richly decorated sword and a fine helm with gilded fittings, on his back a red shield bearing a sacred *valknut* motif inscribed in black, the knot of the slain: a symbol of Odin, and of battle. This man, whoever he was, was no peasant. He could only be another volunteer, reasoned Bjólf, yet none that he had seen were so youthful.

As they approached, the figure turned, unfolded its arms and stepped forward. The face – and the figure – were suddenly startlingly familiar. Halldís. The eyes of all the men widened at the sight. None of them had ever seen a woman dressed in such a fashion. The entire concept was outrageous. But, Bjólf had to admit, she wore it well. Halldís walked up briskly, giving Frodi a look somehow caught between defiance and apology, as if steeling herself for an argument whilst simultaneously hoping she might brazen it out.

"What is this?" Frodi demanded, suddenly stepping into the role of patriarch. Halldís, in response, immediately became the headstrong daughter.

"I'm going with them," she said, her head high, her tone resolute. "That is why I requested you stay, Frodi – to oversee things in my stead."

"But... you cannot..." blustered Frodi, his face red with indignation. "It's... inappropriate. And I made a promise to your father..."

Halldís stood her ground. "My father is dead. Were he here, he would do exactly as I am doing. I rule his hall now. This is my duty."

Frodi, for the moment, was lost for words – Bjólf could not be sure whether because he lacked a suitable argument, or was merely shamed by the fact that a slip of a woman was going to battle while he stayed at home. The *vikingr* captain smiled to himself and stepped forward, folding his arms and rubbing his chin and regarding Halldís with an air of careful consideration.

"Your duty it may be," he said. "But this is my raid, and all here are under my command."

She held his gaze, knowing she was indeed at his mercy, quietly fuming at the thought as she stepped from foot to foot. "You need me," she said. "I promised to show you the way."

"I assumed you meant a map."

"I am the map."

Bjólf gestured to the small party of local men who had joined them. "I'm sure any of these gentlemen could do as good a job in their own land." One of the volunteers began to nod enthusiastically at this, then thought better of it as his mistress shot him a withering look.

She stood for a moment, frowning like a truculent child, unable to counter his argument. But behind the angry defiance, he could see, was a look of desperation – one that fervently implored him to let her do this.

"Give me one good reason why you should come," he said.

"Because my people are worthy of it. Because I have a score to settle with Skalla. Because I am at least equal to an old man or a boy!"

Bjólf shrugged. "All good reasons," he said. "You are free to join us if you so choose." She looked triumphant, relieved.

Her instinct was to throw her arms around Bjólf. This time, she restrained herself.

"What?" protested Frodi. "I cannot allow it!"

"You cannot prevent it!" she replied.

"Then it is my duty to accompany you – to protect you. Nothing can induce me to stay."

"Someone must stay, Frodi," she said, a note of pleading in her voice. "The people –"

"Will carry on as they have always done, whether we are here or not," he interrupted. "Cooking, chopping wood, tending crops and cattle, they don't need us for that. They never have!" She looked momentarily outraged at the suggestion. He tempered his tone. "If we succeed, then their future will be saved. If we fail, and never return... why, all are doomed, and what difference then?"

Halldís said nothing, casting her eyes down to the ground. It was clear to all that the debate would be resolved only one way. Having argued her own case with such passion, Halldís could hardly deny Frodi his place.

Bjólf smiled at Gunnar. "The more, the merrier," he said.

The big man did not look wholly impressed.

"Thirty-seven," said Bjólf in his ear, reassuringly. "Almost back to full strength."

Gunnar frowned and muttered to himself. "Some old men, a woman, and a boy..."

And so the huge, moss-covered bolt was heaved from the gate, the thick tangle of vines and creepers hacked away. Slowly, falteringly the great gates were hauled apart; the siezed, swollen hinges resisting, the last of the creepers clinging to the damp, heavy wood.

Their first sight was a dispiriting one.

Against the right hand gate, as if its owner had expired where he stood whilst clawing to get in, was a human skeleton. The bones were wrapped and intertwined by twisting, grasping tendrils of ivy, which formed about them a weird, surrogate flesh. Who this once had been, and where they had come from, none could tell. Gunnar prodded at it with his axe. From a cavity in its skull a shiny brown centipede scuttled. "Well," he said with a sigh. "At least this one isn't still moving."

Ahead of them, beyond the opening, stretched the long forgotten path, its edges blurred by a profusion of growth that had crept from the forest on either side: bracken, black hellebore, patches of spindly hemlock, and here and there the clustered red berries of cuckoo pints and the collapsed remains of gigantic foxgloves. Above, what had once been completely open to the air had now grown over, the branches meeting and forming a bridge across which the riotous vines had already begun to find their way, threatening to turn the trackway into a gloomy tunnel of branch, stem and leaf.

Underfoot, along the mossy, rutted trackway itself, bindweed had cast a choking web, slowly strangling the few flowering plants that dared to poke their heads through it. Nonetheless, the way ahead was clear, and the obstacles few. The going on this part of the journey would be good. What it would be like when they finally had to plunge into the dark trees that loomed up on either side, they could not guess.

As the warriors passed beyond the gates, Frodi turned back to his two anxious stewards. "Bar the gate firmly behind us," he said. Then, before turning away, added: "Hope for our return, but do not wait for it."

With these gloomy words, the huge, bone-wreathed gates closed behind them with a dull thud, and the party began its long march to a distant and unknown fate.

# CHAPTER THIRTY-THREE

## THE STRANGER AT THE GATES

IN SPITE OF the forbidding presence that pressed in upon either side – or perhaps in defiance of it – the mood of the travellers was bouyant. The steady rhythm and sense of purpose, grim though it was, had lifted their spirits, and for much of the morning – walking two or three abreast, with Bjólf and Gunnar at their head – they set a brisk pace, encountering no other living creature, not a sound of movement other than the creaking and cracking of the great old trees. The only reminders of any kind of human presence were the small, grey way-stones that punctuated the route at regular intervals, half-hidden by the invading bracken. Halldís, who followed close behind with Frodi and Atli, paused to scrutinise each one as it appeared, noting the markings upon them – signs that meant nothing to Bjólf – often crouching to scrape off a coat of moss or lichen. One of these, she said, would indicate their point of departure from the path.

All had agreed that the wisest course of action was to move as silently as possible through the trees. For much of the way, the only noises to be heard were their footfalls and the clink of mail and weapons – sounds that they knew would not carry far in the dead, baffled air of the forest. After a time – with the death-walkers, for the moment, all but forgotten – they began to relax into the journey, enjoying what simple pleasures were offered: the sharp, fresh smell of foliage as it was crushed underfoot and the dappled sunlight that filtered between the gently swaying branches. Now and then, someone would gently hum a tune in time with their step. They even began to allow themselves hushed conversations.

"So," muttered Gunnar, leaning in towards Bjólf. "About this farm..."

Bjólf looked at him quizzically.

"The farm," repeated Gunnar insistently. "To retire to."

"Ah," said Bjólf with a nod. "The farm."

"I can see it in my mind's eye," said Gunnar, going off into a reverie. "Cattle and pigs. Good dark soil. Fresh green pasture. A clear stream running through it, coming down from a mountain. A big solid barn and a big solid woman at the farmhouse door."

"It has a distinct appeal."

"But where is it? That's the part that's frustrating me."

Bjólf shrugged. "Denmark?"

Gunnar wrinkled his nose and shook his head. "Full of Germans."

"Norway then? Vestfold?"

"I have a price on my head, remember?"

Bjólf sighed at the memory. A costly night's drinking that turned out to be. He returned to the problem at hand. "Obviously not Sweden."

"Obviously."

"Iceland?"

"Too far."

"You're not making this easy for yourself."

Gunnar gazed off into the distance. "I always fancied England. Good soil. Nice climate."

"You and ten thousand other Norsemen. The English are more likely to welcome you with an open grave than open arms..."

Gunnar sighed. Before he could speak again, Bjólf halted him with a hand upon his chest. Behind them, the rest of the party stopped short. Up ahead, some distance away, was a figure. Gunnar blinked hard; uncertain, at first, whether he was seeing right. But there was no doubting it. Standing in the middle of the path, staring at the ground where the ferns emerged from the left edge of the forest and turned slightly away from them, was what appeared to be a young woman; naked, pale, motionless but for a gentle swaying, as if she were just another of the trees being rocked by the wind.

"Is she one of them?" whispered Gunnar.

"If she is not," replied Bjólf, "she is a long way from home." He could not imagine what terrible circumstances – what madness – could have driven anyone here in such a state.

Bjólf turned, and, signalling to Fjölvar, motioned him forward. "Have an arrow ready," he whispered. Fjölvar nodded, and took his bow from his back. Bjólf advanced towards her in slow, creeping steps, making his footfalls as light as possible, all the while trying to maintain a clear line between the girl and Fjölvar's bow.

But for the slow swaying, she did not move as he approached. Her flesh, though pallid, appeared entirely unmarked; her long red hair hung loose down her back and over her face and breast, occasionally shifting as it was caught by the breeze. By Bjólf's reckoning she was little more than twenty summers old. He had by now convinced himself that she must indeed be the victim of some other tragedy, some other derangement of mind, and, being close, was about to speak out to her when, thanks to his own wandering attention, something snapped beneath his foot. Her head whirled around.

Now there was no doubt.

Her red-rimmed eyes, once beautiful, were as cold and colourless as a fish, her blue-lipped mouth lolling open. Around her neck, he now saw, was the blue-black mark left by a rope. She lurched towards him, her lips curling back as if about to utter some inhuman cry, when Bjólf felt Fjölvar's arrow hiss past his cheek and her head jolted suddenly back. She stood motionless for a moment, the arrow in her eye pointed skyward, then crumpled awkwardly to the ground.

It was a grim lesson to them all. The members of the party moved forward and, one by one, crept quietly past her body. Fjölvar averted his eyes as he passed, somehow more affected by this than any of the previous clashes. Halldís, too, shuddered as she looked upon her and felt the image burning into her memory. Though trying to resist the thought, she could not help but see herself in this wretched figure. Her in another life, with another fate. She did not want to believe that it was a fate that perhaps awaited her still.

"Do you suppose she did that to herself?" mused Gunnar as they walked, gesturing to his neck. Bjólf said nothing, and focused his attention on the path ahead.

After that weird encounter, all were greatly subdued – reminded of what lay ahead and wary of what still lurked nearby. It seemed the uncanny emptiness of the forest closer to the stockade – normally a source of unease, but today a cause for cheer – could no longer be relied upon. Twice afterwards they heard, from somewhere amongst the trees, the melancholy groan of some dead, wandering thing. They maintained their silence, and kept on moving.

It was not long after that Bjólf noticed Halldís, crouching at one of the way-stones with their indecipherable runes, sigh deeply and give the forest beyond a lingering, apprehensive look. It was the look he had been waiting for. She stood and turned to him, but he already knew what was coming.

"This is the place," she whispered, then indicated a spot just along from the stone, no more than a vague thinning of the dense foliage. "There was a path here, but it will be difficult to follow. We must maintain a course south-east – or we will never find our way." Bjólf signalled to his men and peered into the dark interior, where no sun, no guiding light, seemed to penetrate.

Then he drew his sword and, slicing through the clinging, tangled vines, plunged into the dank, all-enveloping darkness.

# CHAPTER THIRTY-FOUR

## IN DARK TREES

AT FIRST THE way ahead seemed impossible. Even in the cleft where the old path had once passed through, a thick profusion of thorny twigs and decaying brambles, piled almost shoulder-high, clung and clawed at them as they stumbled forward into the darkness, the sharp points scratching flesh, catching onto belts and scraping against metal. Their blades caught as they swung to hack it down, and when they struck at it, the thicket sprang back at them, raising a rank mildewy dust that stung their nostrils and made their eyes stream. Many donned their helms to protect their heads and eyes from the lash of the vicious, thorny briars that arched unseen and whipped about them as they moved.

Then, quite suddenly, the dense, woody thicket seemed to relent. The clinging knot of vines dwindled. The snarling, grasping thorns thinned. The way ahead cleared. Bjólf stumbled forward, unimpeded but almost blind, hand held out before him, his toes catching on exposed tree roots. With each step, unseen things crunched underfoot.

As they moved deeper in and their vision adjusted to the gloom, they found themselves in a strange netherworld. The impression was of having entered a vast, subterranean network of green-tinged caverns. From the huge trees – of immeasurable age – spread a floor of gnarled, contorted roots beneath their feet, and a twisted, vaulted canopy of living wood above their heads.

Here, it was too dark even to support the thorny guardians that lined the forest's edge – but, around the twisting roots, the collapsed skeletons of their ancestors littered the woodland floor, some still writhing along the ground with the semblance of life, others, far older, mouldered and decayed almost to dust. It was these brittle remains that snapped and crunched beneath their feet – but here and there, Bjólf could now see, there were also intertwined the whitened bones of small creatures – the tiny, jewel-like skeletons of shrews, the skulls and backbones of rats. Lying undisturbed where they had fallen, they attested to the utter deadness of this place.

There would be no fresh game eaten today.

When it had teemed with life, bears and wolves had been masters of this wood. Then, when some troubled instinct had driven them away, foxes and badgers had held sway – and, when they too withdrew, their prey had briefly flourished. Now, not even the smallest of furred or feathered creatures chose to make its nest here.

In their absence, other, tinier creatures had taken hold, the last inheritors of this doomed realm. Among the branches, their principal predator – now master of the forest – had built a vast and elaborate empire; everywhere about, between every bough and twig, were the webs of spiders, sticking to the warriors' faces as they advanced. They had grown huge and fat in their unchallenged domain, and swayed heavily at the centre of their silky, fly-dotted homes as the party pushed past, or scuttled off to the safety of the trees where the warriors' passing left them torn and wrecked.

Above them, where only the slightest chinks of clear light occasionally penetrated, the towering trunks of the trees swayed and twisted with the passing wind, their gnarled, interlocking boughs emitting eerie creaks and strange melancholy groans, as if speaking to one another in some long-forgotten language. What they spoke of were strong winds passing somewhere up above, yet beneath the canopy, the air was as still as a tomb; flat, heavy and lifeless.

Into it, charging the atmosphere with their rank odour, great yellow brackets of fungi projected, and vivid red toadstools dotted with white thrust up their poisonous heads in profusion – the only colours that disturbed the unremitting browns and blacks of this weird kingdom.

Bjólf could not tell for how long they silently picked their way through this oppressive underworld. Time seemed to stand still. Death-walkers, if they did penetrate this far, might wander forever and never see daylight – or else end up pinned amongst the thorny brambles of the forest's edge like one of the insects trapped in the great silvery skein of spiders' webs.

They did not stop to eat or rest in this forsaken place. Some of the party chewed on strips of dried meat as they went, each according to their hunger, none able to tell now whether the time for eating was due or had long since past. Even so, the going that day seemed painfully slow. For as long as they could, the party had kept to where the covering of forest floor appeared thinnest, believing this must be what remained of the old path. But after a time, even that subtle distinction utterly disappeared. Finally, Halldís stopped and looked about in confusion and panic, her sense of direction gone, the silent labyrinth of trees seeming to stretch out equally in every direction, offering no clue to their place on the earth. She suddenly was struck by the fear that they had wandered in circles, and would forever be hopelessly lost. In the gloom, Bjólf saw her agitation, and understood.

"Kjötvi!" he called. Kjötvi the Lucky limped forward, his expression, as ever, one of anxiety. "South-east," said Bjólf.

Kjötvi frowned and looked about, squinted up at the distant

glimmers of light up above, then ahead. He gave a sniff, and made a casual gesture. "This way."

Bjólf smiled at the astonished Halldís, and all continued on, with Kjötvi now at their head.

The first sign that Kjötvi's instincts were correct came from an unexpected source. Fjölvar, who was now leading with Kjötvi, stopped suddenly and dropped to his knee. Up ahead, in the semi-darkness, a different shape – the shape of a man. It was big, this one, dressed in a fine red tunic, broadly belted at the waist. Like the woman on the path, it stood swaying, head bowed, apparently without purpose. Was this what the death-walkers did, wondered Bjólf, when they could not scent human flesh?

Gunnar stepped forward, hefting his axe. "Time I had a go," he said, and, without hesitation, without waiting for a reply, started his swift approach. With his axe raised above his shoulder, he accelerated towards his target, bounding forward, his feet picking deftly from root to root in steady rhythm. Bjólf smiled to himself. The big man could be surprisingly nimble when there was a need.

The death-walker had hardly raised its head before Gunnar's axe crashed down upon it, splitting its skull wide open. The figure reeled forward against a tree and slid to earth, leaving the glistening contents of its head splattered upon the trunk. As he approached, Bjólf saw Gunnar turn the figure over, frown at what he saw, then turn it back onto its face.

Gunnar said nothing as he rejoined the others, but, as they continued on their way, he sidled up to Bjólf and spoke to him in hushed tones.

"Something you should know. That one I just killed... I killed him before." Bjólf frowned at him. "A crewman of Grimmsson's. I drove my spear through his heart during the fight at the fjord."

"Are you certain?"

"The spear-point was sheared off in his chest. Still in him. I'd know it anywhere."

"Then we must be close."

"But if we're close, where are the rest of them?" said Gunnar.

Bjólf said nothing. Gunnar had not expected an answer. But he understood. For now, he would keep this to himself.

As they continued to advance, encounters with isolated *draugr* became more frequent. All were dispatched swiftly and ruthlessly; only one had managed to utter a sound before Úlf's mace smashed its head to oblivion, and if any of its fellows had heard its call, they were left far behind. Unsettling as this development was, most felt it a welcome diversion from the seemingly endless torpor of the dark forest, and they understood that it also meant their destination was near.

Another welcome change came over their surroundings as they trudged resolutely on. The trees became less dense, the light stronger, the ground softer underfoot, cushioned now by a carpet of damp leaves. Quite suddenly, it seemed, they looked around and found the whole of the forest had changed about them; the thick, ancient boles of oak and ash had given way to tall, straight trunks of pine and golden-leaved beech, through which shimmering sunlight filtered. The air had changed, too; fresh, now, with the sharp, pleasing scent of the pine needles that they crushed underfoot as they passed. All around, the forest floor was speckled with tiny flowering plants. Spirits were raised, and their pace quickened as they strode out, confidence in their mission growing once more.

The warband moved differently now the landscape allowed it, with Finn and Eyvind up ahead scouting the path, and the rest in a close-knit group behind, keeping the scouts in sight. No death-walkers had been seen for some time, and the sun – which showed it to be late afternoon – was slanting low through the trees when a whistle went up from Finn. The men halted and dropped to their knees, but Bjólf saw Finn turn and wave him on. He stood, leading the party towards the spot where the two scouts now stood.

They were at the edge of a wide open space, their attention fixed on something ahead. As he approached, a great clearing opened up before him. Devoid of trees but dotted with old, rotted stumps and ragged patches of gorse, it was carved in two by the course of a small stream – barely more than a ditch – which cut a deep groove across the space from their far left to the distant right corner. What had caught Finn and Eyvind's attention, however, was what was standing in a bare, sandy patch of ground right in the middle of it, a little way back from the stream. Upright, motionless but for a familiar swaying motion, its back to them and its head on one side as if idly contemplating something upon the ground, was another death-walker, its stark shadow making a long, dark mark across the scrubby soil.

But this was unlike any of the creature they had seen so far. It was a surreal, unthinkable figure – from head to foot so utterly dark and featureless that it appeared as if merely some bizarre extension of the shadow it cast. At first, struggling to make sense of what he saw, he thought it might be a Moorish man, like the dark-skinned traders with whom he had dealt in the southern sea – perhaps a member of Grimmsson's crew. But that couldn't account for the impossibly pitch-black hue, the weird uniformity of it, nor the fact that the entire surface of its body seemed to be moving.

As Bjólf looked on, a strange feeling of disgust rising in him, the man's skin seemed to constantly shimmer and shift in the sunlight, as if it were bubbling.

"Gods," said Gunnar beside him. "What now?"

Eyvind took a step forward, his sword drawn, then paused to look back at Bjólf. Bjólf nodded his assent. "Stay sharp," he said. "Take no chances."

Eyvind moved slowly, silently towards the strange vision. As he drew close, the party saw him shudder, and stop. He looked back, an expression of hideous bemusement upon his face, then turned to the figure once again, his blade raised in readiness.

"Hey!' he called. The figure did not move. Eyvind called to them over his shoulder, a note of baffled incredulity in his voice. "You need to see this."

Bjólf motioned for the others to move up behind with him. "Stay together. Watch the trees," he whispered. As he approached close to where his scout stood, the explanation – the truth that

Eyvind had found so indescribable – became horrifyingly clear. The entire surface of the man's body was covered in millions upon millions of black ants – crawling, moving, clinging to his body and to each other in such profusion that no hint of the man beneath – if man it were – could now be discerned.

"You ever seen anything like that before?" muttered Eyvind.

Bjólf could only gaze in horrified astonishment. He looked momentarily at Halldís, her hand held across her mouth in revulsion. When he turned back, Eyvind was reaching toward the figure, about to prod it with his sword point.

"No!" exclaimed Bjólf. But he was too late. A horde of the ants had immediately swarmed up the blade and onto Eyvind's hand. "Ouch!" he exclaimed, laughing nervously, swatting at them. "They bite!" But the laugh rapidly died away, became a cry of pain, as fresh blood ran where they had taken hold. Flecks of blood flew from his swatting fingertips, and the black mass that covered the death-walker suddenly surged outward from its feet, flowing across the sandy ground like a glossy liquid and up over Eyvind's legs. He screamed in horror as they swarmed into his clothes, over his face, into his hair, covering him in a manic, teeming, blood-hungry carpet of black.

As all the others stood powerless, paralysed by shock and confusion, one man stepped forward to help; Arngrimm, the volunteer from Björnheim who had so enthusiastically supported Bjólf at the gate. He reached out instinctively to Eyvind.

"Don't touch him!" shouted Bjólf. Though only moments had passed, Eyvind had already collapsed to his knees, his hands clasped helplessly to his head, his flesh being stripped from his bones before their eyes. Arngrimm stopped half way between Bjólf and Eyvind, looking from one to the other, suddenly realising his mistake. But before he could rectify it, the black swarm was on his boots, rising up his legs and working its way into every opening and crevice. He turned and tried to run, his face red, his eyes wide in panic. Bjólf and the others backed away rapidly, looking around for some means of escape from this new enemy.

"The stream!" called Atli. "Cross the stream!"

The boy led the way, his burden bumping against his back as he ran, and without hesitation the rest hurried after, hurling themselves across the narrow strip of flowing water and running for all they were worth. Arngrimm, struggling desperately to follow, stumbled, his legs giving way. As Bjólf looked back over his shoulder, he saw the black insect horde swarm over the old man, covering his eyes and flowing into his open mouth until his strangled cries were finally silenced.

# CHAPTER THIRTY-FIVE

## NIGHT GUESTS

For some time they ran, past the clearing and on into the scattering of tall pines beyond. They had just started to slow when Halldís finally called out for them to stop. She was supporting one of the old men from the village; he was sweating profusely, panting in hoarse, gasping breaths. It had been many years since he had been called upon to run while kitted out for combat.

"Rest!" called Bjólf.

The party halted; the old man slumped gratefully to the floor. Few of the rest seemed keen to do the same. Many of them poked about in the loose carpet of pine needles with their sword points, reluctant to sit upon it, or swiped at their clothes nervously and scratched at themselves. They could hardly be blamed. Every step, it seemed, brought some new terror, some undreamt-of threat. Atli sat on his baggage – which he was finally now able to drop – and looked up as Bjólf wandered over to him.

"Good thinking, little man," the captain said, clapping him on the shoulder.

Atli smiled at the acknowledgement. Then, after a moment of thought, he said: "So, when do I stop being 'little'?"

Bjólf looked back in surprise. Some of those within earshot laughed aloud. Atli held his gaze unflinchingly, and for the first time, perhaps, seemed not a boy, but a man.

A smile creased Bjólf's face. "Maybe today. Good thinking, Atli, son of Ivarr..." Then he pinched Atli's arm. "Though you could always do with a bit more muscle."

Gunnar laughed. "Atli the Strong!"

Some of the men chortled at the irony. It seemed to be the way these nicknames worked, either describing the one distinguishing attribute of the individual – Two-Axe, Long-Beard – or stating something that was the complete opposite of the truth – Kjötvi the Lucky, Atli the Strong. Atli didn't mind. He knew how it was meant. To give a name, even in jest, was their way of showing him respect – of showing he was one of them. He was happy to laugh along with his comrades.

It served another purpose, too. To help him put from his mind an image that he had carried with him from the clearing. As they ran, he had looked back. On the ground, collapsed just short of the stream, was Arngrimm – or, at least, the shape of Arngrimm, still writhing and twitching beneath the shifting, devouring shroud of black. Behind him, in a disordered heap, lay what remained of Eyvind. Now mostly abandoned by the insect horde, he had been reduced to a lifeless skeleton, the low sun that, moments before, had shone upon his smiling face now glancing through the gaps between his stripped bones. And then – somehow, the most horrific sight of all – there had been the lone death-walker. Now bereft of its covering of frantically milling legions of ants, the ghastly state of its flesh was now fully revealed. The skin had been entirely removed, and beneath the body had been bored and reamed by a million tiny mouths, leaving some parts barely covered, and others, that had not pleased them, almost untouched. The head was stripped of features – the nose eaten away, the ears gone, only dark, dry pits for eyes. Its teeth and ribs shone white in the sun, and along its limbs, exposed tendons were visible, stretched like wires. And yet – and it was this that made Atli shudder – it still stood, swaying gently, waiting for its now destroyed and useless senses to pick up the scent or sound of prey.

As THEY GATHERED themselves and continued through the towering pines, Gunnar again caught up with Bjólf, who was walking with Halldís ahead of the main group. She look pale and distraught at what she had witnessed. Although Gunnar and Bjólf and the others were no less appalled, they at least had developed their own ways, over the years, of dealing with such hideous events. Gunnar looked at Bjólf, uncertain whether to speak. Bjólf encouraged him with a nod.

"Have you ever seen ants attack the living like that?" said Gunnar.

"No," said Bjólf.

"Poor Eyvind..." Gunnar shook his head, then cast a glance at Halldís. "You might have warned us you had such pests in your forest."

Halldís shot him a fearsome look. "Do you really think I would have kept silent about such a thing? There are no such creatures... and we also lost a man, every bit as fine as your 'poor Eyvind'!" With that she stalked off ahead, leaving Gunnar irritated and bemused.

"They had feasted upon the flesh of a death-walker," said Bjólf, "and so had become of its kind. That is why they so hungered for human flesh."

Gunnar took a moment to absorb the implications.

"It is spreading to the beasts, Gunnar. We must be more vigilant than ever – and thank our luck that no larger creatures remain here."

Gunnar fell into silent, gloomy reflection as they trudged on their way.

As they went, Bjólf began to notice decaying stumps where trees had once been felled, and even occasional indications of well-worn paths. There were signs of habitation here, though how recent, he could not tell.

They did not have to wait long. Quite suddenly, the way before them opened into a broad, grassy glade, its earthy colours glowing in the low, early evening sun. Worn trackways led through it, and at its heart, casting a long, deep shadow, stood a small, solid farmhouse built of pine logs and, opposite, a great old barn. An abandoned cart stood to one side. It was an uncanny feeling, happening upon signs of such ordinary life in the middle of so forbidding a forest; a haven of normality in the midst of a nightmare. Bjólf hoped it was yet another sign that they were near their goal.

Clearly there was no life here now. No smoke rose from the house. There was neither sight nor sound of any animal. Tall weeds grew through the wheels of the cart, and the hay in the exposed loft of the barn was honeycombed with long-deserted rat-runs. Nevertheless, Bjólf felt comforted by the familiarity of the scene.

When he looked at Halldís, however, her expression was downcast.

"What is it?"

She frowned, digging deep into her memories. "I know this place – from my childhood. It is Erling's farm."

"A fiercely independent old man," added Frodi. "He built all this himself. How, I cannot imagine."

Bjólf smiled and looked around. "Erling. That was my father's name."

Halldís sighed. "We are further south than intended."

"Can we not correct our course?"

"Easily. But it means our progress has also been slower than I thought."

Bjólf shaded his eye with his hand and peered towards the sun, already dipping below the tops of the trees. "How far is it? Will we make it before dark?"

Halldís shook her head, gloomily. Bjólf thought to himself, and looked about, then turned back to them, his mood remaining resolutely buoyant. "Then fate has favoured our party, blessing us with a roof under which to spend the night."

"I thought you did not believe in fate," said Halldís.

Bjólf gave her a broad grin. "When it turns my way, I don't fight it."

Before the light had faded, Bjólf and his men had set about clearing and securing house and barn for the night. Both had seen better days, but to the weary travellers, they were luxurious.

The only argument had been over who took the house, and who took the barn. Those in the house would have the additional comfort of a fire – something they could not have risked in the open air – but the dwelling could accommodate no more than a dozen at most. Bjólf had insisted that Halldís and her people lodge there, and that they at least be joined by Atli, Kjötvi, Gunnar and Godwin – the former two because they had served them well that day (and, Bjólf knew, were less robust than the rest); the latter because they would provide good protection for the others. Bjólf himself would join the men in the barn.

And here the argument began. Led by Njáll and stoked by Fjölvar, the men, fighting back mischievous smiles, started to suggest that Bjólf's place was in the house, that he had things to look after there, that the house offered the warmth he needed. Bjólf, refusing to get drawn in, mortified at such comments in front of their noble host, attempted to steer the conversation back to the matter in hand. But the men, seeing him on the run, would have none of it – surely he would be needed to stoke the fire during the night, they asked?

Halldís was not slow to pick up on the innuendo. She feigned haughty offence before him, but, seeing Bjólf's embarrassment, was soon sniggering along at his expense. When he finally realised that she was colluding in the joke, he caved in and accepted his lot, to a cheer from the crew. Afterwards, much to her further amusement, several said a polite "good night" to Halldís – one or two even apologising with rather touching sincerity for their crude behaviour. She thanked them, keeping as straight a face as possible.

Huddled around the glowing hearth, leaning against the thick pillars, they talked and ate their simple rations and laughed into the night – their trials, for the moment, forgotten. One by one, as the food and the warmth of the fire worked upon them, they succumbed to sleep, until finally Bjólf realised he was the last awake. Gently drawing a thick sheepskin more snugly around the slumbering Halldís, he gazed upon her features for a moment before settling himself down for the night. As he drifted off, the last thing of which he was aware was the voice of Úlf, raised in gentle song, wafting from the barn.

BJÓLF AWOKE TO a sudden crash.

Leaping up, bleary-eyed, he whirled around, his sword already in his hand. The interior of the house was still in darkness, but for the fire's dim glow, but he could just make out Gunnar's shape at the window. The shutter was flung wide open, and, slumped through it, Gunnar's axe still in its head, was the figure of a man, his long, neat braids of hair hanging like thin ropes. Even in this gloom, Bjólf could recognise the grey, lifeless flesh of a death-walker.

"It's all right," whispered Gunnar as the others stirred. "I think it's just a stray one." He went to heave his axe from its bony cleft, but as he pulled, instead of the blade springing free, the whole head came away from its body. Gunnar stood for a moment, a blackly comical figure, staring quizzically at the head still stuck upon his axe. "I just need to deal with this," he said, and made for the door.

He had just swung the door open, and was standing with his foot upon his late victim's face, working the axe free, when a look towards the barn made him stop dead.

"Gods..."

"What is it?" whispered Bjólf, stepping up beside him. But now he could see for himself.

Filling the open space between the house and the barn was a numberless multitude of pale, ungainly figures – some mindlessly jostling each other as they crowded into the courtyard, others, in one and twos, still staggering out from the trees to join the tottering throng. Most had been men, well-dressed and powerfully built: Grimmsson's crew. Some were dragging broken or twisted limbs, listing awkwardly to one side or showing other strange contortions that spoke of terrible wounds to their bodies. Others, with no apparent mark upon them, shuffled forward like sleepwalkers. But all were relentlessly focused on the same goal – the place to which all their faces were turned, all their bodies pushed, and all their paths led: the open door of the barn.

A knot of them crushed clumsily in at the doorway, others pressing in behind. Many had evidently already made it inside. From within there were sounds of struggle. A crash. Urgent shouting. Then a scream. The sounds elicited a chorus of moans from the lifeless multitude. Some reached out. Others that had been wandering with little sense of direction now picked up their pace, and started to stagger directly for the source of the pain, the source of food. As they watched, a death-walker flew suddenly backwards out of the barn, an arrow in its neck, bowling several others over. More surged forward to take their place, their sluggish frenzy growing, their bodies funnelling doggedly, unrelentingly into the barn's dark interior, until it seemed the place would burst at the seams.

"Well, now we know what became of Grimmsson's crew." muttered Gunnar.

"We must do something," said Bjólf, the desperate plight of the two dozen trapped men ringing in the night air.

"But what?" said Gunnar in despair. "We cannot fell them all!"

Bjólf turned back into the house and began flinging things about wildly, Halldís, Atli and the others shrinking back from him in alarm. Finally he turned to Gunnar, having found what he sought: three torches, their tops soaked in pitch. "You remember how Ingjald the Ill-Ruler treated the Swedish kings who feasted in his hall?"

Gunnar nodded.

"Find your way around the back and get our men out any way you can," said Bjólf, placing his helm on his head. "Take

Godwin, Atli and Kjötvi with you. I'll take care of the rest."

Gunnar and the others hastily threw their gear about them and broke from the door, heading off into the darkness far to the right. Bjólf, taking one of the torches, thrust it into the fire until the flames took hold, then stood poised at the door, sword in one hand, torch in the other.

"What of us?" said Halldís.

He turned to her, the torchlight illuminating his face, glinting off the metal. "Stay here with Frodi and his men, and make no sound. You will see soon enough whether I have succeeded."

And with his flame roaring in the wind, he was gone.

# CHAPTER THIRTY-SIX

## INGJALD'S STRATAGEM

As HE RAN, his bag weighing heavily upon his back, Atli's mind flashed back to the terrible night before the stockade. But this time was different. This time, fear was no longer his enemy. Moving in a wide arc, they passed swiftly and silently behind the last of the death-walkers, that flocked mindlessly towards the sound and scent of death. Now and again a straggler appeared before them, emerging from the trees, slowed in its progress by some grievous, ugly wound. The axes of Godwin and Gunnar dealt with them.

Soon, they stood at the rear of the towering barn. Within, an arm's length away on the other side of the wooden wall, they could hear the cries of their fellows, the scrape and scratch as they fought for their lives.

Gunnar did not hesitate. "Watch our backs," he said to Atli and Kjötvi, and he and Godwin immediately set about the barn's thick planks with their axes.

Splinters flew. Inside, men heard the blows, and shouts went up. A section of plank flew free. Gunnar stopped his axe short just in time to avoid slicing through the arm that sprang though the gap.

"Stand back!" he bellowed, his cry echoed by the muffled, desperate voices inside.

They set about the planks once more as the limb was hastily withdrawn, chopping through the wall, chunks of wood flying, pulling off another length, then the piece above it, until there was a rough opening half as big as a man.

Njáll appeared through the gap, red-faced and sweating. "Took your bloody time!" he said, and dived out onto the ground.

More followed. One by one they were hauled out of that death-trap, then, as the hole was broken wider, they came bowling and wriggling out two at a time, the cries and groans of the death-walkers growing all the while, the walls creaking and shaking from the pressure of the undead host within.

All could see a moment of crisis was approaching. "Fetch the cart!" called Gunnar. Atli, Kjötvi and several of their rescued shipmates ran to the old wagon and heaved it around the corner. "When I give the word, push it against the opening."

"There's people still alive in there!" said Njáll, smashing a ghoul with his mace as it appeared suddenly in the gap, moments after Halfdan had flung himself through. Death-walkers were pressing at the ragged hole now, plugging it with their own unwieldy bodies, their arms flailing and grasping, Godwin barely holding them at bay with a broken plank. "Whenever you're ready..." he called out. The surrounding walls bulged and groaned under the pressure, threatening to give way.

"We cannot wait," said Gunnar, then muttered under his breath, "May their spirits forgive me..." At his command they rolled the cart hard against the barn, and the last means of escape was blocked for good.

BJÓLF, MEANWHILE, HAD been attending to the more daring part of the plan.

As he had stood in the doorway of the farmhouse, it had been clear that stealth alone could not help him. Fire was his greatest weapon, but it also ensured that his approach could not be hidden. His attack would require speed. As he watched, death-walkers were still cramming themselves into the barn, as if desperate to fulfil their part of his plan. But at least twenty more stood between him and the barn door, scattered across his path. There would be nothing for it but to run the gauntlet of the creatures, forcing his way past them before they had time to respond.

He squinted into the darkness, trying to read the features of the barn door itself, then scanned the open hay loft high above. He had to time it exactly right. The attempt could not be allowed to fail; there would be only one chance.

Suddenly, the moment of decision was taken from his hands. When he lowered his eyes, they met the face of a straggling death-walker turning directly towards him, its attention caught by his flame. It let out a weird, urgent moan, and others turned at its cry, joining it. It was now or never. He spoke his parting words to Halldís, then charged, his torch flaming behind him.

There was no time for finesse. Head low, shoulder forward, he slammed into the first walker, his helm smashing into its teeth, sending it flying. More turned at the sound of the impact. He swung his sword around, catching the second across the side of its neck, sending its head off at an impossible angle – a killing blow. It dropped like a stone, but directly towards him, its full weight catching his legs as it fell, sending him sprawling. The torch spun out of his grip, landing at the feet of another figure; a great bearded lump of a man in a studded leather jerkin. The creature stared at it blankly, then resumed its course towards the meat, oblivious to the flames now licking up its leg. Others, closing in around him, trampled the torch, stamping it out, and Bjólf's hopes were extinguished with it.

He scrambled for his sword, grabbed it by the grip, but something gripped his ankle – the first one he had struck, but failed to finish. He kicked out at it, as the bearded, burning figure lumbered towards him from the other direction, its flesh crackling as the flames now engulfed its body. If he could only regain the torch, relight it from the death-walker's flames... as he pulled, struggling to rise, a death-walker still on his leg and the hulking inferno almost upon him, another grim-faced ghoul – its leg horribly twisted below the knee – suddenly loomed over him, one putrid hand grasping his shoulder strap, the other clawing at his face.

Then, when it seemed all was lost, the thing jerked inexplicably, its head toppling from its body. The collapsing death-walker revealed a figure behind it – torch in one hand, gore-stained blade in the other, mail shimmering in the flame's light. Halldís. Before Bjólf could respond, there was another crunching impact. The grip on his ankle was relinquished – then a rough hand reached down and hauled him to his feet, and Bjólf found himself face to face with Frodi. The old man turned suddenly, delivering a shattering blow to the burning ghoul, sending him tottering away and crashing into two more. He grinned at Bjólf, the light of his own torch flickering upon his face. "An intelligent man may moderate what fate brings, if he is prepared to seek the help of friends..." And with that he turned again and cracked another of the creeping death-walkers across the temple.

Bjólf looked about him. Alongside Halldís and Frodi stood their three volunteer companions, a youthful zeal rekindled in their eyes, all with swords drawn and ready. Halldís stepped over the twitching bodies towards Bjólf. "We know of Ingjald, even in Björnheim," she said, and thrust her torch into his hand.

Together they turned, the fighters from Björnheim forming a flank on either side of the torch-bearer, forcing their way forward through the staggering *draugr*. The fighting was fierce; Frodi was in his element, joyful at tasting battle again. Halldís, her expression set and grim, struck out with no less vigour, never hesitating, her sword blade biting with ruthless precision. With the way ahead clear, two of the men ran forward, slamming the great barn door shut, putting their shoulders against it as they jammed the bolt into place. Bjólf stepped forward, took aim, and hurled the torch high into the hay loft.

All stepped back, keeping in a tight defensive circle – waiting, hoping, for the fire to take hold. Bjólf took the second torch from Frodi, in case it should be needed. For an agonising moment it seemed the flame had died, but as they watched, the glow in the loft began to grow and spread.

"I pray to the gods that Gunnar has done his job," said Frodi, one eye on the barn, the other on the dim figures that still lurked about them in the gloom.

"Trust Gunnar," said Bjólf.

The flames caught rapidly, leaping out of the loft and up to the gables, swiftly spreading the length of the barn.

Bjólf turned from the fire. "More death-walkers will come. We must make for the forest. Find the others there."

Frodi nodded, and he and his men started for the far side of the clearing. Bjólf flung the torch at the last of the approaching ghouls, sending one tottering backwards, and turned to face Halldís.

"I thought I told you to stay put," he said.

"I make a point of questioning everything I'm told to do," she replied.

Bjólf grinned, his eyes glinting in the growing light of the fire, and, grasping her hand, ran with her towards the trees.

# CHAPTER THIRTY-SEVEN

## ÆGIR'S ROCK

THE MOMENT THEY had seen the flames take hold, Gunnar and the main party of men had plunged into the dark forest, the great roar of the blaze and the last unearthly, hollow moans of its victims echoing after them. Finding the farm had been a strange twist of fortune – one that had allowed them to destroy a whole host of the creatures at a stroke. Yet Gunnar knew that among those horrible sounds carried on the night air were the final cries of men they had failed to save. Having to leave before daylight had been a wrench, but all knew they were safer in the trees; the blaze, now visible from all around, would only draw more of the flesh-hungry fiends, and in the forest they could at least hear them coming.

What proved far harder was holding the party together in the chaotic gloom that reigned there. Gunnar's party had entered first, through a parting in the forest's edge – perhaps once an old path. Soon after came Frodi and his men, followed, some way along, by Bjólf and Halldís. But their hopes of mustering once in the forest were soon dashed. Just a short way into the trees, the woodland once again began to thicken, the boles and roots become more massive, the tangle of foliage more impenetrable. Some blundered into death-walkers and became separated from the rest. Unable to rely on fire, they soon found themselves staggering in an inky blackness with only their ears to guide them, uncertain what might lay behind the footfalls close by, unwilling to call out for fear of attracting the attentions of the wandering dead.

For what seemed an eternity, Bjólf and Halldís, their hands never relinquishing their grip, crept forward through the dark, listening intently. Early on, they had often heard the crack and swish of movement off to their left, where they believed the others to be. Sometimes, it could clearly be distinguished from the slow, shuffling motion of the death-walkers. At other times, the distinction was not so clear. When he could, Bjólf had altered their path towards it, or at least tried to keep it close while navigating his way by the brief, bright glimpses of the sky. But, despite his efforts, the sounds only became increasingly distant, or sometimes baffled his senses entirely, seeming to come from all directions but that which his rational mind told him should be right. Finally, he abandoned his dependence upon them altogether and pressed forward according to his instincts, all the time fighting against the thought of becoming like the lost, directionless death-walkers, doomed to wander this place for eternity, and hoping against hope that the shore of the fjord lay before them.

Though almost blind, he could sense that Halldís, resilient as she was, was close to exhaustion – something he also knew she would never admit. His mind was racing, weighing the possibilities, trying to calculate how much longer they could reasonably continue, when, with no warning, a great expanse of clear sky suddenly opened up before them. They staggered to a halt, staring up. The wind had risen during the evening, clearing the cloud, and the whole dizzying night sky that arced above them was dusted with countless stars. Amidst the needle points of light hung the huge orb of the moon, its ghostly light illuminating a small open glade before them, casting their cold shadows upon the grass. Just ahead, filling nearly half of the tiny clearing, was a grey, flat outcrop of rock, rising towards the far end and falling sharply away where the forest once again took over. Bjólf crept slowly towards it as if in a dream, suddenly feeling his own exhaustion wash over him. "We can rest here," he said: "Death-walkers cannot climb."

She did not argue the point. He helped her up onto the rock, then heaved himself up, threw off his helm and the shield from his back and slumped beside where she lay, her body limp, already possessed by sleep. His hand found hers and closed around it. For a moment, he lay with his eyes wide open, his back to the mossy rock, listening to her quiet breathing and staring up at the impossible abundance of stars – too tired now to make sense of whatever they might once have told him. For a moment he had a vivid memory from his childhood, of lying on his back looking up at the night sky, feeling as if the whole universe spun around that one spot. He thought, fleetingly, that he should stay awake, and on watch until morning. Then he let his eyelids close, and a deep sleep took him.

He awoke suddenly to bright sunlight, his head pounding. Only gradually, as he blinked in the sun's unkind glare did he realise that Halldís was no longer at his side. He gripped his sword and whirled around in panic. But it was certain; he was alone on the rock. Cursing his weakness, staggering to his feet, every bone and muscle aching, he climbed to the highest point and looked about desperately. Nothing but the tall trees of the forest greeted his eyes.

"Hey!" The voice made him start – so much so, he almost toppled from his lofty vantage point. When he looked around, the smiling face of Halldís had appeared above the side of the outcrop.

"What in Hel's name are you doing sneaking around like that?" said Bjólf.

"Come on," she said, extending her hand. "I have something to show you."

Grabbing his gear and scrambling down into the grassy glade, he was led into the trees on its far side where, he could see, the vegetation had already been freshly beaten down. They followed the path, and within moments the trees had dwindled once again, the unmistakable smell of open water met his nostrils, and ahead, to their left, rising above a mountainous tangle of briar and elder, was a great dome of grey-brown stone.

Halldís pointed. "Ægir's rock," she said. Bjólf grabbed her and spun her around – weapons, armour and all – laughing triumphantly.

She beamed as her feet came back to earth. "They say the sea-giant Ægir settled down to sleep one night and was disturbed by a pebble under his back – so he picked it up and threw it inland. And here it came to rest!"

With another shout of delight he grabbed her hand and ran forward, both of them almost tumbling down the steep, tangled bank to the foot of the huge boulder. Within minutes, panting with the exertion of the climb, hauling her after him, they had found their way up onto its great curved brow. As they walked forward to its highest point – the great, dark forest that had so tested them to their left, the great expanse of the fjord and its far shore stretching away to the right – a most welcome sight was slowly revealed before them, one that made them shout again with joy: down below was the small bay they sought; there, still tethered, a little way along, was Grimmsson's ship; and milling about on the shore were Gunnar, Frodi, and the crew.

"What kept you?" called Gunnar, waving.

# CHAPTER THIRTY-EIGHT

## BLACK SHAPES

THE REUNION WAS an exuberant one; the men in resolute mood. The discovery of the ship, upon which so much depended, had greatly lifted their spirits. The vessel itself was in good order. The sky, too, was clear, and there now rose a brisk northerly wind to speed them to their destination. Preparations for the journey had begun before Bjólf's return – all eager for the moment of retribution. Now, all the elements were finally in place for their hammerblow against Skalla.

But not all the news was good. As the crew busied themselves ashore, getting their gear in order for the battle that lay ahead, Bjólf walked the length of the ship alone with Gunnar, and broached the subject that had been troubling him since his descent from Ægir's Rock.

"I see many faces missing from our company," he said. Gunnar nodded, a grave expression upon his face. "How bad is it?"

"Bad," said Gunnar. "Five did not make it out of the barn. Egil. Farbjörn. Guthmund. Sigvald. Kari."

Bjólf's frown deepened. "And the rest?"

"Olaf, Ketill and Ragnar were lost in the forest. Ran into a pack of those creatures in the darkness. Skjöld survived to tell the tale. But..."

Bjólf looked up at Gunnar. "But..?"

The big man's expression grew darker. "He had been bitten When we awoke this morning, he had gone, his sword and armour abandoned by the shore. Hakon and two of Frodi's men also remain unaccounted for. What has become of them, we cannot tell."

Bjólf stood by him at the gunwale, the grey-green water lapping at the timbers. "I make that twenty-one of us now," he said. "That was a costly tactic, back at the farm."

Gunnar shrugged. "Without it, many more of us might be dead."

"Can we still do it?" Bjólf seemed suddenly struck through by doubt. "The men are strong, but is that enough? After all this, I can hardly believe their hearts are still in it."

"Wrong. They are more determined than ever. Change our fate or die trying, that's what we vowed to do. That's what we will do."

Bjólf smiled. "That is what we always do."

"We will make this Skalla pay," said Gunnar, his voice suddenly hard as steel. "For lost friends. For everything. Every one of those deaths will be added to his account."

Bjólf turned and looked back along the length of the ship; a vessel built for war. Yes, Skalla would feel the full heat of their wrath. He slapped its thick timbers. "So, now we have this great tub to contend with..." It was not quite what they were used to: Grimmsson's ship was far younger than the *Hrafn* – cruder in build, longer, and narrower across the beam, with fixed thwarts that served as rowing benches. It also had certain decorative features that were not entirely to Bjólf's taste: the red sail, the iron spikes, the upper three strakes painted yellow, blue and red. But since Björnheim and their first sight of Skalla, he had begun to feel rather differently about the arrogant, vain Grimmsson. Perhaps these affectations were not so bad after all. Grimmsson had saved Bjólf's crew at the expense of his own life, and furnished them with their most awesome weapon – a weapon with which they would strike with deadly speed at the very heart of their enemy. When they did so, it would be for Grimmsson too.

"We've loaded stones for ballast to make her steady in the water," said Gunnar. "It was the one modification needed, with there being so few of us. Other than that, she's ready to go. Everything was in place when we found her – it was as if her crew had simply vanished.

"Let's just make sure our fate is happier than theirs," said Bjólf, and turned towards the gunwale on the landward side, catching sight of Halldís amongst the busy throng at the edge of the trees. Then, just as he was about to jump ashore, something strange caught his eye. Glimpsed at the very edge of sight, something of which he was barely aware, it made him pause. He turned southward, towards their destination, then stepped back from the gunwale, taking in the length of the shore stretching away to his right. Shielding his eyes against the sun, he could see, some distance away, a curious, blurry flicker in the sky immediately above the trees – like smoke, he thought, or the heat haze above a fire. As he watched, he realised it was gradually drawing closer, sticking close to the edge of the trees, becoming more solid as it neared – a texture formed of many different movements. Black shapes. The breeze dropped for an instant, and he thought he heard a strange confusion of hoarse, lonely cries – then the wind once again whipped the sound away.

"What is that?" he said.

Gunnar squinted along the shoreline. "Hmm. Just a flock of birds. Rooks or ravens." He made to go ashore, but stopped himself as he suddenly realised what he had said, turning back to Bjólf with a deeply furrowed brow.

"How can that be, Gunnar?" said Bjólf, a note of urgency creeping into his voice.

Gunnar wrestled with the question as the chaotically

swarming flock, its harsh, throaty cries now clearly audible, drew rapidly closer. "It was a raven led us here," he ventured.

"To the inlet, yes," said Bjólf. "But have you seen or heard a bird the whole time we have been near Björnheim, or this part of the fjord? A single one?"

Gunnar stared back up at the approaching black cloud. "Why do they move so strangely?"

Bjólf moved towards the gunwale, his sense of unease growing. "Get everyone into the trees – now!"

He leapt ashore, Gunnar hard upon his heels. "Get under cover!' he called. "Into the trees!"

For a moment, several of the crew stopped and looked at him in bemusement. Then the black mass of ravens fell upon them.

Everyone scattered, heading for the cover of the forest, swatting frantically at the air as the black, ragged shapes flapped and croaked about them. Spiked beaks and claws stabbed and tore, catching in their hair and clothes as they ran. The ravens attacked without fear or caution. Here and there, the crew grabbed at the struggling creatures and flung them roughly away. Some immediately took to the air and resumed their assault; others, broken, fluttered and flopped wildly upon the ground, or scuttled and hopped randomly about, pecking at their feet. Their movement on the ground was twitchy and erratic, like crazed, diseased livestock. In the air they darted more like bats than birds, but their eyes, like those of the death-walkers, were utterly dead; their one clear purpose to pick at living flesh.

The warriors had soon plunged in amongst the trees, where the ravens' attacks foundered upon branches and brambles. But they did not stop. Many caught in the tangle of briar and ivy and flapped and jerked convulsively, hung like moths in a web. Others broke through and hurtled about in their mindless quest for blood.

Bjólf rapidly located Halldís in the dark tangle. With a nod, she reassured him she was unharmed. Like many others, she had donned her helm to protect her head and eyes, but they were struggling to wield their weapons against the creatures in the close confines of the wood. They couldn't stay here. If the ravens were anything like the death-walkers, they would relent only when the source of food was entirely exhausted.

When the creatures had first approached, they had clung to the shore, seeming reluctant to venture over the water. Bjólf could only hope that this reluctance was stronger than their craving for flesh.

"We have the get to the ship!" he cried. "Hold your shields high, and grab whatever gear you need on the way!" Swords drawn, he and Halldís took a deep breath and broke from the trees. As they battered against his shield, Bjólf swung his sword wildly, smashing them out of the air. Others followed suit, swiping with axe, sword and mace, splattering blood, and sending squawking, scrawny, bundles of tattered black feathers bouncing in all directions and littering the floor.

Bjólf hurled himself into the ship, hauling Halldís after him. By ones and twos, the rest of the crew clambered or flung themselves over the side.

"Raise the sail!" bellowed Bjólf, loosing the reefing lines as the croaking mob fluttered and beat about his head. Men flew to their tasks, heaving the yard up the mast. The wind began to fill the sail.

As the ship moved, the attack seemed to abate and a few of the crew cheered in relief. But just when it seemed the crisis was at an end, Bjólf heard another cry go up and saw someone pointing. From the port gunwale he could see, half crumpled on the shore, the figure of Kjötvi. Slowed by his injured leg, he had been mobbed by the main body of ravens, which all but smothered him as he lay hunched in a ball among the twisting roots, his arms protecting his head.

Before he could make a move, Bjólf saw another figure leap ashore. Hrafning ran to his friend, a wooden stave in his hand, cutting a swathe through the swarming multitude, batting them this way and that like in a game of Stick-Ball. He beat them off the fallen man, heaving him to his feet as the birds flocked around his head, wading into the water and finally delivering him to the ship. The ailing crewman was hauled aboard and

Bjólf could see that where Kjötvi's right eye had been, there was now no more than a gaping, bleeding hole.

They reached for Hrafning, but he hesitated. Looking away, along the shore, he turned from the ship, waded to shore, and ran along the waterline.

"What's he doing?" said Bjólf. "If he delays any longer, he'll have a swim on his hands..."

The sail was now fully hoisted and bulging in the breeze. As soon as they were clear of the bay, the full force of the wind would take them. Bjólf threw off his helm and mail, about to head back onto the shore, when Gunnar restrained him.

"The line!" said the big man. And Bjólf saw it; in the water, the line that Gunnar had left ashore during their encounter with Grimmsson, that Bjólf himself had tied to the spike on the ship's prow. As he watched, Hrafning, swamped now by the ravens, struggled to where the line lay anchored drew his knife and sliced through the rope. It sprang free and he collapsed, weighed down by the massing bodies of his attackers. The crew could only watch him die, as the ship caught the wind, turned from the shore and was drawn inexorably away from the last resting place of Hrafning, son of Róki.

Though it had hardly been the start they had imagined for the voyage, they were at last under sail, and drawing closer to their goal. Kjötvi, oblivious to his own injuries, was devastated by the loss of his old friend, but all about him, the men muttered words of deep admiration for Hrafning's final deed. While there had been many deaths, this one, at least, had some purpose. It was selfless, heroic. From a barrel of mead discovered amongst Grimmsson's stores, they drank a toast to his memory, all satisfied that Hrafning's place in Valhalla was assured.

As they did so, Gunnar edged up to Bjólf, speaking in confidential tones. "About Kjötvi..."

"I know what you're thinking," replied Bjólf.

"Those ravens drew blood. Will he be all right?"

Bjólf shrugged. Who could know in these strange times? "If anyone will, it's Kjötv. But keep an eye on him all the same."

Stepping up onto the prow, relieved to once again have the

timbers of a ship beneath his feet, Bjólf looked at the figurehead – an ugly, oddly elongated, impossible to identify creature painted green and red. There was one more thing to be done.

"Boy!" called Bjólf.

Atli gave no answer, but looked about him. "Did someone let a boy on board?" he said. A guffaw went up from the crew and Bjólf took the point.

"Noble son of Ivarr," began Bjólf again with a bow. "If you would be so kind as to grace your captain with your esteemed presence..." His tone suddenly shifted. "And you better not have lost that bag I gave you."

Atli approached, dumping the heavy bag upon the deck in front of him. "If I had lost it," he said, "I could not have shown my face again."

From the bag, Bjólf drew the scorched, finely carved dragon's head that he had salvaged from the smouldering wreck of the *Hrafn*, and climbed high in the prow. Within minutes, he had lopped off the old gaudy, figurehead and crudely nailed the *Hrafn*'s in its place.

There was a cheer as he stood back to admire his handiwork. "Now," he called out. "Does anyone know if this ship has a name?" All looked at each other blankly. In all their deaings with him, none had taken enough interest in Grimmsson to find out his ship's name.

"A ship must have a name!" called Gunnar.

"How about *Naglfar*," called Thorvald. "The ship that takes the doomed warriors to the final battle at Ragnarók!"

There was laughter at that, it was the kind of grim humour that had kept them all sane over the years.

"I have a better idea," said Bjólf. He filled his mead horn and raised it aloft, standing high before the full sail. "*Fire-Raven*!"

"*Fire-Raven*!" they cried back, and all drank in its honour.

# CHAPTER THIRTY-NINE

## GANDHÓLM

With good weather and the wind in their sail, the majority of the crew suddenly found themselves bereft of purpose. For the first time in what seemed an age, there was nothing that demanded to be done – nothing to guard, no one to fight, no threat of death.

It was, Bjólf knew, the calm before the storm. Something for them to savour. He sat with Haldís near the stern, his shipmates scattered about them, but while others relaxed, his mind was still working, running ahead to the challenge that lay before them. It was no more than a series of practical problems to which solutions needed to be found – problems that could be broken down, worked out, ultimately solved. The only issue was, these problems would cost lives.

"Tell me," he said to Halldís, "who are these mysterious masters who Skalla serves?"

Halldís sighed, looked out across the water. "No one knows," she said. "We have had dealings with them, of course. My husband, Hunding – he went there, negotiated with them, brokered the first truce." She fingered the black and red braided bracelet upon her wrist. "That is where this came from." She looked downcast for a moment, then gathered herself. "But even he did not see the masters themselves. Skalla is their only intermediary. Some say they are gods."

Gunnar looked at Bjólf, but Bjólf gave no response.

"You have said little of Skalla himself," he said after a pause.

"There is little to say," said Halldís. "Little that I wish to think about."

"But you spoke of a score that you have to settle," said Bjólf. "This is personal for you."

Halldís stared down at the deck again. "Because of him, my husband is lost." She looked Bjólf in the eye, shrugged with feigned indifference. "Don't worry – I know full well he is dead, although for months I held out hope. But that is not the main reason. Skalla murdered my father."

Gunnar raised his eyebrows. "You kept that one quiet."

"Can you blame me? Do you know what it's like to live with the shame of your father having been killed by his slave?"

Gunnar puffed out his cheeks in amazement. "Skalla was a slave! This just gets better and better."

Bjólf glared at him. Sometimes he thought the big man spent too much time on board ship and not nearly enough among regular people.

Halldís took it in her stride. "It is what made him so dangerous. He had nothing to lose. No rule to follow but his own."

"Tell me of this island fortress – the island Skalla's masters inhabit," said Bjólf.

"We've always called it Gandhólm – the island of sorcerors."

"You say you've *always* called it that?"

"Of course," said Halldís with a frown.

"What are the odds?" said Njáll with a laugh. "An island called 'the island of sorcerors' which becomes a home to sorcerors."

"It's fate," nodded Gunnar. Bjólf glared at him again.

"Maybe Skalla's masters chose it because they liked the name," chipped in Godwin.

"No, no..." said Halldís, frowning more deeply, her expression one of confusion. "Do you not know? Did no one tell you?"

All looked blankly at each other, then back at Halldís.

"There *was* no island before the masters."

It was left to Bjólf to speak. "Perhaps you'd better explain what you mean by that."

Halldís looked about at the puzzled, expectant faces, cleared her throat, then began.


"IT WAS FIVE years ago, about this time of year. Things were quite normal then, as they had been for generations. Then, one night, without warning, all the animals about Björnheim began to bleat and whinny and crow as if some terrible disaster were about to befall. They kicked and bit at their stalls, and just as suddenly fell silent again. The sky lit up, as bright as daytime, but white, like lightning. The ground shook with a terrible roar, as if the earth were turning itself inside out.

"Then the flood came. A great wave, surging along the river. Our dwellings in the village are upon a hill; they survived. But the other farms in the lowlands were not so lucky. Those who lived to tell the tale said the water was hot, as if boiled in a cauldron. That it brought with it strange things. Within days the floodwater had abated, but from that night, Hössfjord had a new island."

"What?" exclaimed Gunnar. "It just rose up one night, right out of the water?"

"Or fell from above," said Halldís.

"An island that fell from the sky? This is madness! A story of a rock thrown by a giant is one thing. But this..."

"I have no explanation for it," said Halldís. "I can only tell things as they have happened."

Gunnar stared at the ground. "I know what you will say, Bjólf, but it certainly sounds like sorcery to me."

"I do not believe it," said Bjólf. "Will not believe it. Where is the evidence?"

Gunnar, still staring at the deck, spoke in a low, quiet voice. "Berserker warriors, raised from the dead?"

"If they are sorcerors, why not destroy us with a wave of the hand? Turn us into toads? And why does the pestilence also afflict Skalla's men? They are no sorcerors, Gunnar – or, if they are, they are very bad ones."

Gunnar fell silent.

Bjólf questioned Halldís further about the fortress – its strengths and weaknesses – but her knowledge was soon exhausted. It remained an enigma, even to her; a mystery that left Bjólf troubled by the multitude of unanswerable questions it raised. Suddenly it had struck him that he was rushing into battle against an enemy of completely unknown powers, and unknown potential – something his uncle had always warned him against. But what choice did he have? Their future, whatever it was, now hurtled towards them with an unstoppable momentum; a confrontation in which all questions would ultimately be answered, everything finally revealed.

WHEN THE AFTERNOON sun was in the sky, Halldís went and stood up on the prow, her attention focused intently upon the left bank of the fjord. She had told Thorvald to keep in close to that shore – only that way, she said, could their approach remain hidden from the ever-watchful eyes of Gandhólm. Then, up ahead, the fjord seemed to bend sharply to the left, its further reaches obscured by a long, projecting spur of land off their port bow. When she recognised the place, Halldís jumped down from the prow, her disposition suddenly agitated.

"Put in here," she said, pointing to a thin, sandy strip in the crook of the promontory. "The island lies immediately beyond this spur."

At the signal from Bjólf, Thorvald leaned on the tiller. The sail was dropped, the mooring lines thrown ashore.

"We reach the far side overland, through the trees," said

Halldís as the gangplank was hastily extended. "Then you will see it for yourself."

# CHAPTER FORTY

## THE GROVE OF DEATH

THEIR APPROACH WAS lined with tall, densely-packed trunks of pine and birch, the soil beneath their feet loose and mealy. On the face of it, these were undoubtedly more pleasant surroundings than the forests near Björnheim, but all were aware that they were in the realm of the black guards now. As they marched, drawing inexorably closer to the source of the evil that had afflicted them, the dead, portentous silence of the place began to weigh upon the company. Halldís, especially, became increasingly withdrawn and anxious.

Her mood infected them all. The forest was open to the sky above, but they were hedged around by the massive trees and the gigantic, primordial fronds of bracken that loomed in between. They were on their guard, alive to sounds of movement, but none came. There was no bird, no scurry of squirrel or shrew, not even the buzz of an insect – only the ceaseless sighing of the trees above them. It was a weirdly sorrowful sound, as if the entire forest were in mourning for the passing of its own life. For a time, in that strange realm, it was as if they were the last animate creatures upon earth – so much so, some even found themselves longing for the shambling presence of the undead.

The sight of a figure ahead made Gunnar start, and the company froze about him. Grey and skeletal, dressed in colourless rags, it stood motionless, framed by the trunk of a huge, rough-barked pine, its lipless mouth grinning without expression, its empty sockets regarding them in hideous silence. Bjólf made a movement towards it. It did not react. As he crept slowly forward, he saw that it was pinned to the tree by a series of rusty iron spikes – one protruding between the edges of its bared teeth. This was no death-walker – at least, not any more. It was the first sign of life they had encountered since their arrival here.

As they moved beyond that grim guardian, the soil became more gritty and dessicated. The monstrous ferns suddenly subsided, revealing that all around, as far as the eye could see, the forest floor was strewn with human bones. In stunned silence they picked their way past until the field of grim relics finally dwindled – none daring to point out the fact of the absence of even a single human skull. The bodies had been decapitated, the heads removed, by whom, and for what purpose, the troubled company could not tell.

None were sorry to leave that place.

Gunnar, intent in taking his mind off these gloomy matters, sidled up to Bjólf as they walked.

"I was thinking..." he whispered.

"Be careful with that," said Bjólf.

"About when this is all over. About that little farm somewhere..."

"Ah yes, with the barn and the woman."

"I was thinking, maybe Ireland."

Bjólf nodded appreciatively. "Very green. Lots of rain."

Gunnar shook his head. "But then I thought: too boggy."

Bjólf sighed deeply. "How about Scotland?"

"It's practically Norway these days."

"The Frankish kingdoms?"

"Maybe, but that would mean living among Franks."

"Normandy?"

"Bunch of fanatics."

"Russia then?"

"Full of Swedes."

Bjólf sighed again. "Sorry, old man, I'm running out of countries."

Gunnar raised his arms and let them fall in exasperation. "You see? It's hopeless. There must be somewhere out there a man can live in peace. All I ask is a small, sturdy house with a..." He fell silent. Ahead of them, just visible through the trees, as if his words had summoned it up, was a stout-beamed dwelling in a clearing. All drew their weapons. Shields came off backs.

Beyond the cover of the trees they could now see a whole complex of buildings, roughly arranged around a dusty courtyard of dry, barren earth, a circular space at its centre scorched and blackened. Dead leaves and ash blew across it. Somewhere, a door creaked in the wind. Everywhere there was an atmosphere of abandonment.

Bjólf signalled silently to his men; a nod briefly to left and right. Without a word, two groups, headed by Godwin and Finn, split off and headed out wide on either side. It was the tactic they had employed at Atli's village, and at many villages before that.

ATLI LOOKED AROUND in surprise, uncertain what he should be doing, baffled at the way the men seemed to know Bjólf's intentions without being told. By the time he had realised what was happening, they were already gone. His place – by default, it seemed – was with Bjólf, Halldís and the rest.

They approached the courtyard slowly, warily, passing the open entrance of the timbered house as they did so. Gunnar investigated with silent efficiency, shaking his head as he emerged. Through the open doorway, as they moved on into the open space beyond, Atli glimpsed the same signs of long abandonment that had been evident back at Erling's farm. They kept moving, the only sound the wind gusting through empty spaces, punctuated every now and then by one of Finn or Godwin's men as they investigated the dank interiors upon either side.

The buildings themselves were strange to Atli's eyes. Some had evidently once been ordinary farm outbuildings, probably of the same age as the abandoned house, but had since been crudely adapted or expanded, sometimes employing materials that he could not identify. There were flat, square roofs; iron rods held together with wire and metal pegs; patches of rust grinning through crumbling plaster and peeling paint; featureless partitions of wood that had warped in the wet and were splitting apart; ragged, thin materials hanging in shreds over open windows. Although these ugly features were clearly more recent than the buildings upon which they had grown, they gave a bizarre impression of more advanced decay. The mere sight of them filled Atli with a feeling of dread.

Ahead, he could now see that the large, blackened area had been the site of an immense fire – perhaps a succession of fires. Strange, lumpy remains – part-consumed fragments of wood, odd bits of twisted metal, and what looked like charred bits of bone – were strewn about its ashy centre, seemingly covered in a dark, oily residue. Bjólf stepped carefully into it, felt the ground, and picked his way back out. Finn and Godwin emerged from the last of the outbuildings and shook their heads.

Bjólf picked up speed, moving towards the two larger buildings that lay directly ahead of them. One looked to be a huge barn – long, like Halldís's hall, but with an entirely straight roof and constructed from thick boards through which the wind whipped and howled. To the right of it as they approached, directly opposite, was a smaller and very different kind of structure; low, squat and square and built of uniform grey blocks, with slits for windows. Bjólf stood in the wide gap between the two, looking to one, then the other, then ahead towards a further, smaller clearing beyond, lined with trees. As he caught up with the rest of the company, Atli peered through the huge open doors into the vast, dark space of the barn. At the far end was another doorway, also open, beyond which was dense forest – yet far enough from the opening to admit a dim light. The interior seemed to be divided up into stalls – for animals, he supposed. Whatever they were, they were now long gone.

Opposite was the door to the grey, squat structure, and different from almost every other door Atli had seen here in two important respects: with its heavy planks and thick iron straps it appeared substantial enough to contain wild beasts. And it was closed.

Bjólf looked at Gunnar. "What do you think?"

"I'm trying not to," said Gunnar. "This place... It's like nowhere I've seen. And it has a bad smell."

Bjólf nodded and said to Halldís. "Do you know this place?"

She merely shook her head, her expression troubled, as if the little she knew from the last few moments were already more knowledge than she could bear.

"Well..." began Bjólf. But before he could say another word, a sound made all of them turn. It was the chink of metal on metal, clear and distinct, from somewhere behind the heavy, closed door.

Bjólf approached slowly and silently, and put his shoulder to the door. It resisted, but shifted a crack. Not locked. Gunnar and the others stood with weapons and shields ready. Bjólf shoved with all his strength. The great door scraped half open before grinding to a standstill. Inside, all was black. The sound came again, louder this time. The air that wafted from inside was heavy with the stench of death-walkers.

Bjólf began to creep inside, Gunnar following close behind. Atli had moved up close to Bjólf, and found he was next in line. He faced a choice: follow behind Bjólf and Gunnar, or stand back and let Fjölvar or Halldís pass. He clenched his teeth and plunged in.

Inside, their eyes quickly adjusted to the gloom. Ahead was a straight corridor with several doorways off it, about which rubbish was scattered, and here and there pools of water into which an occasional drip fell. The *chink-chink* came again, echoing from somewhere deeper inside. As they crept on, they saw that the doorways – through which the only light filtered – were not all wide open as they had initially assumed. Their doors were fashioned from bars of iron: some half open, some seemingly locked shut, but all coated with a fine film of rust. Each chamber had a single slit for a window. Some had damp straw upon the floor, and others were entirely empty; in several, chains hung from the walls. That was the source of the sound they had heard.

IT CAME AGAIN, now much closer. Bjólf raised his weapon, moving between the last two doorways. The door to the right – of heavy wood, like the first – was wide open. Beyond was a very different kind of space from the other chambers; still dark, but expansive, cluttered with furniture, at its far end a great, baffling, bulbous shape like a vast, enclosed pot that, as far as Bjólf could see, appeared to be constructed entirely of blackened metal.

The sound came again, directly behind him. He whirled around, sword ready. As he advanced into the opposite room, he heard a shuffling. Another *chink-chink*. The chamber, like the others, was dark, a shaft of daylight piercing through the slit in the wall, blinding him now to what lay in the deep shadows. He sensed a presence to his right, and turned to face it. For a moment he stood motionless, listening intently, trying to make his eyes penetrate the darkness, to make sense of it. From within the room, out of sight, came a weird, low cry that chilled him to the bone. A cry that was like two cries, in an eerie chorus. Then, with sudden violence, a figure lurched forward out of the gloom, flying at his face. He leapt back – it stopped dead at the limit of its chains, in the full glare of the light, the taut links ringing in the clammy, sickening air.

Bjólf reeled back all the way to the far wall. Seeing his reaction, Gunnar stepped in, ready to fight, followed closely by Atli and Halldís. All gaped at what they now saw. "Gods..." whispered Gunnar, a quiver in his voice.

That it was a death-walker was clear enough. Its flesh was grey and in an advanced state of putrescence – at certain points (its manacled wrists, its damaged knees, the fingers of its clawing hands) turning to the black slime that had become all too familiar. In its empty hideousness, its face, too, confirmed all their expectations of such a creature – the dead, fish-like eyes, the expressionless, lolling mouth, the collapsed, decaying wreck of a nose – all slipping away, by slow, inevitable degrees, from the skeletal foundation beneath.

What raised the sight to a new level of abomination, however, was not any aspect of its deteriorating condition. It was the way in which it had been altered. There, next to that rotting, vacant face – also, impossibly animate, yet with flesh that seemed somehow closer to the bloom of life it had once possessed – was a second head, the neck sewn crudely into a cleft at the side of the first, the stretched, wrinkled flesh, all along the join, glistening and dripping a pustular yellow. And whereas the first face conveyed nothing but the expected blank emptiness, the second, it almost seemed, stared back at them with its own expression of pained horror.

It began to utter another cry. Before it could complete it, as if unable to tolerate the sound, Gunnar stepped forward and smashed it down with two decisive blows.

For a moment, they stood in shocked silence. Then, slowly, as if by some instinct – as if in need of answers to the questions that now troubled them – they moved one by one into the last of the rooms: the large chamber opposite.

The cluttered interior was dominated by a number of broad, flat tables, some of which were darkly stained, others covered with strangely-shaped objects – tools of metal, containers of ceramic and glass, some broken. Rarely, if ever, had Bjólf seen such a wealth of glass in one place. Other detritus lay scattered about the floor, unidentifiable in the gloom.

Slowly they moved through this alien environment, trying to grasp its purpose – or perhaps, simply, trying to believe it. After all, there could be little doubt as to the cause of the dark stains on the great, slab-like tables. Ahead, the huge iron ball loomed. As they approached, the stench of the place – already unbearable – intensified. From its top, a kind of chimney extended up and through the roof. At its front, they now saw, was a thick iron door into its interior. Inside, traces of ash. And, Bjólf thought, bits of bone.

Atli stepped forward and peered into the large, trough-like container to one side of the great cauldron and started back in revulsion. It was filled with severed limbs in various states of decay.

Bjólf looked at Gunnar, his expression dark. "We should leave this place," he said.

"I agree," said Gunnar.

But as they turned to go, Halldís caught Bjólf's arm. "There's something in here," she whispered. They stood in silence, not daring to move, until they heard a movement, somewhere back near the door, in the shadows. They looked, but could see nothing. Again it came – a strange, scuttling sound. It was heavy. Large. Yet, in the shadows – less murky here than in the previous chamber – no figure could be detected.

Gunnar turned this way and that, trying to follow the sounds. "It must be an animal," he said.

"But there are no animals," said Bjólf.


ATLI, HEARING ANOTHER scurrying movement, turned to his right, peering along a row of benches. There, appearing from around the corner of one of the tables, was a low, large shape. He tried to shout out as he looked upon it, but could not. Instead, he simply pointed, staggering backwards, a strangled, incoherent cry escaping his lips.

It was enough. Bjólf, Gunnar and Halldís were around him, blades raised in readiness as the thing crept into the light on its awkward limbs. Where they expected to encounter the face of some wild creature, they saw in its place another once-human visage, another lost soul.

It took all of them a few moments to comprehend what they were looking at. At first it seemed it must simply be an injured death-walker, crawling forward upon its hands. Then the ghastly truth became apparent. The thing had no legs – nothing, in fact, below its waist. But grafted to its torso, in the same crude manner as the two-headed monstrosity in the previous cell, and carrying it along like some grotesque, oversized insect, were two more pairs of human arms. Sensing living flesh, it suddenly gave a hideous cry and darted forward with a horrible scampering motion, its teeth bared. Bjólf and Gunnar set upon it without hesitation, smashing the thing with axe and sword until it was unrecognisable.

They did not linger in that place any longer. All four of them hurried back into the daylight, gasping for fresh air.

Halldís wiped at her brow, deathly pale. "Someone... *did* that to it..." she said, falteringly. "Some human hand..." But such horrors were beyond words.

Atli, his head spinning, wished only to put as much distance between that building and himself as possible. His legs wanted him to run. Instead, he stumbled away as far as he dared, towards the entrance of the great barn, trying to pull himself together, his stomach heaving.

As he returned to his senses he looked about him, peering the length of the huge building, with its rows of stalls on either side. He walked in, looking at the vacant cells as he passed, the freshening wind a welcome relief. They had seemed like they were intended for animals. That was what they all assumed. But were they? He did not know any more. It seemed the distinction between human and animal, once so clear, was suddenly foggy and obscure. This, then, was the masters' ultimate achievement: the annihilation of humanity.

He turned, realising he should get back to the warband. But as he did so, a dark shape – silhouetted in the open doorway at the far end and framed by the foliage beyond – caught his eye. It was familiar and unfamiliar; something he immediately recognised, but which felt entirely out of place.

A dog.

He turned back and squinted at it, trying to make out its features, wondering how on earth it could have survived all this.

It staggered forward as if exhausted, its head low, then stopped. Perhaps there was hope after all. Perhaps there was life here, fighting back. As he watched, another, almost identical shape appeared, its movements similarly stiff and slow. He smiled to himself, debating whether he should go towards them, bring them back to show the others.

Then three more padded slowly into view.

Atli felt a chill run through him. He cursed his idiotic mistake. Not dogs. Wolves.

He began to back away from them, suddenly struck by the terrible memory of the ravens at Ægir's Rock, not wishing to turn his back. But as he did so, one moved forward. The others did the same, their movements loping and awkward, and then all of them broke into a run. Before he turned, he just had time to see their red eyes, their matted fur, their gaping, ragged wounds, before hurtling headlong back towards the doorway. He could hear them now, pounding behind him, drawing closer, a low mournful moan coming from the throat of each one. Ahead, one of the double doors blew closed, slamming in the wind. Atli put on a last burst of speed, knowing that wolves would be faster, hoping that death had at least slowed them. With their yellow-toothed jaws snapping at his heels, he flew through the open doorway and onto the ground.

As he did so, a shield struck the leading wolf in the face, sending it backwards. The doors closed violently on the neck of the second, which struggled and howled, before a foot booted it back and slammed the doors shut. Atli looked up to see Bjólf towering over him, his shoulder against the doors, the creatures snarling and scratching in a frenzy on the other side.

"Don't wander off," Bjólf said, and shut the bolt. Then he turned to Fjölvar. "Go and close the other door," he said. "There's enough to think about without these prowling around." And away he walked.

HALLDÍS, MEANWHILE, STOOD pensively at the edge of the second clearing, considering what now lay beyond. There were no more buildings, no more features of any kind, save the opening of a rough pit in the dry, gritty earth a little way ahead. Past that, the dirt gave way to grass and weeds, a narrow dock with a jetty, and a thin line of trees – the last barrier that stood between them and the fjord. Beyond, across the gently rippling water, sparkling in the sun, she could just make out the dark shape of the island. Gandhólm, island of the sorcerors. Island of Skalla, and of Skalla's masters. As she stood, her future before her, her past behind, she suddenly felt overwhelmed by a deep, all-encompassing sense of despair. Suddenly, she wished only for her tears to flow without end, for her throat to give unrestrained voice to all her for torment, for her legs to give way and the earth to swallow her up so she might sleep forever. She fought to dismiss it, telling herself it was merely horror at all the horrors she had seen. But it would not be so easily dismissed. For the first time, she found herself wondering whether she would ever see her home again, whether, after all this, things could ever go back to the way they had once been.

"We made it," said a voice beside her. It was Frodi.

"This is only the beginning," said Halldís, staring into the distance.

"We will make an end of it," said Bjólf, emerging from the knot of men with Gunnar at his side.

"One thing," muttered Gunnar, a deep frown upon his face. "Where are the death-walkers? The normal ones? I thought this forest would be crawling with them."

"Perhaps even they cannot stand this place," said Bjólf. Deep down, however, the question was also troubling him. Standing next to Halldís, he turned to look upon her delicate face – and saw her frowning.

"What is it?"

"Do you hear something? A kind of rattling?"

Bjólf listened. "Atli found some pets in the barn," he said.

"No," said Halldís. "From over here." She walked across the clearing, Bjólf following close behind. As the wind changed, they heard a strange, ceaseless noise, like hard rain upon the deck. No, more like lots of hollow objects being knocked together. But it was impossible to place precisely. She veered towards the pit, and Bjólf followed. The sound grew louder. They drew up to the edge and peered down, Gunnar and the others closing up behind them.

At the bottom of the pit, deeper than the height of a man, a mass of human heads were piled up, covering its floor, their jaws still snapping, over and over, in a never-ending quest for flesh.

Halldís swayed. Bjólf steadied her, drew her back.

"Is there no end to this?" muttered Gunnar from the pit's edge.

"We will make an end," said Bjólf grimly.

Then, from the far edge of the clearing, Finn hissed a warning. A black boat was coming.

# CHAPTER FORTY-ONE

## HEIMDALL'S EYE

IT HEADED DIRECTLY for them; a long, thin-prowed rowing boat containing perhaps a dozen black-clad men.

"Can they have seen us?" said Njáll.

"If they'd seen us, they'd have sent a ship," said Gunnar.

There were hurried tactical conversations, and then the men rapidly dispersed amongst the trees and beyond the edges of the nearest buildings. Atli found himself crouched in the bracken with Fjölvar and four others at the far side of the clearing, near the jetty. Directly opposite, across the clearing, were Bjólf, Gunnar, Halldís, Frodi and Finn, with two other groups positioned further ahead. They had the advantage of surprise, but they had also seen the black crossbows glinting in the low sun. They would have to hit them hard and fast.

None knew for certain what kind of man they faced. They had seen little of them, save Skalla himself, and that example

made them wary. Atli sensed the tension in those around him.
He gripped his seax, staring at the earth, trying to keep his
breathing slow to counteract his racing heart.

The last few moments of the boat's approach were excruciating.
For what seemed like forever, they crouched, waiting, seeing and
hearing nothing. Eventually, voices could be heard; the clunk of
oars; the scrape of something heavy being heaved off the boat; a
whine of complaint; low laughter. Atli could not get a clear view
of the dock, without moving, but his ears told him that they had
landed. A moment later, they walked into view – two in front,
crossbows loaded and held before them. Five more followed,
some with spears. Four more of the black-clad warriors carried a
large, unwieldy sack between them, and two more crossbowmen
brought up the rear. Only four of those deadly weapons in total.
That was good.

Atli listened to them talk and joke quietly. All seemed cautious,
nervous even, but their chatter showed they were trying not to
appear so. They did not expect trouble. Atli counted thirteen
in all. It appeared they had left their boat entirely unmanned.
A fatal error.

Fjölvar pulled back his bow and drew a bead on one of the
crossbowmen. Across the way, Finn would be doing the same.
He did not even hear the arrow fly, just the dull *thunk* as it
struck the lead man. Before any of them had a chance to react,
the second crossbowman had been felled by Finn. The four with
the sack looked around desperately, panic in their eyes, before
finally gathering the presence of mind to drop it and draw
their swords. One of the two remaining crossbowmen swung
around suddenly, looking directly where Atli was hidden, but
Fjölvar's second arrow cut him down as he raised his weapon.
The other, unexpectedly, turned and ran for the boat, leaving
his fellows in a turmoil of indecision behind him. He got three
steps before Finn's arrow struck.

That was their signal.

The two groups closest to the dock, to the rear of the black
guards, attacked first. Atli could not remember willing his legs to
run, but somehow found himself hurtling out into the open with

Fjölvar and the others. Opposite them, Bjólf's company charged from cover, striking with terrifying ferocity. The clash of battle surrounded Atli on all sides, the black guards huddling in a state of terror as the different groups closed in around them.

For a moment, Atli had no target. The others – faster, more decisive – had taken them all. He turned, and found himself face to face with a black guard who had managed to break away from the melée, sword in hand, eyes wide. Between this man and the boat, there was now only Atli. The boy froze. He knew he had to act, that no one would come to his rescue this time. But he felt his strength drain away, his limbs turn to blubber.

But then he saw something in the other man's face that changed everything. Fear. Paralyzed though he was, he had struck terror into this man. The realisation hit him like a lightning bolt. Atli was suddenly emboldened. In his mind, he knew he had already won. He felt his strength return. The man, in sudden panic, flailed his sword wildly and ineffectually, and Atli deflected it easily with his shield and struck. The seax's sharp point pierced the leather armour and slid between the man's ribs. Blood spilled in the dust. He choked, and fell. Atli stood over the body – stunned, but alive.

In moments, it was over. Not one crossbow bolt had been fired, not one sword blow or spear thrust successfully landed on the members of the warband. Without pity, without ceremony, they began picking over the bodies and hauling them into a heap. None showed any desire to investigate the large sack they had dropped.

"So much for the might of the black guards," said Gunnar contemptuously.

As THEY BUSIED themselves, Bjólf stood at the limit of the trees, staring out, for the first time, at the fabled fortress and its island. The dark, lumpen shape sat squatly in the water, its outer edges rough and muddy and broken – crumbling cliffs of earth from which protruded great roots and twisted lengths of metal. At its western end, facing the fjord, was a crudely constructed harbour where the black ships and other, smaller craft sat. From there, paths wound through the muddy chaos to the weird structure of the fortress itself, obscured behind an elaborate stockade of thick logs, with ramparts and watchtowers, black-painted, like the ships. At its hidden heart, it was topped by a tower of unfathomable design, from the top of which spikes and spires stretched skyward. Surrounding the whole island, some distance out in the fjord, a row of great wooden stakes stood up from the surface of the water – a continuous barrier, punctuated only by two roughly-constructed turrets ouside the harbour.

There was something horrid about the scene – something utterly out of place. Bjólf recalled Halldís' tale about the island's creation. He knew it was impossible, but looking at it now, he could give the bizarre story more credence.

"One still kicking here!" called out Njáll suddenly. A man – his eyes wide with terror, his hands held defensively before his face, writhed and whimpered at his feet. "Not a mark on him. Must've just gone down when the fighting started, pretending to be dead."

"Bring him over," said Bjólf.

The guard looked up at Njáll, pleading over and over, his hands shaking. Njáll looked at the creature for a moment in utter contempt, and then grabbed him by the back of his belt, dragged him to a tree near the dock and tied him to it with a length of mooring rope from the boat. He shook his head disdainfully as he strode away.

Bjólf and Gunnar spent some time questioning their jittery captive. It had not taken much persuading to get him to talk – much to the disappointment of Finn, who had volunteered to help loosen his tongue. In fact, at times, the man had seemed embarrassingly eager, as if believing that he might somehow befriend them, and thereby secure his release. They happily encouraged him in his delusion.

From him, they had learned the times of the watches, the rough layout of the lower levels, and the important fact that there were no more than fifty armed guards within the castle walls at any one time. But beyond this – more from the man himself than anything he had directly said – they had also formed a valuable impression of the fighting abilities of those men, and been encouraged by it.

There remained, however, the question of their equipment – which, in many respects, seemed greatly superior to their own. Among the objects taken from the crew of the boat were several objects that none among Bjólf's company could identify, chief among which was a solid black container on a shoulder strap, which, when opened, contained another, largely featureless black cylinder of unfathomable purpose and baffling design.

"What do you make of this?" said Gunnar, passing it to Bjólf.

Bjólf turned it around in his hands, felt its weight, pushed and pulled at one end, which was oddly tapered. To his great surprise, when he pulled, the thing extended – a slimmer black shaft slid out from inside the first, then a yet smaller one from inside that, until the object was nearly three times its original length, as long as a sword blade.

"Clever," said Bjólf, nodding. He held it by the slimmer end, swinging it lightly. "A weapon?"

"It's heavy enough," said Gunnar.

Bjólf frowned, shaking it more vigourously from side to side. "Hmm. But is it strong? I wouldn't put my faith in it in a fight." He turned. "Godwin?" He tossed it to the Englishman.

"Never seen anything like this," he said. "What is this material? Not metal." He tossed it to Fjölvar.

"Not wood either," said Fjölvar turning it over. "Feels like bone." He tossed it to Úlf.

Úlf scrutinised it closely, sliding the parts back into themselves. "Not bone. Not like any I've seen. But this is fine craftsmanship. Arab, maybe." He tossed it back to Bjólf.

"Well, let's ask its owner." Bjólf turned to the tree, against which the guard still writhed fruitlessly in his bonds. He stopped as he saw Bjólf approach, a look of terror in his eyes. Bjólf presented the black object to him, holding it a finger-length from the man's quivering nose.

"Speak," he said.

The guard looked about him nervously, finally summoning

the courage to speak. "We call it Heimdall's Eye," he said, his voice clipped and edgy. "It helps us see long distances."

Gunnar guffawed. "Really? Well, I suppose more than a few weeks in this place would send anyone crazy."

"It's true," said the guard pleadingly, his knees shaking. "I have no reason to lie."

"You have every reason to lie," said Bjólf.

"I – I cannot explain it..." stammered the guard. "I do not have the art. But I can show you..."

Bjólf drew his seax, eliciting a whimper from the guard, who closed his eyes in panic. When he opened them again, his bonds were cut, and Bjólf was holding the heavy black rod towards him. The guard let out a shaky breath and, relieved at not having been killed, looked about him for a moment, and then bolted for the trees.

Gunnar sighed and picked up the black crossbow. The bolt flew, striking the guard in the left shoulder as he was halfway across the clearing, the impact spinning him around. He began to fall forward, staggered, took a few more awkward steps, then pitched sideways and fell headlong into the yawning black mouth of the pit. The sound of snapping jaws suddenly increased in intensity, only momentarily drowned out by the guard's final, terrified screams.

"Good shot," said Bjólf.

"Hmm," Gunnar grunted irritably, frowning at the crossbow. "I was aiming for his head."

"If this is the calibre of man we're up against, we've only to shout 'boo' at them," said Njáll. "I thought that one was going to piss his pants."

"Well then..." said Bjólf, his eyes seeking out Atli among the men. "Son of Ivarr, you're the brains of this outfit. See what you can make of 'Heimdall's Eye'." And he tossed him the strange black object.

FOR SOME TIME, Atli sat cross-legged, toying with the strange device, puzzling over its strange materials, its obscure purpose.

There were markings on the slimmer end, which rotated, but after endless fiddling it seemed all he could make it do was extend and contract, just as the others had done. Could it perhaps be some sort of measuring device, he wondered? But that hardly seemed to fit with what the guard had said.

He had just given up on it when his own frustration provided him with the answer. As he threw it down onto the gritty soil, a black disc popped off one end and rolled away from him. He grabbed at the loose piece in mortification, hoping no one had noticed, thinking he had broken the precious treasure, but when he looked more closely, he realised that the cupped disc was merely some sort of cover for the wider end of the rod, which was now revealed as having, set a little way back within it, a circle of thick, impossibly smooth glass, its surface curved like a cow's eye. *Like an eye,* thought Atli. *Heimdall's Eye. To see long distances.*

At last, it was making some sense. He turned the object over hurriedly, tried the thinner end. A second, smaller cap popped off, revealing another glass disc beneath. As he held the object up now, extended its full length, he could see that it was somehow hollow, that light passed through it from one end to the other. He held it up to his eye – and got the greatest shock of his life. As clear as if they were within touching distance, he suddenly saw figures of black guards moving about before him. He jumped back, dropping the thing, and blinked ahead of him. The guards were gone. Or rather, they were there, through the trees, upon the island, but now so distant as to appear like ants upon an ant hill. He picked up the object, tentatively, and peered through it again. Immediately, the distant view was magically brought closer. For a moment he he feared that he might also appear closer to them, that *they* could see *him*. But he soon dismissed the notion as foolish. He was still sat here, upon the bank, behind the trees. But then, if they had other devices like this... He scrambled to his feet, and ran off to Bjólf with news of his discovery.

\* \* \*

"HEIMDALL'S EYE..." SAID Bjólf, peering through the device as they crouched at the edge of the wood. "Well, it seems our captive was telling the truth after all. Now we know to stay well out of sight, and also that they may easily see us coming." He turned to Atli. "Good work, once again. You have earned your passage, son of Ivarr."

"But what other marvels might they have?" wondered Gunnar, squinting past the trees towards the distant, grim island.

"Whatever they may be," said Bjólf, "they'll be ours by sunrise."

He scanned the uneven surface of the fortress – partly in deep shadow now, with the sun sinking low in the west – taking in its strange features, then switched his attention to the curious barrier that surrounded the island, far out in the water. He could now see that the two distinct structures on the barrier were watchtowers, and that they flanked a pair of crudely constructed gates. Clearly they could be opened from the towers to allow the black ships access to and from the fortress harbour. But what was it all for? "That endless row of stakes in the water," he said, passing Heimdall's Eye to Gunnar. "Tell me what you see."

"Hmm," Gunnar grunted. "Defences of some kind. Wooden pilings, most likely weighed down with rocks. Looks like thick rope nets strung between them, holding the thing together."

"But not strong enough to stop a ship, travelling at speed," said Bjólf.

Gunnar looked at him through narrowed eyes. "Not *stop*... no, I wouldn't say so..."

"How long do you think we have before those men are missed – enough for them to come looking?"

Gunnar shrugged. "Hours, probably. But night is drawing in. No one is going to head out until daylight."

Bjólf stood suddenly and looked at the boat that had brought the black guards, then back in the direction that the Fire-Raven lay. "We attack before dawn, in darkness," he said. "Soak the sail of the ship. As wet as you can make it. Gather dry firewood and pitch. And someone bring me some rope."

"What's the plan?" said Gunnar.

Bjólf looked out towards the monstrous grey-brown island in the middle of the fjord and the black castle that sat perched atop it like a dark, ugly crown. He thought for a moment of the unspeakable horrors that they had witnessed here, and of the dark power in the fortress that had perpetrated them.

"We're going to arrange a funeral," he said.

# CHAPTER FORTY-TWO

## THE LAST BATTLE

Trani stood hunched in the rickety lookout post, shivering in the cold night air. He hated this watch. It was always cold out over the water, but at night it really got into your bones. No amount of moving around, it seemed, could keep the chill out. Not that there was exactly much room for movement, and he wasn't sure the structure would take it even if there were. No matter how many times Skalla impressed upon them that it was one of the most important jobs on the island, it still felt like a punishment.

He cursed Skalla's name under his breath, then began humming a tune his fellows had made up in honour of their leader. The words mostly focused on the fact that Skalla ate babies for breakfast and had no testicles. Trani sniggered to himself, trying to warm his hands on the flame of the torch. At least he had that. Trouble was, even if you stood up close your face ended up roasted on one side and still frozen on the other. Why could they not simply have put another bracket for the torch on the other side, so it was possible to swap it over every once in a while? As it was, the only way around the problem was to turn and face the island, which defeated the object of him being there. He could not allow himself to do it – though, in truth, he was more afraid of Skalla finding out than of any potential intruder sneaking up behind. There had never been any intruder. Why would there be? No one would want to come here.

True, there had been talk of a crew of *vikingr* being seen somewhere. That, supposedly, was the reason for having the watch extended through the night. But the word was they were all dead now. And even if they weren't, they would be soon. No one could survive out there without the masters' protection. He shivered at the thought.

Never mind. The sun would be up soon and the boat back to relieve him. Then breakfast. He stared into the darkness. A weird mist had rolled in from the north over the past few hours, with the salt tang and the chill of the sea. Now great whisps of it were being whipped towards him on the wind like wraiths. As he looked, he thought for a moment he saw an orange glow somewhere out there in the impenetrable gloom. He wiped his eyes and yawned. He'd been out here too long.

But no, there it was again. A dim light, directly ahead.

He thought, at first, it must be a fire out on the promontory, where the fjord turned northwards. But surely it couldn't be. Who could possibly be out there? Something Reim had said when Trani had arrived to relieve him at the watch suddenly came back to him. "There's a boat due back," he'd said. "Keep an eye out for it." Trani had forgotten all about that. To be honest, he had assumed Reim must have been mistaken. But now...

The glow was growing in intensity, seeming to flicker. A trick of the fog, thought Trani. He looked back to the island, then forward again. It couldn't be from the shore. It was too far out. For a moment he pictured that lost boat, still inexpicably out there, only now returning. He kept his eyes fixed on it, watching it get bigger. Without warning, the fog thickened and the glow disappeared completely. Maybe his mind really had been playing tricks. Ghost stories told by his fellows started to play on his mind – of strange lights that guarded tombs or hovered where treasure lay. In vain, he tried to banish them; he didn't want to think about that sort of thing. It was bad enough being out over this dark water, knowing what lurked below. Anyway, it was gone now. He kept staring at the spot ahead of him, where it had been, just to be sure. But there was nothing.

With a shiver – not from the cold this time – he looked back to the island. "Come on," he muttered to himself, looking longingly for the relief boat. "I'm going to catch my death out here..." When he turned back, his eyes were met by a vision from Hel.

Emerging from the swirling, wind-blown fog at terrifying speed, as if from nowhere, was the towering, spiked dragon-prow of a great death-ship – its grinning figurehead bearing down upon him, silhouetted against a blood-red sail, its whole length lit up by leaping, roaring flames. As Trani stared, open-mouthed, unable to comprehend the impossibility of the sight, the ship ploughed straight into the watchtower, sending it crashing into the dark, icy water with a horrible groaning and cracking of splintering wood, before forging on over it. The final shock – the final unthinkable revelation – was the sound that reached his ears in the moments before the heavy, barnacled hull crushed him down into the haunted, freezing black depths. It was the hoarse, otherworldly baying of wolves.


THE BURNING SHIP did not stop. The wind from the north pushed it on, its flames reddening the sky. The gates fell; the second tower collapsed, dragging with it a whole section of the barrier. One by one, all along its great length, the stakes began to topple. In the harbour itself, a cry went up, but the scurrying guards were utterly powerless to halt its inexorable advance. They could only watch in terror and disbelief as the great ship, flames now leaping the full height of the mast, smashed past the moored black ships, igniting their ropes and sails, rammed into the jetty, splintering it to kindling, and finally, carving the first decisive battle scar into the stronghold of the masters, drove its bows high up onto the island's wrecked shore. As it shuddered to a halt, those within sight – to their horror – saw leaping from its deck crazed, red-eyed, ravening wolves, their bodies aflame, their limbs convulsing, their hideous jaws snapping and tearing at anything that moved.

From the rampart, Skalla watched as the beasts – half consumed by fire, their restraining ropes burned through – took his men apart. Flames leapt, lighting up the whole of the harbour. He did not know where the ship had come from, nor who was behind the attack, but it did not matter now. Somehow, he had always known this day would come. If the fire-ship was meant as a diversion from a main attack, then it had more than done its job. The barrier was in a state of collapse, and all knew only too well what that would mean. He must leave those outside to their fate. They would provide his diversion.

He turned to the panic-stricken lackeys who cowered nearby. "Seal the main gate," he said. "Muster my personal guards. And prepare the berserkers."

WHILE THE WESTERN shore had erupted into fiery chaos, upon the eastern side of the island, all was quiet. Guards stood at intervals upon the stockade, nervous for news of the assault upon the other side of the island, their numbers depleted by the emergency, until now, they barely had sight of each other in the early morning gloom. There was a hiss, and a muffled cry, and one fell out of view. Then another. A third black-clad figure jerked suddenly at the sound of a dull impact, choked, then toppled over the rampart. By the time the iron hooks were thrown over the edge of the stockade, there were no guards left alive to witness them. Moments later, a force of warriors – eighteen in number – stood battle-ready upon the rampart, helms, blades and armour glinting in the light of its torches.

The time for vengeance had come.

The bold strategy had unfolded exactly as planned. But it had not been without obstacles. Kjötvi, against all the odds, had showed no further ill effects from the raven attack (although he now sported an eye patch, fashioned for him by Úlf from a black guard's leather armour). But Folki had fallen without warning into a shivering sickness, his skin pale, a cold sweat upon his brow. Investigation revealed a bite upon his calf, from the night at Erling's farm. Whether Folki had known and chosen to keep it quiet, or had simply been unaware of the wound in the heat of battle, Bjólf did not know or care to ask. All were aware what it would mean. Folki had insisted on staying behind in the grove of death, knowing he was now a liability. Eybjörn, the last survivor of Frodi's men, had volunteered to stay with him. He had said he was too old to make the climb over the stockade wall, but Bjólf knew the real, unspoken, reason he was staying was so he could give Folki peace after he passed. What future it left for Eybjörn himself, none could say. Of all the deeds Bjólf had seen these past few days, this was perhaps the bravest.

The black boat, packed to capacity, heavy with weapons and mail, sat low in the water. Once the *Fire-Raven* had been set on its course, aimed at the distant torches of the harbour, Úlf and Thorvald – the last men aboard – had dropped into the black boat with the others, and thrown a torch into the great pyre upon the ship's deck. With all enemy eyes on the fire ship, they had rowed in darkness to the far side of the island, cut through the rope netting of the barrier and slid the vessel between the stakes entirely unobserved.

Now, from the ramparts, Bjólf surveyed the challenge that lay ahead. Inside the wooden stockade lay a wide open space, dotted with untidy huts and dwellings of all kinds. Here and there, an isolated figure hurried past, responding to the distant emergency. Beyond stood the formidable inner wall of the fortress. Blank and grey, constructed from the same blocks as the squat building upon the mainland, the square, featureless edifice loomed around the hidden heart of the castle, obscuring everything but the strange, spiky tower that sprang from within, its uppermost spire just beginning to catch the first rays of the sun as dawn broke over the distant mountains. This wall was a very different matter from the first; too high for their grappling hooks, with no guarantee of what lay on the other side. They would have to fight their way in.

Slowly, cautiously, they worked their way around the parapet, keeping low, those with bows and crossbows keeping an eye out for any who might raise the alarm. With all attention focused on the disaster in the harbour, none below even thought to look up. As they neared the western end of the island, the clamour of activity ahead intensified. Soon, the harbour itself was in view. Down beneath them, in the fortresses outer ward, Bjólf could now see black-clad men beetling about, barring the stockade's main gate – some hurrying back towards the western end of the grey edifice. There must be a second gate there; and from the way the men were moving, it must also be open. They had to move quickly.

Bjólf gestured ahead to a wide stairway leading down to ground level. But before they could move, Fjölvar nudged him and pointed past the rampart to the glow of the harbour. At first, it seemed that Skalla's men had barred the gate while a large number of their own were still outside it – a curious fact, to be sure. Then he saw that most of those outside the gate were not black guards. Surrounding them – swamping them – was a host of ragged, grey figures, their appearance gaunt and cadaverous, their movements hideously familiar. Some of the guards were fighting, some fleeing desperately back towards the gates that now shut them out. Others had already been overwhelmed, their screams carried on the wind. And, as Bjólf watched, the ranks of the death-walkers were growing, a seemingly endless, swaying army of wet, beslimed figures emerging slowly from the water.

At last, the significance of the barrier became clear.

But there was no time to waste. The sun was rising. Soon, they would no longer be able to rely on darkness to hide them. Waving his warband on, Bjólf hurried down the gloomy staircase, where they mustered in a tight group between a stable and a forge, its hot smell filling their nostrils. A passing black guard – who carried with him an air of authority – stopped at the sight of them, and opened his mouth as if to issue an order. Then a frown crossed his brow. Before he could raise the alarm, Gunnar put a bolt through his neck.

The time had come. At Bjólf's signal, they surged forward silently, weapons raised, shields together.

The guards they encountered had little idea what hit them. Almost immediately, the first three unfortunate enough to be in their path were struck down, before the warband turned the corner, heading for the inner gate, and smashed into the main group of guards, splitting them apart and sending them flying, faces and bodies bloodied. From the heart of the raiding party, those with bows and crossbows scanned the parapet, picking off their counterparts before any of them could ready their own weapons. Now and again a bolt would slam into a thickened shield – one glanced off Thorvald's helm – but once the archers' positions were revealed, Bjólf's bowmen were soon on them.

As the guards panicked and dispersed, the warband split apart to take them down one by one. Resistance from the ill-prepared enemy was weak. Revenge was exacted upon them with ruthless and bloody efficiency.

FROM THE GREY battlement Skalla looked down upon the slaughter coolly. Finally, his enemies had announced themselves. "Get more crossbowmen on them," he said. "And lower the inner gate."

The guard hesitated. "But our men will be trapped out there, with the invaders. Shouldn't we...?"

"Do it," snapped Skalla.

He knew the outer gate would not hold the advancing host of death-walkers forever. Eventually, the wooden gates would give out and they would flood the outer ward. Well, let them have it. The inner gate was stronger. Once it was closed, neither the death-walkers nor the invaders would breach it. They would be trapped together. What would happen afterwards, with the undead pressing in on every side, he neither knew nor cared. Let the masters puzzle that one out. He wondered, vaguely, if they were watching from their sanctuary within, hatching plans of their own.

"REGROUP!" CRIED BJÓLF.

The warband drew back into a tight formation, the last of the uninjured guards fleeing, another limping desperately after them. All around, black figures lay crumpled, some still moving or crying out, others rent apart by terrible blows. Ahead of them now, with no obstacle in their way but the dead, was the open mouth of the inner gate. Beyond that, a walled courtyard, and within, just visible, a group of perhaps a dozen men facing them, weapons drawn and faces set. They did not move or flinch. Behind them, other figures were moving heavy objects into place. These men were of a different order from those they had thus far encountered, but there was to be no going back.

As Bjólf watched, a heavy portcullis of iron began to descend over the mouth of the inner gate. He immediately began the charge forward. The moment he did so, a rain of crossbow bolts hit them from the battlements of the grey wall. Ingolf and Aki fell immediately. The rest were pinned down, crouched beneath shields.

"Knock them out! Knock them out!" cried Bjólf, trying to spot the crossbowmen.

But he knew what had to be done: they must press forward, whatever the cost. Without hesitation, he ordered the charge. Halfdan caught a bolt in the arm and fell as the rest surged forward. In moments, his body was shot through with bolts.

But the tactic paid off. In a few steps they were almost up against the descending gate, too close for the crossbowmen to fire upon them. The black guards within began to move forward, while above them, they could hear the crossbowmen hastily repositioning themselves, their commander barking orders urgently. But it was the turn of Bjólf's crossbowmen and archers now. They fired into the courtyard, felling four men and scattering the rest out of their line of sight.

The way was momentarily clear, but the portcullis was already barely at head height. Without stopping to think, Gunnar threw down his shield and shoved his shoulder beneath the great gate. Had he applied more consideration to the matter, he might have questioned whether he could hold such a huge weight of iron, but it was too late for that.

"Some help here?" he called gruffly.

Úlf and Odo added their great shoulders to his. Their bodies strained, their faces reddened – the gate slowed, but did not halt. Gunnar, the tallest, could feel his shoulder being crushed, his legs about to give way. "Can't hold it for long…" he said.

"Cover me!" said Bjólf, and dived under the gate, shield held high. Fjölvar and Finn followed, their bows ready. The moment he was through, bolts thudded into his shield from above, but Bjólf was too fast. To the left of him, close by, stood two astonished men struggling at a great wheel, the thick shaft at its centre wound around with the great chain that raised and lowered the gate. He was on them so fast that one of the black guards' own crossbow bolts hit the nearest gatekeeper in the leg. Finn's and Fjölvar's arrows flew, and from the inner parapet of the courtyard, two crossbowmen fell. Others scurried out of the line of fire.

Gunnar and the others were crushed to their knees now. Bjólf battered the remaining gatekeeper with his shield and hauled on the wheel with his whole weight. The gate stopped dead – but from the archways around the courtyard, members of the elite bodyguard now emerged from their defensive positions. Filippus and Arnulf, both armed with crossbows, squeezed under the gate and fired off two shots, taking one down and injuring another. Finn leaped forward and added his weight to the wheel. It turned. The gate rose. Gunnar, Úlf and Odo were freed, and the rest of the warband flooded in. Bjólf locked the winch, took up his shield, and drew his sword. All armed themselves, throwing down anything that was now a hindrance to combat: ropes, hooks, cloaks, food.

There followed a savage eruption of hand-to-hand fighting as the two sides tore into each other. It was impossible, now, for the remaining crossbowmen to fire without risk of hitting their own men, and they abandoned their posts on the parapet to join the fray. Freed from threat, several of Bjólf's men discarded their shields in favour of their preferred method of fighting: an axe in each hand for Thorvald, a combination of axe and sword for Gunnar, and for Godwin, the familiar, single, long battle-axe.

Fearless as they were, the inner guard of the black castle lacked the experience of the *vikingr* crew, their slave heritage soon becoming apparent. They fought hard, but wildly – angrily; Bjólf's men, seasoned by many a battle, kept cool heads and conserved their energy whenever they could, watching, waiting for the moment to strike. When they did, rarely did a blade fail to strike its mark. Four fell within moments of the first violent clash, each taken down by single blows. Godwin's axe swept in a wide arc, destroying anything that crossed its path. Gunnar and Thorvald looked unstoppable, striking fear into even the bravest of the black guards. Odo's heavy two-handed sword did not allow his opponents to even get close, cleaving through mail and leather as it struck. By contrast, the sword of Filippus – long, curved, and lighter than its Norse counterpart – flashed at ferocious speed, inflicting terrible wounds upon the unprepared enemy. Atli and Kjötvi followed close behind, finishing them off where they could.

In the very centre, forcing their way forward, keeping steady pressure on the foe, Bjólf, Halldís and Frodi fought side by side, battering with their shields and hacking at those that challenged them. Blood and sweat flew. Teeth and bones cracked. The enemy's shields splintered; their black helms were cleaved in two. Within moments, it seemed, this hammerblow – which had left Bjólf's warband without a single serious injury – had reduced the defending army to a bloodied, disordered handful of men.

Just as victory seemed assured, there came the blast of a horn, and the last few defenders suddenly retreated towards the far wall of the courtyard, leaving Bjólf and his fellow fighters standing. As the black guards fled, they revealed a single figure in the open space before the warband. He stood alone before them, without fear. Skalla, the horn still at his lips. At his waist, hanging from a cord across his shoulder, the lacquered container of white powder, and at his feet, seven huge, black boxes.

FOR A MOMENT, Bjólf and Skalla regarded each other in uneasy silence. Then, Skalla spoke.

"Who are you?"

"I am your death," said Bjólf.

Skalla stared, then chuckled quietly to himself. "You and your men are admirable fighters, to be sure. But am I permitted to know the reason for my death?"

"You are not," said Bjólf. "Let your death be as meaningless as your life."

Skalla glowered at him. "Why you?"

Bjólf shrugged. "Because I can."

"You think so? I do not."

"Then I will!" cried out Halldís, pulling off her helm, her hair flying free. An expression of genuine shock crossed his face.

"Now it becomes clearer." he said. "But still I have my doubts. You see, your will is weak. You could have killed me ten times over as we stood here, but you did not."

"Your crossbowmen could have taken us down as we stood," countered Bjólf. "But they did not. Why? Because they do not act except under orders. They have no thought, no loyalty, no will. And you were distracted by your need to find reasons. By the vain belief that your life has meaning, even though whatever meaning it once had you have long since squandered. You are the weaker."

Skalla did not smile this time. "I think you underestimate the seriousness of your situation," he said. His good eye flicked above the heads of the warband, past the portcullis to the distant outer gate. In the silence, Bjólf became suddenly aware of the distant groans of death-walkers – hundreds of them, risen from the depths of the fjord. The outer gate creaked as their decayed bodies pressed mindlessly against it. "Surely you know this was a suicide mission? The *draugr* are at the gates. Its timbers will not hold them."

"What do I care?" said Bjólf. He pointed his sword at Skalla's heart. "We do not go back. We keep moving forward until we are stopped."

Skalla shrugged, turned to the side, and drew a small flask from inside his hauberk.

"Which brings me to the other reason for my skepticism..." And before they knew what was happening he had flung the clear liquid into two of the great, coffin-like boxes. "If this is to be Ragnarók, in which both sides are destroyed," he said, annointing another three in rapid succession, "then so be it." He tossed the fluid across the last two faces, then retreated hurriedly to a heavy wooden door at the far end of the courtyard.

The first of the boxes twitched. Then the second. A thump came from the third. Involuntarily, Bjólf and his warband found themselves taking steps back.

Skalla watched long enough to see the first grey, gruesomely sutured hand rise from its coffin, then disappeared through the door, slamming and locking it behind him. The remaining five guards – two with terrible injuries to their arms and face – realised suddenly that they, too, had been left to the mercy of the undead berserkers, and began to hammer desperately upon the now locked exit. Within moments, the first of the berserkers – Hammer-Fist, one of the ones they had seen destroy Grimmsson at Björnheim – was on its feet. It swivelled slowly, unsteadily, sniffing the air, attracted by the sounds of the guards, the smell of their blood. A second rose. Iron-Claw. As a third revived, clawing at the side of its box, a spiked ball and chain where its left forearm should be, the first two flew into a frenzied attack upon the guards. As Bjólf and the others watched, the two injured men were torn limb from limb as the rest scattered, the courtyard echoing to the horrible sounds.

Blood splashed everywhere. From behind them, it seemed the hollow cries at the outer gate suddenly increased in volume. The gates bulged and groaned.

"This will be a hard fight," said Bjólf. Five of the ghoulish creatures were on their feet now. "But they are not invincible. Bring them down. Go for the head."

As he finished, one of the berserkers – Axe-Holder – fixed its red eyes upon Bjólf, and thundered towards him.

Bjólf knew that panic would be their undoing. He stood firm, braced and ready. "Get ready to jump..." he muttered to his comrades.

With the huge figure almost upon him, he dropped suddenly to the floor, behind his shield. The creature stumbled, began to topple, came crashing down like a great tree as the other warriors leapt back. Godwin surged forward again with a bloodthirsty cry, bringing his axe down full force upon the thing's neck. It jarred horribly, flying out of his hands, bouncing off hard metal. The full helm had saved the creature. They were suddenly – disastrously – reminded that these were no ordinary death-walkers. Behind these, buried somewhere deep within this ghastly place, were twisted minds.

The creature tried to struggle to its feet, its mouth gnashing and wailing, its arms and axe flailing madly. Bjólf hacked at its leg with all his strength and it collapsed again. Atli, hardly thinking about the danger, leapt upon its back. It reared up, reaching blindly for him, and he grasped the edges of its battered helm, heaving at it, and was thrown to the floor. But the helm was still in his hands. Godwin, hefting his retrieved axe, his eyes burning with anger, swung again. This time, it did not fail him; Axe-Holder's head flew from its body. He shuddered and lay still, twice dead.

Now, they had a strategy. Two more came at them, one with a length of chain swinging from its arm, the other with a trident in place of its right hand.

"I'll take the one on the right," said Gunnar.

Almost before he had uttered it, Fork-Hand was upon him. He dodged and swung around, catching it on the back of the legs with both axe and sword. It fell, but its weapon slashed Filippus in the throat as it went down. Filippus collapsed, gore pouring from him. The creature grasped at the bleeding body ravenously. Thorvald hacked off its arm with one of his axes, and the creature slumped to the ground, face down in Filippus's blood. A horrific slurping sound issued from the fallen creature. Úlf stepped onto its back, hooked the spike of his cavalry axe under the edge of its helm, and heaved it up as Gunnar brought his axe crashing down upon its neck.

Meanwhile, Chain-Wrist had come lumbering towards the remaining warriors. With a cry of "Mine!" Arnulf jumped forward and dropped to the ground at its feet, emulating Bjólf's tactic. But the huge figure, defying expectation, came to a sudden stop, and before Arnulf could move, brought its fists crashing down upon him. There was a terrible cracking sound, and with a roar Arnulf's body – for he was dead immediately – was hoisted above its head, its hands literally tearing him in half as blood and gore cascaded over its open mouth. Halldís leapt forward, and with all the power she could muster thrust her sword point in the small of the creature's back. The blade went deep and the berserker crumpled from the waist down. With its arms and chains whipping ever more wildly and the shock of Arnulf's death still fresh in their minds, the others rained down blows upon its armoured head until its helm was beaten shapeless and all movement had ceased.

There was a moment's respite. Across the courtyard, the remaining guards had managed to bring down Iron-Claw, but Hammer-Fist had smashed one of their number to a pulp and had the forearm of another between its teeth. The man half struggled, half dangled from its jaw, screaming in torment as his fellow guard scrabbled desperately at the door.

The remaining two berserkers – Mace-Arm and Sword-Wielder – had turned their attention to the warband, and now came smashing into them. In the desperate struggle for survival that followed, with the warriors still reeling from previous assaults, strategies were momentarily forgotten. Sword-Wielder ploughed into a knot of men, sending bodies flying as it struck.

By some miracle, all avoided its notched, rusty sword blade, but before any could act, it had grabbed Thorvald and sunk its teeth into his shoulder. He gave a great cry, but did not fall. Others leapt upon the creature, hacking and stabbing at it, but to no avail. Thorvald staggered backwards, taking the creature with him, its teeth clamped around his collarbone, crashing against the wall. Njáll and Finn chopped the creature's legs from under it, bringing it crashing to the ground with Thorvald on top, its sword blade sweeping past the dodging feet of his desperate defenders, its free hand clawing at the flesh of Thorvald's flank, ripping out a great chunk. Somehow, even in his agony, Thorvald managed to draw his seax from his belt. He forced it between his chest and the neck of the berserker, gripped the end of the blade with his other hand, and with all his strength drove the edge of the blade forward against the creature's throat, sawing from side to side. Putrid, oily ichor flowed from the wound, and the creature slumped, inert. The grip was relinquished. Thorvald rolled onto his back, blood pouring from his shoulder and side.

Mace-Arm's assault, meanwhile, had been no less devastating. With the spiked ball-and-chain swinging, it had charged at Odo, who had tried to defend himself with his sword. The chain had wrapped around the blade, the barbed head just clearing his face, but Mace-Arm had then pulled back its arm violently, yanking Odo's sword from his grip and sending it spinning off into the far wall with a ringing of metal. It swung wildly again as swords and axes struck at it, its second pass smashing Odo across the jaw, sending blood splashing across the three men flanking him. He fell, the side of his face a mass of wrecked flesh and bone. Surrounded on all sides now, it swung around in circles, undecided where to strike, keeping all at bay as the deadly spiked weapon hummed through the air in front of their faces.

Their only hope was to disarm it.

Bjólf stepped forward, then, thrusting his shield into its path. The ball struck, the impact almost knocking him off his feet, but the strengthened wood of the shield held, the spikes embedded firmly in its boards. He hauled on the chain, trying to drag the creature off balance. Instead, it lunged for him. He side-stepped, hauling on the chain again, spinning it around, and the shield came loose, its boards split, but Bjólf wound the chain around his forearm, gripping it with both hands, still dragging the creature in a circle as it tried to launch itself awkwardly towards him. He spun it around again and again, pulling with all his strength on the chain, hoping to fling the creature off its feet.

Then, something unexpected happened. Bjólf saw, at the creature's shoulder where there was a crude row of stitching, that the flesh was starting to pull apart. The stitches stretched, snapped, unravelled; the wound widened, and with a great ripping and popping of joints, the creature's body and arm separated, sending it staggering awkwardly towards the gate. It stumbled over a crumpled body and crashed to the ground. The other warriors were upon it immediately, exacting revenge for Odo, for all the losses they had suffered. Its helm was ripped off, its head destroyed.

At the far end of the courtyard, Bjólf now saw that the single surviving guard had somehow succeeded in opening the heavy door – how, he could not guess. It opened further, and he had his answer: within were two of his fellows, gesturing eagerly for the desperate man to enter. But he seemed unwilling to abandon one of his fallen comrades, and was pulling at his collapsed body, even though it was clear to all that he was utterly dead. As the guard dithered, Bjólf shouted to his men. "The door!" he said. "We must get to it before it closes again."

But between them and it stood the last remaining berserker, his attention turned from the guard and focused fully on the warriors.

Hammer-Fist.

For a moment it stood in that bloody, corpse-filled arena, head low, eyes burning at Bjólf, a steady, snorting breath coming from its nostrils like a bull making ready to charge. Behind it, the guard – still not having been persuaded to leave his friend – was being physically hauled through the gap in the door.

"Keep it busy," said Gunnar. And before Hammer-Fist could

make a move, he charged at it with a mighty roar. Almost equal to the berserker in size, he slammed into it, sending it spinning, and thundered on past, jamming himself in the door as it shut against him. A struggle immediately ensued between him and the retreating guards, as they heaved on the door from the far side, and he lashed at them through the gap with his sword. The thing, meanwhile, bellowed horribly, almost as if angered, and flew into a frenzy, pounding towards its attacker.

They had to distract the creature long enough for Gunnar to secure the door.

"Hey!" called Bjólf.

The thing did not react. He ran after it, shouting – then hurled a throwing axe, embedding it in its back. That got its attention. It swung around and, without hesitation, lowered its head and charged at him full tilt, arms and hammer flying as it came. Bjólf stood in the path of the oncoming giant, no trace of a plan in his head. He backed away, made ready to leap, vividly recalling the fate of Arnulf, knowing it would have to be at the very last moment.

Suddenly, the creature jerked and fell forward, its face ploughing into the ground, and came to a standstill at Bjólf's feet. He looked around in shock, and saw Halldís standing behind him, a crossbow in her hand. Then he turned back to the felled berserker. Her crossbow bolt stuck in its forehead, piercing its thick helm.

Bjólf allowed himself a smile. They had done it. They had defeated the masters' most powerful fighters.

His sense of victory was short-lived. They heard Gunnar suddenly cry out. Finn, Fjölvar and Frodi were already racing to his aid, but as they hurried towards the door, they saw him knocked to the ground, limp and bloodied, his helm rolling away in the dirt. His body was dragged roughly through the dark gap, which slammed shut, its bolts shot on the far side. Bjólf pushed past the others and hammered his fists against the door in rage and frustration, but it would take more than fists to get them past the barrier.

Exhausted, but knowing they must fight on, he stalked back

to take up sword and shield again, and as he did so happened to glance at Halldís. She looked past him, up high towards the parapet, and her expression darkened. He followed her gaze and there, upon the inner rampart, lurking upon the upper level, was Skalla, his cold eye watching.

Bjólf, his eyes ablaze, pointed his sword at Skalla's heart once again – surrounded, this time, by the masters' ruined army. A renewal of his warning, his pledge. Skalla stared back without expression. In fury, Bjólf snatched up the huge head of Fork-Hand by its hair, its face smeared with Filippus's blood, and with a defiant roar hurled it at Skalla. He dodged as it bounced against the wall, leaving a dark stain, and backed away slowly.

"Your ruin is coming," called Bjólf, his thoughts now only of vengeance, his whole being, spurred by Gunnar's fall, like some primal force of doom.

"Why wait?" said a voice at his side, and Halldís let fly a second bolt from her crossbow. It struck Skalla in the left shoulder, spinning him around. He cried out and staggered, disappearing back through another doorway, into the shadows.

Bjólf lowered his gaze and glared at the thick door ahead of them, somewhere beyond which – dead or alive – he knew his friend Gunnar lay. He turned to the others. "Chop it to splinters."

Godwin, Úlf and Njáll set about the door with their axes, chips flying, its heavy bolts rattling as their blades battered against it in a persistent rhythm, echoing about the space within.

ATLI, MEANWHILE, STOOD in a kind of daze, staring at the torn and twisted bodies that lay on every side, at the reddened blade in his hand. His feelings surprised him. He did not feel sickened; he did not feel afraid. He felt only gladness at being alive. Here, surrounded by so much death, perhaps only moments from his own, being alive had never meant so much. Then a sharp cracking sound made him glance back past the open portcullis towards the outer gate. It bulged inward, the great bar across it now half broken, showing pale wood where it had split, bending as the pressure from the massed death-walkers increased.

"We have a problem..." he said. Bjólf saw it and, urging the others on as they cleared the way ahead, he dropped his weapons and turned his attention to securing the way behind, heading back towards the winch and the half-open portcullis. But as he stepped past the crumpled bodies, something caught his foot. Bjólf stumbled and fell to his knees, cursing his clumsiness. When he looked up, he saw Hammer-Fist rising, staggering to his feet once more, the crossbow bolt still embedded in his skull, his red eyes half rolled back in his head, but the semblance of life not quite gone out.

Bjólf scrambled to his feet, the thing lumbering unsteadily after him, close on his heels. Its hammer caught him on his shoulder, sending him flying. Something snapped. In moments he was back on his feet, searching desperately for a weapon, when the creature's hand gripped his arm. He struggled, pulling in all directions – the grip tightened...

Atli snatched a grappling hook up from the ground and swung it at the towering figure's head, a length of rope trailing behind. Hammer-Fist shuddered and staggered to one side, relinquishing his grip on the *vikingr* captain. It gave Bjólf a second chance at life, but the creature was not stopped for long. Now, in fury, it turned towards Atli.

THE BOY WOULD not last a moment in the hands of the creature. Bjólf looked around desperately, grabbed Odo's great sword and swiped at the thing's head; the sharp pain in his left shoulder barely registered. Metal clanged against metal. It staggered, its anger growing, and turned back to Bjólf. He hit it again, backing towards the winch, luring it on, one eye on the outer gate, just moments from bursting open. Half blind, it lumbered forward.

"Come on!" he cried, suddenly aware as he spoke that he was echoing Grimmsson's last words. As it kept on towards him he battered it around the head again and again, each blow more desperate than the last, but doing no more than slowing its relentless advance.

Behind him, a sudden great crack, and groan and crash of wood, told him that the outer gate had finally given way. A chorus of chilling moans – hundreds of voices merged together into a single ghastly sound – filled his ears. He did not dare turn. In the next moment he stumbled against the winch, almost fell, scrambled back past it. Beyond the inner gate he could see the host of death-walkers advancing, just moments from surging into the courtyard where the warband stood, watching in horror.

Hammer-Fist, sensing weakness, lurched at him, crashing over the spindle of the winch, its arms flailing past the taut portcullis chain. Bjólf saw his chance. He looped the trailing rope around the creature's neck, around the portcullis chain, and pulled it tight. It thrashed and struggled, unable to right itself, blind to what was happening. He looped the rope again, twisting it around the chain, then kicked away the lock on the winch.

The portcullis came crashing down, cutting the first of the death-walkers in two, the rattling chain hauling the writhing Hammer-Fist up high into the air, smashing its head into the great stone lintel that spanned the gate. It dangled, swinging, revolving slowly, lifeless at last, the crossbow bolt driven deep into its poisoned brain.

Bjólf heaved himself to his feet, walked past the clawing hands of the death-walkers that now filled the outer ward, their bodies pressing against the iron gate in their futile quest for flesh. He said nothing, but merely slapped Atli upon the arm in gratitude as he passed, wincing at the pain shooting through his own shoulder. He took up his sword and shield.

As he did so, the wooden door at the far end of the courtyard caved in, reduced to firewood.

Bjólf turned then to Thorvald, who lay slumped against the side wall, his face pale and sweaty, his mail and tunic soaked with his blood. Kjötvi was tending to him, but stood back as

Bjólf crouched by Thorvald's side.

"I'm done," said Thorvald weakly. Bjólf nodded solemnly, his jaw clenched. They had known each other far too long to dress it up. "I never thought it would end like this," he added. "To be honest, I didn't think it would be this interesting." Both laughed, Thorvald blanching in pain as he did so.

"We can't leave you," said Bjólf.

Thorvald nodded. "I know what you're saying. You're asking whether I want someone to finish me off, so I don't get up again, like one of them." He gestured towards the gate. He shook his head. "I wouldn't wish that task on any of you. Just leave me one of those." He pointed at the crossbow in Halldís's hands. She nodded at him, began drawing it back ready to take a bolt, fighting back tears as she did so.

"Make sure you don't miss," joked Njáll. "You're shit with a bow."

Thorvald smiled. "Go!" he said, waving them away like a parent shooing children. Then his face darkened, a look of pleading mingling with the pain in his face. "Go..."

Bjólf turned his back on Thorvald for the last time, passing through the silent company until he stood before the dark entrance – the goal that had been so hard won.

"Now we finish it," he said, and walked inside.

# CHAPTER FORTY-THREE

## THE DARK CASTLE

INSIDE, ALL WAS black. With no means of lighting their way, they crept forward, along a straight passageway, constructed, as far as they could tell, from the same uniform grey blocks. Occasionally they passed open doorways – all dark, all as dead and empty as the buildings on the mainland. They stumbled upon objects – some familiar, some unidentifiable, all apparently dropped in haste, perhaps only moments before. Ahead, they fancied they could sometimes hear movement, echoing distantly, as if from some deep cave, some great, labyrinthine space. And another sound – harsh and insistent, like a single note blown upon a horn, but somehow empty, repeating mindlessly, over and over. Then, there was a flickering light, dim at first, but, like the sound, growing in intensity as they moved forward, its source far ahead, where the passageway seemed to come to an abrupt end.

The end proved to be a junction with another passageway, that stretched away on either side. But this was unlike anything they had ever seen. The walls were smooth and white, the floor hard and of an shiny, unidentifiable material, the ceiling flat and featureless and as square and smooth as the floor and walls, entirely lacking any visible means of support. Along its centre, they now saw, ran the source of the flickering: a line of light – neither firelight, nor daylight, but some other sickly illumination that had no clear means of production. It stretched the full length of the long passageway in both directions, unbroken, but here and there, sections of the line flashed intermittently like a guttering flame. For a moment they stood, uncertain which direction to take.

A sound of running footsteps off to their left made the decision for them.

As they passed along the passage, more doorways came within view; some rooms dark, others brightly lit. One contained nothing but rows of beds. Another, angular, spindly tables and chairs, and the remains of a foul-smelling meal, recently abandoned. They moved on, the insistent sound ringing ever louder in their ears, never varying, never stopping. It was, thought Bjólf, like the sound of insanity.

Up ahead, three black-clad figures, laden with unidentifiable objects, emerged from a doorway. Seeing the approaching warband, one dropped everything and fled, leaving the others standing in shock. Bjólf flew forward with the others close behind. They hacked down the two guards where they stood. Fjölvar raised his bow to bring down the third, but Bjólf stopped him. "We follow," he said.

The trail led them to a wider corridor with many more rooms leading off it, and at the end a doorway that looked to be made entirely of glass. None could imagine how such a thing could be made, or why.

From a side room came a crash. They followed the sound.

Inside, there were benches like those in the grey, squat building, many of them covered with glass containers, things made of shining metal, weird instruments out of some delirious nightmare. Cowering in a corner was the one remaining guard, Bjólf recognised him as the man who had eluded them in the courtyard. He stepped up to him, putting his sword point to the man's throat.

"Skalla," he said.

The guard pointed a shaking hand in the direction of the glass doors. Bjólf withdrew his sword, not wishing to demean its blade with this man's blood, leaving him to his miserable life.

Beyond the glass doors was darkness, but for a weak pool of light in the chamber's heart, and a scattering of strange, small dots of light – some green, some red. The doors themselves – if such they were – offered no means of opening. Bjólf nodded at Godwin, who stepped forward, spat in his hands, then swung his axe at them. They shattered in a great explosion of glinting shards, scattering across the floor like gemstones.

Bjólf entered first. Ahead, there was another door, some unknown material this time, smooth and featureless. To their left, in a dark corner, completely in shadow, he sensed a movement. There was harsh breathing, and a cough.

"Why did you come here?" came a hoarse voice. It was Skalla.

"I told you my reason," said Bjólf.

"Some pointless revenge? What am I to you?' He paused, coughed again. "Or perhaps I should ask what *she* is to you..."

Halldís stepped forward, her sword raised. Bjólf held her back. He could just make out Skalla's feet now, just beyond the pool of light, where he was slumped against the wall. But he could see little more, could not see whether he had a weapon trained on them.

"Are you dying?" said Bjólf.

Skalla gave a grating laugh. "Perhaps. It's so hard to tell these days."

"Then I will not waste time. The black box you carry around your neck. You still have it?"

"For what it's worth."

"Give it to me."

"And if I do not?"

"Then I will take it."

"So why even ask?"

"Because now, at the last, I wish you to know why we came." He stepped forward, into the light. "To destroy you. To destroy your masters. And to wrest from your dying hand the remedy for the living death."

A strange, throaty sound came from the shadows. At first, Bjólf thought Skalla had succumbed to his wound. Then he realised, as the sound grew, that it was laughter; deep, resounding, uncontrollable laughter, broken only by a bout of painful coughing. "You did all of this, for that?" chuckled Skalla. He laughed again. "Here! Take it!"

The black box skittered across the smooth floor to Bjólf's feet. Halldís snatched it up, opened it, peered at the contents.

She frowned, sniffing at what she saw, then touched it with a fingertip and raised it tentatively to her lips. A look of disbelief came over her. "S-salt..."

"Yes!" laughed Skalla. "That is what you all fought for. That is what you all died for. A box of salt!" There was a movement. "You'd better have this too." From the shadows, the flask slid across the floor, the same Skalla had used to awaken the berserkers. Bjólf snatched it up, tipped its contents into his hand. Water. Plain water.

"It's a trick," said Bjólf. "This is not the remedy."

"You fools! There is no remedy! No respite, no rescue, no escape."

Halldís swayed, suddenly dizzy. "You lie. The white powder... we have seen it work..."

"On the berserkers... of course! Because my masters made them that way. To be controllable. But they are different. It will not stop the living death that is all around us. Not even the masters can stop that."

Beyond the end door came a thump. A scratching. Sounds of movement.

"What is that?" demanded Bjólf.

"My masters. They shut me out. Left me to my fate." He gave a cynical chuckle. "I cannot blame them for it. I would do the same."

The sounds intensified. There was a sudden hiss, and the door slid open, flooding the chamber with light. In the doorway, silhouetted, stood a huge figure. For a moment all stared, blinking at its half-familiar shape, struggling to focus against the glare. Then, with a roar, it flew at them.

The door slid back, plunging them back into near darkness. Bjólf grabbed for the black box – but as he did so, the huge warrior swatted it out of Halldís's hands. It clattered on the hard floor, its contents scattered among the glinting fragments of glass. Staggering backwards, Halldís drew her sword. The creature's swiping fists struck it from her grip, sending it spinning past Atli's head, then battered her shield, splitting it with one blow. She smashed against the wall and slid to the floor, as the members of the warband, as one, fell upon the hulking creature. In the confined space, in the dark confusion, weapons were as much a danger to their fellows as to their enemy. They set upon it instead with their bare hands.

It had no weapon of its own, this one, but all knew that once its fingers grasped them, they would be torn apart. Úlf and Frodi held one arm fast, Njáll and Godwin the other, and with others grabbing its legs they wrestled the roaring, thrashing thing onto its back. Bjólf stepped into the pool of light, standing over it, his sword drawn. Atli, knowing his part, jumped forward, heaving at the gleaming helm upon its head, ready for the killing blow. It flew free suddenly, sending Atli sprawling back onto broken glass.

None were prepared for what they saw. Sword raised and ready, Bjólf found himself looking down upon the face of Gunnar, or what had once been Gunnar. His eyes were wild and red, his blue-tinged mouth foaming, and there was no trace of recognition in his features. Yet, distorted though they were, the features were still familiar, still his friend.

Bjólf hesitated. In shock, the others – for an instant – unconsciously loosened their grip. The creature immediately leapt forward, grasping at Bjólf, sending him flying, his hands slashed by the scattered shards as he fell. It stomped forward, glass crunching underfoot, towering over him, and, with a ghastly cry, reached down and gripped Bjólf's helm. He felt the metal begin to buckle between its huge hands, about to crush his head. In a last desperate move, he grabbed at the floor, felt the grainy texture under his fingers, the sting in his wounds, grasped at it, and flung it in the thing's face. The creature stiffened. Bjólf rolled out from beneath it as it crashed lifelessly to the ground.

All the party stood dazed, no sound but their panting and the harsh note of alarm that still sounded all around them. Halldís climbed painfully to her feet, looking upon the scene with an expression of growing horror. It seemed to Bjólf that her defiant spirit flickered, that her strong heart – feeling, passionate, human – now teetered on the brink of what it could take. But at least she was alive.

As he threw off his helm, a deep thud from the far room suddenly drew his attention. Then a *clunk* which seemed to reverberate through the whole of the floor, as of something heavy being moved. When he looked, he saw for the first time that the sliding door from which Gunnar had emerged had not completely closed. All along one side, a sliver of light broke through. At the bottom of it, wedged in the gap and keeping the door's edge from the frame, was a beautifully decorated golden scabbard.

"Open it," ordered Bjólf. Godwin and Úlf stepped forward. Others joined them, shoving axes, sword grips, anything they could find into the narrow gap, heaving against it.

"My contribution," coughed Skalla as they worked on it, his features now dimly visible in the light. "To help you to your goal."

Bjólf glared at the shadowy presence. "Why would you, of all people, wish to help us? To betray your masters?"

Skalla gave a shrug, heard more than seen. "Because it pleases me. Because I tire of them. Of life."

In response to a final, mighty effort, the door suddenly hissed open, illuminating the room. Skalla lay propped up in the corner, his breathing rough, his black leather armour wet with his own blood, the bolt protruding from his shoulder, and in his limp hand, lying upon the floor, the fine, gold hilted sword of Hallbjörn's ancestors.

Halldís stared at the precious blade for a moment; a blade she had thought forever lost. Memories stirred. He looked back up into her face. She met his gaze with cold eyes, at the man who had destroyed everything she had known and loved, helpless before her. She could not remember how many times she had wished for such a moment. Staring fixedly at him, she advanced slowly. Skalla nodded at the inevitability of it, almost laughed. She bent over him, took up her father's sword from his weakened hand, then turned and walked away. Without a word, Atli took up the gold scabbard and passed it to her. She sheathed the sword, and put it through her belt.

"You do not wish him dead?" said Bjólf.

Halldís shrugged. "I wish it. But what good is there in it?"

Bjólf nodded, then, turning to Skalla, grabbed him by his hauberk and hauled him to his feet. "Well then," he said, "you can come and meet the masters with us." And with that, he dragged him into the next room.

It seemed that in stepping through the doorway they had finally left behind everything that was familiar to them. None could relate anything here to the world they knew, even those with experience from years of voyages. Apart from a single, strange table or bench to one side, the room was featureless – so featureless that it was hard to see it as a real place at all. It seemed as if it were somehow half-finished – a weird, transitional zone between this world and another, as if whatever strange gods had created this corner of the universe had become distracted, and left it, forgotten, unstamped with any clear identity or purpose.

Every surface was as white and smooth as ice, as if all composed of the same impossible substance, a sickly, oppressive light that seemed, inexplicably, to filter from the high ceiling itself, with no clear source. And there, directly ahead – the only distinct feature in the whole scene, set into the white rear wall and almost as high as a man – was what appeared to be a huge circular shield, forged from steel, its metal shining in the light.

All was so strange, so inhospitable, so hostile to life, that there was not one among the company who did not now feel the same deep dread that had afflicted Atli among the decaying, alien edifices in the grove of death.

That the room was empty was immediately apparent. Where the masters had retreated to was not.

"Where?" demanded Bjólf. Skalla nodded towards the great disc of metal in the far wall.

Bjólf understood now that it was some kind of doorway. As he approached, dragging Skalla with him, the lights flickered and dimmed. One by one, the glow from the devices along the benches fizzled out until only a few points of light remained. Skalla looked about him. "They are trying to shut you out," he said. The explanation meant nothing to Bjólf, but he sensed urgency in the words.

"Open it," he said, shoving his captive forward.

Skalla slumped against the wall next to the great metal door, staining it with his blood, his breathing laboured. "Yes, why not," he said with a humourless laugh, coughing.

He raised no latch, reached for no key. Instead, he pulled off his gauntlet and jabbed a finger repeatedly at a strange metal box upon the wall, from which glowed a tiny red light. It emitted a series of unpleasant, high-pitched sounds as he did so. "They do not know that I know this," he said. The fact seemed to amuse him.

The red light changed to green. There was a heavy *clunk*, and, with a deep hum, the huge steel door swung slowly open, bathing them in light.

# CHAPTER FORTY-FOUR

## MEETING THE MASTERS

ATLI HAD ALWAYS thought the worst nightmares were those that came in the dark. He had imagined the darkness filled with shadows, with the threat of unknown, indeterminate creatures, half-hidden or perhaps never revealed, grasping at him from the gloom. With demons, with shapeless monsters, with the hands and voices of the dead. Now he had witnessed these things, seen sights with his own eyes that eclipsed all his most terrible imaginings. For a time, he had begun to believe there were no nightmares left.

The new nightmare – the undreamt of horror – came in cold, sterile light, reflecting off every dead surface, eating into his eyes, into his depleted brain. The shadowless light of the masters' final refuge.

Inside was a fevered, searing vision of ugliness whose weirdly ordered, clean surfaces only made it seem the more delirious, the more utterly insane. Along either side of the room, on starkly white, featureless benches, stood strange things that hummed, and buzzed, and gave off a dead light. Above them on one wall, in cabinets made entirely of glass, were row upon row of vessels – some, like great glass urns, filled with noxious-looking liquids in which were suspended human heads, hands, foetuses and unidentifiable body parts, their lifeless flesh grey and pallid. Here and there, empty eyes stared out, dead mouths lolled open.

At the back of the room, the space opened out into a circular space in which more banks of lights – more than could be counted – blinked and glowed and flicked on or off, arrayed on surfaces in which, here and there, shapes and even pictures – tiny, phantasmic images of people – crackled and moved, as if forever imprisoned behind glass, trapped, like the dead flesh in the great jars, but somehow alive, like shrunken human cattle.

Upon the left side, coming into view as they passed, was a sealed chamber behind glass. Inside, attached to a gleaming metal table, which had been angled upward to give the clearest possible view of what lay upon it, was a man. His body had been cut open, the covering of flesh pulled open by metal clamps, its whole surface pierced by long, steel needles, held in place by complex, shining apparatus. The revealed organs within, still pulsating with life – or whatever now passed for it – were attached to hundreds of tubes through which unnaturally-coloured fluids flowed. Before their horrified gaze, the heart beat, the lungs pumped, and upon his face, the eyes flickered, the mouth moved, seeming to appeal desperately to them from a silent world beyond pain.

None could doubt it now. It was from here that the pestilence had come. It was from here that had spread the unfathomable, inhuman intelligence that had wrought those ghastly creations in flesh – of the dead and the living.

But it was not just these sights, or these thoughts, that so horrified them. It was some other, indefinable quality about the whole of that nauseating interior – this world without shadows, in which everything was revealed, everything too sickeningly evident. The entire room seemed to hum with a kind of dull, aching malignancy that hated life, that sought by degrees to crush and mindlessly consume the spirit. The very air around them – stale and dead, like warmed air spent by corpses – made them feel sick, as if poisoned. It was a place in which life had become an irrelevance, an inconvenience – an anti-world, its physical being so drained and exhausted of humanity that not even its hollow ghost remained to attest to its one-time existence, and merely to look upon its dead matter was to know utter despair, to taste in the mouth the creeping canker of a death beyond death, to feel – as if a shuddering, tangible thing – the ultimate doom of the entire race.

Atli had not thought anything could be more terrible than those ghastly things they had encountered in the grove of death. He had been wrong.


AND THEN THERE were the masters.

As Bjólf had advanced through the opening door into their cursed realm, there had been shouting from within – feeble, terrified voices exclaiming in a strange jabbering language. There was sudden movement, and a loud, repeated, sharp noise – like a log crackling in a fire, but of deafening volume, leaving their ears ringing. He strode towards the circular end chamber, towards its source – an angled, metal tool, the tube-end still smoking, the mechanism now clicking uselessly in the quivering, pallid hand of one of the masters. If this object ever had any dark magic, it was now used up. Bjólf wrenched it out of his weak grip and flung it to the floor.

In front of him, cowering in a corner, his hands raised as if to protect his face, was a small, feeble-looking man in a white coat – his thin, pale, wispy hair barely visible upon the shiny flesh of his barren, balding head, his smooth, pulpy flesh as colourless as a sickly infant. In front of his watery eyes, barely distinguishable from the rest of his bland, characterless face, were two discs of glass, held in place by a fine metal frame. Bjólf plucked them off him. The man whimpered as he did so. He examined them briefly, peered through them onto a blurry world, and, seeing no further use for them, flung them on the floor. The man scrabbled about for them on his hands and knees like a frightened rodent.

Some distance away, behind a solid, white bench, identically dressed, cringed three more puny, pale, smooth-skinned men.

Bjólf turned to Skalla, a look of sickened contempt on his face.

"*These* are your masters?"

"They wielded great power once," said Skalla, a note of apology in his voice.

"I had many reasons for leaving my home, but having great power was never one of them. So why did they leave theirs?"

"It's... complicated..."

"Do I strike you as a stupid man, Skalla?"

Skalla looked into Bjólf's steely, indefatigable eyes, then scanned the bloodied, battle-worn faces that were now arrayed so incongruously in those strange surroundings – faces that spoke of an unconquerable spirit, of a fierce loyalty that Skalla himself had never known.

"No," he said, "you don't." Then he sighed. "Their land is... here. And not here. It cannot be reached by any ship."

"I have no patience for riddles. Speak plainly."

Skalla narrowed his eyes, thought for a moment, then, nodding slowly, began again. "They come from another time. From a future a thousand winters hence. Their world is doomed – overrun with the *draugr*. They fought the pestilence, sought a cure." He shrugged. "Unsuccessfully...

"But they had also devised a means of escape. A mechanism, powered by a great furnace deep beneath our feet. They say it has the power of the sun. Their world fell about them. And so, they flung themselves from it, back here, to an age long before – before the world fell, before the pestilence. They meant to buy time, to continue their work, to find the remedy you yourselves sought..." His voice dwindled to nothing.

Bjólf looked at Halldís, as if seeking some confirmation or denial. She merely stared at the floor, fallen into a withdrawn silence, as if lost to him. For a time all stood saying nothing, the whole chamber seeming to throb with a weird energy that made their guts churn.

It was Halldís who spoke first. "They brought this disaster upon us," she said, her voice low and charged with a mixture of anger and despair. "Their own future was lost, and now their selfishness has doomed ours. There is no remedy. No hope. No respite." She turned and wandered desolately towards the back of the chamber, away from the others, as if seeking only solitude.

"I do not believe it," said Bjólf. "Will not believe it. The future is not set. They have proved it. If they can change things, why not us?"

"How?" asked Halldís, despairingly. "All this might and power..." She reached out and ran her hands across a surface of glass, gazing distractedly at the red-painted metal shape that lay beneath. "They thought they had mastered it. But it has mastered them."

As she stood there, one of the feeble, white-coated men began to chatter urgently at Skalla.

"Shut him up," said Bjólf to Godwin. The Englishman hefted his axe.

"Wait!" said Skalla. Godwin halted. Skalla listened intently to the man's prattling, then turned to Bjólf. "He wishes her to move away from where she is standing."

"You understand their language?" frowned Bjólf.

"Of course," said Skalla. Then, still listening, he raised the brow above his good eye, and chuckled to himself. "Oh, that's good! That lever, the red one behind the glass. It appears that it will send them – this whole place – back to where it came from."

Bjólf could only stare at him in astonishment.

"He is now telling me that I should not divulge these things to you," said Skalla. "But because he never bothered to learn *our* language, he does not know that I already have."

"Such a simple thing can banish all this?"

"As they came, so can they leave. It has been set this way since the beginning. So they could escape quickly if things went wrong."

"And, even now, they have not done so?" said Halldís in

disbelief.

"Christ in Heaven," muttered Njáll. "How much more wrong does it need to go?"

Skalla shrugged. "I believe nothing now would induce them to return to that place. It has become too terrible a memory. They call it 'Hel.'"

Bjólf recalled the way Magnus had used that word, how he had spoken of it not merely as a land of the dead, but a place of eternal torment.

"We could send them back, whether they like it or not," he said.

"And ourselves with them," said Skalla. "There's the catch."

Bjólf looked contemptuously at their surroundings, at the square images on the bench before him, showing the death-walkers swarming about the perimeter of the fortress. "What's left for us here?" He took a step towards the lever and smashed the glass with his fist. The white-coated men jabbered in panic as he did so, seemingly trying to appeal to Skalla. Skalla raised his hand to Bjólf.

"One more thing..." he said. "When Gandhólm is torn from this place, this land will be devastated in its wake. For miles around, all life will be utterly destroyed."

Bjólf hesitated.

"As far as Björnheim?" asked Halldis.

"Further."

It meant the end of everything she had ever known. Her friends, her family, her father's hall, the pastures she had played in as a child. Everything the pestilence had touched.

"Then the infection will be cleansed from this world," she said, and with sudden clear purpose took Bjólf's hand in hers and placed both upon the lever. One of the white-coated men leapt up, rushing at them, shouting incomprehensibly. Skalla swatted him to the floor, leaving the man's soft nose gushing blood.

Bjólf looked into her eyes, then back at his men. From every one of them came an almost imperceptible nod.

"See you in Hel, Skalla," he said.

They pushed on the lever, and everything around them erupted with blinding light.

THEY EMERGED THROUGH grey rubble and choking dust into an alien world.

The sun hung low in the blood red sky. What remained of the fortress sat on a great raft of soil and rock, pitched at a queasy angle like a grounded ship, like a huge clod of earth stuck roughly back in the place from which it had been wrenched. The ships, the harbour, the wooden rampart and all sign of the death-walkers from the fjord had been scoured from existence. Beyond, there were no trees, no sign of green.

In the distance, to the east, a great white structure spanned the valley – a wall of impossible dimensions. Other huge, strangely shaped edifices – some broken and collapsed – dotted the landscape. The fjord itself had disappeared entirely, as if boiled dry. The hard grey covering that the ground had now acquired was buckled and broken, pierced through with pipes and twisted metal and, as far as the eye could see, scattered with the chaotic heaps of rubble and wrecked machines. Where the soil was bare, it was cracked and scorched. It was as if the entire land had been laid waste.

Yet, even now, Bjólf had not abandoned hope. Brushing salt from his old friend's eyes as they had made their way out through the twisted corridors, Bjólf had found that Gunnar was not completely inert, but would stand where he was put, and would walk forward when pushed or pulled in that direction. He had bound him about the waist with a chain, and now hauled him along after them, whether hopeful that he may be restored, or out of pure sentimental attachment, none could tell.

As the ragged company of scarred, weary survivors stepped out onto the great, devastated plain, Halldís looked about her in despair. "How does one carry on in a world like this?"

"Fight," said Bjólf. "Stay alive."

"We do not even belong in this world," said Frodi, appalled at the sights before him.

"Then our fate is truly our own," said Bjólf. He looked about at the tangled chaos. "There must be somewhere out there a man can live in peace," he said, momentarily lost in memory. He looked back at Halldís, then. "And a woman."

"Perhaps we can find a ship," said Atli.

"Or build one," mused Úlf. "I assume they still have forests here."

"Perhaps there is a cure somewhere out there," ventured Kjötvi.

Godwin shrugged. "It could definitely be worse."

As they spoke, from somewhere in the blasted landscape of twisted iron and rubble came a long, low groan. The sound was taken up by other voices, spreading like a pestilence; a chorus of melancholy moans. All around, there were stirrings. Movement. Shuffling.

"What now?" said Skalla.

Bjólf spat into the dust, and drew his sword.

# THE END

TOBY VENABLES is a writer and lecturer in Cambridge, England. He developed a liking for horror early, watching old Universal movies when his parents thought he was asleep. He has written for various media and in 2001 won the Keats-Shelley Memorial Prize (and spent the proceeds on a Fender Telecaster). He now lives in a secure location with his wife, where he is preparing for the coming zombie apocalypse. *The Viking Dead* is his debut novel.

Now read the first chapter in the next
blood-drenched, ass-kicking instalment
in the *Tomes of the Dead* collection:

# DOUBLE DEAD

## CHUCK WENDIG

10th November 2011 • £7.99 (UK)
ISBN 978-1-907992-40-7

15th November 2011 • $9.99/$12.99 (US & CAN)
ISBN 978-1-907992-41-4

ABADDONBOOKS.COM

# CHAPTER ONE

## THE VAMPIRE AWAKENS

THE BLOOD CRAWLED through tight channels and shunted cracks like a rat in a maze. It wound downward through shattered concrete. It crept down along a length of rusty pipe.

Eventually it found an opening and dangled free in darkness before becoming unmoored and falling through shadow.

The first drop landed on the man's nose. Which did nothing.

The second dotted the flaky, cracked flesh of his forehead.

That also did nothing.

But the third drop. The third drop was the magic drop, tumbling out of darkness and falling upon his desiccated lips, from there easing down into his frozen, arthritic maw, moving past rotten teeth and touching the dark dry nub that once was a tongue.

When the blood touched that blackened stub, it came alive with a sharp sound: the sound of a spoon back cracking the surface of crème brulee.

The tongue twitched. Swatches of crispy tongue-flesh fell away like flakes of char. Then the tongue did more than twitch: it flapped, flailed, seeking, needing.

The mouth widened.

The drops of blood from above became a steadier flow. The tongue shot out from the mouth, extended far, too far, *impossibly* far – and like a child catching snowflakes, it caught the blood.

It wasn't long before the blackened tongue was blackened no more. Now it was pink, bright, stained with red.

The mouth opened wider as the blood now fell as an unsteady rain.

THE SOUND OF an animal's cries and the coppery, greasy taste on Coburn's tongue cut down through his dreams like a machete: he reached for them, the animal's cries mingling with a child's cries, the memory of wallpaper and linoleum replaced fast with a wall of darkness and the feel of stone.

He lurched forward. His spine cracking, his bones as brittle as sticks.

Blood fell from above. He cupped his hands (they were hard to move, the fingers like the stiff legs of dead bugs) around his mouth and made sure not to miss a single drop of the sweet stuff. He was a junkie, a blood junkie, a *vampire* who thrived on this stuff and he hadn't had it in – well, he didn't know how long, but judging by the condition of his body, it had been a long fucking time.

What fell in his mouth wasn't enough. Not nearly. He needed more. Would kill to have it (and had in the past, many times, too many times to count).

He tried to speak, but found his voice lost in the dead puckered flesh of his throat, his vocal cords naught but withered strings.

Coburn needed the blood.

And so he decided to climb.

\*    \*    \*

COBURN MOVED AS a spider. Fingers mooring in the cracks of broken cement and crumbling brick, hauling himself up while still craning his neck so as not to miss any of the tiny waterfall of blood. When he found its source – the end of a rusted sewer pipe – he nursed on it like a baby.

It still wasn't enough.

Coburn pried his mouth from the blood – a task that borrowed from his last vestiges of will, a task that set off alarms and screams in his head: *Go back, you're going to miss it, you need it, you fucking ape you can't exist without it, you're a moron you deserve to die – to die for real this time, to die for good.* And yet he persevered despite the cat-calls of his own worst survival instincts, letting the human mind – the one with reason and sense and the ability to see beyond a few drops of blood – take over past the reptilian monster mind that wrenched at the puppet strings.

He swung out, using what little strength his dead body still possessed, and swung along pipe after pipe, a nightmarish subterranean jungle gym.

Then: he smelled it.

A faint breeze from above.

On it, the scent of blood. And a curious smell of rot.

Echoing down through the hole again came the animal's cries, a kind of panicked bleating. Coburn hoisted himself through the hole, his mouth wet with blood, his jaw tight with hunger.


THE HUMAN MIND noticed that nothing here made sense. It was like that old game: *One of these things is not like the other, one of these things does not belong.* But it wasn't just one thing. It was a metric shitload of things. It was *all* things.

Coburn hoisted himself up into an old movie theater that tickled the back of his memory somewhere behind the wall of hunger that dominated him. The theater lay in ruins – the ceiling was half-caved in, the scent of dust and mold sat heavy in the air. The screen itself hung in tatters. Rows of seats had fallen to disrepair.

But the thing that really twisted the noodle was the deer.

And the two men eating it.

Animal was a whitetail buck. Not standing so much as leaning against the broken row of seats, its head thrashing, the creature crying out some sound between a child's whimper and a beastly grunt. One man slumped against the creatures haunches, biting into it the way another man might bite lustily into an apple. The other stood at the front, pawing at the whitetail's face, fruitlessly snapping at the thing's neck – but the animal, still alive (though weakened), kept jerking his head away from his attacker's mouth.

Coburn didn't understand one lick of what was going on.

And frankly, he didn't give a rat's right foot.

Because *sweet goddamn* was he hungry.

With that, he moved to feed. The deer no longer interested him. The blood of beasts was functional, but barely.

The blood of men, however, was king.

Coburn, his skin still tight, still brittle, his bones and muscles still uncertain, stepped up atop a row of seats and almost fell – but he quickly regained his balance and walked across the seat-tops toward his prey.

He came first to the man chowing down on the deer's ass, wrapped his hands around the fool's skull and snapped the head back like it was a Pez dispenser ready to give out some delicious *red candy*.

The smell hit him in the face like a thrown brick.

Rot. Decay. A kind of septic infection.

*We don't drink from the sick*, said that horrible little voice inside Coburn's head but really, hell with that voice, and so he bit down anyway.

Black blood thick as motor oil filled his mouth. It tasted of pus and of pain but worst of all it tasted *worthless*.

See, humans have a spark of something. Coburn didn't care to ruminate on what that spark was: the divine, the soul, a glimmer of sentience, a social security number, whatever. Fact was, *life* was bright and alive inside every man, woman and child, and that glory dwelled—nay, *thrived*—in the blood. It was why the blood of a human was infinitely better than that of a beast: animals had an ember, a spark, but only a fraction of the total fire.

The blood of man offered the whole package. Life in claret sweetness.

*This* blood had none of that. It was dead. Inert. Diseased.

Black as tar and worthless as baby shit.

Coburn's head snapped back, recoiling with the disappointment felt by a starving man who just bit into a plastic fruit. His victim struggled, hissing, the hole in his throat gurgling and bubbling.

The man turned and lunged for Coburn with long, yellowed nails. His face was half-caved in (calling to mind a rotten pumpkin), a gobbet of super-fresh venison still laying flat on his tongue (the meat covered in tufts of deer hair).

The man was dead.

*Dead*-dead. Not dead like Coburn was dead.

But real dead. Double dead.

Shit.

The vampire had little time to parse. The gurgling corpse lunged at Coburn, letting go of the deer. He wrapped his hands around Coburn's throat and turned the tables: Coburn thought he'd be doing the feeding, but this dead sonofabitch was hungry, too. And strong.

That's when things went sideways.

The deer, sensing opportunity, kicked out with its back legs. A hoof caught Coburn's rotting assailant in the temple, and it went through the fucker's head like a broomstick through a block of butter. The buck's leg impaled the rotter's skull, and whatever bullshit facsimile of life managed to animate him before was now gone, and the hands around Coburn's throat went slack.

The whitetail was none too happy about this and continued to thrash. It bucked its head and drove one of its antler points through the chin of the other feeder trying to get a taste up front.

Coburn backpedaled, almost tripped over a seat as the deer panicked. He watched, equal parts starving and stymied, as the deer struggled—it had stuck its attackers at both ends. Antler under one's chin, foot through the other's head.

And it couldn't get free.

It was then that Coburn's veins tightened. His dead heart stirred: not with life, but with a hollow paroxysm of *need* and *want*.

He stood.

He reached out.

He pressed his fingertips together, forming them to a single point.

Then Coburn corkscrewed his hand fast—faster than any human could manage—into the deer's side, up under his ribcage, and grabbed hold of the creature's heart and crushed it like it was a pomegranate.

The vampire removed his fingers, licked them clean, then pressed his face tight against the hole and drank. It tasted of grass and musk and animal stink but he didn't care because at least it wasn't black blood, dead blood, *useless* blood.

The blood filled his throat, and for a moment, all was right in the world.

## COMING NOVEMBER 2011...

TOMES of the DEAD

ANNO MORTIS

Rebecca Levene

ISBN: 978-1-905437-85-6
UK £.6.99    US $7.99

Abaddon
Books

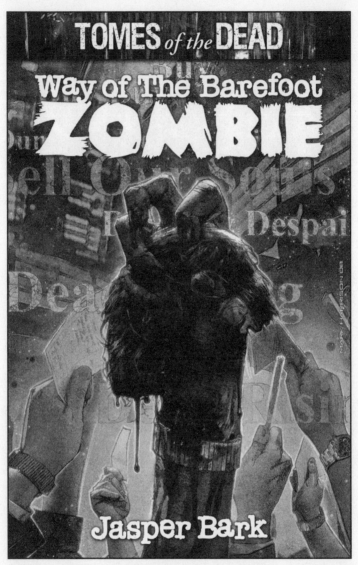

# TOMES *of the* DEAD

# Way of The Barefoot ZOMBIE

## Jasper Bark

Visit www.abaddonbooks.com for information on our titles,
interviews, news and exclusive content.

ISBN: 978-1-906735-06-7
UK £.6.99    US $7.99

Abaddon
Books

Follow us on twitter: www.twitter.com/abaddonbooks

# TOMES *of the* DEAD

# EMPIRE OF
# SALT

## WESTON OCHSE

ISBN: 978-1-906735-32-6

UK £.6.99    US $7.99

Abaddon
Books

Visit www.abaddonbooks.com for information on our titles,
interviews, news and exclusive content.

ISBN: 978-1-906735-26-5
UK £.6.99    US $7.99

Abaddon
Books

Follow us on twitter: www.twitter.com/abaddonbooks

ISBN: 978-1-905437-72-6
UK £.6.99    US $7.99

Abaddon Books

# TOMES *of the* DEAD

## TIDE OF SOULS

### SIMON BESTWICK

Visit www.abaddonbooks.com for information on our titles,
interviews, news and exclusive content.

ISBN: 978-1-906735-14-2
UK £.6.99    US $7.99

Abaddon
Books